PRAISE FOR BRIAN COSTELLO

"If Joyce was right that you could rebuild Dublin by reading *Ulysses*, you could definitely reconstruct a very specific American village of dive bars, record shops and drugstore cowboys from this slab of post-punk tragicomedy [. . .] [*Losing in Gainesville*] traces the emotional arc (or lack thereof) of superslacker Ronnie Altamont, the lead singer and guitarist in his low-rent Florida rock band, The Laraflynnboyles. Set in the mid-1990s, the story captures in intimate detail the wilderness years experienced by many American males of a certain class, age and background. The desolate outlooks of Ronnie and his buddies are weighed down by crap jobs (asbestos removal, pizza delivery, etc.), fueled by the massive and constant intake of drugs and alcohol, and soothed only by the likes of Charles Bukowski, Lou Reed, The Kinks and The Replacements [. . .] It's a big, messy, uncomfortable story but one that captures its milieu [. . .] [I]n the end, the book's real question is whether this beautiful loser is capable of being saved from himself. A rock-and-roll fable about the secret lives ⸢   ⸣satisfied."

⸢*kus*

"A bittersweet, twenty-someth⸢   ⸣ ⸢f angst and longing, riffing on art ⸢   ⸣ amidst the banality and beauty of 90's ⸢   ⸣m portrait of the artists as not-so-young punk roc⸢   ⸣

—Eric Charles May, author of *Bedrock Faith*

"Costello describes suburban absurdities in teeming detail, approaching the self-aware gross-out humor of Tromaville: tumbling forward with the rushing momentum of Kerouac's prose. Nineties counterculture—emo bands, riot grrls, shit jobs, sleeping on floors, warm beer and cold pizza—often provides the punch line. Though funny and poking fun, Costello remains sympathetic to the awkwardness and ambivalence that drives young people, feeling trapped, to struggle to express themselves: that beautiful, life-affirming cycle of broke kids starting bands."

—Tim Kinsella, Joan of Arc frontman, author of *Let Go and Go On and On* and *The Karaoke Singer's Guide to Self-Defense*

LOSING
IN
GAINESVILLE

A NOVEL BY BRIAN COSTELLO

CURBSIDE SPLENDOR PUBLISHING

Published by Curbside Splendor Publishing, Inc., Chicago, Illinois in 2014.

First Edition
Copyright © 2014 by Brian Costello
Library of Congress Control Number: 2014948799

ISBN 978-1-940430-31-7

Edited by James Tadd Adcox
Cover art by Ryan Duggan
Designed by Alban Fischer

Manufactured in the United States of America.

www.curbsidesplendor.com

"He who has never failed somewhere, that man cannot be great."

—Herman Melville

ONE: SPRING

"The trouble with doing nothing is you can't quit and rest."
—Alfred E. Neuman

A REGRETTABLE INCIDENT INVOLVING A GRANOLA BAR

. . . And that's when Kelly leaps from the dumpster, screaming as the red ants bite his tongue.

He tosses the half-eaten granola bar he'd found buried in the rancid smorgasbord of discarded food onto the sizzling black of the minimart parking lot. The granola bar plops between Ronnie's brown hand-to-hand-to-hand-me-down wingtips.

"How could you miss seeing them?" Ronnie asks, bending over to inspect the granola bar, squinting at dozens of red ants swarming over the oats, the raisins, the green wrapper, as frenetic as those vast totalitarian mounds they're always constructing, the bane of the Floridian teenage lawnmower's existence.

Kelly lands, hops, fingers scraping at his tongue. Teary-eyed from the pain, sweat flees his thick brown flat-top, stains the yellowed gauze wrapped around his forehead, gushes down his gaunt face, settles into damp miniature Lake Okeechobees spotting the green medical scrub top he had purchased for a dime in some thrift store back home in Orlando.

"Ow! Ow!" he moans like a novocained dental patient. "Because I'm hungry."

"Buy some food then," Ronnie says, entranced by the ants' movement, still shocked that Kelly somehow missed seeing them. "Please. You're hungry. I'm hungry."

"No!" Kelly winces, face turning that popular Crayola color Food Allergy Red. "It burns, bro. Get me some ice!"

"It costs a quarter." Ronnie finally looks away from the cruel, cruel granola bar, to Kelly's wiry, twitchy form. He wants to laugh at the idea that this could be the proverbial straw to break the proverbial economical bastard's cheap-ass back.

"A quarter?!" Kelly steps backwards, leans against the rusty brown dumpster until the heat of the metal compels a shrugged shove forward. "I ain't paying a quarter!"

"This minimart charges you for a cup of ice," Ronnie continues, standing there with nothing but an ant-infested granola bar between them in the already muggy April air. "There's a sign by the door and everything."

Kelly weighs the pain of the bites versus the pain of spending any money on soothing cool water. The tiny hot welts feel like he's been biting his tongue repeatedly while cunnillinguisting a habañero.

"Fine!" he huffs, pulls a quarter from the front pocket of his multi-stained white painter's pants, flips it to Ronnie before hunching over in agony. "Hurry!"

Ronnie trudges to the front of the Floridian Harvest minimart, feels with each pinched step in those wingtips the swamp-assed taint-chafe particular to being in the afternoon sun dumpster diving in jeans, in Florida. Anemic, sweaty, disoriented from not eating in the two days since escaping to Gainesville, he's delirious enough to mutter semi-coherent ramblings on the order of, "Stupid. Mother. Cock. Shit. Ass. Hot. Food. Dammit. Sucker. Fucker. Cheap. Ass. Hung. Grrrr."

Ronnie pulls open the door, steps inside, hears the welcoming synthetic *Ding!*, the A/C a respite from Out There's heat, humidity, and ant-bitten friends, all of whom tagged along on what Ronnie is starting to think might have been a hasty, ill-conceived move.

Only three nights ago, Ronnie was in his home—a tiny old white shack in the shadows of downtown Orlando's skyscrapers (tall and vulgar and new, breeding and multiplying like the Samsa-sized bugs always lurking in the kitchen, the bathroom, the living room walls)—in A/C like this—not a sprawling Kennedy compound of wealth, space, and luxury, but better than the double-wide trailer he has just moved into off 34th Street—typing away at his soon to be completed 536-page tour-de-force entitled *The Big Blast for Youth*, when the phone rang.

It was Ronnie's friend Mouse, who lived 100 miles north, in the college town of Gainesville—a Charles Manson doppelgänger with penchants for naked performance art, avant white-noise music, and compulsive masturbation. "Ya partyin'?"

"They fired me or I quit at the restaurant tonight. So, no. I'm not."

"You lost your dishwashing job, brah?" (Mouse enjoys aping the Spicoli-tones of the typical Floridian surfer burnout party dude.)

"Don't brah me, brah." Ronnie yelled. "This is serious. I walked out. I can't live here anymore."

Ronnie rose from his desk, turned away from the gray computer screen, stretched with his free right hand, scraped the knuckle against the jagged bumps in the popcorn ceiling. "And the girl I was dating? Maggie? Decided she would rather date other girls. Or guys who aren't broke. Or her cat. Anyone, or, anything, but me."

"Sounds like you should move."

"Yeah?"

"Yeah." Mouse started chuckling, not unlike some sadistic social scientist conducting an experiment on the verge of turning horribly catastrophic. "My old friend Alvin? He needs a roommate. You want to leave Orlando. Sooooo." The sadistic chuckle returned. "He's weird and you're weird and it'll be rad."

By "weird," Ronnie imagined someone who listens to noncommercial music, dabbles in marijuana, and knows a thing or two about foreign films. An unconventional haircut. Some tattoos. You know. Weird.

"Sure. Why not?" Tomorrow would be April Fool's Day, 1996. No job. Most friends had moved away. Five years of college had ended last summer with an English degree Ronnie had no interest in pursuing. He would call his parents and inform them of his decision once he was settled in. He would do the same with the other two guys in his band, The Laraflynnboyles. Mouse laughed his laugh, and Ronnie concluded the call with a "See you tomorrow night," hanging up the phone and returning to *The Big Blast for Youth*, and now, stepping into the maternal A/C that makes Florida habitable in the eight month summer—air-conditioning like this why the state skyrocketed into the Top 5 most populous states, hordes of Rust Belted-exiles taking it from the Crackers and Cubans and Seminoles and Mafioso as the latter half of the 20th century ticked away—Ronnie thinks, Yeah, I shouldn't have moved here without any money. Because deprivation and delirium have heightened senses that were, until then, always satiated, so it isn't just the glorious sweat-drying A/C inside the Floridian Harvest Minimart, and not just the theme song for every dude with a Bondoed Firebird—Loverboy's "Workin' for the Weekend"—piped in over the store's speakers, it's the smells of the juice-glazed footlong franks rotating under heat lamps, it's the *jalapeño y carne chiliquitos con quesos* rotating like overstuffed egg rolls under the neighboring heat lamps, the sausage and egg breakfast biscuits, croissants, and muffins lined in slots, the burnt coffee puddled in caf and decaf pots, even the gnat-clouded bananas, and to see the two aisles of canned goods stacked four rows high—of soups and sauces and vegetables—the boxed and wrapped pastas and ramen and Cheetos and peanuts and ding-dongs—to say nothing of the frozen foods and beer (oh! beer! in cases, in packs, in rings of six, in 12 or 32 ounces. what Ronnie Altamont wouldn't give for just one of you! Cold to the touch, cold down his throat, Spuds Mac Kenzie and the Swedish Bikini Team and Billy Dee Williams and his malt liquor bull all magically appearing before his eyes to help Ronnie forget that he has no food, no money, and no employment in this new town recently awarded "Best Place to Live in America" by the good people at *Money* magazine). The quick gag of the Coke dispensers before gushing Mountain Dew into thirty-two ounce orange and blue (the University's team colors) plastic cups held by skater kids, boards fulcrumed under checkerboard Vans. Ronnie waits for these three 8th grade-looking kids in their requisite black Misfits/NOFX/Pennywise t-shirts and clam digger shorts with the chain wallets dangling below their knees on their left sides. Around the store, sun-fried construction workers punched out for the day enter surrounded by drywall dustclouds, grabbing twelve-packs of Old Hamtramck or Dusch Light, square-shouldered, big boned middle-aged women enter in their blue Wal-Mart uniforms and buy Newports, frizzy hair wet from excessive product and rushed late-for-work showers, college girls in UF leisure wear who will never be more beautiful pump high-octane fuel in their white Honda Civics then pay at the counter and everyone's Finehowreyew, and Ronnie knows this because when the balding brown-haired mustached nicotine-skinned skinny Confederate-flag-shirted gentleman behind the counter asks "Hahhowreyew?" in that uniquely Floridian way, expressing most of the politeness and civility of regions more southern than this one coupled with a bland unenthusiasm betraying utter disinterest in the person's well-being, "Finehowreyew?" is the inevitable answer. The door incessantly *Ding! Ding! Ding!*s with each entrance and exit. Ronnie fills the small cup with ice, turns around, and as always, there's that disconcerting vibe of everyone looking, pointing, laughing, even if they're doing none of those things. It's not just from being what they used to call "punk" way back in 1996, Ronnie Altamont's wingtips the only real difference from the inevitable black Chuck Taylor high-tops, but he wears black jeans, a well-worn white t-shirt with the words NAIOMI'S HAIR across the front in black silkscreened in early-90s squiggles and fingerpaint fonts ("It's a band!" Ronnie yells, when strangers ask, as they often do, "Who's she?"), stained with the gunk of today's foraging, an average less-thin-with-each-passing-year body (the never-popular "Depression and Poverty Diet" doesn't halt this) and a scowling face with black-framed glasses in front of self-consciously bugged out Lydon/Rotten blue eyes making him look even more pissed

BRIAN COSTELLO

off, apprehensive, pensive, surly, and less-than-thrilled to be here than he actually is, topped off with some unnatural hair dye (now, a truly stupid faded purple Manic Panic job) on a shaggy short bristle of unkempt crazy. No, it's not the usual discomfort Ronnie feels from living in this strange, strange state, and it's not the oh-so-nonconformist fashion sense of aligning yourself with the most recent counterculture, it's like these people know Ronnie's story right now. They see the stains, the sweat, the general unemployed dishevelment and the cup of ice, and they know he's up to nothing wholesome. (What Ronnie fails to realize is that any stares, smirks, and hostile undercurrents sent his way have little to do with him and everything to do with how everyone in the minimart has seen Kelly, writhing by the dumpster, both hands gripping his tongue, and the sense they have that Ronnie must be involved.)

You want a piece of my heart? You better start from the start. You wanna be in the show? C'mon baby let's go! the store's speakers command, and Ronnie walks to the counter, ice cup in one hand, a quarter in the other.

"You can tell your friend with the mummy tape on his forehead he's got five minutes to leave the premises before I call the police," says the minimart clerk. No Hahhowreyews for Ronnie.

Ronnie says nothing, too lethargic from hunger and heat to sneer the appropriate caustically witty retort people are supposed to say in moments like these. He drops the quarter, steps out of the A/C, sweat instantly beading his skin. He pops two ice cubes in his mouth to feel some semblance of hydration, before approaching Kelly, who swipes the cup from Ronnie's hand and crams his mouth with ice. Kelly sits by the dumpster, elbows on thighs, eyes closed, moaning with relief. Ronnie wants to tell him how the clerk called his gauze "mummy tape," but thinks better of it. Last week, Kelly was held up by robbers at the dumpy east Orlando hotel he worked at as sole Front Desk clerk of the 11:00 p.m.-7:00 a.m. shift, duct-taped to a chair in the hotel owner's office, pistol-whipped to the back of the head, knocked over, his left ear pressed into thick red carpeting made redder and thicker with his soppy blood. Hence the gauze around the forehead. When discovered by the morning staff, the owner, a racist South African cocksucker, expressed more concern for the stolen money than for Kelly's life. Ronnie had also worked at this hotel, but was fired shortly after calling the owner a "racist South African cocksucker" in the popular opinion column[1] he had written as *enfant terrible* of the University of Central Florida's student newspaper. Upon checking out of the hospital, Kelly, as they say, tendered his resignation, but there was nothing tender about what he wrote, a rant of such acidic fury, it made Ronnie's student column a Victorian declaration of love by comparison.[2] He mailed it off on the way out of town, most of Ronnie's possessions packed in the cab of his truck.

"We need to leave," Ronnie says. "You're causing a scene. I should just leave you here to get arrested for being such a cheap-ass jerkoff." Ronnie turns and starts walking. "I'm going to campus. I think Mouse said something about there being free Hare Krishna food."

Kelly nods, water dribbling out his mouth and off his chin, stands, catches up to Ronnie. From the minimart to the campus

---

[1] See Appendix A

[2] See Appendix B

is a fifteen minute slog down 13th Street, your basic four-lane main thoroughfare—Gainesville's stretch of US 441—past a surf shop, a dry cleaners, and all the restaurants with dumpsters in the back that bore no fruit, only inedible refuse, flies, and the expected smell, your Zesty Glazes and Viva Tacos and Szechwan Gator and McDonald's and Denny's, all through their hour-long tour of Gainesville's finest fast food dumpsters, Kelly rolling around black and white Hefty bags, tearing into the contents, as Ronnie kept lookout from clerks, customers, kitchen crews, police. Kelly wasn't as hungry as Ronnie; at McDonald's, he sipped from a large chocolate shake, at Viva Taco he dipped at a half-eaten basket of nacho cheese covered tortilla chips. But the crème de la trash, at the top of a filled garbage can between the pumps at the gas station on the corner of 13th and University: a Ziploc bag stuffed with barbequed chicken.

"Oh, no," Ronnie had said when Kelly plucked it out of the dumpster. "Please—no, man—don't eat that." Ronnie was hungry, but he wasn't dumpster-chicken hungry, not yet.

Kelly tore open the bag, pulled out a chicken leg, put it to his mouth and bit down. "It's good," he said, after swallowing the first bite, then licking the sauce off his filthy fingers. "You should try some."

Ronnie backed off, laughing from the heat, the hunger, everything. "You're gonna be so sick."

"Actually," Kelly said after picking the bone clean, tossing it back into the trash, sealing up the Ziploc bag (still with two legs and a breast), "the food I eat out of dumpsters from people I don't know tastes better than the food in dumpsters of people I do know." He stuffed the Ziploc bag into his pink fannypack—

yeah, Kelly walks around with a pink fannypack he found on a curb on Alafaya Trail back in Orlando. He washed it. Good as new. It makes his generally fetching ensembles of stained pants and hospital scrub tops that much more fetching. He's 25, has owned a house since he was 21 due entirely to always (until now) working and living as frugally as possible—saving, never eating out, only going to the once-a-month good shows that came to Orlando and opting to shotgun a six-pack in the parking lot before the show instead of buying drinks at the bar, and it goes without saying that the ladies weren't exactly lining up to give the man a blowjob; in spite of how genuine Kelly was, of how genuinely kind and generous he, well, *usually* was (years of friendship having exhausted Kelly's generosity towards Ronnie, especially in a move as poorly planned as this one), it was impossible for most women to get past the "schizophrenic homeless guy/gay orderly" image he had cultivated.

They walk past Gator Plaza, with its salons and drug stores and University t-shirt shops and generic Floridian "cabanas" of watered-down tropical drinks and bikini-clad waitresses carrying plates of oysters. Ronnie recalls the morning, sitting on the front steps of the trailer, strumming his guitar and crooning the words to The Kinks' "This is Where I Belong" in his best Ray Davies intoxicated timbre, "Well I ain't gonna wander / like the boy I used to know / He's a real unlucky fella / and he's got no place to go," and he can't help but wonder right about now—broke and starving with a friend nursing antbite wounds on his tongue—if Gainesville's where he belongs, but a part of him, past all of the right-now troubles, sees the potential—Ronnie already loves how people actually use the sidewalks here, contrasted with Orlando, where everything is so spread out and muggy, the sidewalks are like adornments—future friends everywhere—boys and girls wearing t-shirts of bands he likes, of writers he likes—just that they share these interests at all—if only he could look less, you know, bummish right now. But Ronnie's here for a reason. He has plans, big plans. He recalls strumming the guitar while Kelly told him, "I'm still not going to pay for your food," leaning against his truck, looking at the thick canopy of pines and palms and live oaks that made Ronnie feel he had just moved to the poor part of Sherwood Forest. "I know you want me to pay for your food right now, but it's not going to happen. You need to learn about cause and effect. You need to learn not to self-indulge to oblivion."

Ronnie laughed, strummed, sang, ignored.

"I'm serious, Ronnie," Kelly continued. "We're gonna dumpster dive, and you're going to have to figure out how to live, if this is what you're choosing to do."

Ronnie laughed then, and he still could laugh about it now, Kelly's forays into stern parental life-lessons. They cross University and limp onto the University of Florida, and the poverty and self-inflicted misfortune of the day is replaced by the welcome banalities of a college campus Thursday afternoon. Ah yes, college: the parent-sanctioned, government-approved method to get your child's ya-yas out in just four years before inheriting a bounteous suburban existence. Youth on bicycles, rollerblades, skateboards, rolling up and down the walkways winding between the brick academic buildings, everyone and everything with a purpose, a direction, and in the commons, students sit in clusters doing all the boring-ass activities collegiates do between classes—highlighting textbooks, tossing Frisbees, various permutations of nothing, and

Ronnie already feels a mixture of boredom and self-loathing as they step around all these clusters and approach the Krishna food tables. In purple and saffron flowing gowns, blissed-out Krishnas (are there any other kind?) slop fluorescent curried potatoes and peanut sauce from giant pots onto soggy paper plates. Ronnie and Kelly find a patch of grass in the middle of the commons to sit and try not to look too ravenous, trying to pass for two college students living the life.

"I need to wait until this cools," Kelly says. "My tongue can't take it." He mashes the food, wipes the potato remnants off the clear plastic spork with his hospital scrub, and forces the tines underneath the gauze to scratch his itchy forehead. "What are you going to do about Chris Embowelment?"

"It doesn't matter," Ronnie says, trying to ignore Kelly's violent arm motions as the spork scratches deeper and deeper into the dead skin. The food is at once spicy and bland, a mushy warm gruel that burns the digestive tract. Ronnie doesn't mind it. He's grateful to have something to fight the hunger.

"He might come up here and find you," Kelly says before easing backwards until flat in the crunchy grass, looking/not looking at the cloudless sky above.

Ronnie would laugh if he was less exhausted, less frustrated with Kelly's frugality. (If Kelly would break down and order a large pizza, there would be no problems.) He actually did laugh when, back at his house in Orlando, Ronnie made a final dummy check before leaving for the last time, and Kelly yelled from his jittery maroon Japanese pickup truck, "Nothing you own is worth taking with you. Chris Embowelment is on his way and he's gonna kill you! He's gonna disembowel you with his bass, then he's gonna kill you. You don't want to be here when he discovers you're skipping out on the rent, you dumb dick!"

Ronnie had to laugh, then, thinking, Yes, Kelly is definitely right, on this account, anyway. Chris Embowelment was built like one of those defensive tackles you see on Sunday afternoon television, if said defensive tackle wore green Medusaesque dreadlocks and homemade tattoos covering all skin except the face and played in a touring death metal band called Infestation of Leeches. He had been a practicing Satanist, but lapsed because he found the Church of Satan's canons—such as they were—to be "too tame." From there, he naturally gravitated to a full-throated endorsement of Nietzschean existentialist glory-seeking coupled with a black Randian interpretation of self-interest best summarized in his favorite phrase, "Get the fuck out of my way or I'll rip off your eyelids." In spite of these quirks and the inevitable funereal pallor he brought to his side of the tiny house, Chris was a clean roommate who paid the bills on time. (Which just goes to show that not all guys surnamed "Embowelment" are bad.) Ronnie owed Chris a note of explanation, at the very least.

"Dear Chris," Ronnie began, scribbling in purple marker across the back of an electric bill. "Hey man, I'm sorry, but I walked out on the dishwashing gig, and I can't afford to and I don't want to live here anymore. I think I'm going stark raving batshit, and I need something these surroundings are not giving me. Anyway, sorry I didn't repaint the walls of my bedroom . . . "

(The walls of Ronnie's closet-sized bedroom were covered in permanent marker graffiti. Somewhere between his seventh and eighth domestic beer, he enjoyed scribbling the logos of favorite bands, the Black Flag bars, the blue Germs circle, The Boobs, The

Uncool, The Jerks, The Uncooked Weiners, Butt Butt Butt, Dildos
Over Somalia, The [insert anti-social adjective here] [insert anti-
social noun here] . . . and so on and so forth, and in the middle of
the largest wall was this quote from Richard Hell:

"Rock and roll as a way of turning sadness and loneliness
and anger into something transcendentally beautiful, or at least
energy-transmitting."

Since graduating college, Ronnie had taken solace in this
quote the way friendless Amway distributors find solace in testi-
monials from Double Diamonds.)

"Anyway," Ronnie continued scribbling, "I'm truly sorry to be
sticking you with the rent, for whatever that's worth. I guess what
I'm trying to say is, if our paths ever cross again, I would appreciate it if you didn't disembowel me—"

Outside, the b-flat trumpet of Kelly's truck horn. "He's coming up the road!" Kelly yelled. "I'm leaving!"

Ronnie dropped the marker—cold fear flooding his skin, tin-
gling his balls. He ran out the door, left it open, hopped into his
dinged-up blandy apple green four-door sedan. Squealing into reverse, Ronnie could almost hear the Flatt and Scruggs car chase
bluegrass music as he pulled out of the driveway, shifted the car to
Drive, floored the accelerator down the residential street, as Chris
Embowelment, fresh off an East Coast tour, passes in his tour van
in the opposite direction, about to find the house half-empty, stuck
with all the bills. In the rearview mirror, Ronnie saw Chris Embowelment step out of his van, stare at the open door, figure it out, and—
holy shit!—punch the front of the house, putting a fist-sized hole in
the grimy old aluminum siding. He looked to Ronnie's car, but Ronnie had already turned left towards Highway 441 North, out of town.

Now he's here, in the middle of a university he did not attend, surrounded by dormitories and riot-proof architecture. Hippies of all ages, excessively tanned South Floridian rich kids, the NYC hipsters-in-training with their tattoos-in-progress snaking down their arms, the winter-hating loudmouthed students from the Eastern Seaboard's megalopolises, the unceasing buzz of youthful optimism and energy, and Ronnie, well, eventually, he will go home to a double-wide trailer with a roommate rumored to have two buttholes.

As Ronnie falls asleep/passes out in the commons, leaving Kelly to sit there and scratch his bandaged forehead with a clear plastic spork, he will reflect on how it did not go like this:

At the end of the foolish move, it's Alvin at the front door of the trailer—after a two-hour drive where US 441 North finally escapes Greater Orlando somewhere outside Apopka (You know: Apopka? "The Indoor Foliage Capital of the World?"), and Ronnie actually always loved and will always love this part of the drive— the rundown melancholic old Florida of roadside tourist traps, citrus, moccasins, sweet corn, burned out motels, the violent purple orange sky of the sunsets over undulating pony farms, the live oaks and scrub pines mixing with the palm trees. Driving north in those parts really meant driving South, culturally, and Ronnie, in the car, listening to T-Rex on a worn cassette (*The Slider* on one side, *Futuristic Dragon* on the other), he enjoyed the schizophrenic polyglot of his homeland—of handpainted "REPENT! THE END IS NEAR!" signs nailed to posts holding up billboards advertising "TOPLESS BOTTOMLESS GIRLS 24 HOURS!" Alvin waits in the trailer as the sun sets, as Ronnie and Kelly ride through a vast prairie with tall grasses in all directions into the darkness as the stars and satellites appear overhead. Beyond the prairie, a slow immersion into Gainesville—holistic yoga house here, junk yard there, student apartments, Chinese buffets, the teenage wasteland backdrop of fast food and liquor stores mixing it up with seedy motels and crackwhores . . . and then it's the University, and a westbound turn down Archer Road through vast commercial districts, to the trailer park—a right on 34th Street, then a turn down a lonely little half-lane that crumbles into a dirt path.

No, it did not go down like this—Alvin, welcoming Ronnie into his trailer with one of those three-pump handshakes like the kind employed by Governor Willie Stark in *All the King's Men.* Ronnie climbing the four creaky wooden steps to the white steel door opening into the '70s-muff shag brown living room. Wood paneling covering the walls. Dim yellow light bathing the mess below. Against the far right wall a faded gray cushioned chair with a gaping indentation, giving the sitter the sensation of sitting in a moldy barrel. On the opposite wall—a TV, VCR, and stereo, with a shredded green lawnchair and a punctured red beanbag plopped three feet away. Garbage—used tissues, yellowed Q-tips, discarded fast food wrappers, and crinkled porno—covering most of the dusty carpeting.

"Well. Uhhhhhhh," Alvin did not begin because this never happened, arms outstretched like a realtor in the midst of a hard sell. "As you can see, I never pick up after myself." Alvin stood five feet five inches. He was squat and barrel-chested, with stubby arms like uncooked hotdogs hanging at his sides. He was buck-toothed. Double-chinned. His curly blond hair was short, greasy, and matted, like the pubic hair of a Swedish wino. He wore primary-colored t-shirts decorated with drawings of big fish and captions reading "I'M OUT FOR TROUT." Faded gray sweatpants and velcroed white tennis shoes finished the outfit. Somewhere at UC Berkeley, there was a supermodel astrophysicist, and she was the yin to Alvin's yang, righting the precarious balance of the universe.

Alvin never led Ronnie Altamont forward through the living room and into the kitchen, where the fluorescent lighting heightened the variety of smells, now increased to include rotting food and the earthy stench of an unwashed gerbil cage. The white linoleum was yellowed and sticky. The counters were covered in old newspapers, more discarded microwave dinners, unwashed dishes, glasses, silverware. The sink was filled with the kind of sludgy water you see in the dying industrial towns of the Midwest or Eastern Europe.

"I guess you probably notice that other smell too, pfff!" Alvin never said. Alvin ended most of his sentences with "pfff!" as if to say, "Please disregard everything I just said."

Ronnie would have nodded, if given the chance, sniffing in furtive inhalations, as if to assuage the assault on his middle-class sensibilities from all the mold, mildew, and feces. "What is that?"

"Um, the thing is," Alvin never drawled, "I got two buttholes? And one of them? Well, it's not an anus, but more of a crevice on my backside? Where filth collects? The doctors say I'm supposed to wash it? But I never get around to washing it, pfffff."

"And, just so you know," Alvin did not continue, leading Ronnie out of the kitchen with a gracious "after you" windmill of his stubby left arm, down the dark hallway to the Alabama truckstop bathroom facsimile on the right, where Alvin's stained underwear encircled the rim of the sink, "I never get any women, obviously, so I masturbate pretty much all the time. I'm always watching videos in the living room, pfff!"

"Yeah," Ronnie would not remark. "I noticed that *500 Oral Moneyshots* tape sticking out of your VCR."

"Take a peek into my bedroom, pfffff."

The bed was in the middle. Around it, an island of spread-beaver pictorials from thirty different porno mags.

"Wow," Ronnie would have gasped, a little impressed.

"And here's your room, pfff." Ronnie Altamont's eventual bedroom was at the end of the hall. It was a square, whitewalled room with a closet and a backdoor. It was the only empty and almost clean room in the entire trailer. Rectangular windows lined the top of the far wall. The floor was a white linoleum like the kitchen, only unyellowed.

"I'll take it," Ronnie would have said, adjusting his glasses, running his fingers through the badly dyed hair. "However," he would have loved to have continued, "since we're putting our cards on the table, I should let you know that I have no money, will pay you no rent, and will seldom leave my room, where I will sit and brood while listening to music, drinking malt liquor while trying to write. I won't say much to you when we're here at the same time, and I intend to move out of this dump as soon as a better offer comes up. Sound good? Roomie?"

Here, Ronnie would have extended his hand. Another three-pump handshake. Deal. No surprises.

In the in-and-out of half-sleep, Ronnie compares how it should have gone down with what really happened. The visual part of the tour was essentially the same, without acknowledgements of the garbage, the porno island encircling Alvin's bed, and the rumored second butthole—and that was mere speculation on Mouse's part, a legendary rumor from when Alvin and Mouse attended high school together. Mouse told Ronnie and Kelly about it after the real tour of the trailer. Mouse had followed them from room to room, snickering with every registered look of discomfort from Ronnie and Kelly. In the middle of the living room, a rotund pasty man in his late teens wielded a broom, swinging and jabbing the air with it, yellowed stalks swishing above his head as he yelled the inevitable "HI-YAH!" He was shirtless, wearing only a pair of short, unflattering navy blue soccer shorts.

"Don't mind Stevie—pffff!" Alvin said as they walked past him in the living room. "He's teaching himself karate." Ronnie tried not to laugh at this bit of information, coupled with Stevie's flabby flailings; Mouse laughed, and Kelly squealed as the broom brushed inches from his bandaged head.

When the tour was completed, Ronnie, Kelly, and Mouse stepped outside the trailer, "To talk things over," as Ronnie told Alvin.

"So. What do you think, bro?" Mouse asked, followed by, "Heh heh heh . . . " In the horror-movie night-time silence of the trailer park, Mouse looked criminally insane. Shoulder-length unwashed escaped convict brown hair, satanic facial hair, sagging earlobes from deflated holes that until recently held two cut tubes of garden hose, a sinister face with a false-tooth smile (from when Alvin accidentally knocked out Mouse's front teeth with a golf club back in high school) dark eyes, black eyebrows at 45-degree angles, a white dress shirt with narrow blue pinstripes dotted with multi-hued splotches and blotches, black slacks cut off above the knees, teal flip-flops.

"We're leaving," Kelly said. "This place is disgusting." Kelly, Ronnie was sure, saw nothing but the dark shadows of the live oaks, heard nothing but silence from the surrounding trailers.

"C'mon man. It ain't that bad," Mouse said, picking at the point of his goatee, smiling that smile.

"Fuck that," Kelly said. "It's worse!"

Ronnie turned around, looked up to the dim yellow light inside the forlorn trailer. This didn't feel like Gainesville. Rural Florida, yes, but not the college town Ronnie was hoping for.

"The rent's freee-eeeee." Mouse sang "freee-eeee" like Luther, the leader of the psychopathic gang in that movie "The Warriors" singing "Warriors! Come out to . . . playyy-yayyyy!" "You get started here, join some bands, get a job, finish that book, meet some girls." Mouse laughed and sang, "Girrr-rurrrrrlllls."

"Free?" Kelly said.

"The trailer's 100% paid off." Mouse said. He held out his arms, shrugged. "You don't have to stay in the trailer forever. Get a foothold, brah—a foothold!—and you'll find someplace better."

"Or, you can go back to Orlando and stay with me and do this move right," Kelly said. "Get another job and save up money. Skip this dump altogether and move to Chicago like you've been talking about." Kelly was one of those twitchy-skinny guys who never looked anyone in the eye when he spoke. He was looking Ronnie in the eye.

Back and forth they argued. None of Ronnie's belongings had been moved in yet. Ronnie did consider driving back, finding yet another crap job in Orlando, waiting it out for another year until the money was in place, take the band to Chicago, take the writing to Chicago, where there would be no doubt as to the vast opportunities awaiting. But then again, he would have to be in Orlando for another year, right when he thought he had finally escaped Orlando. Could Ronnie Altamont possibly stand another year in Orlando?

"I'm staying," Ronnie said.

"Now that's the Ronnie Altamont I know and love," Mouse said, arms outstretched to hug Ronnie.

"Don't say I didn't warn you," Kelly muttered before they went back inside to not sign the nonexistent lease. "This is a chainsaw massacre waiting to happen."

Ronnie wakes up to a punch on the shoulder. "Let's go," Kelly says. "I feel weird and old, sitting around here like this."

Ronnie looks around at all the collegiates. "Yeah," he yawns, "I feel it too."

"I grabbed a copy of the student paper here," Kelly says. "Not much in the classified job listings, unless you want to go teach English in Prague."

"I don't," Ronnie says, standing up, brushing the grass off his jeans. "Maybe I'll go back to school."

"Is that why you're here?" They start walking in the general direction of Ronnie's car, parked in a Boca Raton Subs parking lot on University Street.

"I'm going to write and play music," Ronnie says.

"What music? The Laraflynnboyles?" Kelly smiles, almost forgetting about the sweat underneath the gauze, the welts on the tongue. "You're not serious, right?"

"I'm booking a tour. The novel's almost done. I'm mailing it off to get published."

Kelly shrugs. "I need more ice. Don't let anybody tell you different: Ant bites on the tongue are incredibly unpleasant."

"I believe you," Ronnie says, sensing the chance to make the kill. "So is hunger."

They were back on the south sidewalk along University, off-campus, approaching the 13th Street intersection, the true center of town. A turtle-waxy blue Ford F-150 drives past with a UNIVERSITY OF CENTRAL FLORIDA ALUMNI sticker across the back window coasts past, horn honking. Ronnie looks over. A rolled down window and an upraised middle finger.

"Must be one of your many adoring fans," Kelly says.

Ronnie recognizes the truck, the middle finger, the person connected to said middle finger. "He was the Assistant Manager of that Textbook Store I worked at until I got fired for taking a two hour lunch break to, you know, get high, bang Maggie, play 18 holes of golf on Sega Genesis. Not sure why he's still mad at me, I mean, all I did was call him 'a stupid motherfucker who would rather masturbate to the sales figures in his office than do real work' in my opinion column. No need to a hold a grudge, all these months later."

Kelly sighs. They cross the intersection. "I'm too exasperated to laugh. Let's get real food, alright? My treat." To that last sentence, Kelly adds an entirely unnecessary "Duh." Past the corner gas station on the right, Gatorroni's-by-the-Slice, where the punk rockers make and sell the pizza, wearing uniforms of black t-shirts, red bandanas, and tattoo sleeves. "You win," Kelly continues. "You're getting free food from me, but only because we've tried all other alternatives available." From here, approaching the black iron railings around the perimeter of Gatorroni's, Kelly shifts into a barely audible Flintstonish muttering—"Stupid Ronnie. Stupid broke-ass Ronnie. No money and unreachable plans." He turns to Ronnie before they enter the restaurant. "You're nuts, you know that?"

Ronnie suspects he may be, and opts to say nothing that could in any way jeopardize his first real meal as a Gainesville resident.

A BRIEF EXCERPT OF A DRUNK COMEDIAN
PERFORMING AT GATOR GROWL WHO HAS BEEN
ON THE ROAD A LITTLE BIT TOO LONG

". . . Yeah. Keep booing . . . and fuck you too . . . I mean, where the fuck am I . . . seriously, where is this? Lafayette? Lawrence? Columbus? Austin? Tallamuthafuckin'hassee?"

[hearty boos from the audience]

"Look, there's no need to boo me, man . . . all I'm saying is that these college towns are all the same. You think you're so smart. What is this, Eugene? Charlottesville? Athens, Ohio? Athens, Georgia? Wait, what are you yelling? Gainesville? Gainesville?!

"Guess what: Same diff, assholes. Fuck you, I'm outta here."

SLACKIN' OFF IN THE '90s

Maux (actually, in the caustic comic she draws for the school paper, she spells it M-A-U-X, signed at the bottom right corner in angry slashes like black blood dripping in a homicide) grabs a handful of limp ketchup-doused fries from the stack piled on the Burger King bag and throws them at the television. She laughs like she talks—like a twelve-year old boy on the cusp of a voice change—when three of the larger limper fries stick to the screen and gloop downward, leaving three red trails obscuring the movie Maux has deemed "stupid"—some piece of crap Philip (her boyfriend of the week) rented called *Slackin' Off in the '90s*, that one film that's set in a large city in the Pacific northwest where these unwashed nonconformists in flannel shirts and shiny combat boots stand around listening to plodding rock and roll music while trying to date each other and avoid steady corporate employment.

Philip, dough-bodied and prismatically hair-dyed, sits next to her on his old brown sofa, laughing between chomps of sweet-and-sour soaked chicken nuggets spread out across a JFK-era drink tray he found back home in a resale shop—a tray decorated with the outline of the state of Florida circled by drawings of oranges, orange blossoms, surfers, waves, the sun, a compass, palm trees, dolphins, with sweet and sour sauce smeared across the Space Coast. He laughs because, hey, it's funny watching Maux get angry. "If you don't want to watch this," he says, patting his right hand on her left knee, "you can just tell me, I'll shut it off."

She removes the hand with a graceless kick, leans forward. "Look at this shit," she says, pointing to the television with its pinkish pixels glowing through the ketchup trails. On the screen, two "grungy"-looking men in their early twenties wearing flannel shirts and long-hair wigs sit on a couch in a slovenly living room. Posters for bands like Nirvana, Alice in Chains, and Pearl Jam hang haphazardly throughout the plaster-cracked walls. A 1959 black Les Paul is propped against the couch between Grunge Dude #1 and Grunge Dude #2. Grunge Dude #1 slouches and moans, "Aw maaaaaan. It's like, I gotta get laid!" Grunge Dude #2 yawns, stretches, returns to his original hunched form on the couch and says, "Yeah, well, you go ahead. I'm too lazy to get laid. I'll get laid later." Grunge Dude #1 punches Grunge Dude #2 on the arm and says, "You're such a slacker," and punctuates the sentence with a conspiratorial stoner laugh. Grunge Dude #2 says, "Damn right. And proud of it too!" They high-five.

"What? It's good," Philip says, egging her on. "It's what it's like for our generation. It's true-to-life, ya know?"

"I don't know why we're dating," Maux says.

"We're dating?" Philip says, reaching to the remote control to shut off the movie, hoping the silent blue screen of the stopped VCR would keep her riled-up but not so riled up she'd throw more fast food at the television, yelling, ranting, trying to break his things and trying to kick the walls of this dingy duplex he would leave when the lease expired at the end of July, photography degree in hand, bound for anywhere-but-here. No, he didn't want her so insanely rabid that sex—makeup or otherwise—was out of the question.

"No, we're 'seeing each other,' we're 'friends with benefits,' we're 'sleeping together,' we're 'fucking,' we're 'madly in love and ready to exchange marriage vows.'" With each sarcastic label of their relationship, Maux makes "finger quotes" like annoying writers performing at readings. She turns away from Philip, huffs, curls up on the couch, gazes at the wall where he hangs all his matted glossy black and white prints from his photography classes—the inevitable photo major chiaroscuro of his ex-girlfriend (that bitch) in a black dress staring all gloomy-gothic in front of rows of dead orange trees, of straight rural dirt roads trailing off into the flat distance, of close-ups of grass blades, of faded Burma Shave signs painted on old barns, of steaming coffee mugs.

Philip says nothing, steals a nice long look at her body—that body—indigo boots up to her knees, indigo skirt and blouse elaborately ripped and safety-pinned, shortcropped dyed indigo hair, and an emerald necktie. It's sexy to him how she looks like the valedictorian of a Catholic school for wayward mutants. Without that body, Maux's just a cunt—yes, cunt, that word people like Philip only use when prefaced with "Now I'm not one to use this word very often, but in this case, it fits, because that girl is such a total . . . "—and Philip stares at her turned away and feels the half-chub against his boxers, and as always with girls like these (are there any other kind?) he reflects on the lengths he goes to ignore the obvious and compromise his common sense and sell-out his self-respect just to get a taste of that pale thin flesh contrasting all that sexy fucking indigo.

Philip finishes the chicken nuggets, sweet and sour sauce now dipped and smeared from Daytona Beach to St. Petersburg. "So what are we doing then?" he asks.

"Let's go somewhere. Out. Drinks." She uncoils from the couch, turns to Philip, picks up his beloved Florida drink tray. "Otherwise, I'm gonna fling this."

He grabs the round metal tray. They tug back and forth. Smiles and laughter. Philip releases his right hand long enough to titty-twister her left A-cup breast. She screams, lets go, laughs, calls him a shit. The half-chub grows. "Let's stay here," Philip says, holding the tray at arm's length. "Don't you want to see how *Slackin' in the '90s* ends?"

"If it's between that and getting drunk," Maux says, standing, pulling down her indigo skirt, walking to the front door, "I think you know the answer." She opens the door, says, "And if you're not a total douche, you can stay at my apartment for a change."

Outside, Philip hears her car start. He looks down at his erection. "Oh, the places you'll go," he sighs before standing up and thinking unsexy shriveled thoughts of infanticide, cancer wards, and truck-crushed puppies, walks out, locks up.

"You're lucky to be graduating," Maux says. They sit in a back booth during an otherwise empty Tuesday night at The Drunken Mick. The twelve televisions scattered around the room reflect strobe lights bouncing across the unoccupied bar as the bartender takes a white towel to the same already-clean pint glass, and the server is hunched over a crossword puzzle in a booth by the opposite wall, absorbed in finding a seven letter word for "Inter-Gender Wrestling Champion of the World." The jukebox randomly selects "Holiday" by Madonna. "You get to get out of here." Propped between the edge of the table and her lap is her drawing pad.

"Maybe you can come with me," Philip says, yawning, hoping this gets the response he's looking for.

Maux laughs. Philip gets what he wanted. "Why not?" he asks.

"Why?" Maux starts sketching, angry lines stabbed across the paper.

"Because we're in love," Philip says. It has been almost four years since he was a Port St. Lucie dormkid, and everything around here was fresh and exciting and first time. Now, he finds amusement in riling up the easily riled, as Madonna pleads *If we could have a holiday / it would be so nice!*

"We're only together because there's nobody else around," she says, punching dots into the pad. "You're the best worst option."

He watches her as she draws, those mean blue eyes—spiteful, hate-filled—a bitter grin. He hates her. He wants her. And at the end of July, he will leave her. If not sooner.

"Here," she says, sliding the drawing pad across the table. "What do you think?"

He grabs the pad by its spiraled wires across the top, turns it, holds it. It's a one-panel drawing of Philip, wearing a sundress in an open field, holding a bouquet of limp flowers in his right fist. Arrows point to his "'krazy' punk haircut!," "t-shirt advertising some generic southern California pop punk band," "totally individualistic wallet chain," and "camera-for taking 'artistic' pictures." He is surrounded by six speech clouds: "You look nice today," "Let's go watch a movie," "I'm really starting to like you," "This camera is like my soul," "When can I see you again?" and "I miss you." He remembers when he said each of these to her—early in their "relationship"— and the scathing laughter and bitter remarks they engendered.

"C'mon!" she says. "It's funny!"

He smiles, to give a pretense of a reaction. He considers leaving, putting the last two month's absurdity with her to rest already, finishing this pint of Fancy Lad Irish Stout (or whatever you call it) and walking home through the quiet of a Gainesville Tuesday night. Maybe go down to the Nardic Track or the Bubbling Saucepot and see if any bands are playing. Maybe find a porch where friends are sitting around drinking and talking shit. Anywhere but here, with her. But if he leaves, he leaves the indigo, and the emerald tie, and everything underneath. He doesn't feel hurt or offended by the drawing, and he's not sure if it's better or worse that he simply doesn't care.

"You're so ridiculous," he throws out, to the empty space.

"So you're not mad?" She sounds disappointed.

"Why would I be mad? It's a beautiful rendering." He slides the drawing pad back to her side of the table. "I'm flattered."

Maux rips the drawing out of the pad, crumples it up, throws it at his head. He dodges, it lands on the table of the booth behind him. "Let's leave," she says. "Even my apartment is better than this." They finish their pints. She stomps out the door, ignoring the "Have a nice nights" of the bartender and server. Philip slides out the booth when the front door slams. He sees the drawing bunched up into the size of a softball, grabs it, planning on either keeping it or throwing it at Maux's head in the parking lot.

DANCING GIRLS

Meghan sits in a wobbly wooden chair in Mouse's living room, with that bobbed hair and the overbite and the lisp. She trills something flutey on the flute while Mouse rummages through piles of unwashed clothes and porno and emptied microwave dinner boxes for "The tape to record the song I want you to help me with, because I know, when you add what you're going to add, and what you boys are going to add . . . " (Here, Mouse points at Ronnie and Kelly. "Don't patronize us, you charlatan," Ronnie says, sipping from a foamy warm can of Dusch Light on the border of the kitchen and the so-called studio here in this filthy first floor of a rickety gray house on the eastern edge of the student ghetto, while Kelly sits at Meghan's dirty green low-cut Chuck Taylors, oblivious to everything but the February 1996 issue of *The National Review of Titties* opened across his lap.) ". . .it's going to be the best song ever, so . . . " (And here, Mouse hums like a con artist about to con) ". . .doo dee doo dee doo. Let me try and find it here, and you keep doing what you're doing . . . "

"Uh. Mouse? What is this?" Meghan says with that lisp through a retainer (At nineteen and everything! hums Mouse's fevered, feverish brain, because, with the dark bobbed hair, the overbite, the lisp—well, it's better than all the dancing girls jiggling at the tittie bar) as she reaches under the trash-covered table (a wretched uneven example of what you find piled at the end of driveways when the students reach the ends of their leases and upgrade to better homes, better furniture) and pulls out a magazine. On the magazine's cover, a woman with frizzed out 1985 white-blonde So Cal hair, dressed in a pink bikini, only the bikini bottom is lowered to her knees to expose her long, semi-erect penis. The magazine's title, in yellow lightning bolt lettering, is *PSYCH!*

Ronnie laughs at this and Kelly pays no attention, enraptured by the pictures of breasts in all shapes and sizes. "Oh, hee hee, that's nothing, doo dee doo dee doo," Mouse says. "It's something I used for a flier, hee hee hee . . . "

"And what's this?" Meghan says, laughing, pulling out from under the chair a . . .

"Oh! That!" Mouse says. "Hee hee hee. Well, you see . . . " (He strokes his long goatee.) "That's all part of the nothingness too . . . "

"That's a big strange nothing," Ronnie says, stomach empty, behind on meals, feeling and looking underfed, empty enough to already feel the one beer he has finished. "No, really. Tell the nice girl what it is, Mouse."

Mouse's smile grows a faint tinge of a sneer towards Ronnie. "Thank you. I will. See, Meghan, it's just one of those, you know, giant dildos coated in insulation foam to use in some performance art I did at the Nardic Track about a knight in shining bologna?"

"Oh!" Meghan laughs, holds the flute with one hand, swings

the dildo onto the dusty living room's no-longer-white carpeting like Roger Daltrey with a microphone, flinging it to the floor as it lands with a brittle crack.

"I found the tape!" Mouse announces, holding it out for Meghan to see. "Now I'm going to put this in the 4-track, and we're going to start recording, so before you play the flute, I need you to make up lyrics about dancing girls."

"Dancing girls?" Meghan says, the nervousness rattling around her insides, finding an outlet in the right side of her face as a random twitch.

"Yeah!" Mouse sees the nervous tic, and it's that same feeling like at the tittie bar.

"I thought you'd want to sing about poop or jerking off or something," Meghan says. Ronnie laughs at this. He is buzzed on a can-and-a-half of Dusch Light, unsure of what to say but smiling like a cretin.

"Not today. I feel the need to go into a more commercial direction." Ronnie, Kelly, and Meghan laugh at this.

"Ok," Meghan says, free hand's long fingers moving the sides of her hair behind her ears, stands, arousingly perfect nineteen-year-old breasts jutting out against the cotton of the green, yellow-lettered "LARRY'S PAWN SHOP ALL-STARS" softball thrift store t-shirt she wore. The tic fades. "I'll do my best."

"Can we get a pizza first?" Kelly asks, looking up from the engrossing, engorging magazine. "You should order us some pizza for helping you out. C'mon, Phil Spector. Your workers are hungry."

"Didn't you guys just eat? You were at Gatorroni's!" Mouse looks to Ronnie, to Kelly, back to Meghan, regretting the invite extended to the males in the room, but they happened to be there, seated outside at the front patio of Gatorroni's by the Slice—Meghan, the nnnnnugget from the pointless Gen Ed class he was getting through in order to graduate, and the next table over, the study in contrast that heightened Meghan's, well, everything—Ronnie and Kelly—who looked lost, more than a little pathetic—Kelly with the bandaged yellowed forehead, holding an iced-napkin to his tongue, Ronnie, as disheveled as Mouse had ever seen him, picking at the final crumbs and sauce dollops of what had been a mammoth sausage calzone. Mouse was on his bike, pedaling home from the library, saw Meghan sitting there, pulled the bike off University onto the sidewalk and bellowed a goofy "Helll-luuuuuuu" to her, and she smiled that overbitten smile, and—shee-yit gotdamn! The things Mouse could do with her!

The right side of Meghan's face tic'd and tic'd. Mouse noticed the flute case she had there on that greasy gray table, and the plan for the rest of the day formed instantly. (Chance encounters like these happened all the time in Gainesville, part of the thrill of never knowing exactly what kind of youthful adventure you'd get up to.) "A flautist!" Mouse exclaimed. "I need your help recording the greatest song ever made." Mouse flashed his false-tooth smile, and the scraggly knotty brown hair hung to his shoulders . . . and the moustache is bushy-big and his goatee grows to a Satanic point, but that smile! Meghan finds it sooooo disarming, while Ronnie, who watched from six feet to her right, smiled because he knows all-too-well Mouse's m.o. with the nnnnuggets, the way he smiles and will soon rhyme when he says things he knows girls might find creepy. "Yes, that's right!" Mouse continued. "The greatest song ever written, and I'm feeling good, you know—heh heh heh and not just because my friend Ronnie here . . . " (Mouse pointed to Ronnie, who looked up from the calzone's remnants long enough to mumble a "Hi," and that was their introduction.) ". . . just moved to Gainesville, but—and we all need to do this—I was going to go to the tittie bar today for the all-you-can-eat buffet?"

"Oh God," Ronnie said, licking the grease off his fingers. "You're still going on about the tittie bars and the buffets." When Mouse lived in Orlando for two years, a half-hearted student at the University of Central Florida, it was a focal point of many a conversation, and the women around him either laughed or groaned or both, but they never walked away, "creeped out," as Jan Brady might have said.

"But you know how great it is, Ronnie! You've gone!"

"Whatever," Ronnie said, still hungry, looking for any piece of uneaten calzone on the red tray, no matter how small. "It's just boobs."

"Just boobs," Mouse said. "No no no! It's too late today—shit!—but if we could have gotten there before 4 p.m . . . "

". . . And get only one of their watered-down drinks," Ronnie interrupted, having heard this spiel countless times.

". . . Yes, that's right, Ronald, and around 4:30 they get the buffet going, and . . . "

". . . And it's all-you-can-eat buffet food on plates in front of you and jigglin' titties and . . . "

"Yes, yes, Ron—heh heh—and then we go home, and it makes it sooo wonderful when you go home to bang the gong on the ding dong, sing song whack a doodle-doo, hmm?"

"And by that, Meghan, our friend Mouse means masturbate."

Meghan laughed at Mouse's refreshingly weird honesty. Oh,

college! Oh, Gainesville! They don't make boys like this back home in Fort Myers! "I wanna sing it!" she lisped through her retainer, smiling. "Let's make something crazy!"

And now that everyone's here, Mouse hates that he felt sorry for Ronnie and Kelly, and wishes he had left them at Gatorroni's as he stands in front of Meghan, handing her the microphone directly plugged into the 4-track. "We'll eat something soon, after we record this." To Meghan, he rolls his eyes, and shakes his head, unable to apologize more for the cockblocking beer drinking free loading rejects he brought along to this elaborate ruse of seducing young Meghan into his bedroom. "So I'll play you the song in the headphones, and you start singing it whenever you feel it." His hands, her shoulders, a soft too-brief squeeze. "You're gonna be great! Here we go."

Mouse turns to the 4-track, presses the record button, the play button. Through the headphones, audible by everyone—synthesized white noise, low-end keyboard burps and farts, guitar sounds high in the treble range, layered and layered, backed by a mid-90s techno beat (or what passed for a techno beat in Mouse's anti-techno mind—this arhythmical quarter note low-bounce that would clear a dance club faster than live grenades dropping out of the disco ball), all of it working together into an absurd chaos.

"Dancing girrrrrrl," Meghan begins, singing in a creep soprano, headphones burrowed into her hair, big dark eyes looking into Mouse's for encouragement, validation. "Won't you give me a whirrrrrl, won't you make a man out of meeeeeeee . . . "

Mouse laughs at this, standing to her left as she sings—so happy and horny he is to be here—waving his hands and mouthing the word, "MORE!"

"Dancing girl," Meghan continues, the initial nervousness abated, "like a whippo-whirl, won't you hum to me, sensual-leeeeeeeeee . . ."

Mouse smiles his smile and hops up and down, like everything in the world has surpassed his optimistic expectations. Unsure where to go from here, unable to come up with any more lyrics about dancing girls, as overwhelmed as she is with laughter that distorts the recording, she la-las sopranically, ooing and ahing until the beat ends and the song collapses into white noise tracks.

"Was that ok?" she asks. Mouse shushes because the mic is still recording, but he knows he will keep the question in the final mix.

Meghan removes the headphones, and the first thing she hears is Mouse shout "Yes! You're a genius!" He steps up, pulls her in to give her a hug, and he holds her one second longer than the hugs of a friend, and Meghan knows that look, the dude look of "I'm going to kiss you now," that intent, determined, vulnerable glaze they get. She still hasn't made up her mind—this strange, strange boy with his strange, strange friends—she pokes him gently in the ribs with her flute, says, "Let's record this now, hmmmm?"

He's rebuffed, and she's relieved, even if Mouse looks less jovial than before. He forces a laugh. "Yes, the flute! I'll hold the mic, and I want you to play freely."

"Freely?" Meghan holds the flute to her mouth in the horizontal position. "What do you mean?"

"Just follow your gut, your instinct—play it like you don't know the rules. Like a dancing girl, spinning on the pole!"

Meghan nods, the 4-track's tape spins once again, and over the noise and ridiculousness of her lyrics and the singing, Meghan breathes into the flute crazy puffs of swirling bird calls as Mouse holds the microphone, pretending like he's trying to get the perfect spot for the microphone while he stares at her ti-tays, so close to the hand, like the dancing girls who pinch the folded dollar from his fingers and capture it in (Mouse calls it) their Lee Van Cleave. He will try again.

"Now can we order the pizza?" Ronnie asks, still standing in the kitchen's threshold, a newly opened beer in his right hand by his side. Kelly tosses the magazine into a pile of dirty clothes, paces around, eyes downward, scanning the filth and the trash for a magazine he hasn't looked at yet.

"Yesyesyes," Mouse says, not hiding the annoyance in his voice. "Ronnie, since you know how to work the 4-track, on the last free track there, I want you two to sing "Dancing Girls," over and over again while Meghan and I take a walk to the ol' Floridian Harvest Minimart for a 24-pack of Dusch Light and Partini's Party Pizza."

"That's it?" Ronnie says, not hiding the disappointment in his voice. "No screaming? No hooting and hollering? No guitars played through pedals?"

"Just sing it," Mouse says, already out there, Meghan in front of him, right hand across her lower back. "Then you'll get your pizza."

As Ronnie and Kelly (unsurprisingly) nail their contribution to "Dancing Girls" in one take, Mouse and Meghan walk down narrow student ghetto streets, sidewalkless cracked little straight paths the width of the average car. The houses have old white gray porches, subdivided into two to eight apartments, or they're tin-roofed shacks plopped in the far end of the property lines with mulch driveways leading to the inevitable cul-de-sac of parked cars and trucks. No two buildings are ever the same. The trees canopy the streets and shade the sun, which now leaves nothing but a violet twilight.

"How do you know those guys?" Meghan asks, as they walk back, each with a frozen pizza and a twelve-pack of beer, turning left to face University. "They seem a little, I don't know, out of it?"

"Yeah," Mouse laughs. "They're a little shell-shocked moving here. I lived with Kelly when I lived in Orlando, and we all went to UCF together. Ronnie and I ran for Student Government President and Vice-President."

"Did you win?"

"No, but that wasn't the point. It was a dumb college prank, I guess, but one of the ideas of the platform—Ronnie's idea—was to have a holiday called "Big Lug Day.""

"Big Lug Day?"

"Yeah! It was like—" and Mouse sets the case of Dusch Light in the middle of the sidestreet leading back to his apartment. "Put the pizza and the beer down," he adds.

"So on Big Lug Day," Mouse continues. "You get to go up to anyone you want and ask for a hug, and they have to give it to you. You have to do it like this." Mouse outstretches his arms and says, "C'mere, ya big lug." Meghan stands there.

"Sooo, what do I do now?"

"You give me a hug because it's Big Lug Day!"

She laughs through the overbite and the retainer, looks down, looks up and to the right, at the bug-swarmed streetlights over the darkened houses and trees, takes one step forward and they hug, and she laughs again, adds, "Happy Big Lug Day, Mouse," and it's the sound of Meghan saying that into his unwashed shirt that really gets him, makes him think, in the second before the lean in to kiss that this is really and truly better than the sounds of the dancing girls, those strippers looking Mouse in the eye like they actually like him as those black ladies croon *No you're never gonna get it / no you're never gonna get it* through the mammoth strip club PA speakers as they spin away on the poles and slap their asses while he eats practically flavorless barbeque ribs and sips from a watered down vodka tonic. No, this is much much better than those dancing girls in the tittie flop—through the tongue swirls and puckers and his tongue's brushings with that hott-hott-hott retainer, Mouse sings in his head *Happy Big Lug Day to me / Happy Big Lug Day to me*, and while he must eventually thank Ronnie for coming up with the holiday, he must also get them out of the house. Ronnie will sense what's up even if Kelly's too obtuse to understand; as a parting/get-the-hell-out-of-here gift: half of this Dusch Light 12-pack and both Partini Party Pizzas, and it's out the door with those two brokeass brokeasses, so Mouse and Meghan can, you know, do it, while listening to "Dancing Girls" on an endless loop.

ZOMBIE PROSTITUTE

When Nicholas J. Canberry (goes by Nick in class, but uses his full name in the heading to his stories because this is what he wants to go by in the literary world, kinda like Hunter S. Thompson, ya know?) sat down to write the short story "Zombie Narc"[3] for Adjunct Professor Anderson "Andy" Cartwright's Introduction to

---

[3] For the complete story, please see Appendix C

the Short Story creative writing class, it surely never occurred to him that the final product would be the catalyst that would send Cartwright swerving eastbound beachbound on FL-20, chugging straight Absolut from a frozen bottle while throwing stacks of student work out the window of his rusty yellow VW Bug.

Nicholas J. Canberry was actually quite proud of his latest in a semester-long series of zombie-themed stories, among them: "Zombie Cop," "Zombie Prostitute," "Zombie Frat Boys from Hell," "Zombie Sluts," "Zombie Dope Dealer's Revenge," "Zombie Dope Dealer's Revenge Part II: Unkind Bud Strikes Back," "Zombie Librarian," and now, "Zombie Narc." The assigned book for this class—some bullshit short story anthology that was like $70 or something—has not been moved nor opened since he'd tossed it on the window sill by the dorm room bed. ("I don't see the point in reading if you're a writer," is what he tells the ladies at parties. "I mean, movies are the books of today anyway, you know?") One muse is enough, thank you very much, and Nicholas J. Canberry's muse is named Janis—a pink bong he found at a Daytona Beach head shop in the middle of last year's Spring Break (Spring Break!) he christened one night while trying to write a poem about what the Atlantic Ocean means to him[4] for some blowoff poetry class he took last fall and as he sat there at his dorm room desk listening to *Janis Joplin's Greatest Hits* from the CD boombox on the desk's upper shelf, he had the really fantastic magical epiphany that Janis Joplin made the greatest music of all time. (Even better than Bob Marley.) Henceforth, Janis never left the right side of Nicholas J. Canberry's computer (an

---

[4] See Appendix D

off-to-college gift from his realtor parents back home in Newport Richey), and he must have put at least half a sack into Janis's
nug-hungry bowl the night he wrote "Zombie Narc." When he'd
half-finished, Nicholas J. Canberry knew he had something good,
something that would blow Cartwright's farty-ass old punk rocker mind. This was confirmed as he read each page, fresh from the
whirring dot matrix printer:

*"I taught you were our friend, man!" Smokey cried sadly as the cops
put the cuffs on him and took him away. "We did . . . drugs together. Remember?"*

*"I am your friend, man!" Stoney pleaded insistently. "But there's one
thing, you don't know."*

*Smokey spat at the ground as the cops led him away. "I know every-
thing I need to know, man. You're nuthin' but a narc! You're just a narc!"*

*"Not so fast, Smokey!" Stoney announced menacingly. "Watch this!"
The skin of Stoney's flesh was ripped by Stoney's hands. His hands tugged
at his face, revealing . . . A ROTTING SKULL UNDERNEATH!!!*

*"I'm a ZOMBIE NARC!!!" Stoney yelled loudly. "And I'm hungry.
FOR BRAINS!"*

*"What the? No! No!!! Please!" Smokey begged as the top of his skull
was being chewed by Stoney's mouth. Blood shot everywhere, and the
cops shot their guns. They had no affect on Stoney. He grabbed the cops
and ate them up too.*

*"Stoney's brain tastes like chicken!" Stoney reflected calmly to him-
self. "But these cops' brains taste like pigs!" Stoney proceeded to eat his
way through all their brains, ralishing each volumtous bite. The fact is,
Stoney was hungry, hungry for brains . . . "*

. . . These words, one after the other, written by one Nicholas J.
Canberry, provide the unintended catalyst pushing Adjunct Profes-

sor Anderson "Andy" Cartwright to run out of the house with the keys, the stack of student work, the bottle of Absolut from the freezer, and into the car, sputtering down the road, screaming "What am I doing?! What the hell fuck shit am I doing?!" punching the steering wheel, swerving along as the cassette deck plays what it always plays, songs from local legends Roach Motel, circa 1982—young and angry and fun and stupid and great. So long ago. "What am I doing!" Andy (the Department of Tireless Literary Derring-do at the Gainesville College of Arts and Crafts fancies itself cutting edge and insists on the students calling the teachers by their first names. It's very egalitarian that way, lest the students get on bummer authority trips) yells again, not fully aware that he is yelling. He used to be a decent writer—a novel published to not-bad reviews five years prior, some short story credits—before he faced down these mammoth stacks of student work (twenty-five students averaging twenty pages a week—the four students who turn in nothing are counterbalanced by the four engaged in Trollopian, Oatesian prolificness—equals 500 pages per week) day after day, to the point that all this bad, bad writing—stories of dorm room dope smoke, of back seat blow jobs, of unicorns and faeries and mawkish breast cancers and battlefield glory and sci-fi robots out of control and kung-fu peasants avenging their honor and wizards and spell books and all the fear and loathing at the kegger fogged up his brain to the point that working on his own writing was out of the question.

He passes into the next county, the road a perfect emptiness, bisecting undeveloped Florida jungle-woods. He drinks the straight vodka, the sticky cold in his hands and mouth, winces then smiles, grabs a handful of pages of the student work stacked on the passenger seat, flings them out the driver's side window. In the rear view mirror, Andy watches as the pages flip and land onto the pavement.

The stack is smaller now, but Andy lifts what's left and yells "Not small enough!" over the din of the VW engine and Roach Motel. He grabs a page from the middle of the stack and reads aloud as he keeps the wheel mostly straight along the unbending eastbound beachbound road.

"... 'Just because I'm a prostitute from the ghetto doesn't mean I can't have feelings for you!' Angela said, crying like a baby who wants a pacifier.

"'But you don't get it!' Chas said knowingly. 'I'm a banker, and I'm rich. I preside over the country club! This love just isn't meant to be!'"

"Oh God," Andy groans, flings the page out the window. He swigs the vodka, rescrews the top, tosses it to the passenger seat, grabs another page at random and reads aloud.

"... 'The beer tasted like warm piss and it was hot as hell, but these minor and meaningless obstacles would not stand in the way of what we wanted to do. There, in the frat house, I wanted to get Lauren in bed so we could screw all night like rabid and fierce animals in heat...'"

"Out the window!" Andy howls, laughing at the bad joke his life had become these past two years since learning he would not be getting the first tenure track position offered by the Department in several years, laughing at this self-pity and bitterness brought to the surface from one-too-many stories of zombie narcs eating brains in the passive voice. In front of him, the empty white beach and the Atlantic Ocean washing ashore in the choppy gray-green-blue waves under a beach-bright, beach-hot early afternoon. Andy parks in the free dirt lot, finishes the vodka, sees the final twenty odd pages he hasn't thrown out of the Bug, and has an idea.

He takes off his black socks, slips off his brown dress shoes, unbuttons his pink Oxford shirt, tosses each article into the backseat, grabs a large swirled red white yellow and green beach towel with the words CLEARLY CANADIAN in white lengthwise letters, hides the bottle in the towel, grabs the pages, and steps out of the car. In the light dizzy rage of an increasingly savage vodka buzz, he steps quickly over the burning rocky sand of the parking lot, descends the precarious wooden steps onto the beach, and as always, when face to face with the ocean, he recalls Ishamel's lines about people standing by bodies of water, staring to the horizon lines on their lunch breaks with so much wanderlust. The beach and the ocean conspire to give you a proper perspective, to leave you less jaded than you were when you arrived, to remind you that you're a small but necessary part of something bigger, that there's more than these tiny little worlds we've constructed out of money and stress and desperation. So Andy thinks, always reminded of the past when here, of all the great times with girls, with friends, whether overnight in motels or beach houses—days and nights living the Great Floridian Dream of E-Z beach access. It's an empty Tuesday afternoon at Crescent Beach. Along the grainy white sand, strands of seaweed wash ashore. Andy stumbles away from the house and the beach shacks, lurching along to the sounds of the waves and the water. Andy spreads out the towel over soft dry sinking sand, steps to the water as it rolls in on his feet, his ankles, up the cuffed khaki slacks (and these outfits, man, these outfits I gotta wear teaching, I mean, how would these kids not know I was—am, am, I mean, am—punk rock if I didn't tell them!), the waves splash the always jarring crotch region—in a dizzy spin, Andy swings the bottle and sings what he can remember of a long ago Kinks song: "The tax man's taken all my dough / and left me in my stately home / all I got's this sunny afternoon . . . "

Empty bottle in one hand, pages in the other, Andy rolls up the pages, untwists the cap, stuffs the pages inside the bottle. The pages cling in parts to the bottle's insides, but they're in, and Andy replaces the cap, turns to his right, faces the ocean, pulls back his right arm and flings, watching the Absolut bottle's sensual curves flip end over end, the white pages rolled up too tight to move except for those stuck to the insides, vodka/sea water moisture where the black print becomes a blue smudge, it flips end over end in a Saint Louis Arch flight pattern, plopping into a tiny splash a hundred feet away. He stares at that point of impact for a long time, scratches the developing paunch across his abdomen, reflects on the paunchiness of all of this—that gaping chasm that grows with the start of every fall semester, as more eighteen year olds come in as they always do; as Andy once did, way back in 1977. The flabby decision to stick around—the college, the town—part-time professoring, more out of habit than anything else. This life is familiar and comfortable and easy. Two years ago, when the Chair of the Department told him he would not be getting the full-time position, Andy did not want to leave. When people left Gainesville—like his friends had been doing, more and more—so many inevitably returned within the year, tail between legs, wondering what they missed while they were in New York, San Francisco, Chicago, LA. Seeing their returns was a living breathing testimonial to the unstressful simplicity of staying put. The onset of middle-age. Maybe, initially, in the backs of all the minds of creative writing teachers—like touring musicians, bartenders, baseball coaches—you think you've found a fountain of youth, and it means you don't have to give up this life that made you so happy when you were 21, that you don't have to give it up now and go out and sell the proverbial insurance to pay bills. But, at 37, after years of teaching, that cycle of the academic calendar becomes a kind of Sisyphean nightmare of Twilight Zone proportions. You grow up, you try and mature and evolve, but the students always, always stay the same, and right when Andy connects with these kids and starts making real progress, the semester ends. The students' comments, concerns, observations, reactions, to the assigned reading, are unvarying. Standing in the ocean, Andy foresees a bleak future of thankless cheerless unappreciated unrespected decades passing by like nothing. On auto-pilot, spouting the same old tired and obsolete platitudes trying to masquerade as wisdom. For a time, the students will believe it, until they see him for what he is: A failed writer. Chills in the bloodstream as his feet feel the sand tugged away from the undertow. A chill, thinking of this future, his future. A shell of a manchild. Around all this youth, stunted. A writing teacher who does not write. Andy teaches writing, and he stopped writing. The vodkabrain poses the obvious question—So why did you want this, then? And the vodkaanswer is just as stripped away from distraction, with added help from the perspective-giving ocean: He didn't want the job. He only wanted a little office to store his favorite books—Agee to Vonnegut— dusted nightly by the custodial staff—framed posters on the wall of old show fliers and readings he's done (so the students see he's not some typical tweed jacket English teaching stuffed-shirt pipe smoking pedantic bore)—and on the opposite wall his nice little desk with a top-of-the-line Apple computer (because the school knows that if you're going to have quirky artists, you've got to give them Apple computers) stuffed with his short story and novel work, and a file cabinet to the left of the desk to stuff all the student work and in the cabinet of the desk drawer a bottle of scotch to sip with colleagues or alone when the work day is done and to the right a window overlooking the bright campus. To say nothing of the summers to travel, sabbaticals to be left alone, benefits to provide security.

Instead, it's reading 500 pages of student work each week that feels more and more like a massive steaming turd he's required to eat, every single week, living in the same house he has rented for the past ten years. Rented. Now, renting instead of owning seems like a big deal. There are no surprises to the ocean today. Andy remembers being a student—and he'd be in the Student Ghetto with friends as some house party was winding down, and he wanted more, but you shoot out all this energy, and it simply dissipates in these sad southern days and nights. Like his ambitions and hopes. The energy shoots around in meaningless circles, and you want to explode. His old friends would feel this way, and reach the point where they would have to move, and yet they came back. "So burned out," Andy mutters to no one, stepping forward, drunk enough to do it, to walk until the waves rise and fall over his head, drunk enough to pass out, drunk enough to not swim ashore. The chill in knowing Anderson "Andy" Cartwright could be exactly the same person in ten years, in the same house, reading the same stories, dispensing the same tired advice students still—most of them—somehow took so much from—but to him, the words are tedious platitudes, and as a writer (a writer who didn't write, so what did that make him?), he wonders if he believes what he says anymore.

"To pee or not to pee, haw haw haw," he laughs, drunk enough to drown, but sober enough to turn around to push through the water back to the shore, to fall down and get up with each strong-enough wave smacking him in the back, hands breaking each fall digging into the wet sand. In the trip-and-fall out of the ocean back to shore, just another lush singing, the vodkathought, the seaperspective *You could just leave* enters his thoughts. It's the 1990s, and there's prosperity. Work a job, punch out, go home and forget about it, instead of adjuncting two classes a semester, struggling to pay off bills, never really off the clock, or becoming just another tenured asshole with some tiny office, just another dickhead academic on a sabbatical who accomplishes nothing be-cause he's accomplished nothing with his life—like one of those professors who dabbles with the same novel for thirty years. He could leave. Andy smiles at the prospect of this as he reaches the spread-out CLEARLY CANADIAN towel in the dry sand, falls onto the thick cotton, passes out.

Two hours of a dreamless konk-out later, Andy wakes up sweaty, sunburned, and dehydrated. The high tide rolls in, up to pink shins, ankles and feet, the burn not in the painful stages yet, but by tonight . . . Andy's grateful that many of the vodka's toxins have been flushed out from the heat, and the hangover is little more than a disoriented sluggishness. He carries the sandy wet towel to the VW Bug, trying to piece together the afternoon's dance along the edges of a blackout. Wind gusts in short bursts, from all directions, stopping and starting. Sandpipers scurry across the sand along the surf. Seagulls swoop in for trash kills, pelicans float overhead. Rides home from the beach are always damp, sandy, and silent. There's no music when Andy leaves the beach, the little beachy surf shacks and t-shirt shops along the main roads in and out of every beach town, into the jungle again as afternoon turns into evening. It's the Briggs and Strattonesque lawnmowery rumble of the VW's engine and the no-thought of an as yet unprocessed unbrooded upon day.

Well into the jungle-forest, halfway to Gainesville, Andy sees the pages he has tossed. Some are stuck to the road, flattened by traffic, others clinging to high weeds sprouting through the cracks along the shoulder.

He pulls over, parks the Bug, steps out, walks to a stack of the pages scattered by the weeds and a guardrail, bends down to grab one, starts reading:

"*. . . They called us 'Sandwich Artists.' Like Picasso with paint, like Coltrane with the saxophone, so Beth worked with the bread knife, and so I worked with condiment bottles. Artists of the sandwich. On our breaks, one of us would steal a cookie and walk to the far end of the minimall, sitting on the curb in front of the blacked-out windows where the tanning salon used to be. We split the cookie, split a cigarette, held hands, and laughed at ourselves, laughed at our customers, laughed at our ludicrous corner of the world, counting down each day closer to graduation. This was only a year ago, but the path seemed straighter, more clear-cut, than it is now that we're in college. Graduate, one last summer in town as Sandwich Artists, then we're off. For good.*

"*'We're not going to be like them, right?' Beth would say on those breaks, pointing out our regular customers, screaming overweight families voiding packed minivans . . .*"

There is no name on this page, only a handwritten "Page 3" in the top right corner. For once, Andy cannot guess who wrote this. And he wants to know who wrote it, he wants to know what happens next. His head is a stabbing post-vodka skullache, the jungle a stultifying mix of insects and sweat, roadkill and exhaustion. Andy gathers as many pages as he can find—almost optimistic, nearly hopeful—walks to his car, straightens the pages into as close an approximation to a stack as he can make these dirty torn crumpled pages, climbs in, drives home.

THE MODERN DAY WARRIOR'S JOB INTERVIEW

Jeremy Moreland, seventeen years old, wunderkind Assistant Director of Partytyme Pizzatyme Anytyme Affairs for Grandfather's Olde Tyme Goode Tyme Pizza Parlor (the 34th Street location, between Larry's Reasonably Priced Furniture Rental and Le Chandelier Hut, in Patton Plaza) holds in his freckled hands a grease-smudged application where the only information given is the first name: Stevie. No address, no phone, no social security number, no employment history, no references.

"He must figure we already know him so he don't gotta put nuthin' else down," Brooks Brody, the unwunderkind Table Removal and Replenishment Coordinator says to Jeremy when handing him the application. "He just told me to hand this to you when I walked by his booth." Brody stood in front of the counter, holding the gray bus tray filled with yellow plates and clear red plastic cups, in a sweat-soaked, sauce-stained yellow apron covering a uniform middle-scale and lower department stores would call "husky." Brody plays right tackle on the Junior Varsity squad at Buchholz, where Jeremy would soon graduate with a 4.96 GPA. Not that their paths crossed much at school—Brooks Brody being good for little besides plowing open spaces for running backs to sprint through, or parting the overcrowds in the hallways between classes, or lifting heavy objects like free weights or bus tubs. Besides this, he tended to stand there in his short-cropped blond jock mohawk (funny how it was always perfectly acceptable when the o-line or d-line of the football team got mohawks for superstitious reasons or whatever in the middle of the season, but God help anybody else who did it) awaiting his next orders with that blank look of his.

"You did the right thing, Brooks," Jeremy says. "Go finish the rest of the tables."

Brooks grunts an affirmation, swivels a 180 to the unbussed tables. "So, Stevie wants a dishwashing job?" Dale Doar, Director of Partytyme Pizzatyme Anytime Affairs for Grandfather's Olde Tyme Good Tyme Pizza Parlour, says, removing the yellow, red-lettered regulation work cap (the Employee Manual calls it a "party chapeau") and running a hand through receding brown hair he used to comb back into a pony tail. He steps away from the counter, laughs his just-had-his-first-post-work-hit-off-the-one-hitter *heh heh heh.* "I'll let you handle this one," he says to Jeremy while walking to the kitchen, to the back door. "Just give him an interview while he's eating. Make up whatever excuse you need to."

Jeremy stands behind the counter holding the application, in this all-too-familiar perspective of the gold peppermint candy dish and the red plastic "take a penny/leave a penny" tray next to the register, the Elton John/Kiki Dee duet "Don't Go Breakin' My Heart" that the adult contemporary station feels necessary to share with North-Central Florida at least five times a day coming over the paneled ceiling's speakers, the red and white checkerboard-topped tables in the middle, the red vinyl booths—ducttape covering the tears and containing the inner foam—lined along either side of the room, the walls, like everything here, the colors of pepperoni and extra cheese, Polaroids of kids celebrating their birthdays with candles in pizza slices pinned in rows of twenty above friendly posters of "Grandfather Fredo," the jolly cartoon mascot for all three hundred and seventeen Grandfather's Olde Tyme Goode Tyme Pizza Parlour locations, offering litigious-proof advice like "MAMA MIA! BE CAREFUL EVERYBODY! THAT PIZZA! SHE GETSA SO HOT WHEN OUTTA THE OVEN IT COULDA BURN YOUR FACE OR THE ROOFA OF YOUR MOUTHA! OOF MADON!" while spinning flattened circular pizza dough on his index finger like a basketball. The placemats offer the sole nod to the Old Country—between mazes challenging children to "Help Grandfather Fredo ride his gondola through the Venice canals to his Olde Tyme Fun Tyme Pizza Parlour!"—and drawings of mozzarella stix that need coloring—some Italian fun facts underneath the heading "Did You Know?", e.g., "Italy is a country in Europe," "Rome is the capital of Italy," "Dante, an Italian, sent all of his fellow countrymen to Hell in his book *The Inferno!*" and so on. Through the front windows, through the credit card stickers, the "Now Hiring Dishwashers" sign and two-of-these-for-only-one-of-those sales, beyond the compact parking lot, 34th Street leads to Newberry Road which turns into University Street and that leads to Waldo Road to 301 North to Interstate 95 North which gets you to New York. For two perfect seconds, Jeremy Moreland dreams of that day in August when he's clocked out of here for good and walking out that front door, never again having lousy tasks like these pawned off on his scrawny teenage back. Doar had seven years seniority and career ambitions far beyond afterschool/summertime employment, and that's all he had. Doar was a lifer. Jeremy Moreland scored a 1590 on the SAT (only temporarily forgetting that cadaverous: sarcophagus :: billingsgate : Oakland Raiders, a mistake which haunted him for weeks), had effortlessly ascended Grandfather's ranks in just eighteen months—from Dish Machine Operator to Yummytizer Preparation Specialist to Smiley Service Liaison to Assistant Director of Partytime Pizzatime Anytime Affairs. During this part of the lunch shift, when Dale leaves, Jeremy often feels like a virtuous Caesar—the benevolent rulers Gibbon immortalized—as he overlooks what he thinks of as his store and the aftermath of another busy All-You-Care-to-Load-Up-On-Your-Plate-And-Eat-And-Try-To-Enjoy-Because-It's-Yummy-Five-Dollar-Lunch-Buffet, as the Table Removal and Replenishment Coordinators—his Table Removal and Replenishment Coordinators—clean off the tables, and the Smiley Service Liaisons—his Smiley Service Liaisons, are sent home at his behest. Only one customer left. Stevie, who's hunched over stacks of plates, pizza slice in right hand, marinara-tipped breadstick in the other, alternating bites from one to the next. Unshaven and doughy, in a black bulbous Misfits t-shirt covered in crumbs and sauce, working the food like a cud-chewing cow, always in the same booth in the corner, every weekday lunch. And now, evidently, he wants to work here. Jeremy inhales, exhales, indulges in one brief vision of putting all of this in the rear view mirror, grabs fistfuls of the bottom of his red regulation polo shirt with the yellow "GRANDFATHER'S OLDE TYME GOODE TYME PIZZA PARLOR: WHERE EVERY PARTY IS A PIZZA PARTY," with Grandfather Fredo kissing the tips of his fingers, tucks it into his black regulation work slacks, steps up to Stevie's usual booth.

"How we doing today?" Jeremy says, trying not to look profoundly disturbed by Stevie's ravenous eating. "You applied here and I'd like to ask you a few questions?"

Stevie tries speaking, voice blocked by mounds of digested breadstick masticated in violent chomps. He holds out a "Wait a minute" right index finger, moves a stack of plates from what will be Jeremy Moreland's side of the booth, motions with "Have a seat" outstretched arms, tries wiping the grease off Jeremy's side of the table with a couple already soiled and crumpled brown napkins and succeeds in spreading the grease into circular smudges, swallows the breadstick and starts in with this torrent in the cadence, timbre and volume of a Florida used car salesman yelling about bargains in late night TV commercials, "Hey man, yeah, sit down and talk to me you probably know who I am 'cuz I'm in here almost every day so you're probably like 'Y'all, who's that who's always in here tearin' up the lunch buffet?' Well I figured I'm here enough already so might as well apply here since I obviously like the food so much anyway this buffet's the best in town so I saw that sign outside and figured why not?"

Jeremy slides into the booth, looks over the plates stacked five-six high, littered with pizza crusts and the hard ends of marinara tipped bread sticks, overturned dipping sauces (Awesome Valley Ranch, Totally Dudical Honey Mustard, Mama Leona's Fatten You Uppa Sour Cream and Chives, Peter Cetera's Moderate Salsa, Kansas City Dude Squad Mesquite Barbeque Sauce, Paisan Geoff's Zesty Garlic Butter), stray oregano and red pepper flakes scattered everywhere. "So. Stevie. That's your name?"

"Yeah buddy!" Stevie says, swallowing the last of the pizza while finishing the breadstick in his other hand. Jeremy Moreland hears the hick accent, sees the gold brah chain around Stevie's neck and the buzzed black hair and laughs the kind of superior under-the-breath chuckle that comes naturally from the mouths of high school seniors who have been told that they were "gifted" their whole lives. Stevie hears the laugh. "That funny, home slice?"

Jeremy says nothing, pretends to scan the yellow-papered, grease-smudged application for the first time. "And . . . do you have a last name, Stevie?"

"Yeah I gotta last name and a whole lotta other information I could give you, but I ain't gonna share that with you for reasons you know I know and I know you know, so I'm just going to keep that to myself for the time being."

"You're saying you won't give me your last name?"

"That's exactly what I'm saying!" Stevie pounds the table, rattling the plates and the napkin dispenser. "'Cause I heard this thing on the radio that the government takes that information and after that who knows what they do with it man! They get that, and they'll know how to find me, and when—not if, *when*—society collapses, they'll round me up with the rest of you suckers—"

"Well," Jeremy says, starting the scrawny-ass scoot out of the booth, "we can't hire you without a last name, so if you don't feel comfortable—"

"It's Walters," Stevie interrupts, and Jeremy slides back across his side of the booth. "Steven 'Stevie' Raymond Walters."

"Thank you." Jeremy writes in the new information in the appropriate lines. Stevie reaches for his massive red plastic cup and straw-slurps a mouthful of sweet tea. "I can assure you no one here will alert the government of your whereabouts should civilization collapse on us."

"You say that now," Stevie says, "but man, don't get me started."

"I hope not to," Jeremy says, wishing for these three months to move faster, pissed Dale isn't dealing with this. "What's your address, Stevie Walters?"

"Ok, well, that's a whole other story. I was going to Santa Fe Community College, right? But I wasn't likin' it that much so I dropped out. My parents found out about this and they kicked me out—they live out in High Springs now—used to live in Gainesville—but they moved out there when I graduated high school a couple years back. So right now, I'm living with Alvin—he's friends with my friend Mouse—and he's got a trailer real close—but that's not my home *home*, right? So I didn't know if you wanted my home-home or like where I'm living now because I ain't on the lease or any of the bills or anything. I mean, it ain't like my parents would get mad if I was using their address for a job application—they just kicked me out 'cause I ain't workin' right now or goin' to school so they'd probably be glad to see me applyin'—"

"Your address now. In the trailer." Jeremy hands Stevie the application, his pen. "Fill it in, please."

Stevie scrawls in the trailer's address. "So why do you want to wash dishes for us, Stevie?"

"You ever need money for something?"

"No." Jeremy says, trying to make the best of this, indulging both his mockery at those who have never taken Advanced Placement classes and the sumptuous thought of taking money from his savings account for the first time, far away from here, happy and not working for nonworking Dale.

"Well, I wanna kick ass and take names. I like to think of

myself as a modern-day warrior, and if that's what I am, then of course I need to learn karate."

"Karate."

"Yeah man."

"Modern-day warrior." Jeremy leans back in the booth, idea fully hatched. "What does that mean?"

"It means I'm a badass. It means, ok, let's say you hit somebody smaller than you. Not that that's gonna happen but let's just say. You hit somebody who's smaller than you who's defenseless and all that shit—oh, sorry man—didn't mean to swear—but what I'm saying is—if you did that I would hit you and fight you because that's what modern-day warriors do. They kick ass. If I see anything like that I get like 'It's time to take out the trash: HI-YAH!' " . . . And here, Stevie smacks the table with the side of his right hand, knocking two plates off the edge where they land on the extra-cheese-colored linoleum with a loud wobble-wobble. "I'll get that later, don't worry," Stevie continues. "I mean it would be good practice if you hired me anyway, right? So I've been trying to teach myself karate and other bad ass moves like wrestling—"

"You're teaching yourself karate?" Jeremy Moreland laughs in cracked pubescent guttural hee hee hees.

"And wrestling too. It's all part of being a kick-ass badass. It's what I wanna do, and if I get good enough, maybe I can be an instructor or something. Teach kids how to be modern-day warriors."

There's an awkward pause here. Jeremy wants to run to the back and laugh and laugh and laugh, but there's this awkward pause to fill, and filling it is beyond Jeremy's paygrade. He can't wait for Dale to meet this guy.

"Anything else I should know about? Prison time? Drug offenses?"

"No man. Just tryin' to be . . . "

"A modern-day warrior. Got it," Jeremy says. He points to the application sopping up even more grease from Stevie's side of the table. "I just need you to write down your Social Security Number, a couple references, and anything else on there you left blank, and then you're hired." Jeremy slides out of the booth.

"Hell yeah, buddy," Stevie says, extending a grease-laden hand to shake. Jeremy looks at it, smiles, turns away, says, "Your first job is to clean up your booth here." He walks to the kitchen, turns, adds, "And clean yourself up before starting tomorrow at five."

From the open window between the kitchen and the pass, Table Replacement and Replenishment Coordinator Brooks Brody watches Stevie deliver the twenty-odd plates he had used during today's assault on the buffet, walking back to his booth, swinging his arms in irregular unfluid air-karate motions. Jeremy approaches to the left, pats Brody on the shoulder. "You about ready to punch out and go home?"

"Did you hire that weirdo?" Brody asks, watching the same back-and-forth of remnants to the counter, air-karate to the booth.

"He's a modern-day warrior, Brooks," Jeremy says, smiling in malicious adolescent vengeance. "He'll be Dale's worst nightmare."

Brody shrugs.

"Wipe down his table, and you're out of here," Jeremy says, basking in power, in anticipation for tomorrow, for getting out of here in August.

PLAY THE PIANO DRUNK LIKE A PERCUSSION
INSTRUMENT UNTIL THE FINGERS BEGIN TO
BLEED A BIT: THE BAND (NOT THE BOOK)

So the audience stands there with all their tattoos, howling along to the songs, pulling their arms to the sides of their heads like they're in a great deal of trauma. And maybe they are. Even the most privileged members of Western Civilization must get the blues from time to time. The shirtless band—Play the Piano Drunk Like a Percussion Instrument until the Fingers Begin to Bleed a Bit, they are called—you know, after the Bukowski book?—have beards and muscletone and short hair and tattoos and they are one of those—they call them emo bands—who, when they sing, put a lot of feeling into stretching out their vowels. This, ergo, expresses the pain and intensity and uncertainty of life. Whatever they are howling about is very important to everyone packed into the Nardic Track on that Thursday night. To Ronnie, it sounds like they are worked up over paper cuts, like they're singing—"It hurrrrrrrrrrts / paaaaaaaaaper cuuuuut / feeeel the buuuuurrrrrrn / from the fresh copies," but "It can't be that," Ronnie thinks, in the middle of the audience, silently, shyly, observing . . . and the dozens concaved around the band will soon enough be hundreds and soon enough be thousands.

Honestly, Ronnie doesn't get it. He never will. His band, The Laraflynnboyles, sounds nothing like this. He doesn't wax emotional about every stupid thing that has gone wrong in his life. He doesn't want to, and can't imagine what it would accomplish if he did. He isn't sure how "feeling" and "sincerity" means stretching out your vowels when you sing—or, how there is a direct correlation between the two. But that's what Gainesville seems to believe with the fervency of Eastern mystics. Because the way the band sings and the way the audience sings with them and how everyone is on the verge of tears at the minimum and mass catharsis at the maximum has the air of the fervor in a tent revival. At shows, Ronnie used to get bumped by kids dancing. Now, here, he's getting bumped by, to his left, some pork-skinned joker wearing nothing but camo cutoffs half-covering a pair of plaid boxers and at the feet the inevitable pair of black Chucks—he keeps crouching down then crouching up, hands behind his head, pulling his head into his chest—and to his right, some bleach-blonde short haired squat-bodied girl shrieking the words and punching the air at the start and end of each elongated word that's sung by the band. This band will be successful; they will hit thousands of kids all over the world in just the right place at just the right time. Ronnie drinks can after can of Brain Mangler malt liquor, leans against load-bearing poles in different parts of the tiny square room, surrounded by strangers, thinking of what he would sing about if he accepted this as valid, as something he could do without wanting to laugh.

He watches this band, the third of three (the first some pop punk band who sang only about girls around town they had crushes on, with titles like "She's the Publix Cashier Girl," "She's the Zesty Glaze Girl," "She's the DMV Eye Test Girl"; the second some ska band who sang about whatever it is ska bands sing about), thinks about what kinds of songs he would sing if he could indulge in this level of self-pity onstage. Thoughts of Kelly, who left the trailer three days ago, the bandages around the forehead gone with no traces except for a jaundiced peeled look to the covered skin, standing by his truck in front of the trailer in the eerie Jonestown silence of the late afternoon heat and humidity, his parting words: "Good luck, and try not to starve to death." Ronnie laughed at this, in the doorway of the trailer. "Hey, thanks! You too! And the next time you dumpster dive, look out for ants." Kelly winced, still feeling the receding welts across his tongue. "You can always come back," he offered, like an exasperated father, before sighing, looking up to the trees, muttering a final exasperated "Jesus Christ, dude," and stepping into the truck. Ronnie watched as he drove away, back to the lonely house, to another dead-end job, to a comfortable nothing, with one less friend. He deserved a song in the style, subject matter, and presentation of Play the Piano Drunk Like a Percussion Instrument Until the Fingers Begin to Bleed a Bit. If anyone did, it was Kelly. Or in the trailer, Alvin deserves a song. Alvin—who Ronnie imagines sitting there in his moldy barrel living room chair, holding a dandruffy gerbil in his pudgy hands. "This here is Squeaky," he had said the first time Ronnie met Alvin's furry little pet. Alvin extended Squeaky outward with his stubby arms. "Wanna pet it?" "Uh, no. Thank you," Ronnie huffed, haughty, uncomfortable. Stevie was in the middle of the room, sweat marks expanding across his black t-shirt, trying to copy the moves in some Jackie Chan film, bending over to pick up the VCR remote and rewind the movie and show the scene again and again—Jackie Chan hiyahing a bank safe—a sharp pop that instantly craters the safe at the point of impact—Stevie, who, Ronnie thinks, probably deserves an emo song too, was swinging his fists and karate kicking the air in uneven flailings. Meanwhile Squeaky slipped out of Alvin's hands, landing in the dirty shag carpeting, running—ratlike—straight towards Ronnie. "Eeeeeeeeee!" Ronnie squealed, high and girlish, as the gerbil beelined towards his feet. Stevie's hand dropped, fat ninja-like, to the rug, plucked Squeaky by the tail with a hearty "Hi-yah!" and lifted him off the ground. The poor gerbil dangled as Stevie held it between index finger and thumb. Ronnie watched, heart racing, as Stevie walked Squeaky to Alvin, placed him back into his hands, announcing to one and all in that redneck-who-doesn't-know-he's-a-redneck timbre and cadence Ronnie had grown to fear and despise, "Ya see that shit, hoooweeee! I am a badass muth-ur-fuck-er! Ooooo!" Alvin held Squeaky in his hands, pulled him close to his face, scolded, "Pffff. You shouldn't do that, Squeaky. You'll scare Ronnie. Bad gerbil. Bad! Gerbil! Pffff!" The tableau was too bizarre for anything more than a mumbled "I'm going to my room now" from Ronnie. There could be emo songs for Kelly, for Alvin, for Stevie. As the scene in the Nardic Track transforms more and more into something like those cathartic masculine reclamation camps in some desolate part of the Rocky Mountains where men dress in pelts and yell to the heavens until they feel the testosterone again, Ronnie Altamont thinks of himself as a good subject for an emo song, brooding on what happened after the strange incident with Squeaky, when, before going into his room and locking the door, he stopped in the bathroom, giving in to the compulsive need to wash his hands and face several times a day in the brief time he had lived with Alvin and Stevie. He wiped the water off on his navy blue Docker slacks (Ronnie never really tried very hard to incorporate punk fashion into his daily routine, especially in Florida), sized up the Ronnie in the mirror—that faded vermillion dye job (one of the few concessions to looking like the kind of person who listened to the kind of music that obsessed him throughout his late teens and into his mid-twenties . . . and he paid the price for looking so ridiculous, thanks to black hair peeking out where the dye didn't take, neck and scalp stained vermillion where the dye did take), black-framed glasses rusty and corroded at the hinges with binocular lenses caked with gunk along the edges, the unavoidable Florida tan, the scruffy face of an incompetent shaver, nose average in every way miraculously unbroken in light of all the provocative words he'd ranted back at UCF, flabby chin (despite the depression-fueled weight loss), broad slouched shoulders, a fraying old blue t-shirt ready to give up and dethread with the rest of his shirts, bony arms, small hands pressed against the nasty crusty bathroom counter, slacks stanky from freeballing, unfashionable hiking boots given out of pity and charity by Kelly. He too could be a walking talking emo song . . . Hell, even to get into these shows he's had to donate plasma, take the money, buy one twenty-five cent Little Lady Snack Cake for lunch and one twenty-five cent bag of Cheese Canoodles for dinner—so yeah, he could write emo album after emo album . . . if only he could take any of this seriously. Always, always, the desire to laugh in the face of futile despair like this—emo bands like Play the Piano Drunk Like a Percussion Instrument Until the Fingers Begin to Bleed a Bit are indicative of the times—these self-loathing 1990s where people have no compunction about walking around in shirts with the word LOSER or ZERO in big letters . . . where all these "alternative" bands tepidly whine about their lives . . . Ronnie, as the "new kid" in the tiny little punk club where the bands play like this and moments are shared that Ronnie can't understand . . . the only salvation is how they actually laugh with each other between the songs and at the end of the set . . . the way the space between performer and audi-

ence is nonexistent . . . the one thing they all agree on is knowing
that in the end all of this is nothing more than moments between
friends, many of whom could just as easily (and had before, and
will again) plug in and play. These were friends—hugging, arms
around each other, singing, screaming, sweating, palzee walzee
friends, and Ronnie doesn't know where to begin with anyone,
has yet to see any of his old friends who grew up with him in
Orlando then went off to college here and started bands. Everyone in the room is a potential friend, but Ronnie doesn't know
how to go about it, and this is also funny to Ronnie. Not only
the lyrics, but the music was like nothing The Laraflynnboyles
played . . . how all the bands in Gainesville played the octaves of
the chords rather than the Ramones chords and/or the Minutemen 9th chord syncopation he loved.

No, Ronnie doesn't think he will suffer all that much in
Gainesville. He figures he will be broke a lot, be hungry a lot,
lonely, depressed, but he won't mope about it and scream it out at
some show. He will laugh. These bands work in limited spectrums,
and after you've heard and processed, say, Captain Beefheart or
Albert Ayler, it's hard to go back.

Ronnie leaves the Nardic Track, and stepping out of the
muggy show and into the relative cool of the Gainesville spring
is in itself a glorious moment. He walks past groups of sweaty
punk kids standing around in gossipy packs or sitting on the
steps of the Hippodrome Theatre (a beautiful olden Greco-Ro-
man column-heavy building) across the street, staring at Ronnie, not quite in a "Who the fuck is this guy and what the fuck
is he doing here?" but more of a "Who let you in here?" kind
of vibe you get anywhere anyplace the crowd is tight-knit and

everyone in that circle knows everyone else's story. He attempts a smile and a "What's up?" to a couple dudes with skateboards sitting on either side of a girl with shaved green hair and cat-eye glasses. They say nothing.

In the car, Ronnie thinks it's funny to freestyle emo lyrics like he heard tonight: "I don't know . . . anybody heeeeeeeere / I shoulda peeeeeeeeeed before I left the shooooooooooow / now I gottaaaaaa goooooooooooo / man, I gottaaaaa goooooo/my blaaaaader screeeeeeeeeeeeeeeeeeams / to meeeeeee." Through the small downtown, past the closed restaurants and closing bars and grills, the manic action of novice drunk kids acting like novice drunk kids. At Main and University, a flip-flop stepping brunette-with-blonde-streaks skin-covered skeleton girl in an orange and blue University of Florida t-shirt and matching pajama bottom screams "I'M SO DRUNK AND HAPPY I WANNA PUKE EVERYWHERE" while leading a pack of similarly attired friends across the intersection. Ronnie sings as he drives back to the other side of town, past a university he does not attend, down streets he does not know, as the college gives way to the residential neighborhoods. University Avenue begins its slow metamorphosis into Newberry Road, and the plazas and strip malls and apartment complexes begin.

PAYPHONE CALL TO MR. AND MRS. ALTAMONT

"Look, I walked out. It wasn't a fun place to be, you know? The owner was this mustachioed Ay-rab cokehead who was always trying to grope the servers at the end of the night while everybody else who worked there had had a few drinks and I'm back there slaving away trying to wash the last of the dishes and plates so I can go home, because God forbid the lowly dishwasher gets to have a drink with the rest of the crew. I mean, sometimes they'd give me a bottle of Budweiser or something, but I mean, Budweiser gives me headaches, so I can't even drink that. But not only that, it was like, so pretentious, how everyone just had to have their water with lemon, like the lemon makes a difference, and the customers were always calling everything 'fabulous' in like these haughty Newport, Rhode Island inflections, like earning five figures from commissions in the Central Florida real estate market gives you the right to act like you've made it into the upper echelons of the Really Rich."

Right View. Right Thought. Right Speech. Right Behavior. Right Livelihood. Right Effort. Right Mindfulness. Right Concentration. As her son goes through this litany of complaints, Mrs. Sally-Anne Altamont makes a list, in spite of herself, of all the ways in which Ronnie is not following the Noble Eightfold Path. Where to begin?

"Ronnie." Sally-Anne's voice is firm, serious, a tone she hopes conveys how badly she wants him to stop ranting, just this once. But he's always ranting anymore; in recent years, an anger, a caustic bitterness, sarcasm at everything and everyone. Where does it come from? They are retired now, Sally-Anne and her husband Charley, self-described "easy-going vegans, old—not 'ex'—hippies, because we never stopped, and," (for the past nine months, since Charley stole a book called *The Teaching of Buddha* out of the nightstand drawer of the luxury hotel he stayed in in Miami for a three-day academic conference devoted entirely to compound adverbs) "dilettante Buddhists." They retired six years ago, when Ronnie went off to college, and before that lived frugally for decades, invested wisely—ethically, even—used the money to buy a beach house on Hilton Head Island, the ocean to the south, on a quiet section of the beach where they spend their late mornings reading passages from *The Teaching of Buddha* then meditating on their meanings.

Charley emerges from the hallway, pink-red-tan skin, docksider shoes, navy blue shorts, white t-shirt with two oars crossed into an X across the front, that white cap with the yellow rope coiled around the black anchor, not fat but not thin, a quarter-inch short of six feet tall. He looks at his wife—in a teal one-piece swimsuit, white floppy beach hat over the gray-black ponytailed long hippie hair, sunglasses, pink-red-tan skin, not fat but not thin, a quarter inch over five feet five inches—mouths "What is it?" Sally-Anne shakes her head "No."

"And like everybody there was so insufferable," Ronnie continues. "Like, I know this isn't a big deal or nuthin', but like people were always asking for capers on their entrees, even when the entrees didn't need capers. Like they'd just go and ask the servers for capers to show off for their dates, like their taste in capers was gonna get them laid or something . . . "

"Capers?" Sally-Anne repeats.

"Capers?" Charley Altamont says, laughs, gets shushed by Sally-Anne. He shuffles closer to her, fully immersed in the relaxed pace of beach life, no matter what is happening right now.

"Yeah. Capers. Those little salty pickled bulbous Mediterranean things? People would demand them on like honey-glazed chicken. That's pretty nasty, right? You gotta admit . . . "

"Ronnie," Charley says after gently removing the phone from Sally-Anne's grip.

"Dad?"

"You moved to Gainesville, and you're talking about capers?"

"He's on a payphone because the phone in the trailer was shut off," Sally-Anne says.

"Hi, Dad." Ronnie says. "Hi. I was just explaining to Mom what happened and why I ended up in Gainesville."

"No job?"

"It's like this," Ronnie says, over the sounds of screaming babies and arguing couples from the Laundromat next to the minimart where Ronnie found the payphone. "I'm living in this trailer, and there's no rent because the dude who owns it has it all paid off, so like, there aren't that many bills, except the phone—but whatever. The payphone's only like a five minute walk."

Sigh. Right View. Right Thought. Right Speech. Right Behavior. Right Livelihood. Right Effort. Right Mindfulness. Right Concentration.

"How are you eating?"

"Oh, that's fine, Dad. I found this place where you can donate plasma twice a week, and that pays like $40, so I get food money that way."

Sigh. Existence is suffering.

"Plasma." Charley repeats.

"Yeah, see, it's fine because now—"

"Give me your address."

"OK."

"I'm sending you money. Get your phone turned on. Get a job, Ronnie."

"I've been looking. It's the end of the semester though, so nobody's hiring."

"And you moved to Gainesville, why? I know why you left Orlando, what with the pretentious use of capers and everything . . . "

"That wasn't the only reason."

"Why Gainesville?"

"Hang on . . . I need to put more change in the payphone."

Charley waits. Sharp shocks of indigestion he hasn't felt since converting to veganism four years ago. Leave it to his son to give him indigestion, because it sure isn't the quinoa.

"OK, I'm back. I'm here to be a writer and a musician."

"You couldn't do that in Orlando?"

"No, not really."

"Get a job, Ronnie. Use your degree, and get a job."

"This degree from UCF doesn't count for much here in Gainesville."

"Get a job. This is the only time I'm doing this. Write and play music in your free time."

"Sure."

"And no more plasma donating for money. For your mom's sake. Promise."

"Of course. I got a plan here . . . "

"You don't." Charley says. "Otherwise, you wouldn't have moved up there. Give me your address."

SCENES FROM A STOP AND SHOP AND GAS AND GO

"Thankth hon," a haggard blonde lisps to Ronnie between missing front and bottom teeth, grabbing the pack of Newports off the cracked plastic wood counter, shakes what remains of her emaciated frame out the door, in that sloppy strut natural to run-down addicts, as her flip-flops flip, flop, flip, flop out the door.

"That's Crazy Annie," Travis, Manager of the 7:00 a.m. – 3:00 p.m. shift, explains. Travis is one of those short guys with all his fat compressed and isolated into his belly, with salt and pepper hair in a receding pompadour, bushy black moustache centering a bloated face.

"See, she's crazy," Kim, the Assistant Manager of the a.m. shift, one of those thin raspy flame-broiled looking middle-aged women indigenous to the South with sunscarred skin and a frizzy perm circa 1982, the kind who chain smoke Merit cigarettes.

"Hence the name," Travis supplies.

"I see," Ronnie says. It's Ronnie's first day on the job, clerking here at the Stop and Shop and Gas and Go. He had filled out applications all over town, but it was true what Mouse had told him: There were no jobs to be had this time of year, unless you want to join the military, babysit rich kids at Club Med, or teach English in some ambitious country eager to learn the lingua franca from a card carrying native speaker. He lucked out getting hired here—if by "lucked out," you think working the morning shift in a convenience store nestled between seedy motels on 13th Street where beat-to-hell black and white men who stumble in with bloodshot eyes and tattered flannel shirts buy all the cheap wine they can afford to guzzle down on a 72 degree Wednesday morning constitutes "lucking out."

"Cigarettes ain't all she smokes," Kim says, punctuating her comment with a wheezy, coughy laugh, her breath like the stale

"YOUR ONE STOP FOR GAS, GO, AND SHOP!"

smoke/dirty laundry stench of the clothes Ronnie wears to shows and doesn't wash for a month.

"No?" Ronnie says, blue eyes widened in an attempt at Andy Kaufmanesque childlike innocence.

"She smokes crack," Travis says, leaning in close to Ronnie, elbowing him in the ribs and adding, sotto voce. "And dick, if you know what I mean."

Ronnie stares, from Travis, to Kim, and back, trying to look befuddled. "Crack? Dick? Jeez, Travis, this is a lot to figure out for my first day."

"She's a prostitute!" Kim laughs, then coughs. "Smokes dick! Get it?"

"Ohhhhhhh," Ronnie says, in exaggerated epiphany.

The store's walls are covered in fake wood paneling. The floors are a pee-stained white tile. The wet turdish mint smell of chewing tobacco. The eye-watering tinge of cheap bleach. The counter area is an overcrowded island in the middle of the store. Inches above Ronnie's head are hanging trucker's caps extolling the virtues of fishing over working, of the inherent stupidity of women, of cartoon criminals shooting off sparks from an electric chair with the caption, "JUSTICE COMES DEEP-FRIED OR EXTRA KRISPY." Ronnie's first morning behind the counter is a steady hum of American retail commerce; the alcoholics and prostitutes are replaced by the morning rush of the gainfully employed purchasing coffee, cigarettes, gasoline. The rush of the morning passes into the quiet of mid-day.

"Well, here comes Retard Gary," Travis announces as a short bald man wearing an oversized black t-shirt with a silkscreen on the front of a silhouette of a coyote howling at a full moon as lightning and F-15 fighter planes fill in the background, baggy acid-washed jeans, dirty white sneakers and thick nerd-framed glasses parks his adult tricycle in front of the store and limps in from the bright muggy morning.

"Retard Gary?" Ronnie asks, standing in front of the register, Travis to his left, Kim to his right, both managers standing over to make sure Ronnie pushes the right buttons for the corresponding purchases.

"He's a retard," Kim says.

"We was just talkin' about you, Gary," Travis says, wicked yellow smile from his fat face. "Your girlfriend Crazy Annie was here asking about you."

"No way!" Retard Gary says, hobbling to the Coke dispensers. "Nuh-uh. I don't like Crazy Annie."

"So you're a fag then," Travis hollers. Kim snorts, laughs, coughs. "You probably got AIDS all over you." Ronnie laughs—not at the joke, but the quietly desperate laugh you laugh when your boss says something so horrible that you don't know what to do because you need the job because you need the money.

"Shut up, Travis!" Retard Gary says as the ice machine rumbles and delivers a mini-avalanche into his orange and blue extra-extra large ("Thirst Annhilator") 64-oz cup. "I don't got AIDS on me! I like girls!"

"I'm from Missouri, Gary," Travis says, leaning forward to follow Retard Gary's path from the coke station to the register, belly pressed into the counter. "*Show me* a girlfriend."

"And not one of them crackwhores out here on 13th Street neither," Kim says. Travis laughs like a boorish dog from a 1970s Saturday morning cartoon. Ronnie does not laugh.

.

Ronnie Altamont sits on the closed toilet seat, staring at the racist graffiti, body in the pose of "The Thinker" statue and everything. It's like: How far out of your element can you feel in 98 percent of your waking hours? Florida. Fucking Florida. Ronnie. Fucking Ronnie. It's why they call it "work," right? Life must be sustained by doing stressful seemingly pointless tasks like clerking convenience stores because somebody somewhere needs this job done and is willing to pay somebody else something for it.

Ronnie leaves the men's room, returns to the register. Two fishermen—a father and son—son a smaller, less round version of the father—both in matching teal Miami Dolphins sleeveless shirts and two white fishermen caps with hooks encircling the brim—set two 12-packs of Old Hamtramck on the counter.

"It's all you, chief," Kim says, pointing to the register's rows and columns of buttons.

Ronnie punches in the prices, adds the sales tax. The fisherfather and fisherson stare at the trucker's hats dangling inches over Ronnie's faded vermillion hair.

"Hey man," the fisherfather says. "Raise that flap!"

The hat directly above Ronnie's is light blue with white mesh and a velcroed flap reading, in the girlish bubble cursive of hearted I's, "IF GIRLS ARE MADE OF SUGAR AND SPICE . . . "

Ronnie turns, raises his arms, unvelcroes the flap. Underneath the raised flap, the question, "WHY DO THEY TASTE LIKE ANCHOVIES?" above a picture of a dead green fish with white stink squiggles.

Everybody haw haw haws, including Ronnie, who actually finds it funny. He might even buy it if he had the money. But he doesn't, and it would be bad form to steal on the first day of the job.

"Y'all, that's gross!" Kim says, eliciting further laughs from the fishermen.

"Yeah, I'd buy it," the fisherfather says, starting to walk away with the two Old Hamtramck 12-packs. "But I have a feeling his mother," and here, he turns his head to his fisherson, "wouldn't take too kindly to it."

Ronnie does not share these concerns. The hat should be his. It is already so close to his head, hanging there. He was never a thief, never had klepto tendencies growing up the way some kids were always stealing gum etc. from stores. It's only one white trash hat out of dozens that never get sold in these kinds of stores. They're practically decorations anyway. Travis is on his lunch break. If Ronnie is to make the hat his, he will have to do it now, with Travis gone, and when Kim goes off to take one of countless smoke breaks.

The temptation is too great. While Kim stands on the mini-mart's front sidewalk puffing a Merit, Ronnie removes the hat, bundles it up, stuffs it down his "professionally attired" khaki slacks. His blue Oxford shirt is large enough to cover the obvious bulge, and no one can see over the counter anyway.

Ronnie rings up Lunchables and Cokes for the workaday construction or landscaping crews on their breaks. Kim watches his fingers for any slight mis-hit of the register's buttons from Ronnie as she sings along with the Young Country Music from the store's speakers—off-key renditions of tunes tackling topics like memories of the fun had near rivers as a randy teenager, of overly confident rural men with tremendous pride in their country and background, of rowdy bars full of questionable characters who, despite all outward appearances and behaviors, are a swell bunch of folks. And so on. And so forth.

"What kind of music do you like?" Kim asks. "I seen your hair."

Ronnie hates this question. "I don't know, man . . . " he says, unable to hide his annoyance. "A lot of things. Punk? Jazz?"

"That ain't music," Kim says, matter-of-factly. She points to the ceiling, where the Young Country never stops. "Now this—this—is music."

Ronnie doesn't speak to her again.

Travis returns from his lunch break, waddling through the front door, proclaiming, "Hooeee, those were some mighty fine ribs. My-tee fine!" Ronnie immediately steps away from the register, announces "Going on my break now!" He leaves the register island, circling away to the main walkway out the door. "Be back in half an hour," Travis says, and Ronnie blurts out a "Yup!" and pushes open the doors, steps out, hears the sleigh bells taped to shing-shing when anyone enters or leaves the Stop and Shop and Gas and Go.

"He ain't comin' back, is he?" Travis says, rib sauce drying around his mouth and on his fingers, still standing three steps in from the doors.

"Doubt it," Kim says, taking one step to the register, humming along to the Young Country music. "You seen his hair?"

Ronnie's blandy apple green domestic sedan squeals into reverse. He shifts to drive, zooms out of the parking lot, cuts off a dirty white lunchwagon whose driver almost honks her horn. At the next light, Ronne reaches down, pulls out the "IF GIRLS ARE MADE OF SUGAR AND SPICE . . . " hat. He smiles at his reflection in the rear view mirror. He drives towards the University, to the saffron and purple gowned Krishnas doling out free food. He will eat, then drive across town to donate plasma, then buy a real dinner at Publix with the money, try to write something, fall asleep.

WILLIAM RETURNS FROM THE TOUR

Fourteen states, twelve days, three narrowly averted inter-band fistfights, one unaverted inter-band fistfight, one cancelled show, one set cut short because no one showed up and the barstaff wanted to close early, one guitar amp dying a smoky death midway through another set, one instance of the drummer waking up naked with a missing suitcase and no idea where in Columbus he might be, and the final three days and nights spent subsisting on nothing but wonder bread and bologna stolen from a corner store near the Fireside Bowl in Chicago later, you're back in the walk-in cooler behind the restaurant getting high with your equally tattooed and pierced dinner-shift manager, who asks you "So how was the tour, bro?" after exhaling the skunkweedy joint and passing it to you, and you're either not sure or not willing to answer the question, even if your manager asks this because he plays bass in Salo's Children—another band in the hardcore scene—and wants the vicarious thrill of actually playing outside Florida, because you figure your bass playing manager must know, deep down, that Salo's Children suck and will never get the chance to leave F.L.A.

"Never again," you say before smoking, and that's all you want to say right now. You think of the fifth of Floridian Comfort in your car, and you want it now, but you wait, because you know, once you get started, you'll elaborate on "Never again," and the elaborations on the ultimately monotonous hurry-up-slow-down nature of touring, interspersed with the occasional weird and sometimes even wonderful adventures far from home will continue past closing the kitchen tonight and lead you to the usual impromptu front porch party somewhere around here, and there will be no shutting up. The pot keeps you in the moment, heightening the smells of frozen dough and cold sauce, preserved vegetables and damp pasta. Stoned now, you say, "It's weird being back here," and that part of it is even harder to explain—to be back in this tiny walk-in cooler in your black Gatorroni's by the Slice work shirt, dough-stained black work slacks, red bandana soaking up the Florida kitchen sweat—so you don't.

"I'll tell you about it later." You're now high enough to get through the dishwashing, table-wiping, food-serving shift. You pass the manager what remains of the joint, and step out into the hot parking lot and into the hotter kitchen—a five-second change of eighty degrees.

Your ex-girlfriend, now dating your ex-best friend after finding out you hooked up with his ex-girlfriend, stands by the dishtank holding a red plastic tray with two veggie slices. She works the registers with your ex-ex-girlfriend and your current girlfriend.

"Take these to the outside tables," she says, hostile yet non-committal. Deliberately, she's looking to the front of the restaurant and away from you. She has dyed red streaks in her short black hair now, the circle-plus female symbol newly-tattooed on her inner left arm. You're trying real hard to not laugh at these latest developments.

You relieve her of the tray, knowing your streak of going nine days without wishing for the horrific death of your ex-girlfriend has snapped. "The dumbass who ordered them is too drunk to come back to the counter," she says. She flashes a Florida-trade-marked mean-grin, passive-aggressive rudeness couched in the faintest of barely polite smiles. "Even makes you seem sober."

"It's great seeing you again too." She rolls her eyes, returns to the counter. Yes, it's great to be back in Gainesville, back in the kitchen of Gatorroni's by the Slice. Picking up where you left off.

You walk past the counter, smile at your current girlfriend—who smiles back in that nineteen naïve-teen way of hers—all teeth and wide green eyes and dyed blonde short hair with a barrette in the front of the left part and granny glasses and still untattooed and still unjaded. You brood on how long all of this will last until she gets tired of your moods, your personality. You. It's a busy, all-too-familiar night. The booths along the front windows are full, students hunched over text books, half-eaten slices temporarily set aside, families bunched around the tables, moms rocking strollers while dads try to keep their four year olds from kneeling or standing on the chairs in potentially dangerous poses as they reach over to sip from their Cokes. Some cheap hippie spent fifty cents to subject everyone to all thirty-plus minutes of the Allman Brothers' insufferable "Mountain Jam" on the jukebox. The grease-laden underbelly of these red plastic trays, and the burnt cheese/sweaty meat stench of all these pizza pies in and out of the oven to the hungry Gainesville dining public. Outside, dozens of crusty-punks, indie-punks, emo-punks, hardcore kids, so on and so forth, all the little sub-genres too small to hang in their own little cliques, acknowledging each other in the Gatorroni's outdoor dining area—pitcher after pitcher, often on the house thanks to their friends working inside. The humidity that never seems to go away, heightened by the kitchen's heat, red bandana around your forehead not enough to soak the sweat.

It's almost like the tour never happened. You set the pizza down at the drunk guy's table—some Gatorroni Loser who's always out here in his finest street punk leisure wear. He doesn't see the pizza because he's too busy arguing that The Clash isn't "punk enough" for his standards.

Your drunk-ass friends, yelling and bouncing around the farthest outdoor dining table, call your name and wave you over. "We-heh-hell, Bill Collector himself, back from the worldwide tour," Neil says, stepping off the barstool to face you and doff his New York Yankees ballcap—temporarily exposing the stubbled black hair receding higher and higher along the forehead. His brother Paul stands to his right, at the head of the table, pouring their fourth free pitcher into his cup, Neil's cup, and the cups in front of the aptly-named Drunk John and Boston Mike. You know it's the fourth pitcher and you know it's a free pitcher because you're the one who's been walking them over to the table.

"Aw, c'mon," Paul says, finishing the angled pour into Boston Mike's plastic cup. "You know William goes by William now. Bill Collector was PUNK"—and here, Paul punches the table and rattles the cups and the pitcher—"but William, and just William? That's hardcore, dude . . . "

You smile at this. In high school back in Orlando, you were in this band called The Dicks, and your "stage name"—you never played on any stages—was Bill Collector. The band was very short-lived, and not only because there was already a well-known, highly-regarded band from Austin, Texas called The Dicks that you had somehow never heard of.

Drunk John punches you on the right shoulder, a light smack from a scrawny tattooed arm. "We heard all about Bloomington, Indiana, haw haw," he says, and all you can do is shake your head from side to side and say, "Never again," to which everyone at the table laughs at what you can only laugh at from a safe distance. You, curled into a corner of the typical punk house, reeking of post-show sweat and smoke, in clothes long unwashed, rolled into a mutli-stained off-white blanket like a filthy unhealthy burrito on the hirsute hardwood floor—pillowless, but whatever. The post-show party was there, full of denim-clad males mostly who wanted to talk about this record and that band as meanwhile the smattering of women present were surrounded by, on average, five men all going after the same thing—and boy, do the women in these towns know it—and what gets you is how disinterested they were in anything but their stupid town—their stupid towns, because everybody wants to talk about where they live like it matters. You don't think it matters, not anymore. After enough shows like these, all you wanted was a good night's sleep for a change, not another night of listening to the denim dudes talk about the punk rock all night. So at this particular Bloomington, Indiana post-show after-party, you drank enough to find a relatively quiet corner to pass out, pulled the blanket over your head so the music, some hyper-distorted scream you're already overly familiar with, seeped into your hearing slightly less obtrusively . . . As you fall into an unconsciousness on the border between drunkenness and the morning's hangover drain, you sense someone standing over you. You hear sniffles, a conspiratorially whispered, "Yo! Hey!" The only way to get your head out of the blanket is to unroll your body completely from the blankets wraparound, so you roll and roll into this person's steel-toed black boot. The light is on, the records are off, and there is no sound except for the buzzsaw-to-a-swine's-throat snores of your bass player who you can see scored the shredded green couch on the other side of the littered living room. "Look at my face!" the singer of the local band, the headlining band, whispers, standing over you. He wears trash-stenched jeans and a sleeveless jean jacket with CRASS written on the back in black permanent marker. He has Jaggerish facial features, if Jagger had that weird kinda-inbred look some people in Indiana have. A red droplet falls from his face, lands on your blanket, and you now understand why his voice is phlegmatic and novocained as he says, "They broke my nose. We've been backyard fighting!" He smiles—one lead singer to the next—"And you gotta see this shit!" he adds, and you're like, "Fuck it, when will I ever be in Bloomington, Indiana again?" So you step out of the blanket— still in your Docs, but whatever—and you step over discarded beer cans, whiskey bottles, pizza boxes, vomit, gum, clothing, show fliers, records, cds, kitty litter, kitty kibbles, blue red and yellow pieces to the "Sorry" boardgame, the bodies of the other members of your band, MOE GREEN'S FUCKING EYE SOCKET[5], are too-frozen in that way people get when they're trying to pretend to be asleep. Are they your friends anymore? You try not to look too closely at the fliers on the wall of show after show after show after band after band after band—shitty drawings of mohawked

---

[5] You demand all-caps

skeletons and the graffiti everywhere of DK, Circle As, pot leafs, malt liquor bottles, straight edge Xs, swastikas with NO signs, and echoing through your beat-up skull is that line from "Salad Days" by Minor Threat, the core has gotten soft—and the thing is—when the singer said, "you gotta see this shit!" you didn't think he was being literal. In the middle of the kitchen—the once-white linoleum kitchen with the once-teal space age cabinetry and space age appliances, everything now smudged with grime, trash and rodent droppings—you recognize the rhythm guitarist of the headlining band, he who proudly told you at the 6:00 p.m. load-in into the club, "I've been drinking since ten a.m.!" who by 2:00 a.m. was a not-that-interesting mix of whiskey-blackedout belligerence, nudity, and inarticulate, unreasoned arguments on the college kids in this town, the relative pros and cons of assorted pornographic magazines, and how much better society would be if cops weren't around to fuck with everybody—this rhythm guitarist is now passed out in the middle of the kitchen as the lead guitarist and bass player stand on either side of him five feet apart holding a stretch of Saran Wrap. The lead singer grabs a video camera, yells "Go!" to the chunky drummer—one of those too-many-Midwestern-meals-from-Dutch-peasant-stock-already-with-a-tendency-towards-bigness type dudes—who squats over the passed out rhythm guitarist, unbuttons his jeans, unzips his fly, drops the jeans and the boxers, and deuces on the Saran Wrap. You're on the border between the kitchen and the living room, feeling nausea right down to your balls as the turds drop and weigh down the Saran Wrap and the lead singer holds the camera, laughing, asks the rhythm guitarist if he feels something warm on his face. Turd one landed on his septum; turd two on his right cheek. It's a short stumble, steering way clear of the laughter and the bodies in the middle of the kitchen, to the back screen door. You narrowly avoid puking all over one of their girlfriends—some attempted Bettie Page doppelgänger—and hunch by the fence and cough and spit and gag and ask yourself what the hell you're doing so far from home. Not-Bettie Page smokes in a lawnchair, is kind enough to inform you upon your emergence from the pukey darkness that "They don't mean nuthin'. It's just what we do here when we drink too much." You nod, and right about here, you decide to leave the back porch, walk around the side of the house, knock on the van doors until someone lets you in, find space to sleep, hope to remember the blanket in the morning and not forget about it the way you forgot about the pillow in a house much like this one, in Cleveland.

". . . Some people have a weird idea of fun," is all you can say about it to Neal, Paul, Drunk John and Boston Mike. They laugh at this; you turn to walk away. "Get us another pitcher or we'll shit on your face!" Boston Mike yells behind you, and you have to laugh.

For now, you won't tell them, or anyone, that MOE GREEN'S FUCKING EYE SOCKET is finished. From the drive from Louisville to home, no one spoke to anyone excepting the absolute necessity of communicating stops for bodily functions and gas money for the van. You've never been happier to see your own bed, but the rhythms of touring—the drive, the load-in, the hang out, the drink, the finally play, the other bands, the load-out, the search for a place to stay, the after-party everyone insists on throwing, the pass out, the wake up from not sleeping is its own routine, and it's difficult to shake, even if the whole time you missed Gainesville, your house, your girlfriend. But then you're back and here you are again at Gatorroni's by the Slice and realize, you don't miss a thing.

Back in the kitchen, you make more pizza, sneak more pitchers to Neal and all them. The dinner rush tapers off. The students finish their slices and take their textbooks back to the dorms. The families leave their tables unbussed and go home. With an hour to go until closing, your girlfriend with her bleach blonde barretted hair and giant too-young smile who's working to save money so she can have as many tattoos as everyone else working here, grabs you by the arm in the dishtank while you're trying to scrub burnt minced garlic from a skillet, says, "Let's go to the walk-in."

You grab the mop and follow her out the back door, into the hot parking lot and into the walk-in cooler, thinking, Well, there are worse ways to be welcomed back to town. You wedge the mop into the inside door handle to prevent any unwelcome entry.

"I missed having you here," she says, leaning in for a long kiss before grabbing you by the hips and gently pushing you backwards until you're against the cold shelves. She squats down, unzips your pants, grabs, strokes, sucks. Stacked on the opposite shelves are white plastic gallon-sized cylindrical bins where some prep cook lackey wrote "MARINARA 4/16." Your head rolls backwards and your eyes land on these bins. One hand rolls over her hair, over the barrette, and the other hand grips one of the frosty vertical beams of the shelving. You moan. Someone pulls on the cooler and you yell "Go away!" The mop rattles with the violent pulls on the door but does what it was put there to do.

"Welcome back," she says when finished. You smile, catch your breath, say nothing. She removes the mop, hands it to you. "Bye," she says, opening the walk-in cooler as you wipe up with the white towel you keep in your back pocket for wiping down counters and tables. You pull up your boxers, your pants, zip, button. Open the walk-in and step into the heat once again, but instead of going back into the kitchen to start closing up for the night, you run to your car, open the passenger door, unscrew the Floridian Comfort fifth and chug. The booze squeegees and muddles your head. You spin around and look to the clouds and the sliver of a moon and wish you could be ten different places at once and ten different people at once and you want to laugh at this finite life and dance away the unshakable anxiety that keeps you up nights and leaves you a puddle of boozy drool—that this is as good as it will ever be.

You walk back into the kitchen. Your manager asks if you wanna spark another one. You smile, turn around, and it's back into the walk-in cooler, only, this time, you think you can actually start talking about the tour—all of its good/bad unboring/banal glory/futility.

SCENES FROM THE REVEREND B. STONED'S
OPEN-MIC ECLECTIC JAMBALAYA JAM

The wait. The insufferable wait to perform at Reverend B. Stoned's Open-Mic Eclectic Jambalaya Jam here at Turn Your Head and Coffee, an off-campus coffeehouse on the University Avenue entertainment strip. Icy Filet (neé Chelsey Anne Cavanaugh) studies her carefully prepared notecards by candlelight in a far corner of the tiny square room, periodically sipping a soy Americano from a large green mug—this wait a nerve-wracking ordeal of hot and cold flashes, sour stomach nausea rumbles, a general itchiness. Maybe she should cross her name off the sign-up sheet. She looks away from her notecards, mouths the words, and always—always—forgets everything past the first four lines. This is no way to be a freestyle rapper, she thinks, breathes in, breathes out. I need to leave.

"Greetings, to all my brothers and sisters of this funktified congregation," the Reverend B. Stoned bellows in a voice that is one-third televangelical preacher, one-third game-show announcer and one-third stoner-whispering-some-conspiracy-theory-about-the-government (Icy Filet recognizes him from his picture on all the fliers around campus—black beret with the two short black braids sticking out the back, black priest shirt and white clerical collar, pink-tinted John Lennon sunglasses, black fu-man-chu rounding his round face, the tie-dyed kilt and the knee-high combat boots), and the dozen-odd patrons seated in the wobbly round candlelit tables in front of the stage clap politely. "Are you ready to hear gospels of nonconformity and antidisestablishmen-tarianism?" The applause increases, and two of the rowdier audience members Woo-Hoo! to this.

It's too late now to take her name off the list, or so Icy Filet believes—too anxious, brain increasingly manically feverish with each sip from the soy Americano, to listen to the Reverend B. Stoned's opening monologue in which he preaches the virtues of marijuana legalization. Unsurprisingly, no one disagrees; Turn Your Head and Coffee is an inevitably lefty/libertarian coffeehouse. Icy Filet could leave. Why does she want to do this in front of strangers applauding platitudes like "Don't let our dreams for marijuana legalization go up in smoke! Legalize, don't criminalize!"?

As the enthusiastic applause begins to fade, the Reverend B. Stoned preaches into the microphone, "Brothers and sisters: Lift up your hearts and open your mind, soul, and ears to the righteous tirades of my sister in spirit, Miss Hillary X!"

Miss Hillary X steps onto the six inch high stage, approaches the mic stand—a waifish young woman of seventeen with bright blue short hair, a white t-shirt with the word RESIST! screenpainted across in Courier New font. Spiky wristbands on both wrists. Red plaid pants with suspenders between the legs. Combat boots wrapped in chains so they dramatically clunk with each step. A practice-makes-perfect scowl with a Sid Vicious sneer. She glares at the crowd, removes the mic from the stand.

"EVERY DAY . . . I SUFFER . . . UNDER THE TYRANNY . . . OF THE PATRIARCHY!" she yells, monotonical and strident.

"And it's nice to see you too," Icy Filet mumbles to no one, seated in the back, wondering why people can never start things off at open mic nights with nice greetings, simple hellos even, before jumping in with the world-hating.

"I WORK JUST AS HARD AS A MAN," Miss Hillary X continues, standing at attention, head turning from one table to the next, accusing eyes searching for anyone gathered here tonight at Turn Your Head and Coffee who might be in cahoots with the phallocentrists. "BUT I DON'T GET PAID AS MUCH AS A MAN! I WORK SO HARD . . . BUT TO A MAN, MAN, I'M JUST HERE . . . TO KEEP THEM HARD! MY SUBSERVIENT PUSSY! MY MANHANDLED ASS! MY SLAVEDRIVEN TITTIES!" With each yell of her body parts, Miss Hillary X grabs said body parts and shakes them, dramatically.

Icy Filet remembers Hillary Johnson, aka, Miss Hillary X, from high school back in Lake Mary. Two years younger than Icy, she was the notorious editor-in-chief of the school's newspaper—annoying and shrill—muckraking the quality of lunchroom pizza, and how there wasn't enough of a break between classes to get to your next class on time. Somebody somewhere deemed her "gifted," and everyone believed it, and at the end of the day, the principal and administrators were probably all-too-happy to allow her to use her AP college credits to start college one year early. But still, back then, no matter how insufferable she could be, Hillary was never this angry. Icy Filet analyzes potential causes—moving away too young, one-too-many Women's Studies classes, or perhaps something much, much worse. Terrible things can happen in college, or even just walking down the street. Everyone needs an outlet—perhaps this is why we're here tonight, Icy Filet thinks. And if it means indulging dreadful—what? spoken word?—well, it's better than a lot of other ways people deal with their shit.

Miss Hillary Xs rant culminates in a final scream of "MY REVOLUTIONARY BREASTS SCREAM FOR LIBERATION." Miss Hillary X lifts her white RESIST t-shirt, exposing budding breasts, nipples pierced with one glittering silver ring each. She raises her arms into the air, makes what may or may not be Black Power fists, tosses her shirt into the air, landing to her left, halfway between stage and tables. The audience gasps, applauds, woo-hoos, screams ecstatic affirmations.

"Oh God oh God oh . . . " Icy Filet says to herself under the din of the audience. "Please don't let me go on after her . . . " Icy tries recalling her lines, her dope-ass rhymes. Her memory has succumbed to panic. She recalls nothing. "I'm screwed," she thinks. "I should be back in the dorm studying."

The Reverend B. Stoned returns to the stage. "Wow, man, that was truly inspiringly countercultural, wouldn't you agree my brothers and sisters? Let's lighten the mood now with some poetry by my favorite—bud! Heh heh heh!" (Here everyone except Icy laughs.) "Smokey Green!"

Smokey Green, dressed in the obligatory hippie attire, stands onstage in a thick patchouli cloud and reads his poem in the burnout dope dealing raspy voiced stock character in any film from the 1970s:

"See: Bud is my bud

Not the Bud that you drink

But the bud that you smoke

Take a toke

Smell the smoke

This ain't no joke

Breathe it in

Feel the grin

the love will spread

check your head

you're as high as the sky

you don't need to fly

to climb aboard

and be with your bud, bud

Peace."

Raucous applause. Icy Filet groans. She hopes—more than anything—that she will not be called up next. But of course, "And now, sisters and brothers," the Reverend B. Stoned says, black fingernail polished right index finger following the sign-up sheet to the next name. "I believe this is the first time we've had a freestyle rapper here, but that's cool, that's cool. Welcome to our congregation . . . Icy Filet."

She removes the Casio SK-1 from her UF orange and blue totebag at her feet, gathers her notecards off the table. The walk to the stage feels like the walk to an execution. She sets the SK-1 on the onstage barstool, approaches the mic. "Hi, my name is Icy Filet? I'm a rapper?" The audience laughs at this remark. "Um. I'm not trying to be funny. This is what I do. I rap. I'm from the mean streets of Lake Mary." Icy Filet dresses in the "sexless librarian chic" style fashionable among indie-rock women in the mid-1990s. Short black hair parted in the manner of a 1950s accountant. Cardigan sweaters. Slouched postures. Thick nerd glasses. Shapeless black pants. Low-cut Doc Martens. She flips through her notecards, finds it. "OK. I'd like to start with this rap. It's called 'I Eat Pop Tarts.' Thank you."

She turns around, switches on the SK-1. A tinny pseudo hip-hop beat circa 1984 blips and loops out the keyboard's small speaker. Icy Filet turns to the mic, clears her throat, looks down at her notecards (not daring to look at the audience), and rhymes, in a cadence nervous and uneven:

"I eat Pop Tarts
every day now
it's how my day starts
every way now
strawberry, blueberry
icing in my mouth
east coast
west coast
Pop Tarts north and south

toaster oven microwave
Pop Tart flava what I crave
eat it cuz it's healthy
it could even make me wealthy
Yo I know—what I say ain't true
Yo I know—but what I feel is right
Yo I know—Pop Tarts taste stew [And here, Icy Filet loses the
thread, loses her place on the notecards]
Yo I know— Pop Tarts aiiiiight
Word."

She steps away from the mic, the beat blipping its trebly syncopation behind her as she does a practiced nervous dance of one sideways lift from one leg to the next. She cannot look forward, even if the room is dark beyond the candlelight centering the tables. She shifts sideways as she dances, an awkward lurch to the barstool to turn off the SK-1. The beat is silenced between the two and three of the measure. She stands there, awaiting a reaction, applause, something. There's an awkward silence, broken only by a loud whisper of "What the fuck was that?" and Icy Filet wants to cry, wants to grab the SK-1, toss the notecards and never look at them again and run back to the dorm and try and find some answer in her Psych 101 textbook that might explain what kink in her psycho-social development makes her aspire to be the whitest rapper in Gainesville, if not the entire world.

One rapid enthusiastic pair of hands clap and someone yells "Yaaaaaaayyyyyy!" as he runs up to her, and Icy Filet is convinced, irrationally but entirely, that it's Charles Manson and he wants to kill her for what she just did up there, but then she remembers, oh yeah, he's in jail.

"I'm Mouse!" this sudden fan whispers in her ear as he steps onto the stage. With both hands, he grabs her shoulders, adds, "And I'm sorry to have to go after you, because, heh heh heh, that was the best thing to ever happen here, dude! Seriously!" He loops her right arm like a chivalrous Charles Manson. "Let me lead you back to your seat," and he—Mouse—has this goofy grin, and Icy Filet no longer thinks he looks like Charles Manson, but like someone more attractive than Charles Manson.

As they walk away, the Very Reverend B. Stoned returns to the stage, to the microphone, says, "That was . . . interesting," in that sarcastic voice people get when they're threatened by what they perceive as the not-normal. The audience laughs at this, at Icy Filet. She wants to cry; Mouse sees the hurt in her eyes.

"Fuck 'em!" he says before pulling out her seat at the table, then gently pushing her in. He leans in, whispers, "You did great. Don't forget that," and Icy Filet hasn't completely given up yet on performing, on her ambition of the moment.

". . . But I guess you never know what you're gonna get when you come out to Reverend B. Stoned's Open Mic Eclectic Jambalaya Jam! Am I right?! Am I right!" The Reverend B. Stoned raises his arms in triumph, "Number One" index fingers pointing to the ceiling painted to resemble puffy white clouds on a bright blue day. Enthusiastic woo-hoos, all around. "And hey," the Reverend continues. "Thanks to Turn Your Head and Coffee for giving us a space to exercise our First Amendment rights, because? If we didn't have the First Amendment? We'd have a lot of problems, and we couldn't do what we're doing tonight . . . like, uh . . . rapping about Pop Tarts."

Laughter. "Don't listen to him," Mouse says, hands on Icy Filet's shoulders. "I'm nervous to have to go after you."

Before Icy Filet has a chance to ask, "You're doing something tonight?" the Reverend calls Mouse to the open mic to, "Do whatever it is Mouse does, because I don't know if I understand it myself."

Polite applause, over which Mouse yells, "Thank you! Thank you!" and blows kisses to the audience like a venerable Hollywood starlet waving to fans before climbing into the limousine. He runs to the darkness to the side of the stage, grabs an amplifier and electric guitar, carries them to the stage, plugs in the amp, slips the hot pink strap through his head, connects the cable from the guitar to the amp, connects a distortion pedal to the mic cable, connects another cord from the pedal to a coffeehouse amplifier ill-equipped for much beyond the quiet poetic intensity of the average singer-songwriter. Mouse turns everything on. The guitar shrieks violent open-string vibrations, and the distorted microphone howls painful white noise. Mouse shimmies in place to these sounds for five seconds before screaming into the microphone, voice modulated into monstrous distortion. He drops his pants, tosses the guitar in the air. The guitar lands on its body, clanging layers of noise into the tortured amplifier, neck thwacking into the worn red duct-taped stage floor. Under his smudged blue thrift-store pants are diapers. Pants around his legs, he hops like a leprechaun around an Irish spring. He slips out of his teal flip-flops, dances out of his pants. He reaches into the diaper and pulls out a knife. The guitar still howls and Mouse still screams. He grasps the knife handle, extends his arm, stabs his chest repeatedly. The audience screams. It's too dim to know for sure that it's one of those toy knives that sink into the handle with contact. Half the audience, circled around the tables closest to the stage, use this as an opportunity to leave the room post-haste. Mouse screams another psychotic howl—no, um, "lyrics" to any of this, simply extended shrieks and howls—then steps to the amplifier, reaches behind it, removes two bags of flour, a large red bag of Bugles snacks, and three packages of bologna. He tears into the flour bags, shakes them across the front of the stage as the guitar clangs shrill feedback from the vibrations of Mouse's steps. White dust clouds reflect candle light, overhead stage lights. Through the thick flour flying and landing everywhere, Mouse opens the Bugle bag, grabs a handful, smashes them into his plain white t-shirt, stuffs some down his diaper, chews some, spits them out on stage, hurls handfuls at anyone he can make out through the darkness and the low-visibility flour. He opens the bologna packages, wipes his brow with the slimy gray meaty circles, flings them up and out like tiny Frisbees. Now out of food, Mouse removes the microphone from the stand, falls to the stage and rolls around, screaming a sustained guttural banshee screech, body crunching over Bugles, skidding over bologna, flour sticking to damp skin, guitar sustaining an endless rumbling white howl through the long-suffering amplifier.

The audience has long fled the room. Only the employees, the Reverend B. Stoned, and Icy Filet remain. Icy has never seen anything like this in her nineteen years, insides an adrenalized mix of terror and exhilaration.

The Reverend B. Stoned runs to the stage, screaming, "That's enough, man!" as three of the bigger members of the kitchen crew run up to the stage, turn everything off, pull him away and drag him outside by his knotty long Manson hair as Mouse yells back, "C'mon, Reverend, it's all in fun, heh heh—it's freeeeedom, maaaaaan, heh heh heh!"

"Don't come back here, ya fuckin' weirdo!" the Reverend B.

Stoned yells after him. In the empty room, the Reverend stands in front of the stage, kicking at the mess on the floor, kicking up flour clouds. He curses, shakes his head, finally walks off.

Icy Filet approaches the stage, grabs the pants, the guitar, the effects pedal, the amplifier, the cables. It's a cumbersome two-handed carry job, made that much more difficult by general performance-art sliminess caked on everything. She limps like a bag lady out the front door, in time to see the kitchen crew storm past, calling Mouse all kinds of names, and Mouse himself, supine on the curb as the University Avenue foot traffic glares and mumbles as they walk by.

Icy Filet cautiously approaches him. He's covered in flour, Bugle Bits, bologna strands in his beautiful scraggly hair. He still wears the diaper. His face has the purple chubbiness of the recently punched.

"I couldn't find your flip-flops," she says, standing over him now, unsure of what else to say.

Mouse, fetally positioned facing the street, rolls onto his back, moans, looks up, recognizes her—the rapper!—and a slow smile creeps across his face, lips widening, opening to what Icy thinks are two rows of gorgeously mismatched teeth. "Why thank you, Pop Tarts."

Icy Filet looks away, flushed face, sweaty palmed. "That was really amazing," she says.

Mouse smiles, pulls himself up. "Glad you liked it." He stands, plucks a piece of bologna out of his chest hair and tosses it onto the street. "Let me call you sometime."

"What?" Icy Filet says, and it's not that she didn't hear what he just said, but more like all she can think is that if this is his way of meeting girls, it's insanely elaborate.

"Let me call you."

Naturally she's a little hesitant. But then she remembers Mouse, pre-performance, running up to congratulate her after her sucky (her word) attempt at freestyle rapping. "Do you have any paper?" Mouse gestures at the mess he's made of himself, his pant-lessness, and chuckles. "Don't seem to, ah, have anything on me, heh heh heh."

Icy Filet unzips the white vinyly MC Hamtramck pen pouch she found at an Orlando thrift store—her favorite late '80s/early '90s rapper himself, in his trademark crushed velvet purple jump-suit, big glasses, pulse beats shaved into his scalp, with the thought cloud above him (which he points to) that reads, "U Push It Real Good, Wild Thang"—pulls out a notecard and a pen. "Mouse, right?" she asks, handing him the card with her phone number.

"That's right, Miss Icy Filet, my favorite rapper. I'll call you soon, and we'll dance a' dance, take a chance, look askance, you know what I'm saying to you?'

Icy Filet does not, or isn't clear on the details maybe, but says she does anyway. "Bye," she says, waving, walking westbound on University, back to the dorm, SK-1 jutting out of her UF totebag.

"Thanks for getting my stuff," Mouse yells after her.

"Word, yo," Icy Filet says, head and heart spinning in the af-terglow of first-times.

FIVE YEARS

Another Amateur Sunday here at fucking Electric Slim's Used and New CDs and LPs . . . me and Boston Mike standing here behind the counter dealing with lazy illiterate cocksmacks who couldn't find the new Celine Dion CD if you led them by the hand to the "D" section, removed the new Celine Dion CD from the bin, placed the new Celine Dion CD in their germ-ridden unwiped hands, raised said germ-ridden unwiped hands two inches in front of their cattle-blank eyes and said, "Here. Here is the new Celine Dion CD." Sundays at the record store . . . it's like an endless parade of cretinous twats marching in and out through our glass front door . . . me and Boston Mike watch them walk outside along the plaza sidewalk and we see them and pray "Please, please don't come in here" . . . but God ignores us . . . laughs at our petty requests . . . it's the cattle march of the UF student body getting their nose rings—figuratively, but might as well be literally—yanked by our beloved music industry towards whatever insufferable dogshit they've seen fit to mass produce and ship our way . . . it's the ox-dumb rural-ass mouthbreather country folk waddling into town to do their "big city" shopping—fat fucks in NASCAR t-shirts ogling the poster racks in the corner . . . you know, like thong-clad women bending over rows of Camaros as the flame-fonted caption reads, "Haulin' Ass!!!" or the one where the caption reads "Your Tub or Mine?" in watery lettering as the feathery peroxide blonde with the shapily body emerges from a wooden tub painted in the Stars and Bars, all naughty bits strategically covered in soap suds . . . it's old drunks stumbling into the store to stand by the counter and talk loudly at us about how they were fortunate enough to see whatever played-out-not-that-great-to-begin-with classic rock garbage live in concert and everything back in 1979 . . . and speaking of garbage, Sundays are for some reason the big day when the nasty garbage pickers like to come in dragging crates of records with more scratches than grooves, shredded covers reeking of rotten leftovers and roach droppings . . . and then these jerks have the nerve to get all flabbergasted because we won't pay like top dollar for their precious finds . . . real rarities like Herb Alpert and the Tijuana Brass's *Whipped Cream and Other Delights*, Fleetwood Mac's *Rumours*, and *Reader's Digest Presents: Sounds for Easy Listening, Volume Three* . . . in the middle of all this wheezing farting monument to human ugliness, egg-shaped moms stroll in thinking if they hum off-key renditions of the hit song they want to buy for their kid's birthday (on the cassingle format, natch), we'll get all "Name That Tune" with it and help them out . . . our friends who make up our customer base on every other day of the week are nowhere to be found . . . sleeping off last night's parties . . . bicycling from one barbeque to the next . . . but not me and not Boston Mike because somebody's gotta work this counter on Amateur Sunday, and the bills—oh, the damn bills!—never go away, so fuck it, fuck these asshole customers, and fuck me.

Boston Mike stands there on these typical Sundays and calls everything "retarded" in that accent of his that I'm not even going to try to do because I guess it's just—whatever, right?—I mean, Boston's where he came from so of course he's not going to sound like those of us around here who were oh-so-fucking-lucky to be born and raised in the South—and when it gets really fucking unbearable here—he'll elaborate and call the day "wicked retarded."

"Wicked retarded," he says, tongue ring clicking every time his tongue touches the roof of his mouth, standing there in that faded black stink-ass Assuck t-shirt, that smudged-up Boston Red Sox ballcap he wears to cover up his receding hair he thinks women actually care about, spacerless earlobes drooping and sagging like elephant balls, same old piercings across his bearded face, same old tattoo sleeves covering his arms, normally beady brown eyes squinting into that look of hatred fear desperation and annoyance you only see on the faces of jerkoffs like us deep in the existentialist pit of retail hell . . . "Wicked retarded," Boston Mike says . . . and with that, it's the cue to give up on any hope of getting to kill the rest of the afternoon by sneaking a sixer of Old Hamtramck tallboys poured into coffee mugs . . . at least for another hour and a half of this shit . . . and I look over to where Boston Mike's looking, to the front door, and of course that's the source of the "wicked" in his sentence . . . I mean, what else could make this snail-drag of a Sunday afternoon worse?

Boogie Dave.

Boogie Dave is my boss, the owner of the store, a fecal-breathed troll of a man, a pathetic lumpy-dump troll-turd . . . like if a snaggle-toothed crackwhore had sex with one of the larger *Fraggle Rock* muppets, this is the thing that would be shat out in trollbirth . . . he never asks us how we're doing . . . shuffles in in fatguy sweat pants, simian back hair poking out of a sleeveless black Johnny Thunders t-shirt that is given the impossible duty of slimming Boogie Dave's ample man-tittied torso . . . shoulder-length black hair that probably looked alright back when he opened the store during the dusty-denimed/pub glam era of 1973-1974, but now what's left of his mane hangs there around the back of his tumor-bumpy skull like frayed tassels from the curtains of a dying pimp . . . he glares at us as he steps past, sniffles, says "It smells horrible in here!" and I want to say "Great to see you too, Boogie Dave," but all you can do is stand there and look around and make sure your ass is covered and make sure there's nothing under your control that he has to whine about . . . because Boogie Dave is a total whiner . . . if the jerkoff finds one tiny mistake he'll harp on it and harp on it and mutter and complain until you wish he would drop dead . . . he climbs the steps to the upraised front counter slash register area, says "Look out" to me and Boston Mike, who step sideways into what little space we have back here, pulls out—yes, of course—about a dozen sticks of New Age Writer's Retreat incense sticks . . . soon the store will reek of wheatgrass deodorant and tenured patchouli . . . the funny thing is, it never succeeds in covering up the dusty attic smell of all those old records alphabetized in bins in the middle of the store as the CDs and VHS tapes loop around the walls and these fat stupid customers somehow squeeze their fat stupid asses in the narrow spaces between while Boston Mike and I wait for the inevitable Boogie Dave whining about whatever's wrong today with the store before Boogie Dave leaves, now that his twenty minute task of showing up at the store long enough to make his employees feel completely inadequate has been accomplished . . . such a cranky, cadaverous weirdo . . . clinging to this record store even though he hates it, because it's all he has . . . if it's not this . . . it's retail . . . and I sometimes fantasize of going into the electronics department of some large department store and there he is in the regulation blue dress shirt/ khaki slacked uniform of the corporate retail gig . . . actually having to earn a living by dealing with customers for a change . . . and not just customers who normally come in here on non-Sunday days, but the vast unwashed morons who make this record store gig a total can of corn by comparison . . . Sundays times a million . . . he fits the incense sticks into their strategically placed holders on different shelves by the walls . . . pushing through customers who are in the way . . . more likely to say nothing than to say "Excuse me" . . .

"So what do you think's on his whine agenda for today," I say to Boston Mike as we stand there watching Boogie Dave push his way from incense-holder to incense-holder.

"The music, probably," Boston Mike says. "That and he probably found something unalphabetized."

He always finds something, and if he finds nothing, he can always dust off the ol' "You guys need to be more alpha" speech . . . because . . . well, look at him . . . you don't get more Alpha Dog than Boogie Dave . . . he read some book on dogs at one point and has used it ever since as his go-to on leadership and management techniques . . .

I nod, because that sounds about right, and Boston Mike has to repeat his "Wicked retarded," and Boogie Dave approaches the counter, steps up, says, "What did I tell you guys about not playing Beefheart when it's busy like this?"

Sure enough . . . it's the Beefheart masterpiece *Lick My Decals Off, Baby*, and it's one of the more . . . avant parts of the record, where marimbas and saxophones and bass clarinets scream over drums that sound like they're being thrown down a craggy mountain . . . Boogie Dave normally keeps himself scarce on Sundays, but now that he's here, he gets to witness how Boston Mike and me, we like to flip one abrasive record after the other as a passive/aggressive ploy to make the Sunday amateurs leave us alone because we're tired, hungover, and besides that, we're genetically incapable of giving them decent service anyways . . . neither of us says anything to Boogie Dave . . . I mean, I think Beefheart is the ultimate pop music, but hey, that's just me, and a master race of a few thousand who have ears evolved enough to see the epic enchantment in the music . . .

"I never understood how anyone could like this," Boogie Dave says, removing the record right when it was getting even better. "It wasn't good when it came out, and it hasn't improved with age."

He throws on some contemporary alternative rock, some cookie cutter pop-rock filled with gravelly vocals and negative navel-gazing . . . and I can't help but cringe . . . physically cringe from my toes to my head to my balls to my soul . . . at how tedious this music is . . .

"We're not doing as well as we did this time last year," Boogie Dave says, turning to us. Nobody makes eye contact. I pretend to be staring at customers, making sure they're not trying to steal anything (like I care), Boston Mike looks to the front door, smiles and says, "How are you?" to a group of three chattering college broads in short-shorts and half-t-shirts (and you know they ain't gonna buy shit . . . girls like these never linger the way the creeps of all stripes linger in here browsing for hours . . .) who ignore him . . . "And last year we weren't doing as well as we did the year before that." This is not news to me or Boston Mike . . . there are five other record stores within this one mile radius, to say nothing of the mall three miles away . . . "And I'm the only one who seems to care about it" . . . we say nothing to this . . . I mean, honestly—we don't care. Because why should we? This is a minimum wage gig that's usually a cool-enough minimum wage gig except for Amateur Sundays . . .

"What would you like us to do, Boogie Dave?" I venture, knowing there's no point, but feeling obligated to say something, even if I know it won't lead to anything good (the girls who have worked here have all been reduced to tears by this piece of shit at various points in their work-lives here) . . . but I've found it's better to say something instead of nothing . . .

"You guys need to look like you care. You could start there.

You know not to play Beefheart. I told you that, but you do it anyway. How am I supposed to interpret that?" Boogie Dave looks at the clipboard to the left of the counter where we write down the sales of every new purchase . . . "And look," he points to today's sheet. "You didn't even write down that we have Built to Spill in backstock. What if I saw that and ordered a bunch more?" He says this, knowing everyone who works here knows we have plenty of Built to Spill records here because it's a big seller, but Boogie Dave is, to the depths of his soul, a dick, and is like compelled to point out every obviously unintentional mistake . . .

"Things have got to change," Boogie Dave says, sets the clipboard back down next to the counter, descends the counter steps. He shuffles off to the front door like the pathetic sad sack that he is, adds, "You need to figure out how you're going to make that happen, because it ain't gonna go on like this forever."

On top of all this, the customers get to witness Boogie Dave's browbeating, and if you want my opinion, his unpleasant style does more to alienate customers than the music of Captain Beefheart ever could . . .

Boston Mike watches Boogie Dave step into his green VW van, back it out, leave the tiny parking lot, roll away down the student ghetto side street on the north side of the plaza. "I'll buy the beer," he says, and I laugh, feeling the relief of this stressful meaningless day as it reaches the halfway point before we get to go back to my house and really hit the beer . . .

I immediately put the Beefheart back on . . . ring up the customers and their shitty selections, answer whatever braindead questions they might have . . . dreaming of the Old Hamtramck tallboys in the wet brown paper bag Boston Mike is most certainly carrying out of the Pop-a-Top right about now . . . I want to be buzzed, I want to be numb, I want to forget about that fucking asshole Boogie Dave and how the only nice thing I can say about him is that he doesn't have any kids to pass along all his horrid-horrid traits . . .

When Boston Mike walks in with that brown paper bag, I can't help but smile. It'll get a little bit easier here with each passing half-hour . . . as the dickhead customer rush starts to dissipate and the beer starts to kick in.

Boston Mike pours two can's worth into our respective coffee mugs—his a white South-by-Southwest memento that reads "KEEP AUSTIN WEIRD" and mine a yellow Cracker Barrel find that reads in red-letters: "WHEN I GET OLD I'LL MOVE NORTH AND DRIVE SLOW." He toasts with a "To this day being almost over, and to watching the customers start to screw" . . . That's one of his words, Bostonian for "amscray!" . . . and our mugs cheer, and I chug, eagerly awaiting that first rush to the brain. "Ooooooooooo-wooooo!" I howl, spinning my head from side-to-side, like how cartoon characters do when they come to their senses. I know I've been kinda, you know, down on working here, down on the customers, down on the scene so far . . . I know this . . . but you know, usually, it really isn't that bad . . . I mean . . . It's working at a record store! The great American dream of every young rock and roll-inspired twitty-twat! Oh, to be paid to do what you love! Sit around and play music! That reality isn't 100 percent accurate . . . but it is often enough . . . now that the rush is dying down, and the boss is gone . . . I can bask in this bright sunshiney afternoon . . . I mean, look at it! Look out there! It's fucking nice here!

"Hey, this is my friend Drunk John," Boston Mike says to this girl Daisy I've been crushing on since I first started going to shows here, this tall thin curly-blonde covered in tattoos who I usually just call "The Canary Babe" who walks in in eight-mile long jeans and that model walk she has, this sashay that gets me every time . . . it kinda scares me, to be honest, how beautiful she is . . .

Daisy the Canary Babe turns to us, smiles and doesn't break that stride to say, "Yes, I know Drunk John," and she has this stunning smile that's part genuine, part manipulative, and that gets me every time . . . fuck, she's hot-tot-tot . . . "How are you guys doing today?"

"It's getting better," I manage, smiling like a total choad. "I'm glad you're here." and she laughs that soft laugh of hers and says "Thanks, guys . . . " and like any remotely attractive person who comes in here, you know she knows exactly what she wants and will leave as soon as she finds it . . . why can't it be opposite? Where, like, the assholes and amateurs walk in and walk out and the girls like Daisy the Canary Babe stick around?

"How come you never ask her out?" Boston Mike asks. "She seems to like you alright."

"Ah, you know . . . she's hooked up with pretty much all my friends." (Which is true . . . she's been with William, Paul, Neil, Mouse, the Play the Piano Drunk Like a Percussion Instrument Until the Fingers Begin to Bleed a Bit guys . . .)

"So?" Boston Mike scoffs.

"So that's gross."

"But you're into her."

"Yeah! I mean, look at her! She's Daisy the Canary Babe."

Boston Mike looks down, shakes his head. "You're pathetic."

. . . And maybe I am. "Shh, she's coming up here," I say . . . and add a "Fine, I'll ask her out," and descend the steps to stand outside in the heat of the parking lot and wait for her to walk out so I can get her number and you know maybe somehow get to bang her.

I try and force what I hope she will interpret as a smile on my face as I step down to the store's blackened white linoleum . . . she's easily six inches taller than I am, and I wonder what I would do with someone this tall, but I have total faith in my creativity to come up with some amazing answers . . .

Outside, wishing just this once that I was a smoker, so I could you know look like I had a reason to be standing out here like this, feet balanced between the edge of the sidewalk and the concrete curb. Shifting my weight from one foot to the next . . . watching the plaza's customers go in and out of the Laundromat, the greeting card store, and the copy place . . . two beers down . . . basking in the Sunday . . . thinking what I'll say to Daisy the Canary Babe . . . thinking of how everything could stop now, and I'd be happy with it . . . not in an "I've made it!" kind of way . . . but I'm comfortable and happy from my perch behind the counter of Electric Slim's, to be here in Gainesville dicking around my early postgraduation years from that fine-fine institution of higher learning right across the street there . . . time can stop moving . . . just let me woo the shit outta Daisy the Canary Babe when she leaves the store, and the fucking world can stop, ok?

She leaves the store walking that model walk, stops when she sees me, "What are you doing, John?" she asks, smiling, and me, so glad she left the "Drunk" out of my name . . . this encourages me to bounce off the sidewalk and the curb, take the five steps her way . . . "Just taking a break," I say in what I hope isn't a too-tipsy looking smile . . . "Where you headed?" I add when my stride somewhat matches hers, putting that emphasis on the "you" to sound you know classy, like I'm interested in the woman for the woman . . . "I have studying to do. Started seeing this guy," she says.

"Oh yeah?" I say, trying to sound like I barely give a fuck, when inside, that's all I do . . . "Anyone I know?"

"Nobody you know," she says, and I stop a few steps past the laundromat's double front doors, as if I'm unallowed to venture any further due to the high responsibilities of my career in recorded music retail. "I mean—he's not in 'the scene,'" and she laughs at her finger quotes, and the only iron-clad rule I know is that if you openly discuss "the scene" with someone, you have to put it into finger-quotes, because otherwise it sounds tacky coming out of anyone's mouth over the age of sixteen . . .

"Well. He's a totally lucky guy," I say, cringing deep inside at my use of the word "totally." Sometimes, to be honest, I hate everything about myself.

"Yeah, well, I don't know if he sees it that way. Didn't you graduate?"

Graduation. Something I don't want to talk about. "Two years ago," I answer.

"Oh," she says, practically saying "Then what are you still doing here?" in the way she says "Oh." and I realize, it's never gonna happen.

"Yeah, you know," I add, trying to salvage it. "I like it here just fine—not like I want to be at the record store forever, but I like it here."

"I do too," she says, and it seems in the way her voice takes a softer tone, the way she looks at me, then at this plaza parking lot, then turns her head to University, like she actually might mean it. "But I do need to leave. Great seeing you again."

I wave and smile, watch her tall model walking body move down the sidewalk, plastic bag with an LP bouncing against her gorgeously narrow left hip . . . I walk back towards the store, in that adrenal bounce you get after you do something you think is brave, laughing to myself, thinking, As if I ever had a chance . . .

"She has a boyfriend now. Let's get drunk," I say immediately upon entering the store . . . and when I'm back at my perch, Boston Mike pats me on the back. "You tried, bro," he says. "I'm proud of you."

"Yeah yeah," I say, open the third Old Hamtramck tallboy, pour it into my mug, confident this will be the can that transports me to the end of this Amateur Sunday shift . . .

The last hour does fly by, and it always feels great to kick out the final customers in a tone that suggests they are the biggest douchiest fucks on the face of the earth for still browsing after we told them they had ten minutes before the store closes . . . that turn of the lock and the flip of the "OPEN" sign to "CLOSED" are the best things about Amateur Sundays . . . now it's a matter of tallying the receipts and leaving the till in dear sweet Boogie Dave's slovenly back office. Punch out the timeclock, sip the last few swillish drops from the drained Old Hamtramck, take the cans with us so we can toss them in a nearby dumpster, engage the security system, and we're free . . .

It's a five minute walk to my house, with a stop halfway for more Old Hamtramck . . . I carry the six-pack and we walk down the dirt-covered graveled little student ghetto roads to my place . . . the sidewalks don't exist so we walk down the middle of these streets—our streets, it seems, since I've lived in my place for four years now, and that's an eternity around here . . . me, I'm on this like, "Fuck that guy," rant, and Boston Mike's like, "Who?" and I say, "You know who. Boogie Dave. I think I wanna fight him," and Boston Mike laughs and says, "I'd love to see that," and I'm like "He's such a prick," and Boston Mike says, "You should open your own store then. Put him out of business."

I say nothing to this. We're approaching my front porch and I can't shut up about the day, "And Daisy. What's she doing dating somebody outside of 'the scene,' man?" Boston Mike laughs and says, "It isn't right. Maybe she got sick of us."

We step up the three wobbly steps to my gray porch. I hand Boston Mike a beer and keep one for myself before unlocking the front door and tossing these in the fridge and taking outside two pink beer koozies with light pink flamingos raising their left legs at 90 degree angles as the orange-lettered word "FLORIDA" curves around the bottom. Now, we'll sit in lawn chairs and kick back and forget about the day . . . without the background noise of music . . . because, after eight hours of forced music, you want silence.

I can usually go about an hour before wanting to throw on a record. Usually, by this point, the beer has obliterated the bad points of the day . . . that, coupled with me and Boston Mike making fun of all of our stupid customers . . . and honestly, I get sick of hearing Boston Mike's accent. And again, I'm not gonna do the accent, but—and this is going to sound stupid, and by stupid, I mean Florida-stupid—I didn't think people really talked this way. Shows you what I know about the world outside of my little slice of the Sunshine State. English Degree aside, sometimes I think all ally know about is this town, my friends, and the unceasing routine that is SUNDAY! SUNDAY! SUNDAY! at the record store. By now, we're getting pretty lllllloaded . . . and I'll throw on some record . . . on this fine evening, *Jailbreak* by Thin Lizzy . . . why not? . . . you know those dudes knew all about heartbreak, and shitty jobs, and the highs and lows of love and lust among bros like us . . . party bros! . . . post-work brews, sitting in lawnchairs, and all I know is that the night will eventually take us to Gatorroni's for slices and however many free pitchers William can send our way, and by then, Boogie Dave and Daisy the Canary Babe will be long out of my Old Hamtramck-soaked mind.

I live in one of these crumbling old one-story houses in the student ghetto where everything's falling apart beautifully . . . built in the pre A/C Floridian style of practicality, of southern charm . . . patio and house upraised five feet . . . and from this vantage point, you see everyone passing by on foot, on bike, in cars . . . everyone you want to see and everyone you don't want to see. After living here for five years—believe me—it's easy to have plenty in both camps.

It's starting to get really good out here, man . . . Phil Lynott is singing, *I'd come runnin / I'd come runnin back to you again* and you know he means it in ways all these emo shits will never understand . . . and speaking of (even if he is more, you know "hardcore" than "emo," but whatever) . . . here comes Max, riding up to us . . . Max, who I lived in the dorms with so long ago . . . and since those days, he's become this vegan straightedge kid, which—and I hate to say it—basically means he's figured out a way to deal with his dad being a violent abusive drunk . . . these soy-eating nondrinkers come on all pious and sanctimonious, but really, that's what it's about . . . I mean, not to generalize too much here, but you know . . . since he's vegan he now weighs about a buck oh three, and most of that weight's from his big brown beard . . . and the money he saves from not buying three dollar six-packs of Old Ham-town go right into tats and piercings, and fuck if he doesn't already have more than he needs of both.

I want to hide as he rolls up, because I know he'll probably wanna engage in, you know "tat talk," because it's probably the only thing left all three of us have in common (Boston Mike lived down the hall back in the dorm days . . .), our tat sleeves and shin ink. I don't need the piercings, but Boston Mike sure has them. Except for the dirty-ass Sox cap, and Max actually has half-dollar sized spacers in his lobes where, like I was saying, Boston Mike's lobes flap in the breeze all disgusting like—and oh yeah, except for how Mike talks and how Max has this Michigan rust belt emigrant timbre—these two could be identical twins. I want to hide because I hate how humorless Max has become. Back when we'd sneak booze into the dorm, when he wasn't totally averse to eating the occasional cheeseburger, the dude actually had a sense of humor. He had this thing where we would get completely lllllloaded before going to parties, and he'd bring a package of saltine crackers hidden in his bookbag with the booze . . . when he'd see a group of uptight-looking girls standing around at the party, he'd take out a saltine, approach the girls, unzip his fly, pull out his balls, stick the cracker underneath his balls, and say, "Pardon me, ladies, but could I interest you in an hors d'ouerve called Nuts on a Cracker?" The girls screamed and we laughed. He'd do this until he'd throw up in a corner and me and Boston Mike and whoever else was around that we were friends with would have to drag him back to the dorm before fights broke out. Seriously, Max was a lot more fun when he drank.

But it's too late. "Hey," Max says, stepping off his bike, voice weighed down with brooding drama, like he's on the verge of writing some stupid emo song about this meeting, or that he's gonna go off and make a zine about it . . .

"Yo, bro!" I beckon, in full-on party dude voice . . . only a semi-ironical thing for me . . . I mean it's funny to talk that way, like you're one of those dudes who hangs around kegs all night talking shit . . . but at the end of the day, I basically am that guy . . . I raise my can in the air, so very very comfortable in this old lawnchair, on this patio, in this neighborhood. "What's going on?"

He approaches the steps, shows us his right arm wrapped in clear plastic. Through the plastic, three fresh black Xs, circled by the words "STRAIGHTEDGE FOR LIFE." "I got more work done on my arm," he says, as if we're blind or something.

"Aw, pissa," Boston Mike says, and inside, that sinking feeling of pointlessness, like those first fifteen minutes of an eight hour Sunday at Electric Slim's. That everything and everyone is a stale joke, and I'm the anticipated punchline.

"Oh ho ho, the talk of the tat," I say, laughing, then standing up to run inside the house to throw on some record, something Max'll dislike because it's "ironic," and the worst thing in the world for these jerks is irony. Irony is a fucking war crime, but sanctimony is godliness to these depressing jerkoff puritans. Fucking liars. All they joke about is Satan or being gay. Seriously. These people are so unfunny, so tiresome in their ponderous pompous piousness . . . how everything in life is such a be-all-end-all big deal. In the old days, they'd go off to be monks. Now, they show off their tattoos. I hate my tattoos. I don't even know why I have them anymore. To think of all that money I wasted that could have gone to beer, records, and pizza. They're embarrassing because everybody has them now. Everybody.

So I sneak off into my bedroom, throw on Bowie's *Ziggy Stardust* album, and the first song, "Five Years." There was a time when Max and I would sit in our dorm getting high while listening to Bowie when we should have been studying. Ridiculous—I know—but you do a lot of stupid crap when you're eighteen, trying on everything to figure out what fits you.

I strut out the front door, trying to move like Ziggy Stardust—like some kind of androgynous alien robot—and it's that sloppy blissful apathetic-over-all-the-right-things kind of actions—where that part of your self-control that you didn't really want to develop in the first place is gone—and you feel alive again . . . this is why I bother with the beer. I mouth the words and smile, pointing at Max . . . "Pushing through the market square / so many mothers dying / news had just come over / we had five years left to cry in . . . " I drain what's left of the beer and remove it from the koozie. Max glares at me at the bottom of the steps, still standing there holding his bike with his non-new-tat-armed hand.

"What, dude." I say, sick of looking at this sadsack emo kid who used to be my friend. "C'mon man, you used to be *fun* . . . "

"Where do you see yourself in five years, *Drunk* John?" Max asks me, and my nickname sounds strange coming out of his mouth—and not because he says it like a joyless pompous straight-edge kid—the question makes me pause. I mean, I guess I drink a lot—but everybody does here, so whatever. It's just that my name is John, and it's such a common name they had to separate it from Straightedge John, Psycho John, Goth John, Short John. Whatever. I'm not especially proud of my nickname, but it could be a lot worse. Slut Chrissy. Roofie Steve. You get a nickname here, and you're stuck with it. For life.

I answer Max's question with a long, sustained, guttural belch. Boston Mike chuckles at this. I mean—I could lie like everybody else does around here when asked questions about their futures. Say I'm moving to some big city up North. Share some lofty dream of pursuing this or that. We all know how that ends. Those people come back within a year, when the temperature in their new city first drops below freezing. Honestly, right now, I don't want to think about what I'll be doing in five years, or even five months. Five years . . . it will be 2001. I'll be twenty-nine. I don't want to think about it. I unleash a second belch, equally as long, sustained, and guttural as the first one.

I drop the koozie, throw up my hands and say, "OK, Maxie. I'll bite." I spin my hands in a forward motion and affect a dumb guy voice asking "Why do you ask where I'll be in five years?"

Max straddles his bike. "I don't know. It's like, you're doing the same shit you did five years ago."

I pick up the pink koozie and toss it at his pierced, bearded, soy-stuffed head. It bounces off his forehead, lands in the dirt. Boston Mike laughs at this, and Max picks it up, looks at the flamingo and the "FLORIDA," smiles this smile more in line with the old Max, tosses it onto the porch. "Same old John," he says.

"And you?" I gotta ask. "Your big change since the dorms, as far as I can tell, is that you don't eat animals and you got your arms covered in tattoos. What's 2001 look like for you, big guy?"

Max looks right at me, and it's that look he had on mornings after parties where he'd do the "Nuts on a Cracker." The way he'd look when we'd be at Denny's the next morning, eating hangover omelets and trying to look adult by smoking in our booth and brooding over coffee. Like he wants to know something, what he did the night before, and if it was funny, sure, but not just that. Something more.

"I don't know. I'm trying to figure it out." With that, Max pedals away, back towards University, as if he just rode over here to bring me down, and now that he's accomplished that, he can go return to whatever vegan straightedge tattoo parlor he was being all angsty in before he stopped by.

It's a minute of me and Boston Mike in silence broken only by Bowie going on about five years before the world ends.

"Fuckin' sanctimonious prick," I finally mutter. I stumble (I'm stumbling now, but I don't care because I'm drunk so fuck it), into the house, back to the kitchen, grab two more beers, muttering in the self-talk of the drunk, "Five years . . . who cares . . . why can't it stay like this, man? Why . . . the fuck . . . not?"

"Five years from now's gonna be 2001," Boston Mike says, grabbing the beer from me and moving it slowly to his face like the black monolith in that movie while singing the opening notes to "Thus Spake Zarathustra." He pounds tympani notes on his right thigh, sings "Dun-dun, dun-dun, dun-dun, dun-dun, duuuuuuuuun."

"I thought we'd be on a Martian colony by now," I say, trying to forget, trying to laugh it off. "Like we'd be eating protein pills for lunch in zero gravity."

"Yeah, no shit, right?" Boston Mike says. "We'd be time traveling to the Roman Empire for orgies, or to 1965 to see The Who."

We pshaw at the future we were promised at Disney World. "Let's shotgun these and get outta here," I suggest. "To the Drunken Mick, to Gatorroni's . . . shit, anywhere, man."

We both keep our keys looped on the right side of our pants. We unloop the keys, turn our beers sideways, poke a hole, stick it in our faces and try not to choke as the Old Ham-town gushes straight down our throats. Five seconds later, we toss our cans to the side. I run into the house, turn off the lights and the Bowie, lock up. We descend the stairs, walk down this street I know so well, and these old homes I know so well. I know who lives inside these houses now, who lived there before them, and who lived there before them.

"So what do you think?" I ask Boston Mike, feeling the familiar gravel of these barely paved roads.

"About what?"

"In five years. Where'll you be?"

Boston Mike laughs. "Jesus, dude." He punches me in the arm. "I don't know. I don't gotta know. You don't gotta know. We're young. Wicked young." I say nothing, eyes trying to focus on the traffic one block ahead on University.

We turn left onto University Avenue, away from the campus towards the bars and restaurants. The sun sets behind us, the afternoon heat replaced by an easy warmth. The streetlights turn on up and down the street. The lights inside gas stations, the hotel, the restaurants and shops . . . they're bright beacons . . . and all I can ask myself is: Why can't it always be like this? Everything here and now is perfect and comfortable, and why can't it always be like this? Me and a friend after work walking somewhere to get even more lllloaded with more friends, to relax in this relaxing place that feels more like home than anyplace I've ever been . . . because, even if Boogie Dave is a total dick, and Daisy the Canary Babe will never grace my bedroom . . . that's alright, because we're still young—and every moment—every flip of a record, every girl I pass, every waking moment, has so much incredible possibility, and that's life here, and I don't ever want that to change.

And that's the fucking problem . . . it never stays the same—not when you're in the womb, in the house the morning of your first day of school, graduations, college, after college, and on and on until death. This moment is everything, so who gives a fuck about five years? It's another perfect night in a town I never want to leave.

Up ahead at Gatorroni's, Neil and Paul are at an outside table, a pitcher of dark beer in front of them, sipping from plastic cups then spitting out the beer in a long comical mist.

"We're practicing our spit takes," Paul says when I sit to join them.

"Let me try," I say, as Boston Mike goes inside to score two free pitchers from our friends behind the counter.

LIKE STEPHEN KING

"It's all really ok," Ronnie says to no one, walking back to the trailer from the Kwik-Mart, down a side street with the kinds of forlorn little office buildings that always house short-lived non-descript small businesses with names like "KDM Systems Inc" and "Southeastern Solutions." On the right, before the trailer park, two one-level houses, collapsing on themselves in a kind of abandonment most often seen in whole sections of Detroit. "The book will be published soon, and that's that."

Ronnie runs into the trailer long enough to grab the disc holding all 536 pages of *The Big Blast for Youth*, carries the disc—this blue 3" square disc that is his eternally bright and lucrative future—to the car, holding it tight in both hands like the valuable object it is. He hides it in the glove box, drives away, and within minutes is reclined in a gray plasma donation chair by the plasma center's front windows—facing a row of six similar gray chairs occupied by everyone from collegiate ravers, looking blissfully emaciated in shiny track suits, to the black and white poor of this and nearby counties (Alachua, Putnam, Marion, Union, Gilchrist, Bradford, Levy). A four-inch needle drains the, as Lou Reed might've called it way-back-when, mainline in the middle of Ronnie's right arm, and Ronnie squeezes his right hand, sitting there under fluorescent lights as the TVs in the corner play MTV videos of 1990s musicians making money off their perceived problems . . . Ronnie kills the time by imagining how it's all going to go down, because, after all, Ronnie is familiar with that film Drinking is a Really Big Deal When You're a Writer, you know, the one about the poet who liked drinking, so Ronnie knows how these discoveries happen.

It's only a matter of time, Ronnie thinks, sitting there dreaming about how great it will be, once he mails off the manuscript. All that is left to do is to print it out and mail it, once he is done filling this IV bag with amber colored plasma. Soon this whirring machine to his immediate right will stop whirring, will stop separating Ronnie's blood from Ronnie's plasma, and he will get the needle removed from one of the perpetually stoned orderlies who work here, will get the crook of his arm wrapped in gauze from same perpetually stoned orderly, will collect his money, and leave for this friend of a friend of an acquaintance named Chloë, this girl he kinda new back in Orlando who in a chance encounter in a Publix parking lot, told Ronnie she would be more than happy to share her computer, printer, and paper for the cause of *The Big Blast for Youth* getting into printed form and mailed to the lucky editor who would get to read this.

•

"Do you want anything to drink?" Chloë asks, standing in the doorway to her feng-shuied bedroom, smiling. Smiling at Ronnie.

Ronnie sits in a black office chair crammed to the brim with what Ronnie believed to be spaceage polymer plastics form-fitted to practically massage the asses of anyone so fortunate enough to sit down upon it. What a chair; what a chair! Ronnie contrasts this with that rickety wooden chair of Chris Embowelment's, painted black with red pentagrams (of course) that creaked and shifted like it would break at any moment as Ronnie had proofread the novel on Mr. Embowelment's computer ("I wonder how he's doing, or if he's forgiven me?" Ronnie thinks to himself) in the early morning hours of the day he was to move to Gainesville. Before leaving, Ronnie wanted to be sure no revisions were needed. None were needed. It was a masterpiece.

"What do you have?" Ronnie asks, staring at the gray monitor screen on the dust-free white desk, the paper-stuffed off-white printer to the right of the wide and dense monitor with a menu awaiting orders to print the novel that would change the world, as Ronnie makes one last dummy check for any mistakes.

"Beer. Wine." The way she stands there, smiling. Ronnie had always considered Chloë to be like this overweight gothy broad (Yeah, Ronnie thought it was hilarious to say "broad") with the requisite fixations on Morrissey. Here she is now, living in Gainesville, in the

Duckpond neighborhood—this relatively upscale neighborhood of professors and graduate students—standing there, smiling.

"Wine." Ronnie had learned that having a drink or two after donating plasma was the equivalent of three or four drinks.

"What kind?"

"Whatever."

She returns with two long-stemmed wine glasses half-filled with chardonnay (Ronnie guesses), sets his to the left of the keyboard. "Have you ever had a spritzer?" she asks.

"Spritzer?" Ronnie repeats, not taking his eyes off the screen.

"It's wine and Sprite."

With his left hand, Ronnie lifts the glass. With his right hand, he clicks the "print" button with the mouse. The printer screeches, then whirs. The glasses clink.

"Cheers," Chloë says. She makes a big production out of sniffing the wine before sipping it, sounding to Ronnie like someone trying to breathe with a bad cold.

She wears too much eye make-up, Ronnie thinks. It's a painful purple, thick, layered on with a trowel. Same with the lips, the blush, the purple streaks in the bangs of her dark hair, framing her fat pale face, wrapping around the beginnings of that double chin. Still fat, but less gothy, Ronnie decides. Goth-casual? Sure. He decides Chloë is one of those girls who act thirty the moment she obtains a driver's license. That thirtiness only grows worse with each new rite into adulthood. She has one month left in college, and she acts and behaves like Ronnie's idea of somebody's mom. The depleted plasma levels and the lack of food help the wine kick in immediately.

The manuscript prints, one slow page at a time. This house.

The interior decoration is straight out of an interior decorating magazine. Color-coordinated walls match furniture, match plates, match curtains, match clothes. Not green: Avocado. Not purple: Plum. But you strip that away, you have these worn hardwood floors, thoughtfully planted Spanish moss dangled shade trees (in Central Florida, they never considered the importance of shade trees as they were tracting out their own take on suburbia—keeping a palm tree or two (and those don't shade shit) for decorative purposes only), and the distinguished venerable overall charm to the place, with its front porch and soft yellow exterior paint, a house that had weathered more during the past fifteen years than those Central Florida homes had. Ronnie can ignore the feng-shui and all the obnoxious color-coordination, and dream of someday living in a Gainesville house like this, should he ever be fortunate enough to escape the trailer. He tries and fails at recalling the other time he was here, loaded on roofies after The Laraflynnboyles played a chaotic houseparty in the student ghetto, three years ago.

•

It was a tiny little house—Paul's house at the time—so small that the bands played in the kitchen and only about fifteen people could cram into the living room to watch the performance. It's one of those houses in punk rock lore where everyone figures quite rightly that they're going to tear it down in a couple years, so there's really no need to clean anything, to mop away the sticky black grime on the linoleum floors, and if there are cracks or outright holes in the plaster on the walls—why, it's nothing a flier from some enjoyed Nardic Track show from the recent past won't fix. Wille-Joe Scotchgard's drums are pressed as far into the kitchen as possible, with his back to the oven where he has to consciously avoid brushing the knobs that turn on the gas stove's burners. John "Magic" Jensen plays the bass, wobbling from side to side—head a dumbed-down mix of stooge pills and stooge drink—bleach blond glam metal rock-wig atop his head—and Ronnie, without the wine now blocking the vision—if his mind at the time hadn't been filled with stooge pills and stooge booze—one little prod from someone there who does remember—and Ronnie could see the view from the floor, under-neath about ten bodies who dogpiled him gleefully after he made one comical/not comical leap into those who had packed into the room to see them—guitar face-up on the dirty floor, open detuned strings plucked by random hands, as random voices sing into the microphone and mic stand that have also fallen to the floor—the sweat dirt old beer smoke stench—and through the gaps in the legs and arms, Ronnie looks to the rhythm section, who look back—Magic peeking through the feathered-metal bangs of the wig, and Willie-Joe leaning up over the drums to make sure Ronnie's alright, and he's actually better than alright, because his girlfriend is some-where in here, and his friends are everywhere, and he's in a band, and outside in the front yard, they stand in groups of three, four, or five, as the Gainesville Police cars are parked along the edge of the yard, officers waiting for anyone to take one step off the prop-erty with an open container. Ronnie often forgets about this, for-gets about catching a ride (with whom?) to the Duckpond to stay at Chloë's, and they sat in a circle of eight or nine or ten, Ronnie in Maggie's lap, Maggie wiping the kitchen floor grime off his face with a borrowed dishtowel, softly asking, "Why do boys with big brains do such dumb things?" to which Ronnie can only smile be-cause he said everything he had to say in the performance and is ready to pass out like this.

.

Three years later, and Maggie's gone, the band is on a downward spiral, Ronnie has graduated, and here he is in Gainesville, printing a manuscript he feels he has no choice but to believe is his ticket out of this rut. "What's your book about?" Chloë asks, leaning into Ronnie, one fat boob brushing his back.

"Aw, man, I don't know," Ronnie says, leaning away from the fat boob, not taking his eyes off the gray screen showing the novel's title page. He loathes this question. "It's about a lot of things."

Chloë leans in closer, boob brushing his back again, face inches from his right cheek. She smells like the perfume counter at the mall. "That's not a very good answer, Ronnie."

"Yes, Chloë. I know." When sober, Ronnie doesn't entirely dislike Chloë, but now? "It's about Orlando, basically," Ronnie manages.

"Oh. Can I read it?" Chloë asks, wide hips already swiveled to the printer, hands already reaching to the twenty printed pages.

Ronnie moves his hands to block Chloë's. "When it's published, you can," he smiles.

The phone rings on the opposite side of the bedroom. "Be right back," Chloë says, patting then squeezing Ronnie's shoulder.

"Oh hi!" she says—too loudly, too loudly—into the phone removed from its cradle on the nightstand next to the bed. She plops onto the bed, left hand holding the phone, right hand running fingers through her hair. "Ronnie Altamont is over here. Yeah! He's printing out a book! Yeah, he wrote a book! Me neither . . . "

Ronnie sits in front of the computer wishing the book would print already, wishing he could mail it away, ready to flee Florida for the small press that would easily get his work out there. This

Orlandoan notoriety, its final residue manifested in the first and last namedrop, was tiresome, because—really now—he was less than nothing. Some bum, knowing little except not to trust any social acquaintance who speaks of him by his first and last name, because the "glory days" of three years ago, or even one year ago, when his name mattered to anyone, are over.

"Ok! Hmmmm, bye bye!" Chloë says before an indecorous roll off the bed and back on her own two goth casual sensible black-shoed feet. She replaces the phone in its cradle, straightens her clothes. "So. That was Diana," she announces. "She wanted to tell you 'Hi.'" Diana. She went to UCF with Ronnie. She sang in one of those emasculated bands that have one-word names like "Break" or "Collapse" or "Banish." Ronnie honestly couldn't remember. They weren't "punk," and therefore, Ronnie didn't care. At Chloë, he smiles and nods, as is his style when memories are gone or ideas can't be followed.

"Where are you sending the book?" Chloë asks, returning to Ronnie's right side with her mall perfume counter stench and her fat.

"It's this small press in the Midwest," Ronnie says, almost turning to face Chloë, but too enthralled that the book—his book—was actually printing. "One of my," and here, Ronnie shrugs in false modesty, "fans," because he had a few, much to Ronnie's surprise, when he wrote that opinion column of his back at UCF, where he ranted and raved and sometimes was funny and other times was just caustic, and looking back on it now, he suspected the administrators were simply ignoring him, knowing that some-day soon, Ronnie would be out of there, either with a degree or dropped out, and they probably predicted he would be in the exact position he was in now, "suggested this press, and it looked interesting, so . . . "

"Why don't you put it out with Random House or something?"

Because they're not ready for what I gotta lay on society! In Ronnie's head, there lived a burnout hippie, and while most of the time said burnout was just a comic invention, at least once a year, their thoughts coincided. This was that time for 1996.

"It looks interesting," Ronnie repeats.

"Well, that sounds good then." Chloë leans away, smiles. "More spritzer?"

"Ok."

She grabs the glasses, tromps off to the kitchen. She returns, sets Ronnie's to the right, in front of the printer. Ronnie sips. They are, um, spritzy. The printer continues from one page to the next. Chloë pulls up a chair next to Ronnie, grabs the stack of pages from the printer.

"No!" Ronnie yells, grabbing her fat arm. The hostess giggles. Coquettishly. She thinks Ronnie is flirting. She reads aloud from the manuscript. "It's like when Darby Crash howled '. . . dementia of a higher order . . . it felt like a passport away from this futile reality' . . . ?'"

It's the question mark at the end that gets Ronnie. As if she's saying, "What?" He yanks the pages from her hands, yells, "No!" again, much louder than he intends. "Jesus!" he adds before he knows what he's saying, "Will you step off, bitch?!" As he pulls the pages away, he knocks over the wineglass. It shatters on the hardwood floor between them. Wine and Sprite spills across the room.

There are exactly five seconds of silence. The coquettish giggling stops. The smile disappears. "I'm . . . sorry, Ronnie," Chloë says, steps back from the computer, from the mess. "I didn't mean anything."

Ronnie holds the crumpled stack of pages in his hands, as the printer keeps on whirring. "I know you didn't," Ronnie finally says. He holds out the stack of pages, stands, office chair rolling into the shards on the floor. "I'll clean this up. You want to read this? Here." Ronnie offers the stack of papers. "Sorry. I was just . . . nervous. I shouldn't be."

"I don't." Chloë steps away, 180s out the bedroom door. It looks like her shoulders are shaking as she leaves, but Ronnie can't think about that.

The print job is only halfway finished, and Ronnie can't leave until it's done. He wishes the printer would move faster, hopes the ink and the pages hold out. Then he will leave and they can both forget about it. Ronnie can't think about why he doesn't want Chloë—or, perhaps, anyone—reading his book. He can't think about why he's so hateful to this person who has been so kind and hospitable to him. As the print job finishes, Ronnie grabs handfuls of tissue paper from the box next to the phone's cradle on the nightstand, throws the wine glass shards and spritzered paper towels into the garbage back in the next-door bathroom. Down the hall, Ronnie can see Chloë—Chloë's back anyway—seated on her couch watching CNN in the living room, seemingly enthralled, or perhaps moved to tears, by Bob Dole giving a speech somewhere.

Who-knows-how-long later, when *The Big Blast for Youth* finally reaches page 536, Ronnie gathers it up, practically runs out of that bedroom, down the hall, to the front door. In the doorway, Ronnie turns to Chloë's sobbing back. "Um." Ronnie begins. "Thanks for everything. And hey: thanks for the spritzer."

"You're welcome," she says, devoid of feeling, not turning away from Bob Dole on the TV. "You can show yourself out."

Ronnie feels like the chump he knows he is, shrugs, turns and steps out of Chloë's house, carrying his precious, precious manuscript to the car. He never sees her again.

•

Sobering, only a little, on the drive to the post office, Ronnie wonders why he apologized. Who takes pages from printers and reads them without permission? No, really. Who does that? Feelings of guilt dissipate into the near-summer humidity of the Gainesville weekday afternoon.

The line at the post office in the student ghetto is a swift moving nonordeal of students picking up care packages sent by Mom and checks sent by Dad. When it's Ronnie's turn, the bulky ashen black late middle-aged mailwoman weighs the package, assesses the postage, takes Ronnie's money.

"It's the book I wrote," Ronnie says, wishing she would ask about it.

"A book? You mean like Stephen King?" She holds the package for a moment, like it might mean something more than what it is.

"Uh, yeah, I guess." Ronnie shrugs, takes his change. He walks away, wishing he could have told her about how it was on its way to getting published, after so much work, so much writing. And how it only needed one draft.

Do I really need to tell you that the publishers never make it down to Gainesville to track down Ronnie? That they don't even mail a rejection slip? The days turn to weeks turn to months, and the black mailbox bolted next to the front door of the trailer never has its mouth stuffed with advances on future earnings or galleys or proofs or whatever they're called.

Ronnie will sit in his sparse white room and listen to the Germs growl and bleed through hand-me-down speakers at the foot of the mattresses while he broods on the unmagical epiphany that writing—his writing—could no longer be this easy task of writing some stupid column while drunk on Brain Mangler malt liquor for some right-of-center University too conservative to be hip to the gonzo style of Thompson and the other New Journalists Ronnie was blatantly ripping off, as is the style of so many young men sitting down to write for the first time. This novel—*The Big Blast for Youth*—all 536 pages of it—wasn't anything but practice, and it would surely take lots and lots of practice before anything could even begin to happen.

Possessed of such daunting knowledge, the yellow legal pads and spiral notebooks Ronnie used to spend hours filling were left to fend for themselves by the stacked mattresses in his bedroom. For far too long, Ronnie would write next to nothing besides drunken declarations of love and hate for various people, before passing out in the bedroom, and who knows, maybe that is also a kind of practice, even if nothing will emerge from those pages but loose, illegible, self-absorbed notes.

ALVIN AND MOUSE, DALE AND STEVIE, STEVIE AND MOUSE

Pfffffffffff . . .

I mean, I told him not to punch my wall, and I *told* him not to drop his boot on Ronnie's table because if Ronnie sees that, he'll get

mad. So that's what I said to Stevie when he knocked on the door—
pffff—I have the note right here. Ronnie helped me write it. It goes:

"Dear Stevee

you are not welcum heer

you dont cleen your mess and dont pay bills

so you cant stay here anymore. Alvin."

I put what he had into two plastic bags—pfff, he didn't have
much—and left it by the door. Hoping he'd get the hint. No, he still
knocked on my door and it's late at night—so why's he gotta bother me so late? I didn't want to answer—pfff—but he kept knocking,
yelling like, "Let me in man, I wanna talk to you, it's important, I
need to ask you something," and going on and on like that the way
he always does. Ronnie's right, and you're right, Mouse—Stevie
never shuts up.

But he did get real quiet when I opened the door and he
stood there in that stinky black Misfits t-shirt he's always wearing, looking like he just got off of work the way there was new
sweat on top of the old sweat smell of him. He says like, "Hey
Alvin, c'mon man, let me in, this is a joke right?" and I tell him
that no, it ain't a joke, because me and Ronnie, we don't want
him living there.

He's gotta ask me, "Why?" and I tell him. Pfff—I tell him, "You
broke Ronnie's table, you put a hole in my wall, you don't pick up
after yourself, and you don't pay rent." And that's all true, Mouse.
Ronnie had to point it out for me to really see it, I got so used to it.
Around everywhere he sits, there's dented coke cans, used Q-tips,
used tissues, potato chip bags, McDonald's wrappers covered in
ketchup, mustard, and pickles. All of it goes around him in a circle
where he sits and it stays there.

But Stevie doesn't say anything about that, instead he talks like—pfff, "Well Ronnie don't pay nothing." Then he tried stepping into the trailer but I wouldn't let him in and he's going on talking: "Ronnie told you to do this, didn't he? Too good to talk to us, too good to leave his room, and he talks you into kicking me out. Where's his money?"

So I have to tell him that me and Ronnie—me and him—we made an agreement that he would live there, that he was Mouse's friend he brought up from Orlando. Because that's what you and me and Ronnie agreed, Mouse.

Because you should have seen it when Ronnie came into the living room and saw the table Stevie broke. I mean, the table, Stevie broke the glass top in two—right down the middle—but he thought if he could stack one part of the glass on top of the other part of the glass—Ronnie wouldn't notice, but it's the first thing he says, Mouse. Ronnie never leaves his room. He sits in there all day, or if he does leave, he goes out the back door. Stevie was always asking "How come he never sits out here with us when we're watching TV or playing *Sonic the Hedgehog*?" and I always told him—pff—cuz it's always so dirty in here and in the kitchen, and Stevie, he don't say nuthin' to that but like, "So?" and now that he is out, maybe I will try and clean and maybe Ronnie'll wanna be out there now—pfffff. But that's the first thing he asks, stepping out there and he's still got a pen in his hand 'cuz I know you were sayin' that he's a writer so maybe that's what he does all day, but he sees the table and walks over to it, lifts up the porno mags Stevie put there to try and cover the table cracks, turns to me like he wants to kill me and he asks me, you know, "What happened to my coffee table?" and I ain't gonna lie, Mouse, so I tell him. I'm sitting there in my chair watchin' Jim Carrey being funny, and I tell him, and that's when he tells me that Stevie needs to leave and I even told Ronnie that I even told Stevie not to show me his modern-day warrior moves because, pffff! You know he don't know karate.

So Ronnie, he tells me that Stevie's takin' advantage of me—pfff—but I say to him—ok, but how do I get rid of him? He stands there like he's thinking and then says I should write a note, but I tell Ronnie, you write the note—aren't you supposed to be the writer? But he says it should be in my writing and he'll tell me what to say, so he tells me, I write it, and tape it to the door and hope Stevie'll just read it and not knock, and Ronnie leaves me there to deal with him, because when that's done Ronnie says he's gotta leave, and I ask him if I can go with him but he says no because he wants to meet girls, so that's what happened, Mouse.

Pffffffff. Do you need any help, Mouse?

Mouse has been setting up the four track this whole time, plugging in cables and setting up microphones in the dark living room's late afternoon ripe squash sunlight shooting through the old-ass blinds as dusty laser light show beams. Alvin follows him from the living room to the bathroom, where Mouse has a mic stand with a microphone plugged in in front of the toilet and leading back to the four track set on an old red dairy crate. Mouse hasn't caught much of what Alvin's been saying, throwing in "Oh sure!" and "Right!" and "Oh no!" and "Heh heh heh" at times that feel instinctually appropriate. Icy Filet is coming over (!!!), and Mouse is setting up the bathroom for her to bust out her latest rhymes as Mouse takes a slide and plays the upper cosmic frets of a detuned guitar that's plugged into reverb and delay pedals.

Mouse wants to record this, put it out on a seven inch, or barring that, a cassette to sell at the shows.

"Well—heh heh heh—that's too bad, Alvin," Mouse says, walking through the kitchen, to the front door. "I was hoping the three of you would all be friends, you know, like—partners in unemployment? But we'll talk soon," and Mouse opens the door, and Alvin wants to say something, but all that comes out is "Pffffff."

Mouse closes the door. Stevie no longer lives there. That much, Mouse knows, and that much, Mouse can almost care about, even as he's getting everything together for the big date, because Icy Filet will be knocking soon. Among the things that Mouse doesn't care about, and wouldn't have even if he'd known, is what had already happened to Stevie, the night he'd had at Grandfather's Olde Tyme Good Tyme Pizza Parlour before getting thrown out of the trailer.

Mouse had never met Dale Doar, who was in his office that night, that office which also serves as a tiny storage room for dry goods, the time clock, spare aprons, shirts, and hats, and stacks of those orange and yellow Grandfather's Olde Tyme Goode Tyme Pizza Parlour Employee Handbooks, with their thick three ring binders that can't quite stack perfectly. Dale Doar, at his desk, punching a calculator with his left hand, then scribbling numbers into end-of-the-business day forms with his right. Scribbling in the yellow triangle of light from the desk lamp (everyone is ugly under overhead fluorescent lighting after hours of intense restaurant work), smells of marijuana and dish detergent filtering in from the kitchen. The Smiley Service Liaisons had been sent home, The Table Removal and Replenishment Coordinators lined up to punch out—the large figure of Brooks Brody temporarily blocking the white bright of the kitchen as he slid his time card into the clock, said, "Later, Dale, don't work too hard." Dale nodded, didn't look up and didn't lose the rhythm of tapping the numbers on the calculator, scrawling them into the forms. Like every night, he would soon fax these forms to corporate, drop off the money in the bank, then it's home to Arthur the cat, the bong, to Gina next to him on the couch—green Publix uniform unbuttoned but not removed, a white t-shirt underneath untucked, and oooo-mmmm those big ol' . . . and then like David Lee Roth says, in the song "Panama," . . . *reach down, in between her legs . . . see that pus-say . . .* Soon, but never soon enough, he would get to that, and beyond tonight, this was another day closer to getting out of the store, going corporate for Grandfather's—Assistant Regional Director of Quality Pizzarifficness—and up up up the ladder. Not bad for a D student.

The plates and glasses clanked as they were replaced, the silverware rattled in their respective slots, the plastic racks shoved through the dish machine's conveyor now pushed and scooted into what Dale hoped were neat stacks, and then the abrupt unsettling silence of rooms that had only moments before been filled with noise. It was a silence profound and jarring enough for Dale to stop punching the calculator and to stop scribbling figures into forms. The silence lasted only two seconds, long enough for Dale to tap, tap, tap the desk with his index finger, to sigh if only to make a sound, because Dale hated silence for any duration. The radio was loud, the TV at home was loud, the apartment complex was loud, the traffic, the ceaseless chatter of customers and employees, everything. Especially Stevie—*Stevie!*, he thought, with disgust—was loud, but in his case, Dale preferred silence. Dale could hear Stevie stepping closer to the office, whistling circus music, pounding on the wall or the steel of the kitchen's counters while saying "Hi-yah!" in a loud whisper. Dale heard him, talking to himself (he never shut up, that was the biggest complaint from everyone . . . he's a dishwasher, and the motherfucker never stops talking), "Dammit, man, this day is done, done, done, done, done, done, done" (and with each "done," Stevie would hi-yah a new part of the kitchen as each step was closer to the timeclock) "and I want to have fun, fun, fun, fun, fun, fun, fun, because if it ain't five o'clock here, it's five o' clock somewhere, and that's what they say, anyway, right boss?"

Dale found the silence, as Stevie walked into the room, blocking the lights from the kitchen, to be even more jarring and discomforting. It heightened how the only people left were Dale and Stevie, and that made what Dale was about to do that much more unpleasant. He wanted to have the boy genius—Jeremy—take care of it, but he already caused enough problems by hiring this chatterbox weirdo.

"I need to talk to you for a minute," Dale said, filling out one last column before rolling back and swiveling towards Stevie.

Stevie punched out, replaced the time card in his slot, held up his hands and announced, "Look at these things!" He wiggled his fingers. "Pruny!"

"So. Stevie. You've been here two weeks," Dale began, leaning back, folded hands behind head.

"Yeah, buddy," Stevie interrupted. "And I ain't gonna lie, it gets tough back there by yourself washing all those plates and pans, those utensils. I'm always sayin' to the crew 'Y'all! When ya gonna go easy on me back here? You don't want me to karate chop the next person who brings back too many plates. Best believe I'll swing these arms and—" and here, Stevie flailed his arms in opposite circular directions, culminating in two hands pushed out while yelling in a high pitched shriek—"HI-YAHHHHHHHHHHH!"

"That's the problem," Dale yelled over the "HI-YAHHHHHH-HH!" rolling backwards as Stevie's hands pushed inches in front of Dale's head. "You're scaring everyone."

"What do you mean?" Stevie asked, lowering his hands, straightening up.

"I mean, you're scaring the crew. You're scaring customers. And," Dale scrunched his nose and rolled back two inches, the wheels grinding over the dirt and cracks in the concrete floor. "I'm not sure of how to put this, but, you smell. Bad. You really need to figure out a way to do laundry."

"Oh!" Stevie laughed, sniffed, then said, "That!" as if it was a trifling thing. "I'm stayin' with Alvin, and he don't have laundry in the trailer so I'm waitin' to get my first paycheck from y'all so I can launder these clothes, so there really ain't nuthin' to worry—"

"Do you bathe?" Dale asked.

"Well, Dale. That's the thing."

"So no? You don't?" Dale rolled closer, leaning in, face scrunched into dismay.

"It's part of my training," Stevie said, crossing his flabby-beefy arms.

"This modern-day warrior act?"

"It ain't an act, man! Once some money comes in, it's like I told Jeremy, I'm gonna get trained to be a modern-day warrior, a real bad-ass. In the meantime, I'm training myself how to do this, and—"

"You're training yourself?" Dale asked, followed by a short sharp, "Ha!"

"You gotta start somewhere, man! Ya think those Chinese peasants sat around waiting til they had the yen to pay the sen-say to learn how? Ya think they told their friends, 'Sorry about my luck, y'all, but I can't be no martial artist 'til I can af-FORD it? No, man! I'm trainin' myself, and I need to have a stink on me. It's in all the movies. You think animals bathe before they hunt? No! They gotta smell like the environment around them, but I keep my hands and arms clean if you want to smell them, because I know we can't have germs gettin' on everything."

"No," Dale said. "Look. Stevie. Dude. At the end of the day, between all the hi-yahing in the dishtank, your practice chops by the dumpster behind the store, it's just . . . not working out."

Stevie lowered his arms, slouched. "You firin' me?"

"Afraid so, buddy." Dale extended his hand, to shake. "We'll mail you your check. Good luck."

Stevie stepped forward, as if to shake Dale's extended hand.

"HI-YAHHHHH!" he screamed, shifting into a quasi-Bruce Lee position, right arm pulled back, left arm held in front of him, open palms in both hands.

And Dale, he sure did flinch, rolling backwards in his chair, the scream such a horrible contrast to the near silence of the buzzing fluorescent lights in the rest of the kitchen, to say nothing of the fact that, dude, a couple of the guys in the crew did smoke Dale out as the dinner rush was starting to die down. His face winced, turned rightward sharply in the anticipated shot between the eyes.

"Just kiddin'," Stevie said, dropping his arms. "Just wanted to see you flinch."

When Stevie told him it was all one big ha-ha just kiddin', Dale stood, adrenaline shaking him out of the thc torpor.

"Out!" Dale yelled. "You're fired! Out!"

Stevie backed out, turned around, walked towards the back door, leaving Dale there to regain his composure, to straighten up, to look down at that desk calendar with all the Xs through all the days that are done, all the days still in the way of getting out of here. Dale cursed, grabbed a black Sharpie, drew an X through today's date. If it ain't drunks in the dishtank, it's crackheads, and if it ain't crackheads in the dishtank, it's— fucking modern-day warriors. Dale will laugh about this eventually, over after-work drinks with the others in corporate.

Stevie's voice faded away, a steady spiel of, "Alright, man, well, no hard feelings, I guess, I mean—I did like working for all y'all even if you didn't think I was Grandfather's Olde Tyme Goode Tyme Pizza Parlour material, I mean, it is hard to balance the balance between that and my trying to be a modern-day warrior, so I'll let myself out the back here and that's that and I'm sorry if I scared ya Dale with my modern-day warrior chops, but it was funny watching you panic that way . . . "

•

. . . So I don't gotta tell you the rest, Mouse, you know how it went down with me and Alvin. He never gave me no chance to explain nuthin, but that's 'cause Ronnie made him think bad about me. I keep hearing how you can only use the martial arts I'm trying to learn in like self-defense, but I'm like, "Y'all, I wanna kick some ass!" but if that's the way it's done, I guess that means I can never go after Ronnie.

I miss living in Gainesville, even if it's only been a few days, but I grabbed my shit off Alvin's front steps, threw it in my truck, and I had just been fired, so I'm sitting there in my truck thinking,

'The hell I'm supposed to do now?' and, thanks to Ronnie, my only option is to go back to my parents, who're gonna wanna make me go back to school if I'm to live under their roof. High Springs ain't that far away, but I do miss Gainesville.

Maybe it'll be alright, Mouse. I'll go back to Santa Fe Community College—I mean, I'm only nineteen, so I'm sure I'm not that far behind. Besides that, maybe they got free karate classes there.

So that's it, Mouse—I was goin' to town today and thought I'd stop by and see what you were up to, and it looks like you're busy with your girlfriend here in bed, so let me just walk out of here and let y'all get back to what you were doin' before but thanks for lettin' me in and hearin' my side of the story because I guess if I learned anything, I need to make sure I have plenty of room to do my karate choppin', and maybe I shouldn't go around braggin' that I'm tryin' to be a modern-day warrior so I'll just let myself out here and y'all stay in that bed, oh-kay.

WILLIAM AND MAUX

A third shot of some foul-ass octane burn later—some cheap well shot to go with the cheap beer—and your mouth finally liberates the throbbing numb of your thoughts, a steady drooling alkie-babble to Ronnie on your left and Paul on your right as the bar you're seated at rotates and the old wave music buzzes out the speakers hanging in the four corners of the room . . . "All I'm sayin' here—all I'm tryin' to say here—is that it can't go on like this. You know? My band's done, and is that tour as good—as, like, adventurous, I should say—as it's ever gonna be, from here on out? If so, why am I here? Who, in this town, 's gonna settle down with me? And do I even want to settle down. I mean, it's the same as it's been, and it can't go on forever like this. Can it?"

"Look at these nnnnnuggets," Paul says. "Everywhere!" He swivels his bar stool, leans in behind you to say to Ronnie, "You want to be in a room full of nnnuggets, you don't go to the punk rock shows. You come here to the Rotator, to Old Wave Night. They love this shit! Love it!"

"That's all you can say, man?" you moan, and you know you're sounding like a grade A buzzkill, but still—Paul's still calling girls "nnnnuggets." Is this life always going to be one big joke to him, and what happens when that black Caesar haircut turns gray and that black Bauhaus t-shirt paunches out?

"Aw dude, I don't know, man," Paul says, sips his beer, adds, "Just trying to have some fun tonight, unlike you."

"Who's she?" Ronnie asks. You watch him point through the darkness beyond the bar's slowly rotating circle. You like him— he's Central Florida and you're Central Florida—and you want to warn him about what and who to avoid, and you see where he's pointing, and it's no good. This can be a small, childish town, and not everybody wants you to be happy.

"Her name's Maureen, but she spells it M-A-U-X." That name feels so empty in your mouth. When was that? Two years ago? Took her home after some house show. Lately, memories are constantly ambushing you into realizing how much time has passed, how much has changed, between then and now.

"Did you date her, like, in a relationship?" Ronnie asks.

Relationship. "He had a relationship with her poon hole," Paul says, and you try not to laugh. You fail.

One fifty cent mug of beer after the next. The Rotator skirts the border between the college town and the rural hinterlands. It's an XYZ Liquor Lounge officially named JP Mc Jelloshotz. The buzzing sign above the front entrance is a white-light background with a drawing of a bow-tied penguin wearing sunglasses shaped in the odd-angled style of the 1980s. Some impoverished punk rocker discovered they had mugs of beer for fifty cents, and here you are. The stools around the circular bar—and the bar itself—spin a complete orbit in one hour. The more you drink, the faster the room spins. Or so it feels. Aside from the lack of sawdust on the floor, the large square room around the rotating bar looks like a roadhouse in a 1970s film about renegade truckers with CBs riding around the country with precocious chimpanzees. The place oozes with seventies gimmickry; you sense the ghosts of mechanical bulls past upon entering. "The scene" took it over from the old day laborer rent-a-drunks who used to sit in these stools and spin after a hard day of scrapping drywall or whatever the hell they did all day, and your generation will devote their lives to supporting whatever you perceive to be a kind of authenticity rooted in recent history.

"So many nnnnuggets tonight," Paul says. Then, he switches into the clipped cadence he affects when moving into pure sarcasm. "Oh! The nuggets! The nuggets!" His squinty brown eyes dart from one girl to the next—seated at the bar, dancing on the dance floor.

"What's a nugget?" Ronnie asks.

"Aw, you know, dude—cute girls!" Paul says.

"It's a porno mag," you say, facing ahead, an offhand comment to stir the pot.

"William, you know it's more than that." And here, as he has so many times before, Paul holds forth on the nuances of nug-getry, "as opposed to mere hotness" he declaims to Ronnie, that "je ne sais quois" he repeats less like someone with an air of pre-tension, but more as someone with the air of one-too-many 50-cent beers who has come across a phrase he finds funny. You half-listen—having heard this so many times before—and you think of quitting MOE GREEN'S FUCKING EYESOCKET, of quitting music altogether and moving on. To what? A wife? Kids? Thoughts in-conceivable only one year ago. Ronnie, he asked about Maux. She sits on a stool by herself, in the corner under neon signs suggest-ing you drink beer, as if anyone who would come into this place would need prodding in that regard. A pint of Fancy Lad Irish Stout (you know her drink habits—Fancy Lad beer, Van Veen vodka) is wedged between her cream-dream thighs exposed from that short shiny indigo skirt.

"I'll be back in a minute," you say, rising from the stool, step-ping off the rotating bar, feeling like a kid trying to hop off a de-celerating merry-go-round. Paul continues his lecture on nuggets, and Ronnie hangs on every word, mouth agape, nodding.

Maux doesn't notice you at first. She is glaring at the floor. She looks up as you approach, suddenly smiles, catches herself smiling, scowls.

"Why are you here?" she sneers, unclenching the pint glass from her thighs. Head to toe, this indigo vision from the planet Krazy. And who do you think you are, thinking you could meet the marrying kind here in Gainesville, where the women are as crazy and flaky as the days are hot and generally pointless?

"I don't know," you say, pulling up a bar stool and sitting down. For once, you answer honestly. "Why are you here?"

"I don't have any friends, remember?" she says. "I hate people, remember?" You remember. She sips the Fancy Lad from the pint glass, recrosses her legs. "Oh, and I broke up with Philip."

"I'm sorry to hear that," you say.

"No, you're not," Maux says, and you laugh. "This Charming Man" by The Smiths bounces out the speakers, and all the women in the room run en masse to the dance floor.

"You're right," you say. You're not in the mood for the typical Gainesville duplicity.

She empties the pint glass, hands it to you. "Let's get out of here," she says.

Sometimes, like now, Maux has the right idea. "Where to?" you ask, hopping off your barstool.

"What did you say to me when we hooked up?" She slides off her barstool and faces you, knee-high indigo boots, that indigo sleeveless miniskirt, those long lithe arms and that edible neck, the slope of the chin, the cheeks, the indigo lipstick, the indigo eye shadow, the short angry shock of indigo hair. Your erection is profound, this almost leaky menacing high-maintenance wand of hormonal desperation pushing against the black denim of your cut-off below the knee pants, even when she quotes you and imitates you in your Kermit-the-Frog-as-Ian-Mac-Kaye voice, " 'Let's go back to my apartment and listen to music?' Let's do that."

Nothing is long-term, and not much even makes it to short-term here, so who cares. Who cares if your nineteen year old girlfriend, the biggest nothing of all since coming back from tour, is asleep in your bed at home. Waiting for you after closing Gatorroni's.

"We're going to listen to music at your place instead," you say, setting the empty pint glass on your bar stool, and then you think it'll be funny to imitate Maux's raspy teenage boy snotty tone, so you say "There's some dumb stupid horrible band staying with us right now who I hate," and she has to laugh, and you have to laugh, and it's a discreet sneak through the crowd of women dancing to The Smiths. You avoid eye contact with all of them, because if they figured out what was happening, well. The last thing you need is another ex-girlfriend co-worker at Gatorroni's by the Slice. You don't look up and over to Paul and Ronnie, because you don't want them to see you leaving without them, and maybe they see you and maybe they don't. You don't want to have to explain anything to anyone.

You make it out of there without any interactions, stumbling across the white graveled parking lot in this pathetic little corner of this "mixed up muddled up shook up world" (so you sing to yourself from a song the title of which you can't recall) to your hail-damaged white Honda coupe, the racquet-ball-sized hail leaving black dimples on the roof and hood. Maux finds her car—something cold and teutonic—and it's a ten minute drive back to town. You follow the red square tail lights as the darkness of the rural road slowly brightens into college town streets. You arrive at her student ghetto apartment, and you shrug, get out of the car, think/don't think about what you're doing/not doing, and how it's so easy to get into a rut here, and too easy to drink the days and nights away. Easy . . . easy . . . easy. Two steps inside, and Maux has her indigo lips all over the right side of your face.

DOUG CLIFFORD: THE BAND (NOT THE DRUMMER)

Ronnie leaves the plasma center, crook of his right arm bandaged, wallet's emptiness temporarily assuaged with a ten and a five, drives over to William and Neal's coach house, nothing to do on a weekday afternoon, pulls up the dirt driveway, white clouds billowing behind him, parks in front of the white shack they lived in, gets out of the car, steps inside because the door's open and a familiar old record is playing.

"Ronnie!" Neal says, standing in the middle of the tiny dirty beige living room with the low ceiling, shirtless and hairy, in nothing else but blue shorts. The coach house feels like a mid-August afternoon where the breeze—such as it is—doesn't stop the heat. "We're starting a Creedence Clearwater Revival cover band, and we want you to be the drummer."

"Who else is in it?" Ronnie asks, walking the five steps to their battered gray sofa, stepping around Neal and falling onto the couch as John Fogerty sings "Oh Lord/stuck in Lodi uh-gaaaaain" through snap-crackly-popped vinyl.

"Nobody. Yet. Just me and William." Neal moves to the open doorway, looks out to the sand and the dirt of the driveway, air-bass guitaring, turning to his right at the wobbly black disc on the turntable on the opposite wall of the couch where Ronnie slouches with his bandaged arm and the bloody-dotted cottonball pressed into the crook of his arm. If Ronnie wanted to change the music, he could do so almost without getting up from his seat—only a matter of stretching himself over a cracked and ancient orange coffee table cluttered with stacks of random artbooks, a label-free jug of red wine, and an opened

gatefold brown and black record cover—CCR's *Chronicle*—dotted
with tiny green marijuana flakes.

"What's the drummer's name?" Ronnie asks. Like any self-
respecting American, Ronnie loves Creedence Clearwater Revival,
and finds it impossible to fathom anyone—anyone!—disliking
their music. And Ronnie knows he can pull off these rhythms
without any problems.

Neal turns around, steps to the coffee table. "Good question."
He picks up *Chronicle*, flips it over. "Oh! Of course. Everybody knows
it's Doug Clifford." Neal laughs, extends the album to Ronnie's face,
points to the liner note that has his name. "Doug Clifford, dude."

Ronnie laughs, takes the cover out of Neal's hands, stares
transfixed at Doug Clifford's shagginess, the brown mop top and
the relief pitcher moustache. "So I'm Doug Clifford?" he asks.

"The band's Doug Clifford," Neal says. They laugh. Neal adds,
in the shy burnout voice of the musician with the microphone in
every independent rock and roll band ever, "Hey what's up? We're
Doug Clifford? We're from Gainesville?"

Neal flips the record, and they sit on the couch passing the
label-free red wine jug, taking in the sounds, talking about Doug
Clifford, the band that wasn't a band yet, that would, in fact, never
be a band.

William steps out of his bedroom—yawning, stretching—grog-
gy from a hungover nap. Short blond hair in bedheaded clumps,
wrinkled white t-shirt of some old hardcore band with a cheap-o
black silkscreened image of the buzzcut-headed singer in mid-
howl, left hand grabbing the mic, right hand balled into an angry
punk rock fist. William sits between Ronnie and Neal, blue work
pants cutoff below the knees skidding against the worn fabric of

the couch, keys jangling in a right side belt loop. He leans forward, grabs the wine bottle, drinks, studies *Chronicle*.

"Should we grow mutton chops and moustaches for this?" he asks. Ronnie laughs at the idea.

"Naw, dude," Neal says. "We'll just wear flannel. No need to be glitzy." He leans forward, points at the cover. "Doug Clifford would want it that way."

The afternoon dissipates into evening. They empty the wine bottle and *Chronicle* ends, and then Neal throws on *Cosmo's Factory* and then *Willie and the Poor Boys*, and it doesn't matter if some of the same songs are repeated—they are starting a CCR cover band so it is paramount to gain an even greater familiarity with the material.

Paul walks in the door, "Oh, CCR . . . I too can hear the bullfrog calling me . . . " He stops to look at these three giggling on the couch. "You guys are lllloaded!" Paul says.

"It's Doug Clifford's fault," Ronnie says, fully feeling the spirit of the wine, of the music.

"Well I'm going to the Drunken Mick if you want a ride." Paul shakes his head, laughs. "Looks like I got some catching up to do."

"Maybe Paul should be Doug Clifford, and you can be Stu Sutcliffe, Ron," Neal says, as they stand and stumble out the door, leaving the record to end on the bummer jam "Effigy." "You can play other instruments, and Paul only plays the drums."

"Aw, man," Ronnie moans. "I was really hoping to be ol' Doug."

"Well we can't all be Doug Clifford," Neal says as he locks the front door. "Such is life."

Everyone they would see at the Drunken Mick, everyone they would talk to at the Drunken Mick, they would figure out a way to work Doug Clifford—the band that would never be a band—into the conversation. "Doug Clifford drank Fancy Lad Stout, so that's what I'm gonna have too." "Doug Clifford likes girls like you, has anybody ever told you that before?" "Yeah, I don't know if I can see your band this weekend. Doug Clifford said it wasn't very good."

"What's all this Doug Clifford malarkey?" Paul asks Ronnie, sitting at the Drunken Mick as Neal, on the other side of William, serenades all passersby with random snippets of CCR songs, culminating in illogical drunken laughter and a "Doug Clifford!" plea.

"It's our new band," Ronnie informs him.

"Really?" Paul says.

"Sure!"

"Uh-huh." Paul shakes his head. "It's all talk. Next week, it'll be something else."

Before Ronnie can contradict him, the wine and the Irish stout drowning out any counterarguments to the undeniable fact that yes, Doug Clifford will get off the ground and yes, Doug Clifford will be a real band, Neal stands on the bar, completely naked, a gorilla-hirsute body soft shoeing across the mahogany bar, yelling, "This one's going out to Doug Clifford!" He raises his arms in triumph, sings, "I wanna know! Have you ever seen the rain!" He shakes his dong up and down, round and round.

Ronnie leaps off the barstool, laughs, preparing for a fight somewhere, or jail time—something—but instead, the roomful of drunks, scenester kids Ronnie hasn't met yet, collegiate-y types seated at the tables throughout the room, all chant "Doug Clifford! Doug Clif-ford! Doug Clif-ford!" until the bartender—long used to these antics, coaxes Neal down, bundled clothes in hand, trying not to smile.

"He does this all the time," Paul yells in Ronnie's ear over the din of the continued "Doug Clifford!" chants.

Neal squats down, leaps behind the bar, throws on his clothes, yells, "Thank you! We're Doug Clifford! Good night!"

The short squat ginger-headed bartender looks to Paul, smiles. "You know what to do," he says in an Irish brogue exaggerated for greater tips the way female bartenders accentuate their tits.

"Yeah yeah, I know," Paul says, smiling in the familiarity of the routine. "Let's go, little brother," he announces, right hand's fingers beckoning towards the exit.

And in the dizzy-drunk near last-call at The Drunken Mick, Paul leads Neal by the arm, Neal's pants pulled up but unbuttoned, t-shirt coiled around his neck, followed by Ronnie and William, as the "Doug Clif-ford! Doug Clif-ford!" chants fade and they step out onto the University Avenue sidewalk, to the car, home to bed.

.

No, there would be no Doug Clifford. Doug Clifford would be replaced by the next band concept. There would never be enough time to get to all the ideas. You could pull off two or three bands at once, but the others fell away into afternoons and nights like these—frivolous discussion where someone like Ronnie Altamont could believe it would be possible to actually get Doug Clifford off the ground. So many ideas fell to the wayside, getting no further than creative play, self-expression for self-expression's sake, impromptu late-night jams, or the idle talk of the potential members of Doug Clifford. Everywhere, kids talk this way, and they make ambitious plans and announcements and they want to believe that this is the band that will get off the ground, and who knows, maybe this will be the band to get off the ground, but just as likely it won't, it's more enjoyable to talk. Sometimes, the idea itself is better than any possible execution.

And there were no shortage of ideas. Freed from the confines and general horseshit of high school, stimulated enough by college and the young adulthood of post-college, anything seems possible. Brains bloom endless variations on the same four chords, the same 4/4 rock beats, music—in execution or theory—dancing between the gap of thought and expression the Velvet Underground once sang about. It's the limitations Melville lamented at the end of Chapter 32, "Cetology," in *Moby Dick*: There's never enough time, and that's the colossal bummer of life, isn't it?

SWEAT JAM

In the corner of the spare square room soundproofed with red rugs nailed to the walls, Paul pounds eighth notes on the floor tom of his five-piece gold sparkled Ludwig drumkit, hitting the snare on the two and the four of the 4/4 beat. Like all drummers, he's the first in the room to get lost in the music, of this simple VU cavepound, eyes opened but not looking at anything . . . often when playing drums, Paul thinks of streets in towns he used to live, streets in towns he will never return. In Wekiva—the neighborhood he grew up in before going off to college—the twenty minute drive through the mammoth subdivision, the Duckpond to the left, the one-story ranch-styles on side streets that branched cul-de-sacs with bike trails winding through the jungle scrub. Hunt Club Boulevard—that was the name of the main thoroughfare and you don't get much more suburban that that—a four-lane road with only minor curves, winding home after school and yelling "Faggot!" at old people who were dumb enough to walk the sidewalks or "Skateboarding should be a crime!" at the skater kids. With the body memory of the drum beat, his mind wanders down those streets, tries taking stock in what he remembers and what he forgets. Cannonballs into swimming pools, that sensation of hanging in the air—dry—before falling, before the big splash. The hallways of their high school—the high school that has since been torn down and replaced by a newer, larger, nicer, more functional high school—the dirt and grime on the white tile of the old one, the rows of blue lockers, the clang of the lockers, the manic chatter, the drama and secrets and undercurrent of uncertainty masked by everyone with every step between classes, the three bong-bong-bongs of the tardy bell, the cheap portable walls put up to separate what had once been giant rooms, the library in the center of the school, spokes of hallways and classrooms orbiting. In the Fishbowl—the circular steps surrounded by windows of the painting and theatre classes—where the arty kids hung around before the classes started, the goth kids, the skaters, the punks with their liberty spikes and CRASS t-shirts, cliqued up because you needed a group to get through it. Paul pounds the beat and remembers all of this, remembers leaving school, getting in a car, driving down Sand Lake Road through the subdivisions and the open fields that would become subdivisions soon enough, the perpetually sunshiney afternoon of a Central Florida week-day as school lets out and no matter what you think or thought about it it stays in your memories.

Neal stands to his brother's right, picking at a red Fender bass plugged into a buzzing Peavey bass amp. His mind doesn't wander around in memories of past places the way Paul's does—he needs to hold this together—as the bass man, as the bridge, the link, between the drums and the guitars. It's more of a channeling of the spirit of Mike Watt—of the Minutemen, of fIREHOSE—of locking into what's happening and finding the freedom in it and the spaces to not just lock down the rhythm and bridge the gap from drums to guitar—but to figure out ways to get to the top two strings and the upper frets—not to show off, but to find the right sounds, the right counterbalance to the guitars, because everyone knows the guitars want nothing more but to wank and noodle and dick around, so this is an anchor that will give them not just the low notes of the chords they play, but a larger framework to do something that is both tasteful and creative. He puffs out his cheeks and exhales like Mike Watt the way guitarists might windmill like Townshend. He moves in spasmodic forward lurches, backbone sways waving from the base of the spine to the neck as the fingers on his right hand pick-pluck the strings. It has to start with Watt for Neal, because Watt opened up the possibilities of the instrument for Neal, and that led to Mingus, to Jimmy Garrision, to Rockette Morton. Day-to-day life is nervous energy channeled into right and wrong places, but here, with the music, it's all focused on this, and every distraction, every good and bad memory, all the drama of the Great Gainesvillian Soap Opera, fades to nothing.

William, all he wants to do is plug into the Crate amp in the corner and stand to the left of Paul, pedals cranked up all the way, and stab at a detuned off-white Fender Squire so it makes cloudy feedback of dense black and white noise. He doesn't really know how to play guitar, only picking up chords here and there from friends while sitting around some late-night front porch party, so he tries following the cavepound rhythm, smiling in sweat and angular side-to-side hip swivels, never more convinced that MOE GREEN'S FUCKING EYE SOCKET is over, because the simple enjoyment of it, at its base, of making music with friends, died somewhere on that ill-fated and pointless tour. If anything, instead of dreaming of where he was, or where he is, he thinks of where he will be, if he can figure out how to get out of here.

Ronnie tosses around the phrase "Sweat Jam," used by Neal before they went to Paul's gray-teal, wood-rotting, plaster-peeling student ghetto house, walking over from Gatorroni's with a case of Old Hamtramck, as he follows Paul's rhythm and bounces around Neal's foundation, a beat-to-hell black and white Fender Squire plugged direct into a Peavey amp with a small amount of distortion and a small amount of reverb, throttling the instrument with pick strums and fist punches, trying to find new sounds, the high white sounds of life itself. Sweaty forehead, sweat-stained t-shirt, wet hair. Ronnie lived in the all-encompassing now, the brilliantly beautiful now. The music they made in the sweat jam was Ronnie's life—one loud long song jumping around in keys and tempos, bright then droning, repetitive then chaotic, but always loud and always sweaty. Each day, each moment—he thinks as he jumps around in the three foot diameter of space he has between Neal and William and in front of Paul in that tiny red-rugged room—is a glorious sweat jam, a cliffdive into the unknown, no matter what happens with his writing and his band, here in Gainesville.

Life as a sweat jam. Yeah. Ronnie can live with this.

TWO: SUMMER

"Got a car, got a car car car / I'm goin' far, in my car / Got a dog,
got a dog dog dog / I'm a hog / and you're a frog."
—The Angry Samoans

THE LARAFLYNNBOYLES

Here comes another god-damned taint-chafe of a Florida summer, and The Laraflynnboyles, the band Ronnie Altamont left behind in Orlando, are planning a tour, a fruited-plain circle through the Southeast to the Midwest and back.

Each day, Ronnie would pace the trailer's filthy kitchen, shifting his weight from one foot to the other on the unstable linoleum flooring, vibrations shaking Squeaky the Gerbil's cage to the edge of the sticky kitchen counter, corded powder blue phone pressed to Ronnie's ear (Alvin paid off the phone bill with his first paycheck washing dishes for Otis's Barbelicious BBQ's Archer Road location), talking with the bass player—John "Magic" Jensen—about all the wonderful shows they would play, as if the band still existed, as if the tour was as inevitable as Florida summer sunshine. How beautiful the names of the cities sounded in their larynxes, on their tongues, through their teeth, through moving lips! Louisville! Cincinnati! Saint Louis! Columbia!

"Chicago!" Magic says, and, for once, the dude sounds happy, like he's sincerely excited by something. (And no, it matters nothing to them that the show they've booked isn't in Chicago, per se, but in some basement called the "Drunk Skum House" in the far western suburb of Aurora, Illinois.) Because Magic, he's like those guys in college who are always one year away from graduating with a philosophy major he knows he's never going to apply towards much beyond endless sardonic waxings on the human condition between bong swats while slouched in an exhausted blue couch covered in cigarette burns while watching hour after hour of the retarded sexual development of Tony and Angela on *Who's the Boss?* or Cousin Balki's unfortunate mangling of common sayings on *Perfect Strangers* or the incurable nerdishness of one Steve Urkel on *Family Matters*. It is no great stretch for Ronnie to imagine Magic down there in the slow hours of this nasty-muggy June afternoon, a cigarette burning in the right hand, a beer can in the left, waiting for the call from whichever X-ed out raver-junkie had the good drugs this week. Only, on the phone, there's something in the way Magic exclaims (yes, exclaims!) the word "Chicago!" Like it means something. Ronnie can almost imagine the depression that Magic always tries self-medicating away melting on its own. A smile in the eyes behind the black-framed rectangular-lensed glasses, in the normally scowled mouth. Maybe he even straightens up a bit on that blue couch, turns off the sitcoms, combs out the knots in his long black hair, changes out of the t-shirt and cut-off shorts that hang off his skeletal frame, changes out of those clothes he lives in for days, actually looks forward to something beyond the next drug delivery.

"Then we'll still move up there next year," Ronnie assures, because it was always the plan to take the band to Chicago, to get out of Florida and move to Chicago.

(And what do you think they possibly imagine about Chicago, about the day-to-day and night-to-night realities of living there? John and Ronnie had traveled to Chicago once—to visit Chris "Chuck" Taylor, The Laraflynnboyle's original lead singer, an avuncular improvisational actor who lived with six other roommates in a half-built loft space in the South Loop neighborhood filled with the sounds of Orange Line trains taking sullen commuters from downtown through the Southwest Side before stopping at Midway Airport, late nights punctuated by the gang war gunshots, from various exotic firearms, resonating through the streets and alleys. None of that mattered, because it was Not-Florida. It wasn't Chicago, but merely the idea of an immense city of endless possibility.

They knew nothing of crumbling brick three-flats with water-stained ceilings, of parking tickets given out to feed a corrupt machine. About corner taverns and hipster bars where everyone knows everything about nothing much. Ronnie—In that fluorescent-lit multi-stenched kitchen, yellowed and gerbilly—wearing stained khaki pants, a short-sleeved, sweat stained holey blue t-shirt, unfashionable hiking boots, oversized glasses—has no idea. He idealizes the Midwest as some plainspoken, levelheaded tell-it-like-it-is magic land of pragmatism, and romanticizes Chicago as this city full of big booming life bursting with Roykos, Superfans, Blues Brothers, Ditkas, Albinis—when, really, all it is is Not Florida, USA—some promised land where he could be successful at what he loved.)

"We'll play out all the time. Make some money at it, maybe even make a living at it," Ronnie continues, peeling his hiking boots off the floor of the kitchen, looking out the dusty kitchen windows at the trailers up and down the street.

"I'll make sure Andrew's on board. No worries," Magic says, talking about Andrew "Macho Man Randy" Savage, the Laraflynnboyles drummer, an affable stoner with a taste for video games and hanging around doing as little as possible.

"We'll talk soon," Ronnie says, and adds the word, "Stoked!" before he hangs up the phone, runs to his room, picks up his guitar, starts plucking frantically strummed barre chords—looking forward to the near-fruition of a long-held ambition, an obsession going back to adolescence, if not earlier.

•

It starts very young—at four or five even—when it's easy to imagine yourself as the lead singer of a stadium-packing rock and roll band, between gigs as homerun record-setting golden-gloved shortstop, rushing record-breaking all-pro running back, Mars-exploring astronaut, and puppy-rescuing fireman. The rest of childhood to puberty is a potato sack race between vocations. Fireman? It doesn't sound glamorous enough. Football? Those practices are no fun at all. Astronaut? You don't get to Mars with a C-average in science. Baseball was the last to go. Ronnie's eyes went myopic around the time his family moved to Florida, and the new place was too hot to bother with the Pony Leagues, and besides, by that point, music offered some kind of map through adolescence's chaotically inextricable terrain.

Through a combination of practical elimination of childhood dreams, and emerging passion, Ronnie Altamont finds rock and roll. At first, his only source was MTV—the J. Geils Band, Quiet Riot, Van Halen. From there, he tunes into the "Album-Oriented Rock" stations that would later be relabeled "classic rock," where bands like Led Zeppelin, Boston, and Pink Floyd—then, as now—

played in an eternal loop. Compared to the music of the mid-1980s, classic rock was, indeed, classic. The popular music of 1986-1990, Ronnie's high school years, slogged through an endless succession of soulless, talentless swill. Ronnie ignores all of this and obsesses on the *storm und drang* of The Who.

Here's when the dream (Since this aspires to be The Great Floridian Novel, perhaps it should be called The Dream) really possessed Ronnie, because The Who—and Pete Townshend in particular—were accessible in ways the other so-called "classic rock" bands could never be. While bands like Led Zeppelin and the Stones in particular were often essentially saying "I have a big dick and enjoy sex with lots of women"—Townshend said: "I have no idea what I'm doing or even how to express it." Here, for Ronnie, was the teenage wasteland of the mind, heart, and glands.

High school. What was that bullshit but one big daydream of drawing band logos all over folders? Putting the head down on the desk and drooling in sleep as the teachers went on and on about topics that weren't rock and roll and were therefore unimportant? Songs—lyrics, guitar solos, bass lines, drum fills—ricocheted around Ronnie's skull like dozens of pinballs. Waiting for the final period of the school day—marching band—to go bash a snare drum for an hour. Then, it was home, and straight to the bedroom to brood on some inaccessible girl-crush, as The Who played from the nearby stereo, every night and all weekend. That plea: "Can you see the real me? Can ya? Can ya?" *Quadrophenia* as the soundtrack to hours staring at the popcorn ceiling required in all those hastily-built Florida suburban homes, thrown up in an attempt to keep pace with the Great Yankee Migration of the 1980s. Textbooks, as uncracked as they were when he got them in August, rarely left the morass of his locker, where pictures of Townshend and Moonie in leaping drumsmashing windmilling glory adorned the locker door's interior side. High school. It wasn't glory. It wasn't disgrace. It was nothing but a daydream. A Bartlebyesque refusal.

All that changed with the drums. Ronnie constantly practiced, and studied Keith Moon in particular. He absorbed everything about The Who—every Townshend leap, Entwistle flurry, Daltrey pose, and especially Moonie's ability to make the whole kit shout in tumultuous waves. He read every book he could find on The Who, reread those books, owned every Who album (even the bad ones), and, somehow, this led to discovering punk rock (because Townshend liked the Sex Pistols and the punks from that time generally liked The Who). It wasn't through the punk rockers in his high school (although he would eventually be friends with most of them—William, Neal, and Paul, among others), who seemed at the time like another bland choice in the salad bar of high school cliquedom. It was like this solitary quest to find the songs and the bands that got it—"it" being whatever it was you go through as a teenager—right. By the time 1990 came around, the discovery of bands—old and new—local, American, English, whatever and wherever—was Ronnie's drug, the thing that got him high and excited to live. At some point during this time, Ronnie switched to guitar, finding it cheaper and easier to carry around than a drumset.

Bands started and ended quickly in that time, with names like The Adjective Nouns, Murderous Kumquats, and Poop, none of them very good. Two weeks before graduating high school, Ronnie meets John "Magic" Jensen through the singer of one of these interchangeable bands. With Magic, Ronnie finds, for the first time, someone who shares his musical obsessions, who has spent similar hours flipping cassette tapes in his bedroom, supine on the bed, staring at the ceiling. For Magic, these obsessions are eclipsed only by his love for marijuana. Ronnie and Magic are inseparable. Magic taught himself to play bass, loves the music of Frank Zappa and Jane's Addiction the way Ronnie loves the music of The Who and (by that point) The Buzzcocks. Magic turns Ronnie onto the Dead Kennedys, Ronnie turns Magic onto the first two Ramones albums, they both watch the bands in *The Decline of Western Civilization*, and knew that somewhere—not where they were—but somewhere—was a better world of live music and danger and adventure. Magic rarely left his room. The room had his bong, his bass, his music, his pornos, the TV. He would sit in a red recliner, stoned, watching *Star Trek: The Next Generation* on mute, studying Natasha Yaar's tits with the Butthole Surfers providing the soundtrack. There was nowhere else to go and nothing else to do, and the life they saw glimpses of through the music and the TV wasn't where they were, so they were bored all the time (not knowing that there were far worse things in the world than boredom) and they had no idea how to alleviate it—naïve and generally understimulated—sitting in the darkness of Magic's bedroom where the aluminum foil covered the windows and blocked the sun of those insufferably hot days. Magic sits in his room where the TV is never off, and mutters perceived truisms like "Life doesn't suck, it's just boring," and "They're fuckers man, fuck 'em."

Nothing comes of the bands they start because, well, drummers are drummers. And not only that, good drummers were impossible to find. There were plenty of people with drumsticks—and some of them even had drumsets—and some of them could even keep beats—but none remotely shared Ronnie and Magic's interests.

Finally, after they'd both started attending the University of Central Florida, they find a drummer in Willie-Joe Scotchgard, who actually plays the viola, but knows how to keep a beat. School lets out, and early summer is always a terrific time to start a band, so Willie-Joe drives home to Lakeland and brings his drums back to the living room of the second floor of some remarkably tolerant apartment complex in UCF's student ghetto, and it is here, the four of them ("Chuck" Taylor still living in Orlando, an alum from Ronnie and Magic's high school, old friend and dopesmoking buddy from the drama club Magic dabbled in, Magic's interest explicable in that the girls were much cooler and better looking than they were in the marching band) buy six-packs of Falstaff Beer (on sale for two dollars at the nearest Publix), and goof off the evenings and nights beered up enough to play the dumb songs Ronnie and Magic had written.

The songs are satirical, silly. Maybe they're a punk band. Maybe they aren't. ("Jesus, who cares?!?" Magic yelled after Ronnie voiced his concerns, and that settled it.) Ronnie names the band The Laraflynnboyles, after the actress on *Twin Peaks*, because Ronnie sees in her what he never could quite see in all those peroxide plasticine Florida women—someone beautiful with an inner vulnerability, and yeah—goddamn right—it's all projection, but you gotta understand: Ronnie had to find everything alone, the way all kids in exurbs with the guts to think for his/herself must do when slogging through the Great Adolescent American Mindnumb.

The songs: Country-Western odes to their Altamonte Springs hometown (remarkably similar to The Kinks' "Willesden Green"), songs with one-line lyrics repeated over and over ("Sweaty Hands"— whose only lyric was "Sweaty Hands: Whenever I see you I get sweaty hands," a tribute of sorts to Flipper's "Sex Bomb"), the requisite 90s is-this-ironic-or-is-it-not-quite-ironic-but-something-in-between-irony-and-earnestness covers of Kiss ("She") and .38 Special ("Hold On Loosely," Chuck Taylor's star turn, the way he'd point like Elvis and shake his comically avuncular frame at the smattering of ladies in attendance at each show as he sang, "You see it all around you/good lovin' gone bad."), songs about this big white 1970 Chevy Impala driven by a girl Ronnie briefly dated, who would pick him up and take him to all the weird little clubs and bars and (true) chili bordellos dotted across Orlando's landscape as they made the cute little inside jokes boyfriends and girlfriends make while listening to a cassette of Lou Reed on one side and Screaming Trees on the other endlessly flipping back and forth between the two, she politely indulging the "I will always be punk" rants he would veer into from time to time, as was the style of the early-to-mid 1990s), a song Magic wrote called "Chilean Sea Bass" (that being a metaphor invented by Paul to describe cute girls), the entire presentation—when they had shows—layered in a thick Kiss rock and roll swagger, like if Kiss had one too many beers before playing. It was funny to them to act like Kiss—it was funny for Ronnie to howl Paul Stanleyisms like "I know everybody's hot! Everybody's got the: ROCK AND ROLL PNEUMON-EE-YAAHHHH!!!" as Magic shook his fist and growled "Ohhhhhhh yeahhh-ahhhhhh!" like Gene Simmons. They were laughing at their childhoods of bad MTV, bad bands, bad music, at being sold a bill of jiveass rock and roll goods.

Unconsciously, they were trying to link (and reconcile) Kiss with The Minutemen, a Promethean-enough endeavor had they actually known how to play, but by falling way short of either mark, they had their own thing going, no matter how sloppy and ill-conceived. It was funny. It was cathartic. And the music, for its time, wasn't half bad.

They played gigs all over Orlando—living rooms, backyards, coffee house open-mics, any bar or club that would have them. In Gainesville, they played a kitchen where the show ended with Ronnie tackled by all his new/old friends—the kids he never got to know in high school like William, Neal, Paul—as they stole the mic and screamed along to "Sweaty Hands." Friends, old and new, got into the spirit of the jokes, the spectacle, the seriousness of the joke. As for the rest, as Magic was still fond of saying, "They're fuckers man, fuck 'em."

The music and the writing liberated Ronnie. Everything was really coming together—ladies, parties, tons of friends, fan mail about the column he wrote. Quite often, the days and nights spent in that blissfully naïve corner of the world called the University of Central Florida were blissful, languidly blissful. It was around this time when Ronnie met Maggie—who was three years younger, three times more attractive, and three times sweeter than Ronnie—and it was the closest thing you can get to "love" in the emotional immaturity of the late-teens and early twenties. In the middle of winter, Ronnie and Magic visited Chuck Taylor (who moved to Chicago after a year in the band to pursue dreams of improv comedy), and the city felt right, comfortable, even if it was 80-degrees colder than what they were used to. The action and the energy appealed to Ronnie as much as the music scene and his passing familiarity with Touch and Go, Drag City, Thrill Jockey . . . but really, so much of his love for Chicago and his desire to move there was projection, pure and simple, where Ronnie took everything Central Florida did not have—everything Ronnie wanted in a place to live—and tacked it onto Chicago. Besides, in terms of big cities, Chicago at the time felt like the only viable option. Atlanta was too southern for Ronnie. New York never came up. It was in transition from the Snake Plissken nightmare of the past to the Walt Disney nightmare of the future, and no one was moving to Brooklyn in those days. The West Coast was too far away . . . it didn't seem real. There was something about the Midwest that appealed to Ronnie. Pragmatic. Level-headed. Honest. Direct. Tellin' it like it is! Surrounded by people who think they've cornered the market on sanity and reality. He had heard of Lounge Ax in passing, hadn't heard of Empty Bottle or even Wicker Park . . . it wasn't so much about the music scene of that time as it was the idea of a city with so much possibility. Where Orlando felt hopeless, and Florida felt stultifying, Chicago felt and seemed inexhaustible, and Chuck Taylor, through his actions, his talk, his changed demeanor (urban, fast, smart) seemed to confirm all these projections. Drunk on tequila from the bar Chuck worked at, Magic and Ronnie agreed, while sobering instantly from the below-zero windchill on the cab ride back to Chuck Taylor's half-built loft space, that they would move there when they graduated.

In Orlando, they recorded on 4-tracks in Magic's apartment, and continued playing shows, and everything leveled off and that was fine even if the band wasn't really going anywhere. But where was it supposed to go?

Realistically, there were only so many places to play, and only so much you could do in Orlando. Graduation loomed. Willie-Joe Scotchgard graduated first. He moved to Cleveland to study the viola in a conservatory. They found another drummer—high school friend Andrew "Randy Macho Man" Savage—and soldiered on, but there was a decline in effect here, magnified by Orlando's omnipresent drug culture. Roofies were big that year—1995—and they weren't used by The Laraflynnboyle's circle of UCF friends for date rape, no matter what the papers say is its use in the uberculture. They made mean, surly, loudmouthed drunkards out of everyone, no matter how kind and considerate you normally were. Magic found roofies a fine way to numb the empty afternoon and evening hours. They magnified his already profound bitterness. For his part, Ronnie drank more and more, unsure of what to do with himself, especially after graduation, and his newspaper column—this column he had come to rely on so much as his identity—was no more once he graduated and received the diploma he didn't know how to use. Ronnie washed dishes so he would have time to write *The Big Blast for Youth*, and continued practicing with The Laraflynnboyles even if too many gigs ended badly from Ronnie's overindulgence of malt liquor, and Magic's nasty borderline violent (lots of fights broken up at this stage) roofie glaze. In this cloud of post-college uncertainty, as his behavior grew more and more erratic, as the smile on his face disappeared, as he floundered from job to job, Maggie left.

At some break in the clouds, Ronnie took a good look around. The only girls left were bisexual raver junkies. All the dudes he knew were content to be high all the time. He felt Orlando closing in on him. He was back to sitting around in his room, in the house he lived in with Chris Embowelment, playing Who records all night, trying desperately to avoid the thought that it was time to grow up and get a regular job and spend the rest of his days in comfortable, expected middle class, forever nagged by some variation of the question "What if?"

The only thing Ronnie could think to do was to flee for Gainesville. Ronnie and Magic weren't exactly best buds by this point— having little to connect over anymore besides what remained of the band—but Ronnie assured Magic the band would continue, somehow. They had always wanted to tour, and now Ronnie would get them more shows in Gainesville because it wasn't really that far away from Orlando (just far enough), and the music scene seemed better, what with all the punk rock you could shove down your spiky-haired throat and all. A stopgap, anyway, until they could get it together to move to Chicago. But Ronnie needed the change, needed the stimulation of others who weren't all about shitty drugs anymore, to a place that had more going on. Gainesville was all Ronnie could afford.

All of this swum around in Ronnie's quixotic brain as he played his unplugged electric guitar in his room after getting off the phone with John "Magic" Jensen. The tour would make things right again. Getting shows in Gainesville would make things right again. And then, soon enough, packing up and leaving for Chicago would make things right again.

It would be a beautiful and triumphant summer, and Ronnie couldn't wait to jump into it.

RONNIE AND SALLY-ANNE ALTAMONT

Ronnie calls his parents to share the good news.

"A tour," Sally-Anne Altamont repeats, when presented with said good news.

"Yeah! Definitely!"

"You have no money, Ron. You have no job. You're not even in the same town anymore as those other guys, who never exactly struck me as hardworking and dedicated musicians. None of this strikes you as, I don't know, problematic?"

"It'll be awesome."

"Awesome." After a three mile run on the beach, always, a focus, clear candor, often lost in the lazy days of retirement, misplaced in the vagaries of meditation. "It's like you've lost your mind ever since we moved to South Carolina and you went off to college."

"That was six years ago."

"Exactly."

SIOUXSANNA SIOUXSANNE GOES BOWLING

It's "Rock and Bowl Ain't Noise Pollution Nite" at the Gainesville Bowl-O-Rama. Siouxsanna Siouxsanne (an unfortunate nickname, lingering from high school during the peak of a Siouxsie and the Banshees obsession) is here tonight, throwing her sixth consecutive empty frame over on Lane 15. She is a terrible bowler. Most gothic bisexuals are.

The Run DMC version of "Walk This Way" pounds over bowling shoes squeaking across the wood. Swirling jade, black, and vermillion AMF boulders spin down the lanes, thundering like tympanis before grand old school showbiz introductions, until the percussive woodblockish rattle of the overturned pins break the tension, as the ball lands with a mechanical plop into the great unknown/unseen of its mysterious journey beneath the lane to be gracefully unfurled from the gaping maw of the retriever. From the game room, spasmodic videogame queefs. Across the lanes, strobe lights flicker. Black lights glow tubesocks and lint. The disc jockey is Sweet Billy Du Pree, legendary 1970s FM DJ back when Gainesville had a hard rock station called BJ 103: The Tongue.

"This one's goin' out to all the real rock and bowlers who still remember quality rock and roll," the venerable Du Pree rasps through the crackling speakers of the public address system, voice worn low and raspy through a life of whiskey and Quaaludes. The elegiac opening strains to "Magic Power" by the Canadian power trio Triumph fade in and set sail across the lanes on a sonic odyssey of magic. And power.

"Shit! Shit! Shit! Turn right, you stupid goddamn dick ball!" Siouxsanna Siouxsanne yells over the din after yet another ball veers left well before having a chance to knock over any pins. She turns, straightens her posture, recomposes, and all inebriated clumsiness and aggression in the toss evaporates. She is tall, in a long black dress and black stockings, a slinky slide in the walk in faded red white and black bowling shoes unaccustomed to supporting this much grace. There's a relatively austere use of makeup (We can't look like we did in high school now, can we?) across the cheeks, eyelids, and lips of her art school features, a dyed-black salon cut somewhere between a page boy and a bob. Pale. So pale. It takes effort to get skin like this in Florida.

Siouxsanna Siouxsanne loses her footing, unused to the lack of traction as her right heel skids sideways. She flails to the floor in what seems a comedic pratfall, hurriedly rises, mutters, "I'm too llllllllloaded to be here!" over the not-quite-mocking laughter of friends.

Ronnie Altamont is impressed.

He silently observes the bowling and the good time laughter of this distinctly middle class college crowd in their ironed thrift store tees and unholey back-to-school mall pants. Ronnie leans forward against the bowling ball racks, standing on the unfashionably brown plaid printed carpeting on the three steps above where the bowlers sit changing shoes, keeping score, chugging brews. Here are the easy smiles and burdenless leisure of summer vacation, a jarring change from the dismal poverty Ronnie had grown accustomed to, those long muggy hours in his bedroom in the trailer alone, listening to The Stooges and trying to write. School is over, but only temporarily for them, but for Ronnie, he's reminded of how he felt like an interloper that first day he and Kelly set foot on the UF campus to score free Krishna food.

After a sweat jam at Paul's, Ronnie drove William and Neal to the Gainesville Bowl-o-Rama—where some nnnnnnnnugget William was trying to hook up with would be with a few of her friends. They would all be Ronnie's friends soon enough—all twelve of these amateur summer vacationing bowlers—but only Siouxsanna Siouxsanne stands out to Ronnie, in her mix of post-goth grace and sloppy belligerence. Ronnie, not the grown-ass man he thinks he is, still young enough to treat every crush like he is the first person to ever have these feelings. So charming! Siouxsanna Siouxsanne, stomping up to the line to try yet again to knock over a pin—any pin—falling over the line as she flings the ball "granny style," long lithe arms pulling and spinning the rest of her forward until she loses her footing, spins, plops backwards while the ball—chipped and yellowed with white streaks like a dusk thunderstorm—bounces over the first lane to her left and continues rolling two lanes over, sabotaging the very serious play of a muffler shop's weeknight bowling team—where it knocks over four pins. Her friends cheer at this, they clap and congratulate her for finally getting on the scoreboard. The muffler shop's weeknight bowling team[6] has to smile, no matter how jaded they've become to the general misbehavior of college students. It helps that the interference in their very serious league play is from a girl who would be real pretty if she didn't wear so much makeup, if she didn't dress like she was leaving a funeral, if she laid out in the sun once in awhile and got herself a tan. Not that they would kick her out of bed or nuthin'. They're just sayin'.

"FUUUUUUCK YEWWWWWWWWW!" Siouxsanna Siouxsanne brays to the paneled ceiling's spinning multi-colored disco lights. She's on her back, brain floating in and out of booze-fueled, med-soaked half-dreams of car trips with her parents—the only child in the backseat staring out the window from Orlando to St. Pete or Fort Myers or wherever they would go to see family—watching the lakes and swamps and bays and gulfs and oceans—pretending she was some kind of superfast manatee diving in and out of the sharp glittering waters (no matter the color—the pea soup of

[6] "Gary's Superfuzz Big Muffler, 'We Want to Sell You a Muffler,' on Waldo Road, just a quarter mile north of the flea market. See ya there!"

the swamps or the worn concrete of the ocean or the choppy blue of the bay) keeping pace with the off-white wood-paneled Country Squire station wagon and flying out of sight above them when the waters ended until another water body appeared to the left or right as Billy Squier sings "my kinda lov-uh/my kinda luv-uh/ my kinda luuv-uh . . . " Two hands wrap around damp armpits and pull Siouxsanna Siouxsanne upright. She tries walking, but her legs are not taking any orders from her brain. Two friends— William and Neal, actually—lift her along on either side like she's a running back carried off the field after a knee injury to the gracious applause of the audience, only there is no applause, just snack bar stares and beer bar glares. Even the lanes are silent, as these twelve (plus Ronnie—transfixed and fascinated and in love) move en masse toward the exit.

Sweet Billy Du Pree turns down the Billy Squier, announces, "Ladies and gentlemen, you know I used to party hard, but I also used to party safe. Let's keep it street legal out there at the rock and bowl, yadig? Here's another song that could never get old: 'Whole. Lotta. Luuuuuuuuv.'"

Siouxsanna Siouxsanne lollygags her head rightward, yells "You suck ass!" to the DJ booth. Friends shrug at Sweet Billy Du Pree, mouth the word, "Sorry." Ronnie looks to Sweet Billy Du Pree, up in the DJ booth. He wears a red bandana on his upper forehead. A faded black "The Ultimate Ozzy" tourshirt, swollen from the beerbelly. Aviator sunglasses. He nods his head in rhythm to the "du-nuh, du-nuh, nuh" of the "Whole Lotta Love" guitar intro. The rocking and bowling resumes.

Ronnie trails behind this group as Neal and William keep Siouxsanna Siouxsanne from falling to the ground, passed out

and dreaming of childhood manatees. In and out of consciousness, she yells expletives, mumbles unintelligible moans between drools. So beautiful, Ronnie thinks. In the parking lot, two
more friends join in and hoist her into the back of a Volvo station
wagon—one of those relaxed boyfriend and girlfriend couples
you know will be married shortly after getting their degrees—
and off they go, Ronnie watching the Volvo's boxy red taillights
fade away across the mammoth parking lot. In the midst of the
parking lot talk—the shrugs and the "That's Sioxusanna Siouxsanne for ya's," the ride back to William and Neal's where they
will have one more beer while listening to CCR (and still talking
about Doug Clifford like it will really happen), Ronnie wants to
ask about Siouxsanna Siouxsanne, but he knows no one will tell
him what he wants to hear, knows no one will say, "You and her,
you'd be great together, Ronnie!," knows no one will claim that
she isn't as crazy as she was acting at the Gainesville Bowl-O-
Rama for "Rock and Bowl Ain't Noise Pollution Nite." So he holds
it in, "it" being whatever passes for "love" in his heart, mind,
and other, less noble, body parts.

QUASIMODO IN THE DISHTANK

Alvin knocks on Ronnie's bedroom door—three soft, unassert-
ive taps.

"Yeah what?" Ronnie grunts, annoyed, because he's thinking
about maybe doing some writing as he rifles through his compact
discs for something to listen to. He's busy, you understand.

"I got my first paycheck from Otis's Barbelicious BBQ, and

I was wondering if you wanted to go out for Chinese food. My treat, pfffff."

All thoughts of busyness, of thinking about writing while listening to music, vanished from Ronnie's mind, replaced by a massive steaming mountain of pork fried rice. Ronnie hops off the mattresses, leaps to the door, opens it. "Let's go."

The restaurant—The Ancient Chinese Secret—is a two-minute drive down 34th Street. Alvin drives, narrowly avoids sideswiping two cars, honking blurs in the myopic haze beyond the range of his thick glasses. "Pfff. Guess they didn't see me," Alvin says. Ronnie laughs at this, trying not to look at the murderous glares from the narrowly avoided cars, thinking how absurd it would be to die in a car crash simply because he wanted to score a free meal.

They sit in a cool dark dining room in a booth by the window overlooking the broiling blinding plaza parking lot. Alvin talks about his job. And talks. And talks.

"So I wash the dishes, the forks, the knives, the spoons, the spatulas, the bowls, the plates, the storage bins, and whatever they want me to wash, really—pffff!—but that ain't all I do there. I stir the beans, butter the bread, take the clean plates to the bus boys, take out the dirty linen at the end of the night. It ain't bad really, pfff." Yes, Ronnie is aware of the job description here, and not only because he has prior experience in the dishwashing field. Alvin has told him all about the routines of his work several times already. Butter the bread. Stir the beans. Take out the dirty linen. Wash what they take back to me. Pfff. Ronnie is too hungry to listen, to care, to bother with trying to respond to anything Alvin says, because Alvin doesn't respond to what you say, he simply continues talking about whatever the hell he wants to talk about.

As Ronnie waits for his food, Pluto orbits around the sun in one complete rotation, empires rise and fall, Ice Ages come and go and come and go again. Still, no food. Alvin keeps yammering. Pfff. But it's a free meal, and if Ronnie can eat something, he can go to Gatorroni's, where he'll score free beer from William and drink all night. If only this food would get here already.

". . . So yeah, they call me 'Quasimodo' at work, pfff." Alvin mentions in the middle of this nonstop yak.

Ronnie snaps back in the booth, jarred from his impatient reverie. Ronnie huffs. Ronnie is offended. "They call you 'Quasimodo?'" Ronnie huffs once more. Ronnie is offended. "I can't believe that, Alvin. That's so mean."

"Well, it's nothing I ain't used to, pffff." Today, the "pfff" sounds especially resigned, like a deflated tuba.

"No, man . . . that's not right," and Ronnie, he actually tries imagining that there is someone inside Alvin that's real, someone suffering an endless series of slights, guilty of nothing but being born with Swedish wino pubic hair scalp, acne, buckteeth, that smell. Everything is off about him, and he knows it and has to live with it. Ronnie could look around town, could look at himself and those around him, and at the end of the day, no one was stranger, no one was a bigger nonconformist than Alvin. He didn't even try. He was born into it. Everyone else magnifies their nonconformity just enough to get laid but not enough to adversely impact the quality of life they are accustomed to. Beyond a heightened sensitivity and artistic inclinations, they didn't suffer daily the way Alvin suffered daily.

Ronnie manages an "I'm sorry, man."

"Pfff."

Finally, the food arrives. Sweet and sour chicken for Alvin, pork fried rice for Ronnie. After subsisting on little besides Little Lady snack cakes and microwave burritos, Ronnie relishes it all—the taste and the chew, the swallow and the downward movement, the warmth and the fullness. All thanks to Alvin. Shit, Alvin's the entire reason Ronnie's even here in Gainesville. Who else would let him live this way? Rent-free. Bill-free. And all Ronnie does is make fun of him.

"Well, that was great," Ronnie says on the drive back to the trailer. "Best meal I've had in a long time."

"I'm thinkin' about watchin' a movie tonight, pff," Alvin says on the drive home. "Ya wanna watch it with me?"

Ronnie thinks it over as Alvin turns right off 34th Street onto the side street leading to the trailer park. After free Gatorroni's beer, when William gets off work, they'll show up at peoples' houses, see what they are doing, or maybe they will end up at the Rotator. Nothing definite. With some food in his belly, it would make drinking that much easier.

"Naw, man," Ronnie says. "I made plans." Alvin parks the van. Ronnie immediately opens the door, hops out. Oh yeah. He almost forgets to say, "But thanks for dinner." Alvin watches Ronnie get into his car and drive away.

"IT'S THE BEGINNING OF THE BEGINNING OF THE END OF THE BEGINNING," SEZ ROBBIE ROBERTSON IN "THE LAST WALTZ" . . .

. . . is the quote I've been running around in my head lately after watching that movie at some hippie party at UCF (all the little subcultures hang out together on the fringes, so you end up being around hippies, no matter how, like, fuckin', punk rock or whatever you are). At first, I scoffed at it, and I don't remember much of the rest of The Band playing with all their old fart friends—once the roofies kick in alls I remember is a vague steady blunt surly torrent leaving my mouth and the delusion that my brain is finally making some truly wonderful and fearless connections re: my life and shit.

But yeah: What does that mean? I mean, I know it's probably just some cocaine koan bullshit when Robertson says that, but, ok, let's break it down:

We know it's the beginning, but it's the end of that beginning, but it's the beginning of the beginning of that end of the beginning.

I'm starting to think I know what he means by that, as me and Macho Man Randy pull up to what Ronnie tells me is called the "Righteous Freedom House," one of these large old houses people here live in where bands play every weekend, one of those Gainesville punk rock houses Ronnie busts a nut over in his corny punk rock fantasies.

"This better be good," I say before stepping out of Randy's brown-exteriored, gold-interiored 1981 Chrysler Cordoba—you know, the car with the "fine Corinthian leather" ol' what's-his-name from *Fantasy Island* promises, only Randy's car isn't fine Corinthian anything—cloth seats blackened with dirt and tears from lugging amps and drum gear from one end of Orlando to the next, the paint job worn away by the sun—hood, roof and trunk dented by hailstorms—and somebody (Ronnie, probably) started calling it "The Poop Ship Destroyer" after that Ween song. Randy climbs out, looks across at me, over the pock-marked roof as I continue, "I have five roofies in my pocket, and I'm not afraid to take them if this isn't."

Of course, Ronnie couldn't grace us with his presence to load in the gear, and actually—nobody's here right now as we're in that awkward time of after dinner and before the party when you wonder if anyone's going to bother showing up, so Randy and I trudge back and forth from The Poop Ship Destroyer to the corner of the living room that's been allocated as the place to plug in and set up by the scenester (the thing about Gainesville that I never understood was how everybody here kinda looks the same . . . it's like that line in *Quadrophenia*: "it's easy to see / that you are one of us / ain't it funny how we all seem to look the same?" (And now you see why I'm not the singer for The Laraflynnboyles. If you think Ronnie's singing is bad, and it is . . .)) with his black band t-shirt and hair dyed some bright unnatural color and very short on a frail vegan frame and they're all nice enough, I guess—these wannabe prodigies of Ian MacKaye, and you can tell in their behavior, they're always sitting there thinking "What would Fugazi do here?" but we trudge across the small treeless grassless dirt front yard into the large living room covered in (of course) show fliers and (of course) the iconic photographs of like Minor Threat sitting on the front steps of the Dischord House, Jawbreaker sitting on an old couch, some angry singer I don't know doing that "breaking the fourth wall" thing all these angry desperate singers do when they run up to a crowd of equally angry desperate kids in the audience who gather around the mic to scream along to the words they've memorized like solemn Boy Scout oaths of forthrightness to the

Den Leader, interspersed with pictures of Kiss and Iron Maiden and Van Halen that somebody here finds funny, and, come to think of it, I find it funny too, meanwhile Scenester dude stands over us as we plug in and set up asking questions like "So how's the Orlando Scene these days?" and I pshaw and grunt a "Sucks" and Randy shrugs and says, "Yeah," and Scenester dude presses on and asks us about different bands in Orlando and yeah, we've heard of these bands, they all have names like December's February and Car Bomb on a Sunday Afternoon, and I can't stand those bands, but I try to be polite so I says, "Yeah, we're not really into any of that," and Scenester dude gets the picture.

True to form, Ronnie shows up the moment everything is finally set up. He's with William, Neal, and Paul, and it's like some kind of high school reunion with our hearty ha ha has and backslapping embraces. Ronnie seems happier. He looks like hell—disheveled hair, smelly unwashed clothing, an underfed weight loss—but he does seem happier the way he stands around us smiling, looking from me and Randy to the other guys. He always wanted to be a part of something. I think that's why he wrote that retarded opinion column for the school paper. I really do.

Anyway, Paul, who communicates entirely in inside jokes, volleys about five inside jokes my way in about twenty seconds, and it's like we're all seventeen or eighteen years old again having a late night at the Denny's on State Road 434 back in Orlando, only, instead of ten of us taking up the largest booth in the restaurant, ordering nothing but a basket of fries and ten glasses of water, it's six years later, and we're living whatever short-sighted dreams we had back then of playing in bands. It's really all we ever talked about, aside from girls.

Neal steps up to Randy, rubs his recently emerged beer belly. "Looks like Tara's keeping you well-fed, heh," and as he rubs, he pokes Randy's belly and punctuates it by saying, "Heh! . . . Heh!" until Macho Man Randy shoves him away, laughing (the dude doesn't have a mean bone in his body) and says, "Fed and fucked, dude. You know how it is . . . "

"I only know about the second one," Neal says, and we laugh. It really is great being around these dudes again. It almost makes me want to like Gainesville. Almost.

Anyway, they show up with a case of Old Hamtramck, and they're already drunk, so it looks like me and Randy have some catching up to do before we start playing. People slowly start showing up, peeking into the empty living room, taking one look at us, realizing they don't know us, then stepping out to shoot the shit in the front yard. I shotgun three beers in a row, and my friends—oh, my friends!—they circle me and cheer me on in a way that's sincere in its ironical references to collegiate dude squad bro-ham peer pressure. It's like we're making fun of it even though it's exactly what we're doing.

"Watch this, fuckers . . . " I say, feeling what I wanted to be feeling right about now (and those roofies are weighing down my right jeans pocket), and my key pokes a hole in the middle of the Old Hammy can and the beer floods my throat and my brain turns energetic and sluggish all at once as the heaviness of the suds fills my chest and when the can is empty, I crush it against my skull a la Ogre in *Revenge of the Nerds*, and my five friends cheer me and suddenly we're all chanting "Nerds! Nerds! Nerds! Nerds!" for no reason, except, if there's one thing we have in common, it's that we like to start ironical chants with each other after we've been drinking. When the drink takes hold, we love to yell. And now, I'm ready to play, because, honestly, I don't give a fuck if we sound good or not. Fuck these people. Fuck Gainesville. These smirking phony tattooed up scenester types with their identical hair and identical dress, standing in their little clusters of small town self-important drama. What Ronnie sees in any of this, I will never know. Behind the amp, I pull out the roofies and pop three into my mouth, chase it with the beer. Great. Let's rock.

The show goes about how I figure it will. I'm drunk, feeling the pills slowly kicking in, forgetting whole songs as the set progresses, weaving in and out of consciousness, weight shifting from one foot to the other. Ronnie ain't much better, and actually, he might be worse, because he was at some bar for three hours before showing up to play. Macho Man Randy wasn't the best drummer to begin with, and now, he looks green with beer sickness, like he might throw up on the drums so when he hits them the puke hops and leaps the way glitter does in those glam metal videos of our youths. Only Paul, Neal, and William bother watching us, and all they do is yell the words "Rock! Beats!" (whatever that means) over and over again while throwing their empties at our heads. The scenesters peek in through the front screen door long enough to smirk at our band—this band we've been doing for so fucking long now called The Laraflynnboyles—and who even knows what that's referencing anymore?—who even remembers *Twin Peaks*?—and no wonder they're completely indifferent to our stale band with our stale jokes (our Kiss between-song banter of "How's everybody doin' tonight! Yeah? Who wants vodka and orange juice?" or whatever the hell we're saying tonight) pointing out via wornout satire the, this just in, stupidity of the music we call

Rock and Roll. And yet, at the same time, it's like, we're just having fun here, and isn't this what it's ultimately about? See, that's what pisses me off the most about Gainesville. These doctrinaire fuckin'... Gainesville scenester types. So humorless. So unable to relax and have, you know, f-u-n. Yeah, we suck. So what? I'm up here, trying, no matter how drunk we might be right now. We took the time to try and do this, and do I hope maybe someone will like what we do? Of course. It gets nervous; I get fucked up. But when I bother thinking about these Gainesville scenester types, all I can think is: Fuck them. And fuck Ronnie too, if he thinks this is some paradise of music and art. Motherfucker's just trying to relive college. Because, really, what else does he have?

Finally, our set ends, culminating in a grand finale that lasts twenty minutes, everything this rock and roll fermata, where we try and sound like The Who, windmills and all, only, this time, I would really like to smash my bass guitar and be done with all of this. It's an endless volley of beer cans from our friends, and I smile, and I do the math, and I think, yeah, I can afford another bass guitar, so fuck it.

I unplug and keep the fermata going on my bass. I walk out of the living room of the Righteous Freedom House, back into the screen door, somehow navigate the three steps to the dirt yard, and I'm still playing the bass even though it's no longer plugged into the amp, and everyone stops to look at me. I pluck open strings with my right hand and make the devil horns with my left hand, because I know that joke is old and these jerks will hate that as much as they hate The Laraflynnboyles. This is a red Epiphone bass, the only one I have. Six years ago, I worked all summer, busting my ass delivering pizza, to buy the thing. I've spent so many hours playing it, in practice, alone in front of the television, or in front of the stereo while trying to learn a new song, rewinding tapes over and over again to make sure I got it right. But I'm feeling this fermata right now more than I've ever felt anything. I can't stand being ignored like this. My anger and frustration with this audience, with my life, with everything, supersedes my attachments, and I raise the bass with both hands, then my right hand wraps over the left hand at the upper neck and I swing downward. The bass guitar makes a funny sound when you smash it into a dirt front yard. There's a hollow vibration from the wood, from the metal, from the force. I swing and smash and swing and smash as people clear out, some running out to the street, everyone cheering now (they're cheering), but try as I might, the fucking thing won't smash. The dirt is too soft, the neck and the body of the bass are too thick. I can't stop now. I have to destroy this thing. I hear the guitar in the other room stop playing, then an abrupt stop, even the drums stop, and Ronnie and Macho Man Randy stand in the doorway and I'm too fucked up to care how they're looking right now, and I hold the bass aloft once more and yell to them "Thank you! Good night! And goodbye!" just like fuckin' Robbie Robertson in *The Last Waltz*, turn around, run out to the street, and the solid road is all the bass needs to splinter, crack, break until only the strings connect the neck to the body. I'm under a street light, and it's like I'm under a spot light, and I hear enough "Woo-hoos!" and "Yeahs!" from these dumbass scenesters in the yard to know I'm doing right here, that this makes up for our lackluster set. Victorious, I toss what's left of my bass towards a drainage grate across the street, where it almost falls into the hole, but dangles on the edge, a little bit short.

And that's the last thing I remember before waking up outside of Neal's coachhouse in some lawnchair with Randy sitting next to me as The Minutemen's *Double Nickels on the Dime* plays from inside. I come to, ask Randy, "What time is it?"

"2:30," he says. He punches me on the arm. "How ya feelin', Townshend?"

At first, I have no idea what he's talking about, then I remember. The bass. I groan. My heart sinks. I have a nauseous feeling that throbs from my temples to my balls. I lean forward. Hands on my head. I tally the damage. Shotgunned five beers, drank several more, popped five roofies, smashed the bass.

"Think we can fix it?" I ask, knowing the answer. Randy laughs. Yeah. That's what I thought. I stand, stretch, feel the vertigo and the spinning—the black sky and the palm trees, sand pines, live oaks, closing in, here in Gainesville again, in the patch of dirt separating this coach house from the front house, our cars parked at haphazard angles, as d. boon sings "as I look out over this beautiful land I can't help but realize I am alone." I face the street, over and down the small incline of the driveway, the occasional car rolling by, turn around, look into the coach house, where Neal airdrums, air-guitars, air-basses, one after the other, Ronnie behind him, jumping up and down on the couch, William and Paul passing a whiskey bottle back and forth. Neal sees me, yells, "He's awake!" runs out to me, carrying by the neck the remnants of my bass—the top half of the neck, strings linking the neck to what remains of the fractured body, some wood, some wires.

"This was the greatest thing I've ever seen," Neal tells me, and he hands me my bass, my baby, the only thing in life I care about. "You're heroes now. Gainesville won't shut up about it."

"Well they didn't show it." I say, trying to figure out a way to hold what remains of my bass in one hand, without the rest of it either falling into the dirt or swinging into my shins.

"Aw, dude, you know. Extreme times, extreme measures. It was beautiful. Heroic."

"Whatever," I say. "Give me a beer." I shuffle back to my lawn chair.

"You got it, dude," Neal says, runs in, runs out, hands me an Old Hamtramck. I open it, take one sip, and as Randy starts talking about how it "Looks like Gainesville finally likes us," I don't get a chance to tell him why I don't care and why it doesn't matter anyway, because the next thing I remember is waking up, face buried between a musty brown couch pillow and musty couch cushion, the evil morning sun broiling and burning through the blinds.

"IT'S THE BEGINNING OF THE END . . . ," CONTINUED

"Hungover," Magic answers when Ronnie asks how he's feeling as they sit at Denny's before Magic and Macho Man Randy leave for Orlando. Fresh coffees steam out of bottomless mugs. They look out the window next to their booth. The bicyclists and joggers and power walkers of all ages rule the 13th Street sidewalks. The Laraflynnboyles share a communal hatred for the kinds of people who get up to these activities on Sunday mornings like these. "You should move back, man," Magic continues.

Ronnie shrugs. He isn't thinking about the band, or moving back. He's thinking of last night, of Siouxsanna Siouxsanne, of when they finished the show, and suddenly almost everyone decided the band didn't completely suck, thanks to Magic smashing his bass.

He found her outside, leaning against the back of a car parked in the driveway, a bottle of wine on the roof. They talked. She seemed impressed by what had just happened—and everything about the way she looked was so arty, so practiced and tidy and neat and beautiful, like English women in the alternative music videos girls like Siouxsanna Siouxsanne studied obsessively . . . and Ronnie Altamont, he is none of these things—he is disheveled, his clothes anti-fashion, his hair unkempt and uncombed, and he stood there in post-gig sweat and stink thinking maybe he had a chance because he just did something worthwhile maybe, so he handed her the haiku he kept in his pocket, written on a now-damp piece of scrap paper, the kind of haiku he wrote for every girl he had liked for the past several years, each haiku a variation of any of the following:

"siouxsanna siouxsanne

stunning, let's go out sometime

so bee-yew-tee-full."

Siouxsanna Siouxsanne paused to read it.

"Thanks," she said. "I like this. It's funny."

This should have tipped Ronnie off, he now thinks as they sit at the Denny's waiting for their food. These Florida girls, the way they say something is funny without laughing or smiling so you don't know if they actually think it's funny or not. The haiku is always a litmus test. If they laugh at this, they'll laugh and put up with everything else about Ronnie.

"Well?" Ronnie had asked, suddenly painfully conscious of how sweaty and gross he was, post-gig.

"What?" Siouxsanna Siouxsanne said, reaching over to raise the wine bottle, tipping it to those full red lips, sipping, swallowing.

"Do you want to go out sometime, like, uh, to the museum or something?" Ronnie. So articulate.

"No," she said.

"No?"

"I can't," she sighed. "Sorry."

"Oh." Ronnie stepped back, aware of every drop of sweat, every wrinkle in his clothes, the smells. "Ok. Why?"

"Because," Siouxsanna Siouxsanne said. She extended the arm not holding the bottle and the haiku, palm-up hand moving from side to side to take in the yard and its little groups of talkers. "You're just like them. Even if you're not like them, you're just like them."

Before Ronnie could say anything else, she walked away, disappearing into the party, into the Gainesville night, and Ronnie now sits at the booth, brooding on what the hell she meant by that. He feels so out of place in Gainesville, especially amongst these people who are supposed to be so different from everyone else. And Magic's telling him to go back to Orlando.

"It ended up being a good show," Ronnie says. "We hadn't played here in a while. Next time we play, it'll get even better."

"When we play in Orlando, people just have fun and don't take this shit so serious," Randy Macho Man says.

"I don't get so disgusted I smash my bass," Magic says, and the mere mention of his now destroyed bass makes him look down, ashamed. Ronnie looks at Magic. Really looks at him. Everything sags anymore. Self-medicated. Severely depressed. A tremendous sadness in the eyes, hidden behind the glasses. "Just waiting to die" was his typical answer to "How are you doing?"

"That was kinda awesome though," Macho Man Randy says. He can't wait to get home, to tell everyone about it.

The discussion is interrupted by the egg-shaped waitress, who brings their order—Grand Slam Breakfast for Randy Macho Man, Deli Dinger for Magic, Moons Over My Hammy for Ronnie.

"Just come back, dude," Randy Macho Man continues. "Orlando's not as bad as you think." Every time he comes to Gainesville, Randy Macho Man has a good-enough time, but the complexity of it all, in the way people are always around to tell you what they think and what they heard, when all you need is some friends, a paycheck, a place to go home to with a bong and some records and the Orlando Magic winning on TV.

"It's worse than I think, and I'm staying," Ronnie says. "It's a stupid place, owned and operated by stupid people."

"Here we go," Magic says.

"It's the worst of LA and Altanta," Ronnie continues. "Seriously. Orlando wants to be Atlanta and LA rolled into one. What kind of an aspiration is that?"

"You're always complaining," Randy Macho Man says.

"Totally," Magic agrees.

The arrival of the food is a relief for Ronnie. The smells of cigarettes and bottomless coffee are joined by scrambled eggs, butter, syrup, cooked meat. Ronnie doesn't have to fill the silence. He doesn't have to fill the air with forced conversations no one wants to have anyway.

When he finishes, Ronnie continues, "Look, it's cool you want me back, but it ain't happening. I know I'm broke and all that, but I'm . . . ," and here, Ronnie surprises himself with the word, ". . . happier."

Happier. Yeah. Happier. "Yeah, you're happier," Magic sneers. "You don't seem happier."

"I am." Through the hazy torpor of the late morning hang-over, Ronnie smiles. "We can come back and play again, and it'll go better. People are talking here. It'll be better. And then we'll tour. We're a good band. Good things are going to happen."

This is met with a collective shrug from Magic and Macho Man Randy during the final bites of yet another post-show Denny's breakfast. "I'm still getting the tour going. It'll be fun to get out of the state for once." Another collective shrug.

They pay the bill, walk out into the heat, to Macho Man Randy's car.

"Alright, well, we'll talk soon," Magic says, getting into the car.

"Yup," Ronnie says.

"Later," Macho Man Randy says, and that's it.

I.D. 4: THE HOLIDAY (NOT THE MOVIE)

In the early morning hours of the 5th of July, Ronnie, passed out in the backseat of his car, awakens to the sounds of tremendous farting, like stubborn old lawnmowers refusing to kickstart.

Ronnie opens his eyes, disoriented, unsure of where he is, and then he sees—no, it can't be that—two pairs of hairy white ass cheeks, pressed against the windshield as Neal screams, "Ronnie Altamont! Wake up, dude!" while his brother Paul laughs maniacally on the passenger side of the windshield.

Ronnie sees, hears, and processes what is happening, yells "Oh Gahhhhhhd!," the bile rising in his chest. He opens the car's back door and runs to the backyard of the barbeque he had been at since noon yesterday, puking into shrubs two bottles of Straw-

berry Kiwi Boone's Farm (Strawberry Kiwi Boone's Farm? What is he, thirteen?!), vomit like yogurt and power steering fluid. Behind him, laughter, growing closer, louder.

"Altamont!" Neal hollers, rounding the corner of the house. He sees Ronnie, bent over, coughing and drooling. "What are you doing?"

Ronnie rises, stupidly drunk but sober enough to know how stupidly drunk he has been. "I didn't move here to have the banal college experience of puking at some party," he announces, an attempt at sounding smart. Only the thing is, he believes it. Because the college aspects of life here, to interact with college people as they do their college things (and not the music things, the art things, the you-know punk rock things) fills Ronnie with a cold desperate desire to leave immediately, and to puke like this reminds him that his time in Gainesville is limited, because this simply cannot go on.

On the other hand, Ronnie isn't sure if a pair of brothers farting with their naked asses smooshed against a windshield constitutes "banal," but his cheap-wine-soaked mind isn't really up for such fine distinctions. He falls to the ground again, retches.

"Seriously!" Neal yells, then repeats, "What are you doing?"

Paul follows his brother, watches Ronnie bent over the shrubs, says, "Alright, Altamont. Get the last bit out. You're better now. Let's get back to the party and get you a beer."

Ronnie stands, wipes his mouth, nods. He looks away from the shrubs, to Paul and Neal. Neal is completely naked. It's that time of the night for Neal to be completely naked, Ronnie thinks. Paul readjusts his pants. Ronnie wants to throw up again, but merely dry-heaves. That image. Two pairs of asscheeks pressed against the windshield. Oh Gahhhhhd. Half-awake, with the brain ache where the lost inhibitions used to be.

He walks back around the house with Paul and Neal, past his car, to the front yard, as Paul and Neal laugh heartily. From the rest of the party, Ronnie is greeted by tipsy applause from the people who remain—names Ronnie learned and unlearned in a matter of seconds, sitting around the faintest embers of the grill, pulling out fireworks from backpacks.

"Lesser men have died seeing what you just saw," William says, handing Ronnie an ice cold Dusch Lite. Everyone laughs. Ronnie manages a smile. Ronnie opens the beer. That is the closest he gets to drinking it.

Later he sits in a lawnchair and tries piecing together what happened as almost everyone else runs out onto the street to do battle with bottle rockets. Five to a side, they crouch behind mailboxes, cars, trees, light the wick, the seconds of waiting, the scream, the whiz, the explosion, the laughter, the screams of pain, of triumph, the smoke trails, that acrid firework Independence Day stench. In out-of-sequence images, Ronnie recalls showing up thinking it would be funny to be the guy with two bottles of Strawberry Kiwi Boone's Farm, drinking them from the bottle, quickly, because he is nervous, surrounded by all these people he does not know, who circle the grill with beer and whiskey and the kind of languid summertime conversation you hear once all small talk and latest news has been exhausted. There was Siouxsanna Siouxsanne, as drunk then as she is now, not at the bottle rocket fight but walking around yelling "We're not friends anymore, assholes!" to the warriors fighting on the street, no one listening because she says this every weekend and they find it endearing, somehow. In a social scene filled with quirks, kinks, and eccentricities, this is what Siouxsanna Siouxsanne does. Oh, and Ronnie remembers William, at one point, taking Ronnie aside and asking, "You all right? You seem a little quiet today."

"Uh, yeah," Ronnie managed, numb, not fully there. The alcohol shut him down, rather than animating him.

"You should eat something, dude," and William pointed to a blackened paper plate next to the grill, piled with charred soy hot dogs. "Cool," Ronnie answers, yawns, and shuffles off to the back seat of his car where, on the floor, an old copy of the school newspaper, where Ronnie studies the cartoon from Maux (he tries remembering where he had heard that name) of a pantsless hillbilly straddling the Florida panhandle as the rest of the state dangles between his legs like a limp penis. Inside the state penis are tiny drawings of New Yorkers fighting Cubans fighting tourists fighting surfers fighting rednecks fighting state troopers fighting the elderly. As an added touch, the Florida Keys drip like urine from the bottom. Everyone holds a pointed gun. The caption reads, "Greetings from Florida," drawn in postcard lettering. "Try not to get killed!" The postcard was tilted sideways to look like it was pinned off-kilter to a bulletin board. Ronnie smiled at it, thinking of how unpleasantly funny—and uncollegiate—such a girl must be who would draw something like this.

This is all Ronnie remembers before waking up to Paul and Neil's asses and thunderous farts.

"I absolutely hate these people," Siouxsanna Siouxsanne says, stumbling around the grill. "Farting on windshields? Shooting each other with bottle rockets? I don't know why I bother trying to be friends with anybody here."

"Yeah," Ronnie says, rubbing his temples, thinking of his bed, or the stacked mattresses in the tiny trailer bedroom that passed for his bed.

"Why are you here?" Siouxsane Siouxsanne asks.

Ronnie looks up at her. "You kinda look like Nico. Anybody ever tell you that?'

"Yes," Sioxusanna Siouxsanne says. "Now answer the question."

"Aw, man," Ronnie says, in a weary way, like Dylan in an imagined press conference. "Because it's the Fourth of July, and . . . "

"No," Siouxsanna Siouxsanne stops, stares at him. "Here. Gainesville. You're not going to school here. So why bother?"

Ronnie looks away, throws up his hands, mumbles, "Aw dude, I don't know." He shifts in his chair, drunk enough to throw out, half-serious, to the empty windless air, "To meet girls like you."

Surely, in this giant world where all possible outcomes have already occurred, there have been plenty of moments of ill-timed vomiting, but Siouxsanna Siouxsanne, not triggered by Ronnie's words, but by all the drinking, those pills (whatever what's-his-name gave her), this all-encompassing weariness and wariness with Gainesville and these parties and these people, moans and moves, scurrying to the back of the house to throw up in the very same suffering shrubs covered in Ronnie's violent earth-toned regurgitations.

"Jesus," Ronnie mumbles, over the steady din of the unceasing bottle rocket war, "When I tell women I like them, they puke." He leans forward, regains his footing in that awkward precarious way people do when they rise from lawnchairs, trudges to the back-yard, where, thankfully, Siouxsanna Siouxsanne has found shrubs past Ronnie's defiled shrubs, seemingly free of what Kerouac once called "sentient debouchments."

"This isn't about you," Siouxsanna Siouxsanne says between violent retchings. "You're ok . . . Just don't ask me out anymore." She coughs, spits. "See you later."

Ronnie needs to leave. He walks back to the side of the house, to his car, to the front seat this time, Siouxsanna Siouxsanne's puke-cough fading away, the moon and stars spinning, trapped in the eyeache of a cheap wine hangover. Ronnie pulls out into the street, honking, smiling, waving at near-strangers as he weaves through one side of the bottle rocket war. Fireworks bonk the trunk and rear window, faded laughter decrescendos into the silence in the emptiness of the student-ghetto streets, and Ronnie drives home, listening to Gary Numan sing "Me! I Disconnect from You," and Ronnie wants to feel alive, and he could almost turn around and tell Siouxsanna Siouxsanne that that is the reason he lives in Gainesville now. Not to feel younger, or to extend the first taste of adulthood freedoms via the college lifestyle, but to feel alive. He could turn this car around and tell her this, but Ronnie knows this isn't a pressing concern for Siouxsanna Siouxsanne right about now, assuming she even remembers the question.

EATING BAKED POTATO WITH A JELL-O STRAW

Mouse stands before Ronnie Altamont and Icy Filet, wearing a tattered brown and green bathrobe, holding a cassette tape, smiling that smile, preparing to speak. Ronnie has just met Icy Filet, having come to Mouse's to escape that depressing trailer, where maggots collect on the rotting food left in the kitchen before transforming into dozens and dozens of flies, where the summer smells have taken on a humid raunch, where the shade of the Sherwood Forest trailer-trees cool nothing.

"Icy as in, you know, cool, and Filet, as in, you know, our state's abbreviation?" Icy Filet had explained to Ronnie when she greeted him at the door in an oversized faded green button down long-sleeved shirt, stained and torn and obviously belonging to Mouse, shirt hung low like a miniskirt, exposing squat legs and bare feet tromping through the dirty kitchen to the perpetually cluttered living room, where they sit facing the mammoth speakers ten feet away, with Mouse in between, preparing to speak.

"Welcome, Ronnie. Now, as you know, I've been trying to write a hit song, something that will get on the airwaves. Something commercial. Something lucrative." Between right index finger and thumb, Mouse raises the cassette to his face. "This, my friends—*this!*—is the song." He steps to the stereo, left hand holding the cassette outward, right hand behind his back, looking down like a professor reaching the apex of a lecture he knows is brilliant. He dramatically turns to Ronnie and Icy Filet, points to Icy Filet, who sits "Indian-style," tugging at the shirt she wears. "But with this here lovely lady," and Mouse steps to her, leans down, kisses her on the barrette holding the frosted highlights of the ruby-dyed left-parted short hair; Icy Filet smiles, a ruby lipstick smile stretching across her face, and looks away, adjusting her cat-eye glasses. Mouse returns to the stereo, bookended by the mammoth speakers, ". . .we have the makings of a hit song, something with what they call in this business of music, crossover appeal. So without further ado, let's hear our song, and Ronnie, I look forward to seeing you blown away by this, and I look forward to hearing your thoughts."

Mouse turns, inserts the cassette, presses play. Foreboding tape hiss, then screeching white noise, followed by a slow synthetic 4/4 hip-hop beat—bass drum, snare, closed high hat cymbals opened on the eighth note after three then closed at four—repeated. A simple four note bass line on an endless loop, and then Icy Filet's voice, an awkward, lurching, talk-speak that doesn't quite lose the rhythm no matter how hard it tries:

I'm in my room watching Sanford and Son
faking heart attacks, Elizabeth it's the big one
drunk like Grady workin' power saws
eatin' baked potato with a Jell-O straw
we got astrophysicists down the hall
German swimmers and people throwin' Nerf balls
aphrodisiacs circled on my plate
do I have free will or is everything fate?

As the verses stop, the beat continues—the bass line, the white noise guitar—as Icy Filet interjects "Word" and "Aw yeah" here and there. The next verse:

Floridian Wizard of the rhyming scheme
Icy Filet is everything she seems
sortin' it out in a laundry bag
chicken fried rice and a can of Black Flag
roaches on the ceiling fishing for the sounds
of Icy Filet, Mouse, and the Get Downs
candy apple bottom with a tig ol' bittied face
like a Sharpie in your mind that can never be erased

The song soldiers on for five more seconds until the beat stops. The white noise of the guitar fades away into the tape hiss. Mouse stops the tape.

"Well?" Mouse asks, leaning in towards Ronnie, that insistent smile and subtle nod simply begging Ronnie to say it was anything less than completely brilliant.

It is ludicrous, awful, stupid, terrible, cheesy, moronic, sub-par, puerile, painful, insufferable, not-good. Ronnie clears his throat. "Completely brilliant!" he proclaims, smiling. "It sounds a lot like Beck." (In Gainesville, it is always important to tell everyone what you think everything sounds like. It shows you know what you are talking about.)

"Beck?" Icy Filet leans backwards, lightly pounds Ronnie with her tiny right fist. She pshaws. "That's bogus, yo. I mean, I like him, but that's not what I'm going for. I want to be whiter than Beck, if that's possible."

Mouse removes the cassette from the stereo, places it back inside its case, tosses the case aside, near a stack of yellowed underwear. "We'll go back to it. It has potential. Ronnie thinks so. Right, Ronnie?"

Ronnie smiles a charming used-car-salesman smile. "I do." Yes, Ronnie believes the song is horrible, but he also believes that, in a perfect world, songs as amateurishly strange as these would be the staples of commercial radio and played with the same unceasing regularity as Pink Floyd.

"Good," Mouse says, readjusting his bathrobe, a wavy flick of the wrist preventing encroaching nudity.

"What do you do, Ronnie?" Icy Filet asks, as they rise to stretch, to step out of the slovenly living room.

"He does nothing!" Mouse says, stepping into the kitchen. "It's why he has no money!"

"I'm a writer," Ronnie says. "I'm also a musician." They follow

Mouse into the kitchen, where Mouse opens three green-bottled beers while howling and laughing, "He doesn't write! His band is a hundred miles away so they never play anymore!"

"That's not true," Ronnie says, grabbing one of the cold green beer bottles from Mouse, chugging, mulling the idea that Mouse is probably right. Yes, probably.

"Mouuuuse," Icy Filet whines a scold to her newish boyfriend of two-and-a-half months, who looks as hangdog as a guy who looks like Charles Manson can look. She turns to Ronnie, puts her arm around him. "It's ok. I believe you're a writer. Do you believe I'm a rapper?"

Ronnie smiles. He can't say "No," no matter what he really thinks. "Yes. I do."

"Thank you," Icy Filet says, hugging Ronnie before grabbing the beer from Mouse's outstretched arm. "You look hungry, Ronnie. Let me order us some pizza. How does that sound?"

"Of course!" Mouse laughs. "Ronnie doesn't eat much, and he needs to."

Ronnie could not disagree. The money is gone. He would be four months behind on rent, if Alvin bothered collecting the rent, to say nothing of the other bills. Ronnie tends to blow the plasma money as soon as he gets it—on beer, on eating out, on enough gas to get to some party and back. He is tired, hungry, exhausted, can't think of tomorrow, or the day after that, and definitely not next week, and don't even mention next month. In the Sweat Jam life, you take whatever resources are at your disposal at that immediate moment and use them to your fullest advantage, to suck the most fun you can out of that moment, because, tomorrow? You will be tired, hungry, exhausted.

When the pizza arrives, Ronnie's hunger pangs temporarily retreat. He finishes the beer and eats his fill, walks into the living room, finds the cassette case dangling at the edge of the dirty underwear pile, removes the tape, places it in the stereo, hits play, then stretches out across the long-unvacuumed floor, falling asleep to the music of his friends, deep in the sleep of one who is exhausted doing absolutely nothing with his life, and having a wonderful time doing so.

WHAT PART OF "DON'T LOOK BACK" DON'T YOU UNDERSTAND?

Kelly stands in the threshold of the opened front door, watching the sprinkler's jets slowly rise, prismatic droplets refracting the sun before splattering across his crunchy parched brown lawn. He lives in the back of a 1950s subdivision in a tiny, pastel blue cinderblocked one-story house in a large corner lot. Across the street, a massive water tower hovers over everything like a UFO on the verge of shooting lasers at unsuspecting earthlings in some long-forgotten drive-in movie. High fences topped with barbed wire thick as bass guitar strings cordon off the opposite side of the street, separating the construction workers, plumbers, and mechanics who live in the neighborhood from the University of Central Florida Research Park on the other side.

Under the driveway's silver awning, a gray Volkswagen Rabbit is parked with its hood opened, perpetually awaiting whatever repair it needs to return to life. Next to the Rabbit is a brown Chevy Celebrity, jack propping up the left front tire side, also perpetually in wait for the repairs that will/might return it to the roads. In front of these on the driveway, Kelly's still-functioning rusted maroon Nissan truck. A blandy apple green four-door sedan rolls up and stops inches from the truck's downward angled rear bumper.

Ronnie shuts off the car, steps out, awaits the inevitable "Told ya so" from Kelly.

Instead, without taking his eyes off the withered brown grass, Kelly sighs, announces, "Take what you want to make sandwiches. There's beer in the fridge too."

Ronnie nods, fifteen footsteps a brittle crunch across the grass, stepping around Kelly, then entering the house. Over the sprinkler's spray, Kelly hears the opening of a beer can, the frantic rattling of glass containers, the rustling of wrapped deli meat. Shortly after this, the sounds of *The Incredible Shrinking Dickies* album on the stereo. Loud.

Kelly continues watering what remains of his lawn, wondering if anything will ever change, or if life will always go on like this, surrounded by friends living a hand-to-mouth existence filled with one or all of the following: beer, dope, acid, Xanax, roofies, mescaline, ecstasy, heroin. Time measured between shows, the once or (if we're lucky) twice a month wait, filled with work, sleep, then any or all of the preceding. Kelly watches Ronnie step out the door, a beer can in each hand, draining the first, opening the second. He is much thinner. Disheveled hair, not in the fashionable sense, but in the "two weeks in a Greyhound Bus terminal" sense. The pungent, musty smell of unwashed clothing.

"Jesus, Altamont," Kelly says, stepping back. "What the hell up and died on you in Gainesville?" He takes another step away, scrunching his gaunt face in disgust. "Besides your soul?"

"The trailer tub is covered in mildew. Mold. Dirt." Ronnie says. He walks the ten steps towards the sprinkler. He takes off his t-shirt, drops it, sets his glasses on top of it. He falls on all fours on the wet grass, leaning directly over the sprinkler, the water shooting his face and hair, wetting his hands, washing the dirt away. In the midst of all the idleness—the parties, shows, general drunkenness—the money ran dry. Therefore, reluctantly and temporarily, Ronnie went back to Orlando. He survived three and a half months without steady work, but after the pizza with Mouse and Icy Filet, he didn't eat for three days. On the third day, he made the two hour round trip walk, from the trailer off 34th Street to Mouse's first floor student ghetto apartment in that gray three story dilapidated house, to borrow twenty dollars, enough for gas money and a meal. Not even Mouse could laugh about it, or say much beyond, "Hurry up and get back here. We'll miss you, buddy," shaking his head as he stood in the living room listening to his latest recordings made with Icy Filet. Ronnie took the money, bought a double cheeseburger and fries at the Checkers behind Mouse's place, on University Avenue, ignoring the glares generated by Ronnie's smell (he stunk like the trailer now, like summer at the season's sweatiest worst) and general demeanor. From the payphone outside the Kelly's Kwik-Stop, Ronnie talked to Kelly long enough to tell him he was coming back for a little while, hung up, packed a few clothes, some books, and a journal, threw them in the car, filled up the gas tank with the money he had left, and kept the speedometer at 80 mph, forsaking the sentimental journey of olde-tyme Florida southbound 441 for the touristy blur of Interstate 75 to the Turnpike.

Ronnie crawls, even with the sprinkler's trajectory so he is always getting wet. His khaki pants turn green at the knees from the grass stains. Between the payphone call two hours ago and now, Kelly secured Ronnie a job. His neighbors own an asbestos removal business. The work is at a school near the beach. Ronnie will sleep in Kelly's spare bedroom for the next month, work the asbestos job, earn and save money. The pay is $7.50 an hour, more than Ronnie has ever been paid for anything.

Kelly goes into the house, returns with a bar of soap and a towel. "Here," he says, tossing him the soap. Ronnie lathers up.

Oh, to be clean again! Kelly tosses him beer cans as the others are drained and tossed. Drunk and drenched in the blazing summer sun, as the Dickies' cover of "Eve of Destruction" howls from the living room and out the open doors and open windows, Ronnie stands, smiles, raises a beer to the great water tower in the sky, because Florida—Central Florida—is at this moment everything it is allegedly cracked up to be. An escape. A new start. Another chance.

•

Friday night. Ronnie borrows a twenty from Kelly before Kelly leaves to his new job, night auditor at some hotel, only this time he's working in relatively safer Lake Mary—where the worst things he will deal with are one-night stands and sloppy drunk insurance salesmen unwinding after long hours of teleconferencing. Ronnie takes the twenty—promising to pay it back when that first asbestos-removal paycheck comes in—and drives off to downtown Orlando, hoping to run into anyone he knows.

Downtown Orlando in 1996 is a five block unvibrant stretch of Orange Avenue, rave clubs and meat markets populated with the most vapid people this side of southern California. Oppressive booty bass and the macho growling of scruffy alternative rock fill the desperately festive atmosphere. Bike police ride in slow predatory packs, shrieking whistles and writing tickets to jaywalkers. The homeless are cordoned off into approved "Panhandling Zones." Douchebags with Mardi Gras beads in July, screaming for no discernible reason.

Ronnie parks on a sidestreet, steps into the anti-carnival of Orange Avenue. The good times from the past attack in the unlikeliest of places: furtive makeout sessions at that ATM machine, holding hands while serenading passersby with Dead Milkmen songs on that sidewalk, fits of laughter over "you had to be there" jokes on that corner. It didn't really start to suck until this past year.

He crosses Washington Street, passing bars that used to be decent enough, past venues for live music that were now gross dance clubs. Too many memories here, and many of them good.

"Ronnie Altamont?" A familiar girl's voice yells as he waits to cross another street.

He turns around, sees his ex-girlfriend Maggie. Everything inside him spins, falls. She is with her best friend Lauren, and Lauren's boyfriend Karl. The four of them used to spend most of their waking non-working hours together, sometimes in these downtown bars, other times in each other's apartments around the University of Central Florida.

"Uh . . . hey!" Ronnie manages, followed by a strange awkward cackle that has never left his mouth before or since. "How are you guys doing?"

"I'm fine," Maggie says, tone a perfect blend of suspicion, nervousness, happiness. "What are you doing? Here, I mean." She looks around at Orange Avenue, the almost-skyscraping bank buildings, the near-bustle of the foot and car traffic, the Orwellian sounds of prefabricated leisure. "I thought you moved away finally."

God, she looks so good. The song "Little Doll" by The Stooges pops into his head, like it used to whenever he was with her. She has grown out her black hair to her shoulders, bleached the bangs, gentle waves he never had the chance to see before (she had always kept her hair short in the two years they dated, Ronnie's last two years in college), and that smile matches the suspicion, nervousness, happiness, in the voice, but it's a self-assured smile—Ronnie can contrast the smile to the anti-depressant smile of late-morning weekends—the teeth she would always try and hide because of their lack of symmetry—hated her whole body, actually—she thought her breasts were too small, her ass too bony, legs too skinny—to get pictures back from the Eckerd Drugs Photo Lab was always an ordeal of self-loathing and Ronnie's constant assuagement that she was, in fact, beautiful, because she was, goddammit. And she is. Only, now, she knows it. Purple combat boots, short plaid skirt, a tight pink t-shirt exposing a bare midriff (and a navel piercing, another new development) where between the small yet proportionate breasts there was a drawing of a retro looking female cat with long eyelashes, womanly cheeks, a jeweled necklace, a coquettish smile. Karl and Lauren stand to either side of Maggie, glaring at Ronnie—Karl in all black, and the kind of all-black that can't even be considered post-goth anymore, but the kind of all-black waiters wear at restaurants that aspire to urban chic; and Lauren, well, she has armpit hair—two black cotton candy tufts emerging from a white tank top, and that's all Ronnie notices about her—but they are no doubt remembering the last time they saw him, drunk and on roofies at some party, stumbling around in a KISS t-shirt and purple hair, Ronnie loudly, obnoxiously hitting on Lauren as they sat on the couch—awkward gropings, lunging kisses, lewd suggestions as Maggie seethed to his right and Karl seethed to Lauren's left—culminating in Ronnie yelling for a ménage à trois, or, as Ronnie called it that night, a "double-team." As in: "C'mon Lauren, double-team us! It'll be awesome! We're hip! Let's do it!" An ugly scene ensued—Karl lunging at Ronnie over the couch, Lauren running off to cry, Maggie somehow separating the two before relatively sober heads prevailed. Ronnie passing out shortly afterward was the only thing that saved him from a deserved ass-whipping. Sincere apologies and pathetic pleading accomplished little; their friendship was never the same. Ronnie and Maggie broke up less than a month later, as Ronnie fell into a foul attitude upon meeting the real world after graduation—a real world that cared nothing about his opinions or the opinion column he wrote back in school—and at the same time, Maggie, just turning 21, was beautiful enough to try anything with almost anyone, because almost anyone was nicer and newer than Ronnie was anymore.

"What am I doing here." Ronnie sighs. Throws up his hands. "I don't know." There is so much he wants to say, wishes he could say. With all the sincerity of his being, he adds, "It's great seeing all of you again."

Karl looks at his watch. Lauren yawns. "We gotta go," Maggie says, starting to walk away. "Bye, Ronnie."

"Wait!" Ronnie smiles. "Let's go to the Holy Goof Lounge. Like we used to. We'll get caught up."

Karl and Lauren are already walking away, Karl holding an upraised left middle finger behind him.

Maggie steps back. "Take care of yourself, Ronnie."

"Heyyyyyy," Ronnie says in his best Fonztones, holding out his arms. Maggie tries not to smile, hurriedly bounces the few steps needed for the hug. It isn't as long as Ronnie wants and needs, but it is long enough. The smell and the touch are so familiar, so warm and welcoming, so why can't it be like it was?

"Be good in Gainesville," Maggie says, stepping backwards, smiling at Ronnie—an unexpected smile, a tolerant, indulgent smile to their past—before turning around to catch Karl and Lauren.

"I'm trying," Ronnie yells after her. Maybe she hears him, and maybe she even believes him.

Ronnie Altamont hangs around the Holy Goof Lounge with its cavernous walls and predictably beatnik décor as the jukebox plays the soundtracks to various spy films. He stays at the empty bar long enough to guzzle three beers in ten minutes. He steps back onto Orange Avenue, into the sea of *Cat and the Hat* hatted, pacifier sucking, raver youth. He finds his car, drives back to Kelly's, eastbound through all the empty miles of Colonial Drive, to that subdivision on the opposite side of the UCF Research Park, where he will climb into a rickety guest bed, think, and not sleep.

•

John "Magic" Jensen opens the door to his first floor apartment, sees Ronnie and Kelly standing there, the traffic of four-lane Alafaya Trail whizzing twenty feet behind them.

"We-heh-heh-heh-heh-hell," Magic says. "We-heh-heh-heh-heh-heh-heh-heh-heh-heh-hell. We-heh-heh-heh-heh-heh-heh-heh-heh-heh-heh-heh-heh-heh-heh-heh-hell."

"Shaddap," Ronnie says, smiling.

"The prodigal son returns," Magic says, arms akimbo. "We-heh-heh-heh-heh-heh-heh-heh-heh-heh-hell ... "

Ronnie and Kelly step around him, into the living room. Saturday night. Beers at Magic's before leaving for a collegiate party. A left turn from the entryway, and it's the familiar smells of old cigarette smoke and stale junk food matching up perfectly to how Ronnie remembers this hazy long rectangle of a living room. Stained uncleanable brown carpeting, flashing Christmas tree lights running around the top, MC Escher prints on the walls everywhere you turn, broken up only by the collage art poster from the Dead Kennedys album *Fresh Fruit for Rotting Vegetables.* The L-shaped blue couches—sagging, cat-clawed and burn-holed. The stereo plays The Flaming Lips. The television plays *Saved by the Bell.*

A right turn from the entryway, and it's the fluorescent kitchen, with its gray walls covered in thrown pasta strands stuck like flat yellow hairballs, the unintentional science projects lurking in abandoned pots and pans on the stove, the case of Dusch Light in the fridge. Ronnie and Kelly go straight to the otherwise empty white Kenmore.

"To old time's sake," Kelly toasts, one cold damp easily-dented can into the other.

"To a regression to blissfully banal college weekends," Ronnie toasts.

Magic stops laughing, steps into the kitchen, opens the fridge. "To dreadful parties filled with South Florida rich kids in striped Tommy shirts playing drinking games around coffeetables until someone inevitably throws up."

"Ah, college memories," Kelly says, and everyone laughs.

Andrew "Randy Macho Man" Savage sees Ronnie and Kelly from the opposite side of the rectangled apartment, sets aside the

whizzing Spin Art machine and the yellow paint he's been gloop-
ing into it, runs towards them.

"Ronnie!" he yells, kissing Ronnie on the lips. "Oh wow! It's
so great you're here! This is going to be the best night ever!" He
grabs a glass from the cabinet, pours water, drinks, runs back to
the Spin Art machine.

"Ecstasy," Magic says. "But he didn't buy enough to share."
Ronnie laughs, watching Randy Macho Man as he follows the
splotchy yellow circles the Spin Art machine makes with each
drip and drop, sweating even more than is normal on a Florida
summer evening, eyes involuntarily rolling upward, but smiling,
always smiling.

"So. Yeah," Magic says, standing in the kitchen, hunched like
he's too tall for the kitchen's short ceiling. "You better get ready,
Ronnie. This party is going to be so great, you'll move back here,
post-haste."

The three of them move to the L-shaped couch. "So did you
find a job up there yet?" Magic asks.

"No," Ronnie says, feeling the familiar contours of the couch,
cushions that rewarded slouching.

"That's great, man!" Randy Macho Man says, running from
the kitchen and back every two minutes, filling and refilling
a green glass of water. Ronnie sits between Kelly and Magic,
Randy sits on the small part of the L-shaped couch, twitching
with joy.

"So basically you're the same brokeass you were before, only
now you're doing it a hundred miles away?" Magic asks. Kelly
laughs at this. "And this is why the band is over? And this is why
you've moved back?"

Ronnie sighs, chugs five greedy gulps from the silver Dusch Light can. "I can't stand it here. Gainesville's better. By far."

"I love both places!" Randy Macho Man says, sweating and rolling his eyes to the back of his head. "You should buy some X, stop arguing, go to this party, meet some women."

"Quite the to-do list," Magic says.

"Goddamn UCF sausage parties," Kelly says, and nobody disagrees.

"I wanna kill this case before we leave," Magic says, crushing the empty Dusch Light with his fist. "I want to be good and drunk before I get there . . . "

. . . And really now, there isn't much that's more pathetic than drinking too much before a party to the point that you can't go to the party. Magic broke out the stooge pills, and now it's a black gap of four hours later, and there is no party, and it's only Ronnie driving Kelly back to his house, rambling on about, "If this was Gainesville, we could have walked to that stupid party, but you gotta drive everywhere here."

"Don't blame me because Magic had stooge pills," Kelly says, in and out of consciousness in the passenger seat, weaving forward and back, side to side, with every bend and bump in Alafaya Trail.

"Yeah, yeah—too many stooge pills, too many crap drugs . . . did you see it in there?"

"Yeah, I saw it. I see it every weekend."

"Mumbling slurring idiots, and Randy acting like everything was the greatest thing ever."

"So nothing's changed since you left."

"No. It hasn't." Ronnie drives down Alafaya Trail, past his jungled alma mater, the bright shiny new apartment complexes and the bright shiny new plazas and hotels. They enter Kelly's neighborhood. "Meh, the party would've been boring anyway."

"Yup."

A throb and a drain as the beer and stooge pills leave the body. The empty 4:00 a.m. streets, weaving through the verdure.

"It's all over here," Ronnie says. "I mean, I admit that I did have some great times, you know? The school, my column, you guys, Maggie, everything? That campus over there . . . it used to be mine. So many warm afternoons doing nothing but writing, skipping class, sitting by the reflecting pond, talking to girls. Right when you settle in—comfortable—the world changes and it's another flying leap into the unknown. The time is too short, too short. And transitional times like these, Kelly. Do we grow up? Get older? Mature? Evolve? What? I can't go back. It can't be done. What will happen to us? Do you wanna be the 25-year-old suburban burnout who buys Bacardi for the high school party? Of course not. Do I wanna be a 40-year-old with a mohawk? Fuck no! I mean, it's just, what are we supposed to do here, in this too-short life filled with these tiny epochs you're always having to shed? What do you think?"

Kelly snores, mouth agape, leaning against the passenger window, drooling.

"Well. Alright then," Ronnie says, as they pull into Kelly's driveway. He leaves him in the car, unlocks the front door with the key hidden beneath the welcome mat, stumbles and lurches through the house to the guest bedroom, climbs in, passes out/ falls asleep.

ASBESTOS REMOVAL FOR PROFIT AND CHARACTER BUILDING . . . THE BEST PLACE FOR THE PUSSY . . . STRIKING OUT IN THE BUSH LEAGUES . . . LOST ON THE FREEWAY AGAIN

"Cain't ya see? Ohhhhcain't ya see? What that woman! She been doin' to me!"

Every bright beautiful morning, the undeniable smell of old spitcups, and the sounds of The Marshall Tucker Band's *Greatest Hits* playing from a worn cassette. Eastbound on I-4, watching the billboards scroll by with oversaturated regularity. Up ahead, the asbestos removal gig, in some elementary school in sleazy old Daytona Beach. Ronnie rides bitch in a dirty white pickup truck between two recent high school graduates with soccer scholarships named Tommy and Bassanovich. Neither can harmonize, but the sentiment is clearly heartfelt as they wail "Cain't ya see? Whoa whooooa cain't ya see? What that bitch! She been doin' to me-heeee!"

The job interview was a formality. Kelly got him the job. The bosses, a husband and wife three houses down from Kelly, were cheerful enough. They were more southerners than Floridians, which meant that when they asked "How're yew?" they actually meant it. The State of Florida required all prospective asbestos removers to take a test showing knowledge of asbestos, its power, its evil, and once Ronnie sat in that yellowed warehouse office and watched the required Nixon-era slideshow about the dangers of asbestos, he was sent off to work with the other "College kids like you," as A.Q., the husband boss, told him, and Ronnie didn't feel like correcting him.

So Ronnie rides between Tommy and Bassanovich—between two soccer scholarship earners leaving for school in Kansas somewhere within the month. Tommy always drives. He has the lanky grace of a forward, which he is. Bassanovich has the squat strength of a goalkeeper, which he is. It is impossible to determine their hair color or style, as they both are never without blue ball caps pulled down over their foreheads. They try growing five o'clock shadows, but their faces are still stuck in a baby-smooth 2:30 in the afternoon.

Every morning, they pass the Speedway, then get close enough to the beach to smell it—out there somewhere beyond the garish hotels forming a pastel wall between the land and the sea. Living in Central Florida is the feeling of having to work while the rest of the world vacations.

In the summer, the asbestos removal gigs are in schools. The buildings are from the 1950s, and the floor tiles are always old, urine-hued, and presumably asbestosy. The school they are driving towards is in the middle of a rundown Florida beach neighborhood of tiny duplexes and dirt front yards.

Asbestos removal is, theoretically, simple: Remove every single floor tile from the school—the classrooms, hallways, offices, storage rooms, bathrooms, auditoriums, gymnasiums—so there is no longer even the slimmest chance of kids breathing in and catching asbestosis. The tiles are removed using special heating machines. Ronnie, Tommy, and Bassanovich each have their own machine. There is a metal handle on each pushcart. In front of the handle is a green console with digital times and readouts of the temperature of the heating unit. Between the four wheels is the three-floor-tile-by-three-floor-tile heating unit, three inches thick. When the machine is hot enough, they push over nine floor tiles, waiting the 15-45 seconds it takes to melt them and unglue the tiles from the concrete floor beneath. When melted (discernible by a death-like tinge of burning black smoke), the machines are rolled to the next nine tiles, and as these are heated up, they grab long metal scrapers and force them under the melted tiles until the tiles are scraped away.

Sometimes, it is like "flipping pancakes" (the oft-repeated comparison during the training session), but other times, to Ronnie, it is like scraping blackened and burnt asbestosis-laden death by chemical warfare, especially when the tiles cling stubbornly to the floor below. It is scraping and occasionally stabbing the floortiles. When separated from the floor, the tiles are placed in black garbage bags covered in skull and crossbones warnings re: the toxic waste contained inside.

"Hey Altamont," Tommy asks as the three of them stab with their metal scrapers at a particularly nasty patch of tiles stubbornly glued to the dark concrete flooring of a second grade classroom. "How's the pussy in Gainesville?"

Working in a dude squad scene like this, sweaty with an idle brain, of course they're going to talk women. Something about the question struck Ronnie as absurd. Like equating pussy with the weather, or fishing, but it was no time to be cerebral, so he shook his head from side to side like he was imagining this second grade classroom, with its A-Z penmanship lessons scrolled around the upper walls, its blackboards, its overhead projector, its cartoon animals offering sage wisdom on everything from crossing the street to washing your hands, was full of vagina—a pulsing pink sea of orgasmic vaginas gaping and spreading.

"You know the best place for the pussy?" Bassanovich says between grunts as they continue stabbing at the floor tiles that will not break, will not melt, will not separate from the floor.

"Where?" Ronnie was genuinely curious.

"Lincoln, Nebraska," Bassanovich answers.

"Really?" Ronnie wants to laugh, but for all he knows—seeing how he's never been to Nebraska—Bassanovich could be right.

"Yeah man! That's what the other players told us when we visited their campuses last spring. They say the pussy there is like . . . like swarms of flies."

"Flies with tits," Tommy adds.

Ronnie thinks of Gainesville girls, horny work thoughts, as he counts down the days until he can go back.

The summer sun is unrelentingly brutal, reflecting off the cars and the sandy yards surrounding the school. The work is hard, but it feels good to do something physical, something that does not require thought. To do something—anything—after months of latent, dormant energy dissipated in unlucrative pursuits.

At 3:30, the work is done. The rides to Orlando are the same as the morning rides to Daytona, only they are tired, and there is more traffic. Everything about I-4 reminds Ronnie of the past, of high school road trips to and from the beach, goofing off in backseats while a friend drives, blasting The Who as Ronnie stares into a girl's eyes, some bronzed flirtatious Florida girl starting to learn of the power her body wields, Ronnie as among the first of many in a long line of teenage wastelanders at the mercy of mania and confusion and angst and various internal and external forces seemingly beyond their control.

Now, it is dirtier, sweatier, and definitely minus girls—only old Big Gulp cups half-filled with tobacco juice (this is the summer when Tommy and Bassanovich take up chewing tobacco), and the Marshall Tucker Band singing "Heard it In a Love Song," until the familiar Colonial Drive exit appears, and it is back to Kelly's, to scribbled journals and television, X-ing off another day until his return to Gainesville.

•

The Daytona gig was finished. A.Q. transferred the boys to the schools of Crescent City, Florida. One hour north of DeLand. Forty-five minutes southeast of Palatka. Near Pierson, San Mateo, and Welaka. Never heard of it? Well, sorry about your luck, and you obviously know nothing of bass fishing, because Crescent City is "The Bass Fishing Capital of the World."

They were put up in a motel along the shores of a beautifully large blue and presumably bass-filled lake, with ten dollars per diem for meals. All Ronnie cared about was that he was one hour closer to Gainesville.

Before leaving, Kelly gave Ronnie a gift: A gray typewriter he stole from the hotel where he now worked.

"Don't you worry they're going to miss it, and suspect you?" Ronnie asked as he received the gift.

"Not really," was Kelly's answer, and that was enough to satisfy Ronnie. "Just put it to good use when you get back to Gainesville."

With that, Ronnie got into his car and left Orlando, bags packed, with no intention—seriously this time, like not even for a week or a month or anything—of ever going back to live.

In Crescent City, the hours are too long—12 to 14 hour days of scraping and stabbing and pounding on old-ass floor tiles in eerily vacant classrooms—to fraternize with locals and to find out what was beyond Crescent City's small-town façade. Crescent City, for Ronnie, was work, in miserable humidity heightened by the green machine's 500-degree temperatures melting the tiles. Crescent City was horrid, shitty work in quiet backwoods, and with each passing day, Ronnie loved it, more and more.

Not necessarily the work itself, but the work ethic. The effort felt good. Necessary. Thoughts while working hard like this, so clear now: The novel was unpublishable. It was awful. *The Big Blast for Youth* was awful. The Laraflynnboyles were over. The tour wouldn't happen. It didn't matter. There will be new books, new bands. Ronnie will return to Gainesville, buff from all the work, with legions of adoring women suddenly noticing him, noticing his pockets stuffed with cash for the first time . . . There would be no more brooding. The discoveries of life would happen through doing rather than thinking, and if these long hours weren't "doing," nothing was, even if asbestos removal wasn't exactly a career path Ronnie would seriously consider, even if this would be over soon. Because, before Crescent City, Ronnie was unsure of whether or not he could actually bust his ass at something. At anything. Now he knew he could, as the sweat poured and muscles ached and the curses rained upon the stubborn floor tiles as Ronnie, Tommy, and Bassanovich stabbed with their metal scrapers.

Beyond these lucid epiphanies, Ronnie, Tommy and Bassanovich filled the endless hours with talk, lies usually, of this girl or that girl they banged that one time. Then, Ronnie would buy beer and whiskey, and together they drank and life was one big dream for the future, a future filled with soccer, of touring bands, of records and goalllls and songs. There was no room for doubt.

Spit cups filled. When the booze kicked in, Ronnie played his guitar, and all three sang the classic rock Tommy or Bassanovich would request, culminating in:

"Cain't ya see? Ohhhh cain't ya see? What that bitch! She been doin' to me-heeeeee!" Nobody else stayed at the motel, so it was easy to be loud, to sing out to the silence, as the sun set beyond the IGA grocery store across the street. And when the booze really kicked in, they would make up their own songs, songs with titles like "Asbestos Removing Motherfucker Blues" or "No Pussy in Crescent City." When the exhaustion of the day matched the drunkenness of the night, they would pass out as Olympic athletes competing in Atlanta won or lost on TV. After not enough sleep, they would start it all over again, waking up to the phone's jarring wake-up call.

·

"Oh," Randy Macho Man adds. "Also, Tara's moving in with me. We wanna get serious."

Sometimes, others have to tell you things you already know. Things you don't want to admit to yourself.

"I quit," Ronnie says, hanging up the phone. Not that booking the tour was going all that swimmingly anyway—expensive motel calls to far-away cities and various show booking punk rock types with varying levels of sincerity, forthrightness, and competence. He rolls off the bed, stands, looks out the front windows at the empty motel parking lot, the quiet road, the streetlights illuminating the late summer silence.

At the Denny's in Gainesville, that post-show brunch where they sat in silence save for the occasional pleas to return to Orlando, Ronnie knew it was over, but he kept mailing off cassette recordings, kept bugging these people listed in the *Maximumrockan-droll* "Book Your Own Fucking Life" directory who set up shows in clubs, basements, living rooms, trailers, drive-ins, Laundromats, wherever. Long gone were those calls between Ronnie and Magic, when they'd dream and plan and practically be on stage already, in Chicago, in each city, playing, touring, living this dream Ronnie has had since forever. Of course, the drummer would be the one to overtly flake out on the whole thing—tracking down Ronnie in his Crescent City motel hermitage to tell him that like he's gotta work, dude, and that like it's time and money he doesn't have and not only that but you don't even live here anymore anyway so what's the point? Ronnie could hang up on Macho Man Randy, could curse him and all drummers as flaky and flighty and completely unreliable, but in the end, all Macho Man Randy did was tell a truth no one else would verbalize. Magic was too passive-aggressive to say anything. Ronnie was too deluded.

Ronnie grabs his guitar, opens the front door, sits on the motel sidewalk and strums. Tommy and Bassanovich had left an hour before to check out the night life of Crescent City. Ronnie, down-stroking Ramones chords, listening to them bounce off the emptiness of the teal and salmon stucco of the motel, off the palm trees, the swamps, the lakes, the bass inside the lakes, guitar sounds as incongruous to the environment as Ronnie felt. "53rd and 3rd" was a long way from Crescent City, Florida.

Ronnie strums, thinks back to six years ago, to June of 1990, of entering Club Space Fish night at the Beach Club for the very first time, leaving the quiet of open black suburban night space for downtown, on westbound I-4, parking on Magnolia, walking up Washington to Orange, and hearing the live music for the first time, screaming out of the amps from the tiny stage, and it was nervous like anything's nervous the first time you do it, but really, it felt right, to be seventeen and seeing bands, and Ronnie laughs at how they would mosh, even to bands who weren't really moshing bands, but they thought that's what you were supposed to do, and enough people joined in that it wasn't the worst thing that they moshed like that, and the way the last band played, the way they jumped and sweated and yelled and sang and lost themselves in the moment, opened up this new reality for Ronnie: more than anything, he wanted to be on that stage, he wanted to be the one with the guitar singing and strumming and playing his own songs, in his own band, with friends who rehearse in spare bedrooms littered with empty beer cans and obligatory posters of inspirational bands and playboy centerfolds and all the usual crap bands hang on walls for inspiration or humor or horniness' sake. And that last band who played . . . what happened to them? Nothing. That's what happened. They quit. They got regular jobs. If they're not married in 1996, they will be married soon enough, with kids and a mortgage to follow. If that's what happened to them, why would The Laraflynnboyles—a band nowhere near as good, Ronnie readily admits—be any different? What did Ronnie think would happen? It was a band started for fun—in college—and now that college is wrapping up, to continue is pointless. Years later, once he will actually finally go on tour, Ronnie will realize that to tour with Magic and Macho Man Randy would have been a goddamn nightmare. But here in Crescent City, Ronnie strums Ramones chords and feels as lost as he did as a teenager, sitting in his room strumming Ramones chords—lonely, bandless, directionless. He needs to play in bands. More than writing, it gives him an identity, a social outlet, a creative outlet. Without bands, Ronnie is depressed, unfocused.

Tommy and Bassanovich return with a 12-pack of Old Hamtramck and a fifth of Floridian Comfort whiskey, Tommy tall enough and therefore old-enough-looking to pull off the ID that says he's 22.

"Might as well've stayed here, for all we could find going on," Bassanovich says, leaning against the back of the truck as Ronnie plays.

Ronnie says nothing, only stopping the strumming long enough to sip from the whiskey bottle passed around, to sip from the beer can to his right. Between the life he had in Orlando, and the life he sorta-has in Gainesville, there's the Crescent City life of right-now, of finding that the only way to bury all thoughts of going nowhere fast is to move, to do, to be, and even if that doing and being was playing random riffs from the first four Ramones albums all night, as the rural stars glitter overhead and the stirring sounds of the Olympics blare from the television behind, so be it. Through callouses and blisters and sweat and soreness and perceived exhaustion you work, and you work, and you work, with nothing behind and not much ahead.

•

"Ok, Mom, so, the tour's not happening, and you were right, about all of it. Happy?"

"Of course we're not happy! Didn't want to burst your bubble, but—c'mon. You knew. You had to have known."

". . ."

"Ronnie."

"..."

"Ronnie."

"What, Mom."

"Where are you."

"Crescent City."

"What?"

"Work."

"You live there."

"No. I'm going back to Gainesville now. Why, I don't know, but it's the best option."

"We'll book you a flight. For here. For home. "

"South Carolina isn't my home."

"Where we live. You can stay with us 'til you get back on your feet."

"I'm on my feet. I'm packed up and headed back to Gainesville. Talk soon."

•

No hope! / See? That's what gives me guts! That was The Minutemen lyric bouncing around Ronnie's head, as he leaves Crescent City, the Bass Fishing Capital of the World, for Gainesville, Money Magazine's "Best Place to Live" for 1996.

After fourteen consecutive days of asbestos removal, it was the end of womanless summer, and there was nothing left to say to Tommy and to Bassanovich but to wish them luck with college, with soccer, and yes, with the pussy.

"And good luck with the bands and the writing," Tommy says before they got into their vehicles to put many miles of wasabi green fields, jungles, and ferneries between them and Crescent City, Florida, through tiny towns with churches, Circle K's, roadhouses, down two-lane lonely roads. Ronnie nods a thanks, feeling no hope nor optimism, as far as music and writing are concerned. For so many, adulthood happens when the dream dies. It's worked away, it's drunk away, it's put away in the back of closets, passed on to children, posted as distant memories in photo albums and computers.

Still, Ronnie isn't there yet. That's what he thinks. Ahead, Gainesville, somewhere at the end of this westbound county road, below this brilliant Florida sunset dotted with pink and violet clouds and that massive orange Florida summer sun that never goes out quietly. Ahead, a temporary solution. Ahead, a place to flounder. Ahead, a place to give up these ambitions, to stop trying and to see what—if anything—emerges.

Lost and uncertain, Gainesville is all Ronnie Altamont has.

THREE: FALL (BUT NOT REALLY)

*"I gave my ring to you (wahh-oooo) / with all of my har-heart /
you said that you loved me (wahhh-oooo) / said we'd never par-hart /
are we really going steady? (wahh-oooo) / or was I just a foo-oo-ool
from the stah-hart (wah wah wah oooo)."*
—King Uszniewicz and His Uszniewicztones

GAINESVILLE GIRLS: 1996-1997

With your pocket flasks of vodka, and your shaved heads, your
pink/black/green/red dyed locks, your granny glasses and your
indie-rock cassettes, your dad's burnt sienna Le Sabre, your old
maroon softball t-shirts from Goodwill, your bikes you ride, your
feminist theory, holding hands with each other at shows to keep
the boys away, working the counters of Gatorroni's, Floridian
Bistro, Sister Chorizo, El Jalapeño del Gordo, your pills and your
shitty drugs, your Doc Martens, your memorized jade tree lyrics written in long lines inside cassettes instead of broken up
into verse/chorus/bridge/repeat, the stories behind the tattoos
on your arms, legs, shoulders, lower back, left ass cheek, right
ass cheek, chest, stomach, mons pubis, your boyfriend's bands,
your ex-boyfriend's bands, your ex-girlfriend's bands, your old
band, the band you're trying to start now, the languages you're
learning, your major, your minor, the films you've seen, the
books you've read, your soy pot roast bubbling in the crockpot,
cheat on me, cheat on you, your nude bodies in early morning

showers after one-night stands, your lost Zippos, your laughter, your idealism, your pettiness, your practiced posture and your ever-watchful eye from the barstool of an outdoor patio, your Hal Hartley video collection, your phone numbers ripped from the pages of spiral notebooks, your bass guitars propped in the corners of your bedrooms, your tolerance of empty wallets and afternoon laziness, your summer roadtrips to the big cities of the north and west, that southern accent you put on the "o" in "Chicago," your bathroom party secrets, the packets of cocaine you rummage your purse in search of, the patches safetypinned to your backpack, your back windows covered in bumperstickers, your kisses, your tongues, your hands, your rejections, your friendship, your fights, your conversations, your hopes and future plans over malt liquor on the roof, looking at the constellations while listening to the quiet sounds of the neighborhood below.

RONNIE AND MAUX

"Don't do that," Maux says, shoving Ronnie away. "I hate holding hands."

Deeper into the student ghetto, weaving in forward and lateral lurches through the narrow streets and dilapidated southern houses with their warped front porches and peeling paint, the silence taking over from the party sounds—Ronnie's housewarming party—behind them (sounds of drained kegs and gossip, uptempo drums ricocheting off the houses, Paul standing in the middle of NW 4th Lane yelling "You're leaving?! Your own party?! Now?! But we're going to Denny's, ya sellout! How can you leave your own party when we're going to Denny's?! You're a sellout, Altamont! A sellout!")

Back and forth, they pass Maux's hip flask of straight Van Veen Vodka back and forth, a cold stainless steel silver reflecting the streetlights like flashbulbs, flask's contents a cheap burning inside their bloodstreams. In the darkness, the brittle thwack of palm fronds and the shush-shush of the sand pines through the languid Florida breezes. Ronnie loves the Florida nights most of all, and these are the nights he will miss when he finally gets it together to leave.

"So. Your boyfriend. He's cool with this?' Ronnie asks as she leads him onward through the parking lot of her studio apartment building.

"That's a stupid question," Maux says, and Ronnie laughs, because he knows it's a stupid question, and furthermore, duh, he doesn't care about the answer. Boyfriend or not, after a woman-less summer coupled with a long night of downing cup after cup of Old Hamtramck keg beer followed by pocket flask vodka swills, Ronnie is in no condition to argue or even think this could be anything less than a brilliant turn of events.

"We broke up tonight," Maux continues, leading him up the clangy stairs. "I just haven't told him yet."

"And this is why I live here," Ronnie thinks. "And this is why I love Gainesville." One moment, you're in the kitchen of your new house, trying to make this girl laugh, this nnnugget with her in-digo skirt and indigo blouse and indigo hair and emerald tie, because you know her scowling is all one big ridiculous act the way everybody needs to have one big ridiculous act to stand out, as she stands there around the keg talking about how she hates this and that, thinks the band playing in the living room (Ronnie's new living room) sucks, and this sucks and that sucks, and Ronnie laughs at her, because he knows it's an act, and she knows he knows, but he is a new face in town, and even if this Ronnie is too much of a goof to be suckered by her persona, Maux still knows he is hers, anytime she wants, like any boy in this pathetic town is hers, and as Ronnie laughs at her snarled list of hatreds and responds by breakdancing—by backspinning and pop locking and moonwalking around the kitchen on the grimy hardwood floor as the impassioned and overwrought emo band plays in the living room, Maux knows, all she has to do, is look down at Ronnie when the backspin stops, look into his eyes through those ugly glasses and say, "This party sucks. Let's go." And that's what it's about here in Gainesville. One moment you're doing all that, and the next, you're led by the arm by this nnnugget with indigo everything through her dark living room, kicking bottles and stepping on paperback books before stopping and finding lips in the pitch black, kissing in some dump that smells like old cigarette ash and spilled gut-rot booze.

Maux leads Ronnie to the bed. They continue kissing, and here comes the groping, the tentative but not-that-tentative post-awkward post-collegiate movements of hands towards the good stuff, the sweet stuff, the pa pa pa oo mau mau papa ooo mau m-mau stuff as the vertical prepare to shift to horizontal . . .

"Did you hear that?" Maux whispered, turning towards the door.

"No," Ronnie lied.

"That knocking? There it is again."

Ok, ok, Ronnie did hear the heavy throbbing pound at the front door. "Don't answer it." Ronnie says, knowing it's either the friends who saw him leave with Maux who want to laugh at him for going home with her, or else it's Maux's ex-boyfriend who doesn't know he's an ex-boyfriend. "Seriously. Stay here and don't answer it," Ronnie says, hands on shoulders.

"Oh, I'm answering, Ronnie Altamont," Maux says, wiggling free from Ronnie's clutches, rolling off the bed, tromping off across the cluttered floor, kicking books and bottles along the way. "Yeah. I'm answering."

Ronnie opens his eyes. Stares upward at the darkness. "Don't let him in!" he yells.

"Who is it?" Maux barks, voice like a bratty almost-pubescent boy's.

"You know who it is! Let me in!" a cracking, slurring, young male voice whines from the other side of that door.

"Don't open it," Ronnie whispers, pulling the covers over his face. "Don't open it."

"Stop pounding!"

"I'm sorry!" A tear-choked voice implores from the other side of the door.

"I don't care!"

"Are you with someone?" A whine, a moan, a sniffle.

"Yes! I don't want to see you anymore. Go home!"

"But I'm sorry!" Full-fledged crying.

"You didn't do anything! Just . . . go home. Write an emo song about it . . . something. Just go."

Maux trudges back to the bedroom. There's one last loud pound on the door, followed by a soft slap, a hand skidding downward, one graceless kick, and that's it. Ronnie stares into the darkness, all the keg beer and bargain bin vodka churning and swooshing in his bloodstream. The room spins clockwise for a revolution, then spins counterclockwise for another revolution. This is what it's all supposed to be about, Ronnie thinks. I moved here to be in beds like these, with girls like these. What does all of this mean? Ronnie laughs.

"What's so funny?" Maux says as she enters the bedroom, climbs into bed.

"It's all very funny," Ronnie says. "And you're a nnnnnugget."

"And you're drunk," Maux answers. She pulls him in. "Sleep with me tonight, ok? Sleep?"

Ronnie nods, realizes it's too dark for Maux to see his nod, laughs again, says "Ok."

"Why are you laughing?"

"Nothing, man." Ronnie yawns. "Good night, lady."

Ronnie turns away from Maux, broods on his life, not as a sweat jam, but as a series of ridiculous, obligatory, meaningless exploits. Growing up, you don't think you'll be this lost, this adrift. You think everything will follow neat patterns from school to marriage to career. It isn't until later that it makes sense to be in strange beds in strange towns.

The booze takes that gnarly late-night stop at a crossroads where you can either pass out brooding this way, or act out through ranting, violence, and unleashed unashamed emotions that way. Like that kid—whoever that was—banging on the door. For Ronnie and Maux, the moment, the potential, is shot for tonight, and there is no getting it back.

Besides, Ronnie wants to pass out and deal with it in the morning. And so he does.

THE NEXT MORNING. A TOUR OF THE MYRRH HOUSE.
THIS IS ROGER. HE IS RONNIE'S NEW ROOMMATE.
HE WILL TELL"THE TALE OF THE PORTRAIT OF OTIS"
BEFORE RONNIE AND MAUX LEAVE FOR THE BEACH.

"Let's go to the beach," Maux says to Ronnie first thing after coughing and hacking out of dreamless sleep, the noon sunshine bashing through the shut blinds and closed black curtains. "I need to get out of here."

She flings the thin white holey blanket—this sad childhood relic resplendent in faded rainbows, unicorns, and pleasant elderly wizards—away from Ronnie's aching head and sluggish body.

Ronnie grunts, moans, opens his eyes, studies Maux's face, sideways, from the left. The morning sun's glare off her indigo hair is beautiful, he thinks. Through the fatigue of the hangover, she is as beautiful as she was the night before, with that short-cropped hair and pale skin and dark eyes. Ronnie is profoundly relieved.

"C'mon, jerk. Wake up!" she says through vodka breath, slapping him lightly on the right side of his face. Her voice is like the voice of those weasely kids you always find riding in the back rows of middle school busses, the kids who poke holes in the seats with their pencils and yell "Faggot!" at pedestrians waiting to walk across the intersections.

"Naw, babe," Ronnie moans in a manner he thinks of as "Dylanesque." "I wanna stay heeeere. With yewwwww."

Maux rolls onto her back. "Don't call me 'babe.' I hate that word."

Ronnie heaves forward, sits up, arms wrapped around legs. "That doesn't surprise me." He looks around, thinking how you can't beat waking up in a girl's bedroom when you're marginally hungover on a weekend afternoon, even when her floor is covered in inside-out t-shirts, crumpled jeans, sparkled skirts, discarded paperbacks, colored pencils, overturned tampon boxes, spare change, the walls tacked with dozens of pencil drawings on pages ripped from sketchbooks—angry, belligerent scribbles, caricatures of the old and the young of Gainesville.

"I've seen your stuff," Ronnie says, looking around. "In the school paper."

"My stuff?"

"Yeah, you know, your drawings."

"Oh," she says, sitting up. "*Those*." She swivels left, plants her feet on the floor, stands, pulls her slept-in indigo skirt downward. "I'm not happy with any of that."

"I liked what I saw," Ronnie says. "I mean, it's funny and—"

"And I don't wanna talk about it," Maux interrupts. "I just wanna go to the beach. Is that too much to ask?"

Ronnie laughs, yawns, drawls, "Naw. It isn't."

"Then get up and get out of here so I can change, then we'll go to your house, get your shit, and go already."

"Yup," Ronnie says, terribly amused by all of this.

Maux now wears a white t-shirt over a pink one-piece swimsuit, cutoff shorts, sockless low-cut green Chucks. It's a quick walk to Ronnie's from Maux's dreary motelish apartment building—across two parking lots, a trodden grass trail between apartment complexes, NW 12th Street, and then NW 4th Lane, a small block of four old houses. Ronnie's is the biggest on the block, in the middle, on the right. A patch of dirt separates the gravelly road from the front door.

The front windows are bordered with chipped blue paint on the rotting sills. The exterior of the house is white vinyl with fake vertical grain. Two locks open with a rusty twisting. The door creaks in that way particular to old warped wooden doors painted in sloppy gloopy dark red stain.

The upper half of the front door is a large window framed by the red. Covering this dirt-smudged, spider-cracked window is a poster of Myrrh, a quartet from the exurbs of Detroit, Michigan who played a militant left-wing prog rock in the late-1960s (their first record, eponymously titled, spelled out "Myrrh" with bongs; their second, "Myrrh II," was a close-up painting of a woman's tongue on which the members of Myrrh posed, standing on a square tab of acid), a clean-living yet still wild and spontaneous group of hard rockers in the 1970s, a commercially viable band of hair balladeers in the 1980s, and militant right-wing militiamen slash children's hunting-camp counselors in the 1990s—"The Myrrh Militiamen," to be exact—who relocated to Montana and advocated the imprisonment, for treason, of (to quote one of their manifestoes) "President Clinton, and her husband!," occasionally resurfacing these days to cut albums of bland anthems about the sanctity of the Second Amendment and other far-right verities. Ronnie had long been fascinated by this band—more for their epic journey from one end of the political spectrum to the other than for their music—and had sent away years ago for a series of brochures they'd published, featuring lots of pictures of kids "Ages 7-17!" pointing and shooting rifles at painted targets ranging from hippies, to Muslims, to butch lesbians. "Fun for the whole wang-dang-sweet-blood-thang family!" the brochures promised, referencing one of Myrrh's most famous hits that is still a staple of classic rock radio. But his poster—a joke birthday present from Maggie two years ago—was from Myrrh's 1960s acid rock heyday: In stark black and white, four stone heavy late-era clearly nonpacifist hippies standing in front of an American flag, right fists upraised in the Black Power salute, left fists clutching burning draft cards, shirtless in tight jeans, button flies unbuttoned enough to show there's no underwear where underwear should be, long unkempt hair, guitars at their feet covered in paintings of Mao and Marx and Lenin, and in the uneven black block lettering of the 1960s hippie press mimeograph, the words, "MYRRH WANTS NIXON'S CORPSE."

The poster hung, their house became the Myrrh House. That poster represented, to Ronnie's mind, something like the ultimate symbol of 1990s-youth awareness of the cultural cesspool that was the 20th century. Pop culture was the most accessible target. Ronnie saw the 1990s—and obviously he wasn't the only one—as a final kiss-off to the stupidity and mediocrity of prior decades. The smug laughter and sneering excitement that used to possess Ronnie and Maggie when they hit the thrift stores and came across anything Myrrh-related was only a small example of this, as the Great Alternative Nation, heralded by Nirvana et. al, temporarily won the neverending battle for cultural supremacy over everything that dominated before it, and for "the kids" who cared about such things, this meant going to sleep at night secure in the knowledge that they would never be stupid and mediocre enough to buy into anything as ephemeral as the crap people valued in the '80s, '70s, '60s, '50s, even as so many others went around dressing in bell bottoms, or as mods, or as rockers, or as Bettie Page . . .

Through the front door of the Myrrh House, a large wide rectangle of a living room, easily large enough to accommodate 100 people crammed in to watch two to three bands, under high ceilings stained with (Ronnie would come to find out) rat piss. To the right, a wobbly end table where the cordless phone charges next to the answering machine. On the other side of this, a dusty yellow loveseat left behind by the previous tenants, one of those thrift store pieces that always look like they've been upholstered with your grandmother's bathroom wallpaper; this in the corner by the steps up to Ronnie's bedroom. To the left of the front door, the drumset and amplifiers from last night huddle together, the sole remnant of last night's mess. Six large windows line the left wall, separated by peeling white plaster. Bombastic dark trim runs along the floor, borders the windows, and with the deep reddish brown of the hardwood flooring—remarkably solid compared to the usual cracks and creaks in student ghetto flooring—the overall look of the living room is that of a shabby Rocky Mountain ski lodge from 1979.

Along the right of the room, past Ronnie's bedroom doorway, a large long rectangular mirror over a mantle too ornate for such a crumbling house. Assorted French New Wave film posters, Roger's doing, hang in the gaps between the mirror, the doorway, and the ceiling-high built-in bookcase that Ronnie has ecstatically used for his many books and records, previously boxed up since graduation.

Roger's large beige couch—more of the no-longer-fashionable hand-me-down variety rather than the stuff of Goodwill—divides the room in half, his smaller beige couch cordoning off a square enclosure for the TV and record player, positioning all of this in the far left corner of the large room. The TV and record player lean against the far wall that rises waist-high below the opening into the kitchen.

Maux follows Ronnie into his bedroom—a smaller, thinner version of the living room, only with powder blue tuxedo colored walls between the six windows along the front and side of the house. Each step is a wobble over pink floorboards adorned in the repeating purple and gold crest of some unknown royalty.

"Well," Ronnie announces, standing in the middle of his new bedroom, arms outstretched, mouth pressed into a Letterman smirk. "As you will find out soon enough, this is where it all goes down. I look forward to spending many an evening with you, here, in this very room."

"Shut up," Maux says, standing in the doorway, trying not to laugh—at Ronnie, at the arrangement of the relatively spacious room.

Ronnie's mattresses are stacked, parallel to the two front windows. A long ("early colonial," Ronnie thinks it's called) wood-framed couch—another "gift" from the previous tenants—decorated with faded tan cushions depicting cowboys riding the dusty plains, is pushed into the four-windowed wall. The wall opposite the windowed outside wall will later become the Haiku Wall, where visitors tape up haiku written at parties Ronnie and Roger throw.[7] This is also where Ronnie keeps a found white computer desk and the typewriter he received from Kelly. On the wall opposite the front, the closet, the "master bedroom" bathroom, and a fluorescent green loveseat where Ronnie often

---

[7] For a sample of haiku from the Haiku Wall, please see Appendix E

sits reading books, looking up from the pages to survey the room and NW 4th Lane beyond the front windows before thinking, "I've arrived." Into the bathroom, a purple-walled, pink-tiled not-spacious area, just large enough to accommodate both a tub and a shower stall.

Ronnie grabs his American flag swimtrunks from the closet and drops his pants. Ronnie has long since given up on underwear, finding Florida's humidity not conducive to that extra layer. "You don't mind if I change in front of you?" he says to Maux, dancing the Macarena as he says this, smiling, swinging the right hand out, palm down, then the left hand out, palm down, then flipping the palms—right, then left.

Maux tries not to stare, tries not to smile. "I'll be in the living room. Weirdo." Ronnie steps into the swimtrunks, singing *"Dale a tu cuerpo allegria Macarena, por tu cuerpo para darle alegria cosas buenas, dale a tu cuerpo allegria Macarena, ayyy, Macarena!"*

He ties up his trunks, leaves the bedroom, follows Maux through the living room to the kitchen. He counts the steps from the bedroom to the kitchen, two steps down from his room, the step-step-step of one dirty bare foot followed by the other, and they keep going, Ronnie has never lived in a house with a living room this large (almost as large as the loft Chuck Taylor lived in by the Orange Line in the South Loop of Chicago), twenty steps from the front of the house into the kitchen. The cabinets are an old metallic green, the counters a soiled old white. The oven has the quaint curves of the 1970s. The kitchen plaster surrounding still more windows is the color of dark mustard. The sink faces the living room. Roger's bedroom connects to the kitchen, an eternal mystery behind an always shut brown door.

Roger sits in the kitchen at the yellow kitchen table, eating a breakfast of oatmeal, bananas, blueberries, and raisins, sipping from a glass of orange juice while flipping through the latest issue of *Cinematic Pedantry*. He's dressed for work—the electronics section of the department store two miles north on 13th Street—black slacks, white Oxford shirt—talking with Maux in the inevitable post-mortems of last night's party. Roger talks with his hands, flinging oatmeal and fruit remnants from the spoon he holds in his right fingers and thumb with each gesticulation. He has a burnt-tan surfer complexion, bleach-blond stubble scalp, glaring black eyes that stare like a remarkably gifted fish thoroughly engaged in its surroundings, a smiling mouth with glaring white teeth.

"So I cleaned up, Ronnie. You're welcome," Roger says, when he sees his new roommate standing in the doorway, in American flag swimtrunks, a faded orange t-shirt with the drawing of a windsurfer navigating a difficult wave as the word "FLORIDA" scrolls below in the art deco style of the mid-1980s, registers the knowing smirk of someone trying to convey the impression that he made sweet love the night before.

Ronnie hadn't noticed, actually. But yes indeed—everything is as spotless as it was before the party started. The amps are neatly stacked with the drums and guitar cases in the corner by the front door.

"Nice work," Ronnie says.

"I also kicked everyone out at four, broke up a fight, and kept a nice couple from consummating their love in your bed. You owe me, dude." Roger says. Ronnie nods, promptly disregarding Roger's words. Roger. Their mutual friends: Paul, Neal,

Mouse, Icy Filet, William, Siouxsana Siouxsanne. Roger finds this place. Needs a roommate. Paul suggests Ronnie.

"He's weird!" Paul told Roger at some party, one of those summer parties in Gainesville where those who don't go home between spring and fall semesters spend all their time, inseparable, ending each night llloaded on someone's porch. "He's like this writer. Or something. Plays in bands. You'll like him. Or maybe not. I don't know. But you should ask him."

Paul called Ronnie while Ronnie was still scraping floor tiles in Crescent City, a call to the motel room like a message from a distant paradise as Ronnie sat on a caved-in mattress covered in the day's sweat and dirt and asbestos.

"Roger's weird! He wants to be a movie critic! Or something. You'll like him. Or maybe not. I don't know. But you should ask him."

"What the hell's this?" Maux asks, pointing to the large portrait hanging above the fake fireplace in the kitchen.

"Otis!" Roger says, as if that alone clears everything up.

In a large golden frame, a picture of a man who could be nothing else but a good ol' boy nowhere else but in these southern Yew-nighted States—new jeans, giant oval belt buckle with the name "OTIS" engraved upon it behind a bulbous belly held inside the kind of western shirt the practitioners of the "Dusty Denim" musical genre of the early 1970s wish they could have found at Nudie's. The neck ain't the only thing that's red—red covers every patch of skin. Short brown hair, flat-topped. A fat proud face expressing pure satisfaction with his way of life. In the background, a ranch; in the foreground, a wooden fence, where Otis has placed his thick ringed fingers. Except, on the left hand, a stump where the middle finger should be.

"Otis?" Ronnie asks.

"Yeah! You know, as in Otis from Otis's Barbelicous Barbeque?'
Roger stands, clearly excited to actually converse about this conversation piece.

Ronnie laughs, recalling Alvin's endless work tales of butter-
ing bread, stirring the beans, washing the dishes—pffff!—at the
Archer Road Otis's. "Ah," Ronnie says. "I know it well."

ROGER TELLS THE TALE

Ronnie pours a cup of coffee, joins Maux at the table, as Roger
wolfs down two spoonfuls of oatmeal and fruit, before the pac-
ing, the nervous rubbing of his hands, the rapid gesticulations, the
rapid-fire spieling, begins.

"Ok, so this is last year, and we got finished with this completely useless class in Azorean Cinema of the 1970s, right? So we
celebrate, get lllloaded, then decide to get dinner over at Otis's
Barbelicious Barbeque. We need to eat enough to sober up because
we still had another final exam or two before the semester really
ended, and the all-you-can-eat buffet seemed like just a fine idea,
Ronnie, a fine, fine idea, and we were so happy that stupid class
was done, we had to celebrate somehow. Now if you go to enough
Otis's, you see these portraits inside every restaurant, right there
in the entryway on the wall behind the cash register and the spinning pies and cakes under glass . . .

"Anyway, we're sitting there at the table, and I'm drunker
than I thought, even as I'm sipping sweet tea, eating from the buffet, and I can't stop thinking—can't stop obsessing—on this por-

BRIAN COSTELLO

trait. Can't stop picturing how perfect it would look where I was living at the time. It gets to the point to where I know I'm going to have to steal it. Not like I'm a klepto or anything—I'm not—but it was just one of those things. I mean, look at this guy smiling down at us . . .

"So I whisper to the dude who drove us to Otis's that I wanna take it, and I ask him if he'll help me out and pull up his minivan right to the front door of the restaurant, so I can rip Otis off the wall, run out the entrance, and dive through the open side door of the van. He won't stop laughing about it, and nobody else thinks I'll do it, and of course, there's this girl from the class who I want to impress, so there's no backing out now.

"We finish eating, and I'm starting to sober up, starting to get second thoughts, but as Gibby Haynes says in *Locust Abortion Technician,* 'It's better to regret something you have done, than to regret something you haven't done,' right? I'm even in the men's room while they take care of the bill and walk out the door, looking at myself in the mirror all like, 'You gotta do this. You wanna be a film critic, you gotta be daring!' I look down at the sink, back to the mirror, and say, 'Let's do this.' And I'm off.

"I'm standing there in the front of the restaurant, waiting for the hostess to lead the next group to their seat, and the restaurant's busy, and I'm like casing the area, you know? Like, what jewel thieves do before a heist? Outside, they're hitting the minivan horn, but inside, I'm trying to play it cool, standing there skimming through one of the complimentary copies of *Auto Trader,* like I'm doing nothing but looking for a nice used car as I stand by the front door.

"Finally, this group of six old ladies walks in. The hostess smiles, counts out six menus, leads them to the dining room. Here's my big chance. I saunter up, sneak and weave behind the counter, yank the portrait off the wall with both hands, and bolt for the door.

"Somebody behind me screams 'Hey!' but I'm already leaping into the minivan sidedoor and my classmate floors it and we're speeding away. I look behind, and there's the hostess, the manager, and behind them three guys from the kitchen crew who sprint after us, but we're already turning right onto Archer Road. I'm laughing, the class is laughing, and the girl I want looks impressed, like I'm brave or something. And so the unintended consequence of it is that I hooked up with one of the only film studies nnnnuggets in the whole class, if not the department.

"And then, like two weeks later? We did something else with the portrait. The semester ends, and our financial aid runs dry and I don't have a job yet for the summer. I'm with another broke friend, and we're hungry, so I get this idea.

"I called that same Otis's and ask to speak to someone from the kitchen. They put me on.

"'Hello,' I say, and I'm talking through my hand to try and disguise my voice to make it sound like, you know, someone who might take hostages? 'We have your portrait of Otis. Here's our list of demands. Write this down.' And the dude who's on the phone is laughing, like he's in the spirit of the thing, because, I don't know, if you work in a kitchen like that, I imagine you need to take the laughs where you can get them, right? So he's like, 'Ok, shoot.'

"I tell him we want—sealed—four plastic plates each of beef brisket, barbeque pork, barbeque chicken, mashed potatoes, corn, biscuits, and fried okra—inside four to-go bags placed on the blue curb in the handicapped parking spot. Me and my friend figure we can park there long enough to check the food, make sure it hasn't been turded on, or whatever, and there's enough open space and traffic between the parking lot and the front door to prevent us from getting jumped by the kitchen crew or whatever. We tell them we'll be there in forty-five minutes. No funny business. When the demands are met, we will leave Otis in the spot where the food is. We have him read back our order. He does it, laughing the whole time, and I'm thinking, you know, they're cool, they're in the spirit of the thing. He could have hung up on us, could have told us they have a replacement portrait of Otis already hanging up anyway, but they're playing along. So that's cool. They're cool.

"We get there, pull into the handicapped spot, and sure enough, there are four to-go bags, greasy with barbeque right there on the blue curb. I open the door, carrying the portrait, and slowly approach the bags of food, looking around for any funny business.

"I lift up the first two bags, but I'm sensing something isn't quite right, and sure enough, I look up and see, hiding behind the bushes and shrubs and hedges all along the Otis's Barbelicious Barbeque building, the kitchen crew, and they start yelling, 'Ambush!' and I wanna laugh, but I gotta book it because who knows what they'll pull if they catch me. So I keep one bag, drop the other so I can continue holding the portrait as I hop into the open passenger side door of the car, and yell 'Go!' at my friend, and he backs out and speeds away a second before the kitchen crew stops us.

"I was bummed we only got one bag for all that trouble, but hey: Still got this portrait, right?"

•

"Your roommate is weird," Maux says, later, at the beach.

"Yeah, well, you should have seen my last roommate," Ronnie says.

"He never shuts up!" Maux continues. "His stories are weird and pointless and he doesn't care if you're listening or not!"

Ronnie yawns, stretches across an old red blanket he brought along. He sips from an Old Hamtramck poured into a blue plastic cup, supplies purchased in a backwoods Circle K, at Maux's behest. After last night, Ronnie has no interest in drinking, but downs two beers anyway and watches the usual action at the beach: Paunchy old men with metal detectors. Bronzed surfer teens in groups of three. Floppy-hatted ladies reading best sellers. Families splashing along the water's edge. Boogie boards. Frisbees. Pro-Am Kadima.

"I hate the beach," Maux says, scowling at the Atlantic Ocean like it's everything in the world that has ever caused her grief. "It's boring."

Ronnie shrugs. "It's the beach. Whatever." Ronnie had quit going years ago. It wasn't, you know, *punk* enough.

Ronnie watches Maux, sitting next to him with her short-cropped indigo hair, pink swimsuit, sun on white freckled skin, her sinewy frame, her hatred for the world. How did he get so lucky? A new house, new girl, new life.

Maux points to the ocean and starts laughing like a weaselly twelve-year-old boy. A morbidly overweight nine-year-old in a red speedo, running into the water, had just been knocked over by a wave. He emerges from the water crying, wailing, "Mommy! The water burns my nose!" The boy's mother, also morbidly obese in a teal monochrome one-piece suit, yells—to Ronnie and Maux's left, ten feet away, sitting under an orange and blue beach umbrella— "Christopher! It's salt water! It's supposed to burn! Get out!"

"Poor kid," Ronnie says, sipping the beer, suds already warm from the heat. "I feel bad for him."

"Well I don't," Maux says. She grunts two final heh-hehs. "Fat people are funny. That's all they're good for. I hate everything else about them."

Ronnie has only known Maux for twelve hours, but he has already noticed how "I hate" starts off an incredible number of her sentences. It is quite the achievement. But Ronnie ignores this, distracted by her beauty, her eccentric beauty that trumps everything else, her hair and her glare, a contrast with all this gentle seaside normalcy.

They don't stay at the beach for long. Ronnie tries holding her hand as they walk off the beach onto the scorched mid-afternoon parking lot. "I hate that," she says, flinging away his hand. "It's stupid and disgusting."

The drive home (home!) is silence except for a cassette recording of "Tiger Trap" by Beat Happening, and Ronnie's perfectly ok with letting Calvin Johnson's mono-bass vocals do the talking as he drives and watches the same lush rural jungleside that had blurred past on the triumphant return to Gainesville from Crescent City. Only now, it's so much better, because it feels like a much less alien land than before, because Maux's here, and the fall holds a promise of all the possibilities he hadn't yet experienced in his short stay so far in Gainesville. The students are back, and with them, the bustle of the college town and the promise of parties, after the tease of it in the dire spring and purgatorial summer.

"Let's go inside," Ronnie says when he pulls his car into the dirt driveway to the right of the house. He doesn't even need to ask because he knows Maux will stay with him.

"Not now, Ronnie Altamont." She leans in for a long kiss. Her lips are salty and sandy and sun-cracked and everything right about this part of the world. She backs away. "I'll call you later in the week."

"Oh. Alright." Ronnie shrugs, tries not to look surprised, watches her open the car door and walk away down NW 4th Lane. She turns the corner, crosses 12th Street—indigo hair, white shirt, blue cutoffs, pink skin, green Chucks—disappears through the walkway leading to a parking lot.

Through the windshield, Ronnie stares at the vines, weeds, and scrub weaving through the fence in the back separating the Myrrh House from the glass company the next block over. Ronnie, alone, is suddenly overwhelmed by vertigo, by the anxious skittish feeling of having nowhere to turn in a foreign-enough land. Even now. Especially now. He hurriedly steps out of the car, enters his new house and falls asleep—in sandy damp American flag swimtrunks—on the mattresses stacked in his bedroom.

THIS DALLIANCE WITH THE MAGGIE'S FARM THAT IS LIFE IN ADJUNCT ACADEMIA IS NOW OVER

Another year for me and you / Another year with nothing to do . . . Professor Anderson "Andy" Cartwright has always found in Stooges lyrics what his colleagues find in, say, Toni Morrison. He sits inside his sputtering VW bug, engine coughing out death rattles, A/C cranked almost as high as the stereo, looking through the bug-stained windshield at the faculty parking lot. Returning to the familiar, to the first faculty meeting of the fall semester, one week before classes start. *Another year for me and you . . .*

And so it begins. It's a potent mixture of dread, resignation, and relief when the students come back to UF, to Santa Fe, to the Gainesville College of Arts and Crafts. The adjuncts return for yet another go-around, somehow surviving yet another broke-ass summer. Out of their aged cars they trod across the lots, shuffling off to take their seats in the auditorium, to await this year's wisdom passed down from on high, wisdom that will surely sound remarkably similar to the wisdom passed down from on high last year, and the year before that, and the year before that. The administrators also return, to the next and closest lot to the campus, driving freshly-waxed status symbols, each with a bumper sticker on the back giving lip service to their leftist idealistic childhoods. Tanned, bright-eyed and flabby from their vacation homes somewhere far, far away. *It's another year for me and you / another year with nothing to do*, Iggy sings in a weary wisdom well beyond his 21 years.

This routine is such a contrast to the wide-eyed first-time lives of the students back on the streets and sidewalks in and around campus. Mom and Dad are here to help with the big move, as their freshmen children, zitty and apprehensive, wear their senior year high school t-shirts as they lug clothes, compact discs, and keepsakes from the minivan to their new home, the smaller-than-expected dormroom. They are nervous and awkward, fearful yet hopeful of the unknown immediate futures. Already, sorority pledges are led around by the neck from leashes held by future sorority sisters, as fraternity pledges run across busy intersections completely naked with the word "PLEDGE" painted on their backs in a nasty shade of poop brown body paint. Others less desperate to fit in immediately take to University Avenue, exploring their new city, freed from the cliques and drama of the hometown high school adolescent past. Book stores. Record stores. Thrift stores. Cafes.

At the start of every academic year, Andy observes all of this, as he plays the role—an anonymous extra in the Big Picture, really—of the struggling adjunct professor waddling off to sit through a meeting he finds pointless, carrying a yellow legal pad and pen to take notes for a meeting he knows will not be noteworthy, but the meeting pays, and he needs the money.

He should shut off the car, should fit the cardboard sunshade across the dash, and walk across the faculty lot, the administrator lot, onto the campus and to the meeting. But he can't leave The Stooges for this all-too-predicatble routine.

They will file into the white-gray auditorium and take their seats. They will sigh, "Ready for another year?" and sigh their responses. They will joke of how they already need a drink. Andy does not dislike his colleagues—and even personally likes most of them—but in the auditorium for the first meeting, it's impossible not to feel as if Andy is sharing a miserable experience with them that nobody signed on for—busting ass for a Master's degree only to work a no-future gig with a limited career trajectory. And yet, it's somehow more comfortable to soldier on—year in and year out—than to actually find a teaching job with benefits, or to simply find another job that pays better, or to move away for more meaningful opportunities. And when the meeting starts, the administrators will take their turns at the podium, and they will say what they think the adjuncts need to hear, and the overall effect is the opposite of what is intended: Instead of making the adjuncts feel like they're a part of the Organization, they are made to feel even less a part of the Organization.

Andy can't think about it too much; it leads down too many dark and depressing trails. And he knows the worst is when he's teaching in the classroom, and it's firing on all cylinders, and he's at his best and that miraculous eye-wonder the students get when they connect the dots is in full effect . . . The worst because lingering beyond that magical moment, he knows it won't matter to anyone in the department and in the institution beyond the department. To the institution, he is a cipher, in the ledger under "Seasonal Help." That's what gets him—loving a place and a job and an institution that doesn't love you back. Andy imagines that most people, they're mostly indifferent to their jobs and the jobs are mostly indifferent to them, but as long as those paychecks and benefits keep coming, it's ok. But this gig is different. It's an avocation, an opportunity to inspire and be inspired, even if everything circling around and outside it is dreadful, and you're left feeling like you have no future, and that you're not growing, as it looks to Andy when he observes his colleagues as they walk along to the first meeting of the semester, as it looks to Andy observing the administrators as they wait out the clock to retirement, as it looks to Andy when he observes himself.

In the car, as The Stooges switch to "I Wanna Be Your Dog," fear shoots from Andy's brain to his extremities, settles into the pit of his stomach. It's the contrast of these new students and these old teachers. It's the fear Andy will never be the writer he wants to be, at the rate he's going. That he will never amount to anything, especially if he sticks around. The politics of the place, the complexities in the politics of the place, the complexities in his relationship to the place and the people employed by it, will drive him crazy if he keeps thinking about it. It is this fear: That there is nothing—and will be nothing— new under the sun. This career is going nowhere, but he will not, cannot, leave Gainesville.

In the summer, Andy found work painting apartments. What he loved was the simplicity of it. He'd work all day, then go home and write. The work stayed at work. There was nothing to take home except old paint-stained clothing. His mind was free while the body worked, and when he got home, there was the typewriter. Unclogged and liberated from the hundreds of pages of student assignments each week, the lesson plans, the student conferences, the futile meetings, the phone calls, the letters, the thousand-and-one impositions on his time that the Department and the Institution demanded, Andy could devote all of his energy to what he most wanted to do. And there was so much to show for it—literally hundreds of pages of short stories only a draft or two away from being submittable, and he knew, sitting there in the car as the speakers blared Ron Asheton's sacrosanct wah-wahs, and the A/C howled through the vents, and the dichotomy of the very old and the very new shared space on-campus, he will have no chance to return to any of these stories, no time to revise, hone, and yeah, craft.

The idea to simply leave, to walk away and not look back, isn't really an idea so much as it is an instinct. Painting apartments paid the rent and the bills. At the end of the day, the life of the adjunct is minimum-wage work. It is work he loves, yes, but that's all it is, and even that, obviously, only goes so far. And it drains him of all creativity. The adjunct's life is a perpetual limbo, and if he doesn't leave now, he will never be a real writer, will never be what he believes he is put on this earth to do.

The Stooges' first album transitions into the extended creepy slow chanting of "We Will Fall." Professor Anderson "Andy" Cartwright shifts the car into reverse, backs out of his spot, shifts to drive, smiles, sputters out of the parking lot.

Ahead is the brilliant uncertainty of a future not carved out in semester-long increments. Ahead is the great not-knowing. The fear dissipates. The anxiety and resignation are no more. Andy has rejoined the kids on the sidewalks, each second a new beginning instead of a downward spiral. To assert control again, to welcome the new, to be reborn into the image of what he wants to be, needs to be. This is all that matters. Andy pulls into the driveway of his house, immediately shuts off the wheezing Bug and the whirling pound of the Stooges' "Little Doll," and in a succession of 1975 Carlton Fisk World Series victory hops from the car to the front door, reenters his house, back to the story in the typewriter, back to life.

DRUNK JOHN MEETS A GIRL

The girls coming into the store today are—"Don't make me say 'pissa,' John. I don't talk like this to amuse you. They look fine, ok? Fine," Boston Mike says, and I couldn't agree more.

Measuring our time in 20 minute album sides. Me and Boston Mike, together once again on a beautiful Sunday morning in late August, and it's beautiful because the kids are back in school, and by kids, I mean girls, and by girls, I mean nnnnuggets.

We're making the best of it, stuck behind this depressing-ass counter. Mike throws on Avail, I throw on Archers of Loaf. He throws on the Wipers, I throw on Royal Trux. When that's over, I scour our used bins and pull out a not-mint copy of "Street Hassle" by Lou Reed, and goddamn if this isn't hitting me just right.

As Lou Reed talk-sing-moan-pleads, "Leave me leave me leave

me leave me leave me aloooooone," Boston Mike and I sneak sips of Old Ham-town tallboys and assess the new wave of nnnnuggety freshness taking their first awkward parentless steps off-campus into Electric Slim's to find their deplorable ska or emo or major label poppy punk, wallet chains a' dangling, so fresh-faced and uncorrupted by the drama in this scene to which they shall surely succumb.

"Hey Mike," I say. "See the bleach blonde in the stupid Candlebox t-shirt and the acid-washed denim shorts? In two months? She'll have a mohawk, maybe even her first tattoo. She'll be the biggest Play the Piano Drunk Like a Percussion Instrument Until the Fingers Begin to Bleed A Bit fan in town."

Boston Mike laughs. "These freshmen, it's always at the halfway point in the semester when they get their first mohawk, right?"

"Yup. Just in time for Thanksgiving. It's like 'Take that, Mom, Dad, and Suburbia! I make my own rules now!' Oh, and see the dyed black short stuff with the December's February t-shirt flipping through The Cure CDs? It's such a minor sideways step in the ol' youth culture to go from goth to emo, right?"

"Naw. We gotta cure her of that."

"It can't be done. Nobody takes us seriously here," and I'm right. But suddenly man, it's like, all at once, the summer, and the feeling like the town is yours and yours alone ends. The parties pick up, old friends come back, and everything's no longer at the mercy of summer's lethargy, it's at the mercy of that giant university there across the street. Yeah, I earned my degree there, two years ago, and like all English majors, I now work retail. Sorry about my luck, right?

"What record is this?" this uber-nnnnugget asks, all punk

rock and everything. Short black hair. White skin. Black t-shirt of one of those Oi bands where the lettering is all army stencil and spelling out all kinds of working class anarcho-syndicalist platitudes. She peers up at me behind the counter with these big dark eyes.

I really hate that cliché about love, you know, the one some knowing authority who's inevitably like a fuckin' sassy urban single lady in her mid-30s spouts off between sips of boxed wine and handfuls of Hershey's Kisses, all like "Honey, you'll find love when you least expect it." Because, you're at a bar, you're at a party, you're out buying groceries or walking around, it's always on your mind. It's like when you're talking about blinking and you can't stop paying attention to when you blink, you know? Shit, it's why I go out at night. You think I go out and drink this much so I can talk to my dumbass friends? No. I keep hoping to meet somebody, but I've met everybody here and I know everybody here that's worth knowing, except for this tiny-tiny window when there are new, heretofore uncorrupted girls like this nnnnnugget looking up at me—here at work when, I can tell you, love really is the last thing on my mind—standing here at work—sipping beers and flipping records—head and mind in a hungover daze and mindlessly checking out the new girls in town like it matters.

"It's 'Street Hassle,'" I try to smile, as the backing vocal ladies on the record harmonize "Hey nonny nonny, hey nonny nonny, hey nonny nonny, hey nonny nonny." These nonsense words convey it so much better than I ever could, and the beer's no help. "Lou Reed," I mumble, reaching over and down to hand her the record cover.

"Cool," she says, turning it from front to back, smiling a giant, hundred-tooth smile. "Can I buy it?" So pure, so unmired in the maelstrom of Gainesville's bullshit.

"On CD or vinyl?" You're no doubt expecting, since I'm a record store clerk and all, that this is some kind of coolness quiz on my part—like, if she says "vinyl," I'll know she's perfect, and if she says "CD," I'll forever look down on her for wanting the medium preferred by the stupid masses, but honestly, I don't give a shit if she wants the thing on a fuckin' CD, LP, betamax, 8-track, 12th generation cassette dub. But it does my heart good when she does say "Vinyl," after all.

I remove the needle from *Street Hassle*, place the record back into its unwieldy cheap plastic sleeve, and it's me staring at her staring at Lou Reed staring at her through aviators and holding a cigarette.

"He looks serious," she says, and she laughs this laugh, a soft girlish giggle, and I have to laugh, a soft drunken heh-heh, because she's laughing, and the beery bravado—why do I even bother drinking?—isn't needed, and I'm as vulnerable as I've been in a long, long time.

"He is serious," I laugh, taking the record cover back from her and inserting the sleeve. "Serious dude," I add—sounding as inarticulate as ever. Fuck.

I feel like I need to do something to make her laugh, and all I can think to do is hold the cover of *Street Hassle* to my head— I'm one of those idiots who gets a kick out of sticking album covers where there's a life-size headshot of the performer up to my head—and saying in a goofy voice, "Hey, look at me, I'm Lou Reed! I'm crazy! I'm taking a walk on the wild side!"

I can't hear any laughter; I hate myself. This constitutes a "good idea" in my dumbass head. I lower the record, and Boston Mike is giving me one of those looks he gives when he's amused at my failed attempts at interacting with the world at large. I can't even lower the album enough to face the nnnnugget, assuming she hasn't walked out, freaked out over whatever it is I'm trying to do here.

But then I do set the record on the counter, and she's still smiling, looking at me, grabs the record and says, "I wanna do that."

She holds *Street Hassle* up to her head, and it's the head of Lou Reed, glaring at the camera, over the body of this young punkette in her oi band outfit, who's laughing out, "Heyyyy, I'm Lou Reed. I smoke cigarettes and wear sunglasses. Look at me, guys."

We're laughing at this, and when she lowers the album, all eyes turn to Boston Mike, who shakes his head at both of us all like, "I'm not doin' that. No way."

She extends her hand. "My name's Sicily," she says.

"Sicily?"

"I'm Sicilian."

"Ok." I feel stupid and awkward and as you can probably tell, I wouldn't know how to talk to girls if you stood behind them with cue cards and gave me an ear piece through which you could tell me the perfect Casanovan expressions. I think that's why I earned the "Drunk" in my name. Drunk John. After a few beers, I stop caring about how I don't know how to talk to anyone.

"And you are?" her expression like she'd expected me to volunteer this information earlier. I tell her.

"Nice meeting you, John." She sets *Street Hassle* on the counter. "I think I wanna buy this."

"Yeah?" I mumble.

"Yeah. You sold me."

"I am a professional." Ha ha ha. But she giggles at my stupid joke anyway.

I hit the cash register, give her the ten-percent-off friend discount, rounding down and knocking two dollars off on top of that. "Two dollars," I say.

Our hands touch as she hands me the two singles. In a record store, like all used retail, you touch a lot of nasty people, with a lot of nasty possessions. Everything's dusty, grimy, germ-ridden. This little touch—as fleeting as it is—is a welcome respite.

Put the record in the plastic bag. Hand her the plastic bag. "Thank you for choosing Electric Slim's," I announce, trying to sound corporate or something.

Sicily still laughs at my lame attempts at humor. "And thanks for the Lou Reed," she says. "See you soon."

"Yup." I shrug. Hem. Haw. Twitch. Tick. Sicily leaves the store. And that, my friends, is how I talk to girls. Smooth, right?

"She likes you," Boston Mike says.

"Ya think so?"

"No shit I do." Boston Mike looks away, towards the front window, then mutters "Dumbass . . . "

I take the price gun, fully intending to return to what I was doing before, pricing stacks of used records, but with a head awash in Old Hamtramck, and a body awash in adrenaline from what just happened . . .

"I should go talk to her, right? Like, right now?" I ask Boston Mike.

Boston Mike, I can tell, is building up to a flurry of furious

Masshole cursings, but before he gets started, we're rudely interrupted by one of our regular wino-ass garbage trawlers entering
the store with a large stack of damp torn moldy jazz fusion records to sell. And it ain't the good jazz fusion either, but like, the
shit you hear at Kinko's. Just awful. And this guy likes to chat us
up while we go through his found shit, like he struck gold out in
the crik and can't wait to reap the rewards. "That's Spy-row-gy-
ra," he informs us. "That's a popular band from back before you
were born probably. And that copy looks like mint condition, you
ask me."

Oh Lord. It's like: How many stacks of limp-dicked, weak-
grooved noodly records with ridiculously dated 1983 silver sequined, piano-scarved, kee-tar playing mew-zish-ee-ans must a
record clerk thumb through, before you call him a man? The answer, my friend, is blowing out Kenny G's tasty sax. But I digress,
because, while I'm about to help sort through this latest delivery
of slimy, smelly mold-vinyl, Boston Mike grunts, "Yeah. Go. Now.
Do it."

I hop down from the register and run out to the sunny-muggy
outside of this tiny plaza parking lot.

She's almost to University when I yell, "Sicily! Hey!"

She turns and smiles, and it's all so easy and so not cool, so
totally corny having to put yourself out like this.

I jog to her. (Yeah. "Jog." Awesome.) "So you're new
here, right?"

"Basically. I transferred from a community college in Orlando."

"Orlando?"

"Yeah. You know." She shrugs and I nod. We all have com-
plicated, ambivalent relationships with this state and her people

and her cities. Love, hate, frustration, joy, bitterness, splendor, despair. There's no place like it, but every place is like it.

"Well let me show you around. Let me call you."

Sicily laughs. "So you do this to all the new girls who come into your store? Swoop right in?"

"Nooo!" I say this a little too forcefully, like the dork I am.

"I'm kidding," she says, opening her black purse (The purse, it's covered in a bunch of buttons of bands I can't stand, but I can fix that, right? Of course!), taking a scrap of paper and writing down her number.

Of course, a couple jerkoff friends of mine on bikes have to ride by in the parking lot, cutting through from University to the student ghetto and yelling, "Drunk John! What's up, man! You drunk? You gonna be drunk at the party later?" and I feel my whole being deflate into some like shriveled forsaken pool toy.

"Why do they call you that?" she asks.

"It's a joke," is the first thing that pops into my mind. "It's a long dumb story. I'll tell you some time."

"Sounds good. Call me," she says, and I say, "I will," and she smiles, turns around, crosses University and steps onto the now-hectic campus.

And me, I stand out here wondering if my luck is going to change, or how will my bad luck continue. Could this be a change for the better? Not that things are bad now, you know, but I keep thinking of how it can't stay like this for much longer. I'm getting old, man. Twenty-four? Shit, time to collect my punk rock social security, retire, move to Florida. Oh wait.

A WELCOME STABILITY, A SHARED LOATHING

Ronnie finds a temp job at one of the off-campus used textbook stores. For 24 consecutive fourteen-hour days, he assembles photocopied articles taken from academic journals, fits them into brown plastic binders, then shrink-wraps them into copypacks assigned to upper-level classes from all disciplines. The hours are long, but after dish washing, plasma donation, and asbestos removal, sitting on his ass in an air-conditioned office with two kindly southern-accented grad students is the proverbial can of corn. Beyond this, skimming literally thousands of published thesis papers all day—with their constant usage of words like "bathetic," "epistemological," "tautological," "psychosociopolitical," and "post-Joycean"—is enough to inspire Ronnie to consider going to grad school. Why not?

By the time work is finished, it's generally 9:00 or 10:00 p.m. Ronnie punches out each night, then walks straight to Maux's apartment, or else she's already at the Myrrh House waiting for him. They hang out, drink vodka, watch old movies, sleep (and only sleep), then Ronnie leaves for work the next morning, and Maux eventually leaves for class. There is a welcome stability to this. Ronnie is as settled as he has ever been in Gainesville, happy to be with a girl again, even if all it is is "hanging out," even if she puts on this cold, spiteful, abrasive persona that Ronnie cannot take seriously. She tries so hard to hate everyone and everything, and it only makes him laugh. If this hatred was real, she would have ulcers, Ronnie thinks. She would be on her deathbed. It's protection. It's hiding under self-invented identities. Everybody around them does it to one degree or another, including Ronnie, especially Ronnie.

Living closer to the University, it is easy to see the effect tens of thousands of students have on the town. Shops empty in the summer are now packed. The sidewalks are no longer deserted. Gainesville offers those away from home for the first time unfettered adventure, and those away from home for the first time offer Gainesville unfettered adventure.

Each day, Ronnie makes new friends. They attend his parties. He attends theirs. Each night, leaving work, he runs into these new friends on University Avenue's sidewalks, and they tell each other what they know and what they've heard about this or that person, this or that band, this or that girl.

One night while sunk into the old gray quicksandy couch in the living room of her cluttered might-as-well-be-a garret, Maux shows Ronnie the scrapbook in which she keeps all the comics she has drawn for the student newspaper. Her first published comic, from September, 1994, is a one-panel of a group of beret-clad "smug poetry majors" (so says the cartoon cloud above them, with an arrow pointing) standing on stage in a circle, reading "swill" (so says another cloud), holding journals with their left hand while their "dead-fish handshake" right hands stroke their "tiny dicks," while their "self-satisfied" audience sits behind tables observing the moment with glowing smiles. The caption above this scene reads "THE REVEREND B. STONED'S ECLECTIC CIRCLE JERK."

"The hate mail for that one was glorious," Maux laughs.

Page after page, a balancing act between satire and misanthropy. Everything and everyone in town (she never bothers with politics or celebrity) is a potential target for derisive, mean-spirited laughter. And yet, it is still funny. Ronnie enjoys it—laughs from the gut, laughs out of shock, laughs because it's good—even if he feels he needs to wash the nihilism off of him when they're finished. It reminds Ronnie of what he used to do and who he used to be at UCF, columns veering between silly and caustic, writing about what he thought he knew, inspired more by zines than anything he read in English Comp fiction anthologies, trying to be gonzo and almost succeeding, except it ultimately didn't matter because Ronnie didn't want to pursue journalism in any form after graduation—not like anyone in "the real world" would have him, and besides, there was the band and the novel-in-progress and Henry Miller saying "Always merry and bright!" and his girlfriend to sustain him through the penniless post-graduation months, except when they didn't, and here he is now, with someone currently experiencing the same notoriety he once knew.

She turns to a page that instantly catches Ronnie's eye: This typical Gainesville scenester type hanging from a gallows, his wallet chain used as the noose wrapped around his neck, quite dead, holding a pen in one hand and a coffee mug in the other as vultures swoop in on a collision course with the eye sockets and rabid coyotes and laughing hyenas wait drooling at his feet. Below this, the caption reads, "THE COFFEEDRINKER FANZINE SUCKS," in letters drawn in the same cut-and-paste "ransom note" font as the local punk fanzine itself.

"That's hilarious!" Ronnie howls, pointing. "That guy hated my old band." It sounds weird and unpleasant, Ronnie referring to the band in the past tense, to not be in a band at all. Indeed, Ronnie remembers the lower-case stream-of-consciousness review of their show at the Righteous Freedom House in the pages of *Coffeedrinker*: "The Laraflynnboyles are typical of the insincere irony of Orlando and their cornball act doesn't inspire me to fight the problems plaguing our ugly world."

"*I* hated your old band," Maux laughs. "But yeah, I used to date him. Briefly."

"What? That guy?"

"He said he liked my drawings. Really, he just wanted to get in my pants. Can you imagine? A male with ulterior motives? Whatever, he was terrible and awkward in bed." Maux lightly punches Ronnie in the arm. "You should be glad he hated your band. Wear it as a badge of honor. In a town of emo whiners, he's the whiniest."

Ronnie laughs, sips from a glass filled with far more vodka than tonic. "Yeah, why is everybody so emo here?"

"I don't know. I hate emo."

"Finally. A hatred we both share."

Maux laughs at this, closes the scrapbook, tosses it to the floor, shifts closer to Ronnie.

"Could they be any more passive-aggressive?" Ronnie continues.

"Such a narrow definition of what constitutes sincerity," Maux says.

"All that whining and moaning and groaning." Their thighs touch, fingertips moving ever-so-closer.

"Could they take themselves and their oh-so-precious feelings any more seriously?"

"Wahhhhh. I don't live in a ghetto."

"Wahhhhh. I don't live in a developing country."

"Wahhhhh. I don't get to live in a concentration camp and instead I get every material need fulfilled."

"Wahhhhh. I don't have a terminal disease."

"And so full of false modesty, always like, 'Oh we suck, thanks for enduring our set . . . ' "

"Phony self-deprecation."

"Jeez, Maux," Ronnie says, leaning in, hands on Maux's thighs, faces inches apart. "I'm so . . . turned on right now."

Maux whispers, "Me too," before passionate kisses, a sprint to her bedroom . . .

In bed, after they've finished, Ronnie turns to Maux and says, "Just promise me one thing."

"What?"

"Promise you won't draw me as a dead man if we stop hanging out."

Maux laughs that pre-teen weasel laugh of hers, punches Ronnie in the arm. "It's my ace in the hole buddyboy. That's why you better treat me right."

Ronnie laughs, wondering if he will treat Maux right. He has his doubts.

THREE MILE MORNING RUN ON THE BEACH

"Do you think he means it?" Sally Anne asks her husband, five steps into walking off the three mile run on the beach. She's thoroughly unwinded as Charley, still catching his breath, has actually been thinking the same question, the answering machine message replaying in his head.

Was their son sincere when he left the message on their answering machine last night saying he was happy? They didn't hear it until this morning—out for dinner the night before as Ronnie called, heard the recording of Sally Anne's "Hahhh! We cain't come to the phone right now, but if you leave a message, we'll call you back thanks!", cleared his throat and after an extended "Uh-hhhm" that almost went on for too long, said, "Yeah hey! Mom and Dad . . . just calling to say hey. Things are going pretty good here. Working, making friends, started hanging out with this girl, so that's cool. Settling in. You know. But yeah—feeling happy to be here. Happy. Yeah. Everything's good. Enjoying Gainesville. [sigh] Definitely. Alright, well, talk to you soon."

The run—from their house, past the other beach houses, turning back once they get into the part of the beach where the hotels and the hordes of tourists start dotting then crowding out the sand—was, for Charley, a reflection on this message. You need a decoder ring trying to figure out what Ronnie actually means, what's true and what isn't, the inflection behind the voice—if it's a forced brave front or if he really and truly is what he says he is. More to the point, if existence is suffering as the Buddha says, has Ronnie learned to accept this? He could never put that into words to his son, how conditions would never be ideal, and would often be nowhere near ideal, and for Ronnie's generation, the answer was to wallow in it, to writhe in it, to get angry but to do nothing constructive about it. Maybe he was wrong about the generation—he loathed such blanket generalizations on age groups born in a certain time—but Charley had read some of Ronnie's old columns for the school paper. Where did that come from? The cynicism, the sarcasm, the despair, the bitterness? Like the saying goes . . . send 'em to school and buy 'em books . . . the un-finished part of that expression, of course, hangs out there to be filled in by every member of the older set witnessing the lack of commonsense and experience in children. There are people in the world who will always need something to complain about, who aren't content unless they're, well, *bitching* about any old thing. They could own their own island in the South Pacific, with their dream home, and one thousand harem women of all beautiful shapes, hair color, skin color, and charming personality, fulfilling every material, psychological, and—yes—sexual need, and they'd complain that the sky wasn't the right shade of cornflower blue. Something. Anything. Charley has spent the last few years wondering if their son was becoming that kind of person. And so, the rare upbeat answering machine message, after so much sulking and brooding and sneering, is unexpected.

When he has finally caught his breath enough to answer Sally Anne's question, Charley shrugs, smiles, slaps Sally Anne on the ass. "Let's go inside," he says.

TIME'S UP

Ronnie has knocked several times on the front door to the trailer. No answer. Alvin's van isn't parked on the dead-grass makeshift driveway.

It's a Sunday late-morning day off, the first day off in weeks. Roger is at work. Maux is studying. At the kitchen table, drinking coffee and thinking about nothing much at all, Ronnie remembers he still has the keys to the trailer.

He had forgotten to return them during the hasty move out of the double-wide. In the sweat of August, in under half an hour, Ronnie tossed his possessions into the cab of the pick-up he borrowed from William, taking out everything except some plates and, more importantly, his vinyl copy of the Buzzcocks' *Spiral Scratch* EP. He figures he can return the keys, remove (and presumably, scrub the months of filth off of) the plates and find that copy of *Spiral Scratch*—whose songs had been burning holes in his mind as lyrics like "they keep me pissin' adrenaline" and "I've been dying in the living room" have ricocheted around his mind for weeks now.

Into the dying blandy apple green sedan. The old drive back from "the action" to the trailer. University to SW 2nd Avenue, winding through football practice fields and law schools and the great Floridian verdure. From there, side streets bisecting softball and baseball fields, and the Harn Museum of Art, where, last summer, broke and underfed, when he should have been looking for a job, Ronnie studied the Lachaise sculptures on display with William. Up ahead, good old 34th Street. It will be great seeing Alvin again. He was so understanding about Ronnie's situation. Anyway, it will be a chance to say a more relaxed and lengthy goodbye to the trailer and its many smells.

Ronnie reaches into his right front pocket of his jeans, pulls out the keys, finds the trailer key, puts it into the lock, when he hears the unmistakable pump of a rifle, followed by a loud, authoritative "FREEZE!"

In the chest-caving, ball-tingling panic of the moment, Ronnie recognizes the voice as belonging to the Gulf War veteran butch lesbian neighbor, she with the rusted brown truck parked outside adorned with the "TED KENNEDY KILLED MORE PEOPLE WITH HIS CAR THAN I HAVE WITH MY GUN" bumpersticker. Hands shaking, Ronnie drops the keys.

"Step away from the door, sir!"

Ronnie steps back, slowly steps backwards down the stairs, hands up, because that's how they do it on the TV when characters get guns pulled on them. A surprisingly rational and calm mindset takes hold inside Ronnie. He has a rifle pointed at his back. Pointed at him to prevent his retrieval of a Buzzcocks EP.

Ronnie turns around. The woman stands to the immediate left of her trailer, like she just emerged from around the corner, rifle raised to shoulder blade, angry eyebrows furrowed over the rifle stock, finger on the trigger.

She lowers the rifle. "He don't want you comin' 'round here no more." Her hair is buzzed spiky, blonde-gray. She wears a black sleeveless t-shirt that reads "DYKER BIKER" in white iron-on lettering, and camo cutoffs.

Ronnie's voice, never as brave as his mind and body, even on good days, struggles to leave his throat. He chokes out, "I'm here to pick up what I left behind."

She shakes her head from side to side. "Oh no. No way. He told me to keep an eye on you in case you snuck in."

"And that's why you have a rifle." The panic subsides a little bit, replaced by a rising anger that someone would resort to this over something so silly.

"It's in the Constitution."

Ronnie isn't in the mood, nor is he in the condition, to debate the pisspoor sentence construction of the Second Amendment. "I'm leaving," he says. "Let me get my keys, and I'm gone."

"And don't come back," the woman yells after him as he climbs the steps to the front door, bends over, grabs his keys.

Ronnie walks to his car, looks at Alvin's neighbor. "Jesus," he mutters, climbs into the car, starts it, backs out, and peels away in quadruple time, finally feeling his hummingbird pulse, itchy with burst sweat glands. And to think, Ronnie was hoping to finally get the chance to say "Thanks for everything!" to Alvin, and yes, "everything" entailed living rent and bill-free. The blandy apple green sedan has never gone faster than when Ronnie accelerates out of the wooded trailer park and the rundown sidestreet, back on 34th Street, too crazed to note once again the mix of sad southern poverty and hot pastel collegiate lifestyle apartment living.

Ronnie will never see Alvin again, and eventually, when the shock wears off, will be of the mind that, in the big picture, he probably deserved to have a rifle pulled on him for his actions and inactions of the summer.

Mouse will hear third-hand rumors from time to time, and pass them along to Ronnie. Alvin was arrested in a not-elaborate meat-stealing scheme with a grocery store butcher. Alvin finds a girlfriend at Waffle House one night who immediately moves in and makes Alvin her pimp, even bringing up her friends from South Florida to turn the trailer into a double-wide of ill repute. Alvin finds work as a camp counselor for disabled teens. Alvin moves to Alaska to work in a cannery. Alvin finds work roadying for the classic rock band Nazareth on a reunion tour. At the end of the day, any and all of these rumors were as absurd as the rumor that Alvin had two buttholes. Ronnie preferred imagining Alvin moving up to a duplex, or an apartment complex with a swimming pool and shuffleboard, maybe even a small home somewhere, as he and a wife who understands him quietly sit in the living room and watch television, expressing their skepticism regarding the veracity of the commercials breaking up the sitcoms with a nice long "Pfffffffffffffffffffffffffffffffffffff."

TEST TUBE BABY FROM A WALLA WALLA STREET

"It's not funny! Fuck!" Ronnie yells, standing in Mouse's bedroom, telling him and Icy Filet what happened. Strangely enough, Ronnie feels more panic-stricken than he did when the rifle was actually aimed at the back of his head. Heart still racing, the unrelenting sensation of being on the verge of hyperventilating, exacerbated by their laughter, their absorption with each other rather than what happened to him twenty minutes prior. "I could have died!" They giggle as Ronnie acts out the action, giggle at each turn and twist of the story like it's some kind of hilarious joke. In bed, in underclothes, fetally conjoined like bed-bound John and Yoko not taking their eyes off each other—Icy Filet stroking Mouse's goatee, Mouse's dentures reflecting the late summer sun through the bedroom's soiled windows as he har-harrs. Mouse runs his fingers through Icy's short black-blonde-red-green-blue hair.

"She wasn't going to use it, Ronnie," Mouse says, still not looking away from Icy Filet. "It's for show. She wanted the chance to justify having the rifle, and you gave it to her."

Ronnie looks to the low ceiling, the gargoyle masks and sloppy collegiate abstract art on canvases nailed to the walls. "Jesus," he says. "You guys are high."

"We sure are," Icy Filet laughs, still stroking Mouse's goatee. "But that's not the point. You should play him the tape, Mouse."

"Heh heh—yes!—heh!" Mouse quickly rolls out of his nauseatingly loving position in bed, hops one foot at a time into the living room, presses play on the tapedeck of his stereo, laughing like a gleeful sadist. "This is the best one yet, brah!" Mouse proclaims. "Listen to this while I run off to sit on the toilet, heh heh heh!"

"Oh no," Ronnie says, looking to Icy Filet, who continues gazing into the direction of where Mouse's supine body once laid.

"You really do need to get high," Icy Filet says to Ronnie, not moving her head to speak in his direction.

Before Ronnie could tell her why that is a terrible idea, the music starts. The frequencies are lower than Mouse's previous efforts, like an artified attempt to replicate the low-rider truck bass throbbing out of the subwoofers of any given Floridian weekend night. Initially, there is nothing but this rhythm, rattling the windows, and then, Icy Filet's speak-sing:

"Armor All-ed interior on a turtle wax face
steppin' in the club like you came from outer space
a Sun Ra Saturnalian with a Plutonian mind
bitches steppin' up thinkin' that they fine
Peter Paul and Mary, Don and Neneh Cherry
your trunk is full of junk and you look like Cousin Larry
jammin' on the one, run Forrest run
Coffeemate creamer and a bear clawed sticky bun"

Between the rhymes, the beat continues, the windows rattle, and over the din, samples from the television program *Perfect Strangers*: Cousin Balki, proclaiming over and over again, "A stitch in time saves ten." Icy Filet resumes:

"Test tube baby from a Walla Walla street
Icy is my name and Mouse provides the beats

we got a Coleman sax with a Danko bass
American birth and Floridian grace
Carol and Mike Seaver, Doctor Johnny Fever
chillin' in a hot tub with Eldridge Cleaver
Terminator X, reps on the Bowflex
Chex Mixmaster with a hankerin' for Tex-Mex"

The song is over in three minutes, finishing in a frenzied orgy of low bass beats, the opening bass line of The Band's cover of "Don't Do It" from *The Last Waltz*, and the opening harmolodics from the Ornette Coleman album *Free Jazz*. When it ends, Mouse sprints out of the bathroom, leaps through the bedroom doorway and dives onto the bed. He, stretches, reclines, laughs, turns to Ronnie. "Yeah? And?"

"Your songs . . . these raps . . . they're really starting to get better," Ronnie says. "You know, it's still very Beck, very Beckish and all, but there's a bit of Doctor Octagon and Dylan thrown in."

"Oh, Ronnie," Icy Filet says, pulling in Mouse to cuddle. "Such the little critiquer."

"Aw, well, you know," Ronnie says, blushing, looking away from the bed. "It was actually kinda soothing, after getting a rifle pulled on me for the first, and, I hope, last time."

"Soothing!" Mouse repeats. A frenzy of smoochy-smooch lip thwacks between Mouse and Icy Filet. Between kisses, Mouse says, "If we keep at it, we'll be sensations. Sensations!" Mouse uncuddles from Icy, rolls out of the bed, stands, announces, "I'm getting beer. To celebrate. Hooray for beer, heh heh heh!"

"Sensations," Icy Filet says to Ronnie. "It's plausible, right?"

"Why not?" Ronnie says.

Mouse returns with three cans of Dusch Light, hands one to

Ronnie. "Nah," Ronnie says. "I'm going home. I need to forget this stupid day. See what Maux's up to."

"She's crazy, you know," Mouse says.

"Totally," Icy Filet adds, reaching across the bed to grab a Dusch Light can from Mouse. She opens it, chugs, turns, rearranges the pillows so she's upright enough to drink.

"It's what they tell me," Ronnie says.

"Good luck with that," Mouse laughs, like he did when he offered Alvin's trailer as a terrific place to live.

RIDING ON THE METROGNOME

You set the Metrognome to the left of Ronnie's front door, bang on the window, as the Myrrh poster with its black power salutes and burning draft cards glares at you like you're The Man they've become. (And nevermind how you got here, how you lugged this three foot tall Metrognome—with his painted red boots, blue pants, green shirt, white beard, wise blue eyes, cherubic cheeks, and red hat with one upturned flap. You can always piece it together in the morning.)

"Ronnie!" you yell. Bang the door again. Now that you've stopped running, everything spins. Dizzy, you step away to barf in the dirty side yard. It's a rational barf, one of those barfs you've learned to anticipate, when your body tells you, "You know, William, I do believe I am going to vomit now," and your brain responds, "Yes, body, I understand. If I could get you to give me a minute to find a decent place to throw up, that would be terrific, 'kay?" When you find the spot, a patch of grass between red ant hills, it is simply a matter of bending over, "Bleeeeeeeeeahhhh" gags, splatter. You're not doing this on the street, in a car, in front of the door, on someone's rug. This is a good place and you are reasonable and logical—considerate, even—in your blacked out state.

"William? You alright?" you hear after the front door half-opens.

"Yesh! Hang on!" you manage between heaves, one index finger upraised. "Uh minnit, dude!"

That's it: Once more, and you're done. You always feel better after you throw up the booze. You turn around, try rising to a standing posture.

"Rrrrrrrronnnie!" you announce as you round the corner. "Ya gotta let me in. I got something for you!" You point towards that heavy-ass gnome you've been lugging all the way from . . . somewhere.

"Get in here," Ronnie says, laughing. Laughing at you. Of course he's awake. As you know, the blessing and curse of living in a party house in the student ghetto is that people come by at all hours. Tonight, or, this morning, that someone is you.

"This is important Rrrrrrrronnie!" You lift and hold this twenty pound . . . fuckin' . . . whatevertheshit . . . dehhhhhh . . . then you set it down again.

"Oh yeah?" he says as you stumble through the door.

"Ronnie, Ronnie, Ronnie Altamont," you continue, standing in the entryway. "What I have here is a gnome. But . . . but . . . it's not just any gnome. It's a mmmmetrognome."

Familiar girlish weaselly laughter from the back of the living room, and when you step in, you see Maux. She laughs her mean laugh as she stares at you. "You're ridiculous, William. You drink like a dumbass, dumbass."

Ronnie carries the metrognome into the house, sets it in the middle of the living room. Roger rises from the long couch, hops over it, runs to the metrognome. "Let me rub it," he says when he arrives, bending over to pat its stomach. "For good luck."

The three of you stand around the metrognome, but Maux, she glares from the couch. Through the booziness, her seething unrelenting dislike shoots across this large living room. She hates you now. Why? You don't care. It's just her style. But you, you have a metrognome. And you're drunk. So. Whatever.

"Alright, William," Ronnie says in an indulgent tone. "What exactly is a metrognome, and how is it different from regular gnomes?"

"See, that's the thing," you start to explain, but as you begin putting it into words, all like "See, you got this gnome, this gnome I stole, from somewhere, then you put a metrognome inside it in the hole there at the bottom, then stick some mics around it and . . . voila!" you realize what a stupid idea it is.

Ronnie laughs, repeats the word "Metrognome," then asks, "You want a beer?"

"Of course I wanna beer," you say, but by the time Ronnie walks across the living room and into the kitchen, you're on the floor, sitting next to the Metrognome, stroking its ceramic beard. Ronnie sets the Old Hamtramck tallboy between you and your Metrognome. You lean back, stretch out, lay on your back.

"Maux, you suck," you yell, turning, left side of your face on the cool dirty hardwood floor. "Everybody knows it except Ronnie. You're a mean person!"

"Thanks, rummy!" Maux shouts from the couches.

"And Roger," you continue, because you've made these connections now and you need to share them because they need to know these things about themselves because you won't say it in the morning and you may never say it or even think it again. "You want to be a film critic? If that isn't duller than dogshit, I don't know what is."

"Hey! Thanks! Thumbs up! Two big thumbs up!" Roger says, back at the couches with Maux and Ronnie.

"And Ronnie? Well, you're ok, for now, because you took me and the metrognome in when nobody else would answer the door."

"Yup. I am one of the good ones" Ronnie says, smirking at Roger and Maux. "Better than these dicks, anyway."

"What? We're the dicks and Ronnie isn't?" Maux says.

"Yeah," you slur. "That's about what I'm saying . . . right now." You think how Ronnie better appreciate it, as the floor feels grimy and grainy and footsteps approach and a blanket falls on your curled-up nausea-twitched body. Ronnie, yeah, he is one of the good ones, you think, but that's only temporary, because, because, beeeecause, he'll like get corrupted by . . . fuckin' Gainesville . . . but the metrognome . . . oh metrognome . . . oh, metro, metro, metro, metro, metro, metro, metro, metro, gnoooome.

•

You open your eyes to a purple early morning. You are on a floor staring at the pointed red boots of a garden gnome. Disoriented. No past nor present. The images of the last few hours begin to sharpen into clarity. You recognize your surroundings—Ronnie's living room—and why you're not in your bed. Beer. Tequila. Whiskey. It was Neal's idea, at the Drunken Mick. The Metrognome.

You scoured the neighborhoods west of the university, Neal driving, your head outside the passenger seat window, scanning, in search of a gnome, any gnome, to steal, to use, for, um, performance art?

"We'll out-Mouse Mouse!" Neal ranted. "It'll be the greatest performance ever!"

"Yes! Yes!" you agreed, imagining setting the Metrognome on a barstool at the stageless performance corner in the Nardic Track with a microphone placed close, the hidden metronome inside the Metrognome. Nothing but the click click click sound, through effects pedals cranked over the cranked PA. Brilliant.

When you found the gnome, in the middle of this large front yard in front of a house that even had the audacity to look like a cottage from the British countryside, you knew you would open the door as Neal's car still coasted along at a fast-enough speed. You tried a military-style rolling out, but fell sideways then rolled into the grass from the road, and that's why your pants are stained at the knees and your shirt is filthy. You run across crunchy Augustine grass blades until you put your arms around the gnome, lift with the knees, then run. Only, it's more of a gasping gallop across the crunchy Augustine grass. It's silent except for your panting, Neal's idling sedan, and the late-night sprinklers across all those lawns. It was too funny and too ridiculous to ask why this is funny and ridiculous. You toss the metrognome in the back, return to the passenger seat, and off you go, laughing-laughing-laughing.

Hours later, you lift yourself up from Ronnie's living room hardwood floor, and you're not sure if the joke is even all that funny, or if it's anywhere near as funny as you thought it was last night.

You had gone with Neal to his house to drop it off, but then you had what you thought was a better idea. A better idea!

"Later," you yell, at the intersection on University, where the stadium—the swamp, Oh! The Swamp!— is on your right. You open the car door, step out, reach into the back for the Metrognome, your Metrognome, hoist him, and sprint away. Neal shouts after you, "That's ours! That's our metrognome!" but you keep huffing and puffing down University before taking a left into the Student Ghetto. From there, the drunkenness increases, and how you avoided pursuit by Neal and how you ended up at Ronnie's will remain a mystery.

Now, you leave the Myrrh House. You walk down NW 4th Lane, turn left on 13th Street. The metrognome will stay at Ronnie's; you're too tired to lug the stupid thing back to your place. Neal will ask about it, will give you grief that you didn't bring it back to the coach house. Let him get the stupid metrognome. It was his idea anyway, the dick.

Throbbing head. Burning stomach. A head full of regrets. Unfocused eyes. How many times has this happened, and how many more times does it happen?

Walking, shuffling, stumbling, limping past all these quiet apartments and houses where people had the sense enough to at least make it home and not sleep on someone's dirty-ass hardwood floor. Home. Sleep it off. There will probably be a party later on tonight. No, there will be a party later on tonight. You can pick up the metrognome later. Or, you won't. Who cares.

THE AMBITIOUS FILM CRITIC AND THE
FLOUNDERING ORLANDO EMIGRANT

Roger clears his throat, lifts the hand-held tape recorder to his mouth, begins speaking in his "serious academic" voice:

"What is immediately apparent in *Sympathy for the Devil* is Godard's fervent belief in art as revolution, be it the evolution of a Rolling Stones song in the studio, graffiti on the walls of a bank building, the whole love and consumption diaspora of contemporary life, art as a realm in which to critique the most fundamental elements of modern Western Civ—Ronnie! You need to wake up! I can't concentrate with you snoring."

"Sorry, dude . . . sorry." Ronnie abruptly jolts awake on the smaller of the beige couches pushed together to form an L. He yawns, stretches, reclines. "Why don't they cut out all that agit-prop bool-shit and show only the Stones footage. That's the only good part in this."

"See, Ronnie? You're too ignorant to understand." Roger would say this often to Ronnie's deliberately obnoxious questions. "These films cannot be expressed any other way." As Ronnie would learn, Roger plays the Film Theorist Superiority Card as gratuitously as a New Yorker playing the countless variations on We Can Get a Bagel at 3:00 a.m. and You Can't.

"Pshaw," Ronnie pshaws. "Wake me up when the Stones are back on. I'm liking those pink pants Bill Wyman's wearing." Ronnie turns away from the television, head buried in the cushions, falls asleep.

When the semester begins, Roger spends his nights watching two to three films on TV, on VHS tapes checked out of the univer-

sity library. He scribbles notes in a journal while speaking volumi-
nous thoughts into a hand-held recorder. On off-nights from going out or spending time with Maux, Ronnie tries watching these
films, increasingly convinced that they are nonsensical forays
of self-indulgence, and their only real appeal for anyone is that
they aren't Hollywood blockbusters. Not a big movie guy, Ronnie.
These films lull Ronnie to sleep, stretching out on the small beige
couch as these invariably French characters move about scenes in
the slowest of pacings. Movies affect Ronnie the way books affect
many people—they make him sleepy.

Ronnie's snoozing and snoring irritates Roger to no end.

"Ronnie, you gotta wake up now!" Roger would say, eyes fix-
ated on the twenty-four-inch TV screen, hunched forward, pen
in one hand, hand-held in the other, thick journal opened on the
coffeetable, pages filled with frantic, coffee-fueled penmanship.
"We're coming upon a very important scene here!"

Ronnie mumbles, does not wake up.

Roger shrugs, heavily sighs, eyes returning to the screen, pen
hand scribbling, mouth talking. Why should Ronnie understand?
Roger thinks. In his current state, such artistic work is beyond his
comprehension. He pauses the hand-held, grabs the journal off
the coffeetable, scoots, settles, sinks into the couch. With his right
fingers, he pushes his hair—some girls in town describe it as "Kurt
Cobainy," and while he would never admit to being a Nirvana fan,
he considers it a compliment nonetheless—behind his ears.

In the short time they have lived together, Ronnie has been
drunk most nights of the week, and when he isn't drunk, he's here
on the couch, using these films Roger loves to get caught up on
sleep. Roger thinks on this, leaning forward to sip from the glass

filled with the blueberry smoothie he blended an hour ago, the blueberry smoothie a crucial aspect to the routine of every night's movie watching. Why is Ronnie even living here in Gainesville? There is no reason for it, as far as Roger can tell. They pass in the mornings—Roger eating his fruit-packed oatmeal, Ronnie zombie-hobbling in glazed-dumb hangover faces and postures as he enters the kitchen for a glass of water. How does Ronnie live like this? To live without any kind of purpose, to be here for no reason, floundering, goofing off over beer after beer after beer?

He thought they would be better friends, better roommates. But Ronnie is in his own mindless world. Soon, he will roll off the couch and stumble into his bedroom and throw on *Marquee Moon* by Television, leaving the cassette on repeat, faint fluttery guitar solos resonating throughout the otherwise silent 3:30 a.m. house. This is how he lives, Roger thinks.

Roger leans forward once again, resumes scribbling notes into the journal as the film "seamlessly drifts from scene to scene, challenging previously cherished conceptions of narrative and characterization." He does not want to think about how he could be like Ronnie in a year or two, after graduation. Will they want another film critic, out there?

Finally, inevitably, Ronnie does roll off the couch, stands. "Good night, dude," he mumbles, and off he goes. In seconds, from Ronnie's room, Roger hears the opening chord to "See No Evil," the first song on *Marquee Moon*. Roger sips from the smoothie, leans closer, scribbles notes, unpauses the hand-held, resumes talking of every impression crossing his mind about this film, locked into the present to avoid brooding on the future.

ON AN ISLAND

"Look at these assholes," Maux says, glaring and pointing at this fat drunken parade of football fans trudging down University to the big Florida Gator football game. Maux and Ronnie had made plans to meet for lunch at Gatorroni's by the Slice, forgetting that today is a gameday.

"Yup," Ronnie says, trying to ignore it as he eats a Portobello pizza slice, sitting next to Maux outside on barstools at high tables facing University Avenue. These orange and blue facepainted barbaric hordes, numbly intoxicated and stumbling, assuming, quite correctly, that binged beer coupled with football gives them the right to act like howling dumb dicks.

"I hate football," Maux says, scowling, short indigo hair glowing in the sunshine. She wears frayed blue cutoffs, a pink t-shirt with "WHO CARES?" written in black Sharpie permanent marker.

Ronnie grunts a second "Yup" between pizza bites. In the short time they have been together, there is simply no limit to what Maux dislikes. Maux hates Lou Reed. Maux hates old people. Maux hates kids. Maux hates babies. Maux hates teenagers. Maux hates rednecks. Punk rockers. Jocks. Frat boys. Sorority sluts. Middle-aged people. Fatsos. Bums. Religious nuts. Retards. Cops. Handicapped. Teachers. Dogs. Cats. Birds. Rabbits. Celebrities. Scenester girls. 98 percent of all scenester guys.

Each day, some new, unexpected hate. "I hate fishermen." "I hate crossing guards." "I hate those kids who dress like submarine sandwiches and stand at intersections waving at cars."

The football fans run up and down the sidewalks, cram into the cabs of honking pick-up trucks.

"Orange!" one side of the street yells to the other.

"Blue!" the other side yells back, in imitation of what they do in the stadium, where opposite sides yell the team colors back and forth.

"These people suck," Maux says, lighting a cigarette. "People suck."

Ronnie yawns, wearied as much by Maux's redundant worldview as the tableau of grown men and women in orange and blue facepaint vomiting on the curb.

So much of their time together is little more than her waxing sardonic on the human condition. When Ronnie takes her to parties, she finds the most isolated corner, sits, and sketches in her pad while chugging straight vodka from that flask she always carries. Ronnie endures it all, glad a girl likes him. And she is beautiful, for a quasi-nihilist.

"Let's leave," Ronnie suggests. Ordinarily, Gatorroni's by the Slice is an ideal spot to enjoy the afternoon, to run into friends walking by, but on gameday, friends hide in their houses, or split town, or at least try to make some money off the invasion by working the overflowing restaurants.

They finish their pizzas, step out of Gatorroni's and onto the sidewalks, shoving through the orange and blue throngs. With each step away from the stadium, north on 13th Street, the crowds thin out. Passing Gator Plaza on the left, Ronnie reaches out to hold her hand. Maux pulls away. "Stop that," she says. "You know I hate holding hands."

Ronnie laughs, speaks in a parodic bark of Maux's voice. "Look at me. I'm Maux. I hate this. I hate that. I hate everything."

They cut through the Zesty Glaze parking lot, into the relative calm of the student ghetto, where residents sell their driveways to the highest, drunkest bidder going to the game.

"I hate you," Maux says, punching Ronnie in the arm, a solid thwack. Ronnie laughs harder. He pretends to shadowbox, hopping around Maux as she stomps towards the student ghetto sidestreets. "Let's box, lady. Ooo! Ooo! I'm punching the air! Lightning! Bam!"

Maux refuses to smile at this, even if she finds it somewhat endearing. Ronnie, she thinks, is another aimless goof, the kind who always bounce in and out of her life—smarter than he thinks, smarter than he knows. This won't last. It never does.

By the time they reach her apartment, the streets are desolate. Only the far off cheers from the stadium penetrate the student ghetto silence.

"I hate making out," Maux says, after they step inside and go straight to her bedroom. The noise and pandemonium that has overtaken the city on gameday doesn't reach this unmade bed in this darkened room.

Ronnie backs away from her mouth. "I know, I know, you hate everything. I get it."

"Yeah," Maux says, reaching behind his head, left fingers and thumb ensnared in the disheveled knots of his brown hair, pulls him back. "I can't stand you," she whispers, breath a mixture of cigarettes, beer, and greasy pizza. "But this? I guess it doesn't . . . I don't know, totally suck?"

That afternoon, they create an island the size of Maux's bedroom. Gone is the sneering, the sarcasm, the professed hatreds. On this island, they are vulnerable, affectionate, real. A fleeting moment when nothing else in Gainesville exists. Her façade is gone.

His façade is gone. They no longer have to try; they're together, and that's all that matters.

Afterwards, Ronnie watches her sleep. He likes it when Maux sleeps. It's the only time she seems happy, when the smile on her face isn't a mean grin. Ronnie, wide awake, sweaty and inspired, wants to go home and write. He hasn't felt this way in months. When not binding copypacks at the temp gig in the used college bookstore, when not with Maux or at some party, Ronnie has taken to sitting in his room and listening to the Television album *Marquee Moon* on repeat all night. He stares at the ceiling and basks in the bittersweet ache of the music. It is the soundtrack to this uncertain time. Delving and lost inside the sounds of the album, it never occurs to Ronnie to try and write.

Football is underway now; tens of thousands of screaming tools are off the streets, compressed into the stadium. There is a rare stillness to the student ghetto on gamedays, once the game actually starts. Ronnie needs to be out there on those streets, needs to get home to the pen and paper. He needs to breathe in the emptiness and the silence before floating into the Myrrh House to daydream, to find his journal, to sit on the front steps, and write for hours, as *Marquee Moon* fills the air.

He kisses Maux on two strands of indigo hair across her cheek, steps back, continues watching her sleep. She would hate being kissed like this, would hate being stared at like this. Ronnie steps out of her bedroom, tiptoes through her crummy apartment and carefully walks out the front door.

Outside, out of the island, walking the Student Ghetto streets. It's the no-surprise heat of 85 degrees, tempered by subtle breezes shaking the sand pines, the palms, even the live oaks.

The skies are a cloudless Florida blue. No one is walking nor driving these streets. In the distance, marching bands, cheering, whistles, air horns, but here, it's Ronnie Altamont and only Ronnie Altamont. This moment, as fleeting as his time with Maux, he feels the Student Ghetto is his. He is post-coital, triumphant and invulnerable.

The Myrrh House is empty. Roger is at work. Ronnie opens the doors and the windows, turns on *Marquee Moon*, grabs his journal and his pen, sits on the front steps, and writes, an ecstatic counterpoint to the stillness of NW 4th Lane.

MOE GREEN'S FUCKING EYESOCKET'S LAST SHOW

Tonight at the Righteous Freedom House, Moe Green's Fucking Eyesocket will play their last show. This evening, Ronnie hurries through the copypack binding so he can punch out earlier than usual. He buys a twelver of Old Ham Town at the XYZ, lugs it back to the Myrrh House, unlocks his front door, steps in, opens the first can, sips, calls Maux, asks if—

"I can't," she cries. No really—she is blubbering into the phone between sobs. "It's my birthday."

"Oh! Happy birthday! I had no idea."

"Oh! Happy birthday!" Maux mimics. "Fuck off, Ronnie. I'll call you later, when it's not my birthday."

Stark silence, then the fast shrill-toned eighth notes of an off-the-hook phone. These are the last years—very brief, in the overarching course of human history—in which human beings will know what it's like to stand with a large cordless telephone in one's hand after the person on the other end violently and abruptly ends the conversation by throwing their large cordless telephone against their living room wall. Ronnie, of course, does not know that Maux does this with her phone, but he stands by the still open front door of the Myrrh House, twelver at his feet, holding that stupid phone to his ear, this dense-enough/weighty-enough antennaed beige plastic wonder of late 20th century technology, looks out the front windows at NW 4th Lane, mutters your basic *frickin' frackin' frickin frack*, can't decide if he should laugh or be angry. He chooses to laugh, chooses to drink away any lingering concerns, drinks the first six in quick succession while slouched on the cowboy couch in his bedroom while listening to *Marquee Moon*, carries the other six on the fifteen minute stumble-and-weave to the Righteous Freedom House.

Three to four times a year, a band will break up, inevitable when one of the members graduates college and/or finds a real job in another city. (Or, in the case of MGFE, when the strains of touring end close friendships, everyone drifts apart, moves on, grows up.) On the front windows of the smaller businesses that can get away with it are handwritten signs reading, "Closing early tonight. Go to Righteous Freedom House for MOE GREEN'S FUCK-ING EYESOCKET'S last show!" In the Gainesville music scene, the last show of a highly-regarded local band is something akin to an Irish wake, minus the Catholic overtones and, naturally, with a bit more punk rock sentiment. Some will tear up, many will sing/scream along with the band, a few will set off fireworks to siss-boom-bah between songs and band members. And, for those non-straightedge in attendance, there's lots of drinking.

And there really is something special about it, Ronnie thinks, as he squeezes into the front door, maneuvers around those already packed into this living room to see the end of another band. It has been like this for the six years Ronnie has been making the drive up to see shows in Gainesville. Because, they are your friends up there, even if they are not your friends—not yet—making music they created to express their lives. These are your friends, even if they are your enemies, surrounding you in these muggy house shows; even if they are your enemies, you share this bond over the love of music. Another era ends. Life moves on, and in Gainesville, it moves in an endless five-year cycle, because MOE GREEN'S FUCKING EYESOCK-ET will be replaced by some younger band. Always younger.

The music howls in amplified barbaric yawps, as Ronnie joins, sweats on, bounces into the throng. He opens one beer, gives away the rest. Through the gaps between bodies—friends standing in a semi-circle around the band, transfixed by the spectacle—Ronnie sees William, ten feet away, screaming into the microphone, face the color of a ripe tomato. The band jabs at rhythm like furious underdog boxers pounding punching bags. Friends grab the microphones, scream along.

Where do we go after this, when the set is over, when the months and years pass? And where do you go after this, William? When your life has been, up to now, entirely focused on the immediate? You scream to all these friends who know the words to these songs like you know the words to their songs, and the only coherent thought in your mind is how fleeting this is. You run out of breath, you roll on the floor, writhing as others grab the microphone and sing your lyrics. In the midst of this entropic cataclysm, you ask yourself if you could ever put your entire being into something or someone the way you did with playing in this band. You'll never sing these songs again. This meant something, even as the law of diminishing returns exacts its slow painful cost. Even as you're now hardly on speaking terms with the others in the band, and you were once the best of friends.

What happens to these memories? Ten, twenty years down the line? This song's about to end. This set. This band. This life. You leap in the air and fall to the filthy hardwood floor, look up at your friends, standing in knowing half-smiles like they're in on the secret, watching this life—this part of your life—end.

You won't talk about any of this when it's over. There will be overlong caught-up-in-the moment sweat-stained embraces with those who have been there all along. Still winded, you will briefly nod to the rest of the band as they start to unplug and break down their gear. They will return the nod, and that's as deep as it will be. You will get drunk, and eventually everything will be a goofy joke again. Nobody takes themselves or their "art" all that seriously, at least not on the surface.

But this moment. You know, and Ronnie knows, and just about everybody else that's here knows. There really is something special about it.

MEH

Kelly: So pleased with himself on this next mid-afternoon's post-mortem of last night's shenanigans.

(Yeah: Shenanigans.)

In hungover shame: Ronnie half-listens to Kelly's rehashing of last night's sexcapades.

(Yeah: Sexcapades.)

No: Ronnie really really really really really does not want to hear about the blow job on the Myrrh House roof, about how Kelly, in the peak of whatever drugs he saw fit to bring up with him from Orlando, couldn't stop with the rolling steady stream of pointing out and naming planets, stars, constellations, even as he's you know feeling her mouth, tongue, hands, up/down, 'round and 'round his engorged peninsula. They're on the front patio at Gatorroni's, and Ronnie is trying—trying—to eat a Portobello slice, and trying not to listen to Kelly, and trying not to piece together what happened, because really now, who cares?

Yes: it's one of those torturous hangovers where the head throbs, the forehead is clammy, perceptions are hazy, dizzy, out of focus, and if all of that isn't bad enough, Ronnie also has the song "Take It to the Limit" by The Eagles on repeat droning on and on in his skull, but not even the whole song, just the chorus, and not even just the chorus, but the one chorus at the end with the high harmonies. And slowly, slowly, brief flashes of moments from last night pop up, things Ronnie said/did, shame flooding his nervous system in the form of nauseous dread with each flash.

Take it to the limit: One more time.

Well: What does he remember so far?

There was the loveseat by the answering machine: Ronnie slouched there, laughing, as the girl—whatshername—falls onto his lap, puts her arm around him, points at the answering machine and asks, "Is this anyone?"

The answering machine message: "Ronnie! Where are you?!" Maux. "Call me. Fucker."

Ronnie: "Naw naw naw . . . haw haw haw . . . just my crazy friend . . . you know."

They kiss: Tobacco tongue. Booze breath. Long. Lithe. Nineteen. *Hey Nineteen.*

She unsmooches her lips: "Wait a second," she whispers, smiles, trots off across the living room.

The Who: On the stereo. *Pictures of Lily . . . Lily oh Lileee . . . Lily oh Lileee . . . pictures of Lily* and that fucking French horn solo that slays him every single time he hears it.

Kelly and Caroline: That's her name. Caroline. She was the girl who was "older." Twenty-one. That's how they all met. They bounce up and down on couches, trying to match the rhythm of the songs.

Kelly: A frenzy of sweat and rolling eyeballs. Chemically-induced happiness.

The fifth: Floridian Comfort. The bottle is on the coffeetable. The girl—*hey, nineteen*—she weaves around Kelly and Caroline, reaches for the bottle. Glug, glug, glug.

That's how they met: Kelly took the weekend off. Fled to Gainesville with a wafer of ecstasy and a dot of mescaline. Fueled accordingly, he charms—and later, he quite literally charms the pants off of (hey-oh!)—Caroline, who's in the XYZ Liquor Store buying a fifth of whiskey for her underage friend, who waits outside in the car. Kelly tells her there's a "party" at Ronnie's, and she believes him. (Later, in less-trusting environments, Ronnie will think back on moments like these, when you could simply talk to a couple girls at a stupid liquor store and somehow get them back to your house on the flimsiest of pretenses, and maybe it isn't even the environment, but the age, because the immediate shame of the next day will pass, and years on, it's a fond memory of capital-Y Youth.) Ronnie and Kelly, they walk back with the twelve of Old Hamtramck, Kelly going on and on about "That Nnnnnugget!" Ronnie didn't get a look at whatshername, and what is her name? At Gatorroni's, as Kelly still goes on and on about the different things that happened—this antic, that antic—her name comes back to Ronnie.

Her name: Laney. Of course! Laneylaneylaneylaneylaney-laney! Oh, of course! Yes.

Anyway: Laney skips (yes, skips) back to Ronnie, stops in front of him, raises the bottle to her lips, drinks. She tells Ronnie how much she actually likes the burn of the Floridian Comfort. People are always talking about how they hate the burn. They can't drink the way Laney drinks. To which Ronnie, drunk and giggly, replies, quote, "Haw haw haw yeah!" She's back on his lap, and Ronnie, who doesn't really have an opinion one way or the other about the burn of Floridian Comfort, glug glug glugs, sets the bottle on the end table, stares at the blinking light on the answering machine, and Maux and her message contained therein, burps, mutters the common Floridian axiom, "Fuck it, dude," kisses Laney's neck, up to the side of her face, and then she turns, opens her lips, and again, the tobacco tongue, the booze breath.

As The Who mixtape plays on: spiders named Boris, pictures of Lily, teenage wastelands, squeeze boxes, and whoooooo are youuu, who-who who-who, who cares, because this is it—too easy, too perfect, too Gainesville—and it's Ronnie and Laney there on the loveseat—Mwah! Mwah! Mwah!—her tongue the sour ashy taste of bilish alkeehal and too many cigarettes and Ronnie loveloveloves it, his brain spinning "Wheeee!",

"Yeeeessss!" his heart pumping "Goooooooooooooooooo!" and The Who calls it a bargain, the best I ever had, and Moonie's drums crash and smash and pummel.

Kelly: Tells Ronnie how this was one of the best nights of his life, no shit, dude, as Ronnie sits there in a throb-stab hangover and "Take it to the Limit" still bouncing around in his head, unable to comprehend how last night was that big of a deal. This is how it goes anymore. Kelly tells him how it seems like "amazing" things are starting to happen for Ronnie here in Gainesville, noting that he even bought the food today, and Ronnie has to acknowledge that, yes, it's better than it was, but still.

Meh: Ronnie, he wants to shake Kelly and scream, "So what!?" Maybe it's the "come down" The Who are always singing about in *Quadrophenia*, or these things you slowly learn over time that have to be experienced over and over again before one can actually question the heretofore foregone conclusion that getting llllll-loaded and getting into some sexual (to use the clinical term) hanky-panky is innately fascinating and worthy of so much of your time. Because Ronnie, he feels like the wild oats, maybe they're finally sewn. And this is the age when one should be fighting the good fight, you know? Join up with the Anarchists in the Spanish Civil War. Teach and inspire a class of underprivileged children. Manage a ragtag scrappy underdog little league team and take them to the championships. Something. Anything. To put ideals into action. To put aside whatever the Bible said about "childish things." Hedonism. Guilt and shame over this bandless, novelless floundering, of having lived this kind of life several lifetimes over, sweating and groaning in the stupid pointless hungover imbalance of the late afternoon after.

What Ronnie doesn't tell Kelly: How, much later in the night, well past the time the condom performed its final float and bob in the toilet water before being spiraled away forever, hours into the curled away post-coital pass out, Ronnie wakes up to the sounds of Laney's violent heaving and vomiting of the Floridian Comfort. So much for loving the burn.

Something else Ronnie doesn't tell Kelly: How the early morning sun shone through his windows like a tawdry blue leisure suit.

And another thing: Her tattoos suck. Same with the nose ring. They mar this otherwise beautiful girl. *Hey, Nineteen.*

And: When Ronnie shut off the tape that had been flipping back and forth all night, she asks, in a soft voice, not worn ragged and haggard—yet—from one-too-many nights likes these, "What is this we've been listening to?" He told her. Flipper on one side. Television on the other. "Never heard of them," Laney said. "Of either of them." Yup. *Hey, Nineteen.*

Actually: The morning ain't that bad, really. They mumble smalltalk. Some laughs. She writes down her phone number on a piece of scrap paper on his desk, but they know, they both know.

Ronnie's bedroom: It reeked of everything wrong and everything stupid about last night.

Kelly: After pizza, they walk back to Myrrh House. Kelly goes back into his truck and drives off, away, back to Orlando, still so so so stoked about everything.

Ronnie: Stretched out on the couch, waiting for the hangover to pass, cursing the meh of it all. Ok, maybe not profound acts of heroism, but the unrelenting thought that he should be giving something back to the world, already. This life in Gainesville, it can't last. As good as it is, as good as it can be, too much of it is downright purgatorial. It can't go on like this. There's too much to see and do and be.

CLOWN VILLAGE

Ronnie wants to be left alone. He wants to hide in his room and read this Henry Miller book. He wants to stretch across this old brown musty cowboy couch, listen to Flipper and Television, crack open the novel, get to the part when ol' Hank goes off on wild tangents on the cosmology of vaginal desire, or whatever. His room is the only place to hide; to even set foot in the living room means having to hang out with Roger; to even set foot onto NW 4th Lane means running into neighbors; and don't even think about walking down 13th Street or University. The acquaintances are everywhere, and they will distract Ronnie from Serious Business. Ronnie considers himself, at his core, to be a Very Serious Person, with Very Serious Concerns. He needs more quiet nights. Instead, he wastes time with strange women, goes with the flow, passively follows along for the ride.

Ronnie Altamont is undisciplined. No shit, Sherlock.

The people who surround him now, many a year or two away from college graduation, never seem to do anything—sitting around for hours and hours watching movies, talking about nothing much at all besides this little world and the people who populate it—but they still pull off straight As and keep near-4.0 GPAs. Ronnie was never that kind of smart. Only by shutting himself off from the world could he get anything done. When he thinks of all the writing he needs to do, but not only that, all the necessary reading he needs to do, the imagined work takes on the shape of a mammoth, stratospheric pile, because he must read, to figure out how he can tell his stories and what he should tell about his stories and even if the stories are worth telling. Nights like these, Ronnie regrets not following Kelly's initial advice, and moving straight to Chicago instead of this Gainesville detour, because, really, what can Gainesville teach him that five years at the University of Central Florida hasn't already? And to even think about what is really worth telling, because nobody thinks goofs like him ever have anything meaningful to say about the world. This life in Florida, it lacks depth, importance, what DH Lawrence called "le grand sérieux." It's a sheltered life in a part of the world many consider to be "paradise," where his only true escape and source of adventure has come through playing in bands, which in itself is a kind of luxury many in the world don't get. There is nothing to see here, nothing to tell. Ronnie has been giving serious thought to giving it up. "It has all been said before," he thinks, and laughs to himself because "It has all been said before" has been said so many times before.

Ronnie closes the Henry Miller, closes his eyes. He starts to fall asleep when he hears a pounding on the front door, followed by squeals from a recorder, maraca shakes, clanky pots and pans, and Paul's voice, singing in the same melody as Andy Williams' "Moon River," "Clowwwwwwwwwwwwwn Villlllage!" Feminine laughter. Cacophony from the recorder, the maraca, the pots and pans. Paul's voice, again, only this time, imitating Luther from *The Warriors*, "Alllltamahhhhhhhhhhnt. Come out to . . . play-yayyyyyyyyyy!"

"Why does everybody imitate that guy in that movie?" Ronnie thinks.

"Please don't open it," Ronnie whispers, staring at the plaster cracks in the ceiling, hearing Roger's heavy-fast trod to the front door.

The door opens. "Where is he? Where is he?" Paul yells, stepping through the Myrrh House front door. He knocks, opens, steps inside Ronnie's room, flanked by Icy Filet on one side, who shakes an avocado-shaped maraca, and Siouxsanna Siouxsanne, blowing into a recorder.

"He's reading!" Paul says, pointing at Ronnie. "Reading!" Paul steps to the couch, stands over Ronnie. "Altamont! There's no reading in Clown Village! We're getting you out of here." Paul pulls at Ronnie's left arm, sings, "We're taking you back to . . . Clooow-wwwwwn Villlllllage." He bends over, picks up the Henry Miller book off the floor. "Reading!" he scoffs. Paul tosses the book to his left, where it plops onto the loveseat between the closet and the bathroom.

Ronnie sits up, stands, sighs. "There better be beer in Clown Village," he says.

"Rrrrrronnie Altamont, we're lllllloaded," Siouxsanna Siouxsanne says, punctuating this with shrill free jazz recorder squeals. She takes Ronnie by the right hand. "You have a fun name to say, Rrrrrronie Alllllllllltamont. It's as fun as singing Clowwwwwwn Villlllllage! I'm lllllloaded."

Shaking off the sleepiness and the solitude, Ronnie follows them into the living room. Roger stands in the middle of the room, looking through a video camera. "I think I need to document Clown Village," he says.

"You fucking better," Paul says, then sings yet again, "Cloww-wwwn Villlllage!"

"Clowwwwwwwn Villllllllllage!" Ronnie repeats.

"That's it, Altamont! That's the stuff," Paul says, and the five of them step out of the Myrrh House.

"I llllllllike you," Siouxsanna Siouxsanne says, still holding Ronnie's hand.

Clown Village is two blocks east of the Myrrh House, and it bears a striking resemblance to Paul's house. In a tiny dingy living room with white wallpaper made out of 8½" by 11" show fliers from the six years Paul has lived in Gainesville, fifteen people—among them, Neal and Mouse—smoosh around a battered coffeetable crowded with several large jugs of cheap wine. Randomly, people yell-sing "Clowwwwwwwn Villlllllage!" in different keys, different tones, over the din of maracas, pots and pans, crash and ride cymbals on stands, drum sticks, tambourines, kazoos, slide whistles.

Ronnie steps up, joins in, bellowing "Clowwwwwwwwwwwn Villllllliiiiiiiiidge" in the falsetto timbre of Jello Biafra from the Dead Kennedys.

"Best Jello Biafra imitation in town," Neal announces, running to Ronnie, raising his right arm in the air like a cham-peen prize fighter.

Everyone cheers. Ronnie is sincerely honored by this.

Siouxsanna Siouxsanne is seated to Ronnie's left. She wears a green knee-length dress, barefoot. Ronnie turns to her, smiles.

"I'm llllllloaded!" Siouxsanna Siouxsanna announces, holding a glass coffee mug filled with red wine in her non-recorder holding hand.

"Oh yeah?" Ronnie says, stepping closer, standing over her.

"Yeah, Rrrrronnie! I am!"

"Good! Because, tomorrow, I'm taking you to Long John Silver's for brunch!" Ronnie grabs a jug off the coffee table, hoists it in a "Cheers."

Siouxsanna Siouxsanne stands, wraps her arms around Ronnie's neck, kisses him on the left cheek. "I lllove this guy!" she announces. "At first, I wasn't sure, but now?" She falls backwards onto the couch. Her eyes close, her head bobs up and down like somebody's uncle trying not to fall asleep on the couch watching the sixth inning of an unremarkable baseball game.

Ronnie laughs, steps through his friends yelling "Clown Village!" meanwhile making an unlistenable cacophony of percussive clanks and honky squonks. He finds the tiny bathroom. The mirror is above the toilet. He catches his reflection as he empties his bladder, and the thought—wine-fueled as it is—hits Ronnie so hard, he has to say it aloud:

"This is our music."

Ornette Coleman said it, and Galaxie 500 said it, and now Ronnie Altamont is saying it, and while he always knew what it meant—now, he really and truly knows what it means. He squirts out the last of it, flushes, zips up, washes his hands, keeps repeating, "This is our music . . . this is our music!" loving how you can vary the accented word, and it always works.

He rejoins the party, screams "Clowwwwn Villllage" still in a Biafra timbre, because he accepts that this is his role in this mess. The song has taken on a dirgelike quality now that everyone is beyond drunken stupor. What is the point of it? No one knows, nor cares. When Ronnie asks Paul a couple nights from now over

BRIAN COSTELLO

at Gatorroni's what he thinks Clown Village meant, he shrugs and says, "I was bored. It sounded like a funny idea at the time."

Ronnie is so taken with this idea running through his head and what it means, he doesn't care that by the time he returns to the couch, Siouxsanna Siouxsanne and Neal are kissing, fooling around. He needs to leave Clown Village, walk back to the Myrrh House, and ponder the epic possibilities of "This is Our Music."

Which he does, wine-drunk and beyond happy, as the shredded voices and worn-out arms fade with each step away from Clown Village. The fog, the angst, the self-doubt disappear like the deep dark puddles on the roads those Florida summer afternoons when it rains for one hour and one hour only, and just as quick, the roads are dry again. In the Sweat Jam life, the stories are here. Right here. This is what he has and this is what he knows. Our music is the racket of Clown Village. Our music is the way Siouxsanna Siouxsanne says the word "lllllllllloaded." Our music is Maux's studied misanthropy, Paul's slacker buffoonery, Icy Filet's hip-hop ambitions. It's these flailing, brooding, self-absorbed, jovial, worry-free, generally happy motions up and down this good-enough purgatory along the one-lane streets of the student ghetto of Gainesville. Our music is All of This, and while none of it seems the stuff of Great Literature, it's Our Music, and here is the time and place. They have their music, and Ronnie has his.

It's this. It's All of This.

One would think Ronnie, upon entering his house, would immediately run to the typewriter and begin to try and tell his stories, liberated as he believed he was from all litmag ambitions and English Department hang-ups on Big Lives and Big Themes. And indeed, inspired as he was, he ran to the kitchen, grabbed an Old

Hamtramck tallboy from the fridge, took a seat at the desk in his bedroom, turned on the typewriter, opened the beer, drank the beer, and typed

"THIS IS OUR MUSIC"

in all-caps, because it was very important and should be typed as such. Unsure of what to say next, he turned on the Flipper/Television dubbed tape on the stereo, walked to his mattresses, plopped over, and passed out.

SHIT FROM AN OLD NOTEBOOK

"September 9, 1996. 9:30 p.m.

"There is no future in rock music; writing is where it's at. I don't want to be 35, with my life over, reminiscing about a tour, some records, etc. Reminiscing and living in the past is not the way I want to live. The past, and the people who were a part of it, tend to go their way, and I go mine."

PORTLAND PATTY

Portland Patty wants to believe Ronnie Altamont is different as she watches him roll out of her bed and shuffle across the creaking hardwood floor on bare feet, out the bedroom into the hallway light, used condom between thumb and index finger like the tail of an unwanted fish on the verge of getting tossed back into the lake. She hears the toilet flush, the spray of the faucet, on, then off. Squeaking footsteps returning. His naked silhouette does not reveal the crumpled, unwashed clothing, the dirt eating into the sides of his glasses, the stubbly short black hair, the wine stains and condiment flakes caked around his mouth. What can she do with someone like this? So typical of Gainesville, but then again—maybe, she hopes—not at all.

Ronnie climbs back into this queen-sized bed that has been half-empty for far too long. While this little house and this little patch of dirty flat front yard conspire with the palm trees and the sunshine to remind her she is a long way from home—in distance, in time—here in bed, she can almost believe she's back home in Portland, but only if Ronnie Altamont is really and truly different.

"Are you staying?" Portland Patty asks.

"Is that ok?" Ronnie asks through the narcoleptic groan of wine-sleep.

"Sure," she says, trying to sound unconcerned, noncommittal. She stares into the darkness, a long way from home. "I mean, I don't mind, but what are you going to say to Maux?"

Portland Patty looks to her left, to Ronnie. His answer is a snore, a phlegmatically redundant inhale and exhale. In her own wine-spiral, Portland Patty remains unsure of what, if anything, she can possibly do with a boy like this.

•

"Roger says you're sleazy," Portland Patty says, the next morning, as Ronnie stretches out his legs and yawns, trying to piece together how he ended up here in this bed, an actual bed, off the ground and everything, grateful for the Saturday morning and its lack of merciless snooze buttons. Portland Patty reclines to his right, hand propping head up. "He also says you drink too much, and you're moody. Other than that though, he says you're a nice guy."

"That so?" Ronnie laughs. "He told me you were an acid casualty." He turns to face Portland Patty. Green eyes peeking out of lower back-length straight blonde-brown hair. He had forgotten what it was like to be with a girl with long hair. Lanky-long, with tattoos covering all the skin from the right wrist to the right shoulder, swirls, patterns, reds, blacks, blues. "He says you're weird and kind've a hippie and that you've done too many drugs and they scattered your brain."

Portland Patty laughs a hearty insincere "Oh ho ho then!" and adds, "Must have. Why else would I have ended up waking up next to you?"

"Hey-ohhhh!" Ronnie says, in his best Ed MacMahon bellow, tossing the thin red blanket over her head, this blanket that had provided unneeded warmth as they slept off the drink through another night of Florida's endless late summer.

"But he also said you were nice," Ronnie added.

"With friends like these . . . "

"Um, who needs dildos?" Ronnie finished.

Portland Patty laughs, sincerely laughs this time, at the stupid-strange joke. There is a refreshing lack of awkwardness to this morning-after. In bed, unclothed and hungover, talking in a leisurely back-and-forth.

"So why do they call you 'Portland Patty?'"

"Why do you think?"

"You're from Portland?"

"That's right, Ronnie Altamont. I am from Portland."

"Oregon? Maine?"

"Oregon."

"That's a long way to go. School?"

"I had to get out of Portland," she says, conspiratorially. "I had a lot of trouble in that town. "

"Really?"

Portland Patty laughs. "No. It was school. I wanted to live someplace different. And it doesn't get much different than this."

"Fine, but why not just Patty?"

"There's already a Punk Rock Patty, a Puking Patty, a New Orleans Patty, and a Heroin Patty. Having a Portland in front of my name separates me from these. It makes it easier to gossip, as people like to do here, as I'm sure you've noticed."

"Yeah. Totally." Ronnie leans forward, shakes his head. "Sleazy? My roommate called me sleazy?"

"What's this I hear about you and Maux?"

"He told you about her too?" Ronnie rolls his eyes, blurts out "That *fucker!*" before he can stop himself.

"No. He didn't. She's crazy."

"She's not crazy. She's ludicrous. How do you know about it?"

"I've seen you two around. At parties. At shows. She's crazy. If she's not crazy, she's mean."

"Nah, she's just ludicrous. And I should break off whatever it is we've been doing. It hasn't been much."

"Do what you want," Portland Patty says.

"Right now? I want to go back to sleep," Ronnie says. Instead, he stretches out in bed once more, still trying to piece together what happened yesterday, and how he ended up here.

Portland Patty leaves the bedroom, steps into the kitchen to make coffee, too sleepy, too hungover, too soon, to decide if Ronnie Altamont is different.

•

Yesterday. Ronnie was relaxing across the larger of the two beige couches in the living room, reading some book about the seven habits of highly effective Celestine Prophets. As the perfect fusion of the self-help and pop mysticism genres, this was a popular book in the mid-1990s. Not that Ronnie wanted to be like a highly effective Celestine Prophet; one of Ronnie's co-workers at some point (in one of the dozens of jobs he blew through at the time) lent it to him upon finding out that Ronnie Altamont enjoyed reading. These are always the books co-workers lend you when they find out you like reading. It was an otherwise boring Friday afternoon. With the semester underway, the temp job at the used college bookstore was winding down. Ronnie was reduced from a high of 60 hours three weeks ago, to 20 hours this week, with ten next week, and it'll be five after that, before a somewhat sad parting, as it's been one of the better gigs Ronnie has held.

On the smaller of the two beige couches, Roger leaned into his handheld tape recorder, communicating valuable insights, as some Finnish film played on television.

"As a metaphor for nuclear holocaust, Djkajollskjoldj's masterful use of taxidermied animals in an abandoned hunting lodge suggests the indomitable force that is life itself, even in the midst of such large-scale annihilation. Furthermore, when—"

"We gotta go," Ronnie said, closing the book, flinging it behind him into the open space between the front door and the couches.

"You made me lose my thought, Ronnie," Roger said, setting the microphone onto the coffeetable, turning off the tape recorder. "I have a paper due."

"It was a bad thought anyway," Ronnie says, standing. "Let's go to Orlando."

Roger paused the VCR, freezing the Finnish film on the split image of a mushroom cloud and a stuffed grizzly bear towering over a crying little girl with blonde braids. "Orlando. Why?"

"It's Friday?" Ronnie said.

"That's not a good reason," Roger answered, moving to unpause the remote.

"I need to pick up a final check I never received from the asbestos gig. If I pick it up today, I can cash it. I'll buy you dinner."

Roger stopped the VCR; the TV screen changed to blue. "Let's go. Whatever. That was a dumb movie anyway."

"There ya go, dude . . . That's the stuff, the spirit, the ol' whathaveyou," Ronnie said, grabbing his keys off the mantle.

They stepped out of the house. Ronnie locked the front door. This girl with long brown-blonde hair, a black t-shirt with the stark fundamentalist white lettering of a local hardcore band, and frayed black pants cut off right above the knees pedaled up to them on her bike. There were always people like her in the Gainesville Student Ghetto, riding down these streets, looking for something to do, people to talk to, conspirators in the time-killing.

Roger waved. "Hey Portland Patty," he said. "We're going to Orlando for the afternoon. Ya wanna go?"

"Ok," she said. With that, she locked her bike to a post holding up the roof's overhang above the front door.

"Don't think about it," Roger muttered to Ronnie as Portland Patty moved ahead of them.

"Think about what?" Ronnie said, already running to the car to unlock it for Portland Patty, to open it for Portland Patty, to turn on the charm and introduce himself to Portland Patty, who smiled and shook his hand before climbing into the back seat of the blandy apple green sedan.

"Good," Roger said.

Southbound. Gainesville gives way to Payne's Prairie, and the immense prairie gives way to the horse farms. Through the rear view mirror of his blandy apple green sedan, Ronnie steals glances at Portland Patty. The omnipresent Florida sun has given her complexion a brown-freckled tint around her green eyes. Freckles dot her long narrow nose, and the lips . . . the lips the lips the lips . . . neither thick nor thin but with a kind of citrusy juiciness, exaggerated perfectly by an overbite and two slightly bucked front teeth.

Portland Patty stares out the window at the passing scenery. All three of them are silent, lost in the reverie of the trafficless road winding through the jungles, the open spaces, the giant skies, the hotels, the motels, the timeshares, the billboards, the swamps, all the wonders of an almost-homeland viewed through dirty windows, their silence layered by the sounds of the full-blasted air-conditioner, and the Arizona-echo of the Meat Puppets' second album, its cavernous country-punk ricochets bouncing and rolling through the hiss of an old cassette, always the perfect soundtrack to the Florida countryside.

Not until they enter Greater Orlando, as the hypnotic tranquil countryside is broken up by the spectacle of the endless commercial districts, does anyone speak.

"So. How do you like Orlando?" Ronnie asks, looking at Portland Patty through the rear view mirror as they wait at the 87th stoplight at State Road 436.

"I feel like a part of my soul has been stripped away," she says, as off-handedly as if she were discussing a slight change in the weather. "Not to sound too dramatic or anything."

"No," Roger says. "There's a lot of nothing in this everything."

Ronnie takes in the intersections, the gas stations and churches and plazas and parking lots. "I can't beat it up anymore," he says. "I've lived here. I know what it is. It's a city of cheap salesmen, of swampland realtors who pitch their mission statements like eighth graders bullshitting their way through book reports."

Traffic scoots forward, ever-so-slowly. "Yikes," Portland Patty says.

"Not to sound cynical or anything," Ronnie adds, smiling, fearing he's blown it.

"Can I use that in one of my screenplays?" Roger asks. He turns around to face Portland Patty. "You know I write screenplays, right?"

"No, I didn't," Portland Patty says.

"Yeah, I've written several so far. Mainly, I'm concerned—perhaps even obsessed to a fault, with the struggle of the individual in a consumer-driven . . . "

"Yeah, you can use that in your next screenplay," Ronnie interrupts, turning up the Meat Puppets. Portland Patty laughs.

Ronnie finds the asbestos removal office, located in the back of an industrial park. There's no one there he recognizes. AQ is on a site. Tommy and Bassanovich are in college now, presumably learning the truth about the pussy in the great Middle Western college towns.

Ronnie cashes his check, takes Roger and Portland Patty to an appalling Mexican restaurant on 436 called Jalapeño Larry's. Roger sits across from Ronnie, Portland Patty to his right. Jalapeño Larry's was close enough to UCF, and Ronnie would often take Maggie there for dinner. They basked in the ridiculousness of it. Mexican restaurants are always bad when they have a Spanish name every gringo can understand. Ronnie loves the idea of taking Portland Patty and Roger here. So bad, it's great.

The server is one of those insanely unreal polyethylene types you find in almost every restaurant in Orlando, trained to pretend like the very idea of serving you your food and reading lines from the script dictated from Corporate is putting her on the verge of the greatest orgasm of her life. Hot sauce on the table with names like "Sandman Unsane's Tex-Mex Weapon of Ass Destruction" and "Colonel Capscium's Dirty Dawg Poblanogeddon." Lite alternative rock on satellite radio. Walls of televisions, literal walls of televisions making laser noises as they go from one sports highlight to the next, reported by some smug douche from the Northeast. This dining area, one of countless autopiloted nightmares masquerading as a good-time party atmosphere here in Central Florida.

On the back of the menu, "El Statement del Mission." Ronnie flips his menu over, points, says, "Here. Read this. Everything you need to know about Orlando is right here."

The chips and salsa are served. Ronnie, Portland Patty, and Roger read "El Statement":

"Jalapeño Larry's is an Acapulco-style cantina del fiesta specializing in distinctive frozen drinks. These drinks are created by an expert team of experienced bar operators and are hand mixed with pride.

"The décor of Jalapeño Larry's is designed to inspire laid back thoughts of an amazing tropical environment. The beautiful faux roof around the bar is reminiscent of sitting on the porch of a Mexican bunga-

low, and the mix of tropical colors and light woods creates a relaxing and welcoming feeling. Tongue and cheek warning signs about the potency of Jalapeño Larry's frozen drinks add humor to the walls, along with photographs of partygoers of the past and present. Lighthearted Acapulco-inspired artworks cover the downstairs dance floor walls as well as the balcony upstairs. With over 55 televisions, a sound system, and a state-of-the-art intelligent light show, Jalapeño Larry's is the perfect location to have some drinks and dance until morning.

"For lunch or dinner, la cocina at Jalapeño Larry's can't be beat. Our tacos, burritos, and quesadillas are made-to-order, and for the health conscience [sic], there are many vegetarian options, including our world-renowned Caeser [sic] Salad.

"While you are sitting at the bar you will notice the famous wall of frozen drinks. Perhaps the most well-known (and well-consumed) of these celebrated concoctions is something we call "The Suicide." With five liquors and five fruit juices, you have never experienced a frozen drink like this.

"Although Jalapeño Larry's is an easygoing hangout spot, by nightfall the nightlife party atmosphere in Jalapeño Larry's can rival any local entertainment venue. Whether it's "fantastico" food, "loco" DJs, drinking games, talented local musicians, unique frozen cocktails, famous drink specials, titillating servers and bartenders, or just a place to have a drink, Jalapeño Larry's is what you're looking for."

"I was thinking about maybe getting a distinctive frozen drink from the famous wall—and maybe even having the unique experience of drinking 'The Suicide,'" Ronnie says, "But that sign over there says, 'Slippery When Wasted,' and I don't want to hurt myself."

"Relax, Ron," Roger says. "It's a tongue and cheek sign. That means you won't—really—get slippery when wasted."

"Yeah, Ronnie," Portland Patty adds. "Relax. You should be inspired to have laid back thoughts by the design."

"You're right," Ronnie says. "I'm a little worked up here, but who can blame me? I'm in anticipation of the intelligent light show. I'm so sick of light shows that are a little bit on the dumb side, if you know what I mean."

"Who isn't?" Portland Patty says. She's never been to Orlando before. It seems like the type of place where irony was your best defense. "For my part, as a vegan and therefore health conscious, I want my only option, the, uh, See-zer Salad."

"But the dressing probably has anchovies," Roger says, "and it has paramesan--"

"Yeah, I know," Portland Patty says. "Guess I'm guacin' it."

As they talk like this, their "titillating server" arrives, announcing, in the loud sportscaster tone of the Very White, "Alright, Señors y Señorita! Here are your implausibly extreme frozen drinks!" Ronnie receives his plastic cup of Rebel Yeller, described in the menu as "A muy loco blend of FloCo, SoCo, Margarita Mix, with a dash of casselberry juice." Roger receives his plastic cup of Fun y Spontaneity, described in the menu as, "Jalapeño Larry sez: 'Me gusta this intoxicating mix of Everclear, Lime Gatorade, and Absolut Nectarine vodka!'" Portland Patty receives her plastic cup of Hace Mucho Calor y Frio, described in the menu as "So cool, it's hot, so hot, it's cool, this certifiably awesome blended drink combines Crème de Menthe, Crème de Cacao, vermouth, tequila, and a few secret ingredients from our 'Instituto del Bebido' that is guar-olé!-teed to leave you in an ecstasy of sweats and shivers."

Ronnie raises his plastic cup, smiles. "To Gainesville," he says.

"Cheers," Roger and Portland Patty say, pressing their cups into his.

"So why did you take us here?" Portland Patty asks after a wincing sip from her Hace Mucho Calor y Frio.

"What?" Ronnie extends his arms, looks around. "You don't like it?"

"It's fine, I guess," Portland Patty says. "I don't know, I'm thinking there has to be better places. Does this have sentimental value for you?"

Ronnie looks away, to one of the unavoidable TVs. What he doesn't want to talk about is, how when these stupid drinks kicked in, how hard they would laugh, how every volley back and forth between Ronnie and Maggie was some kind of comedy gem in a language only they could understand. They were the kinds of inside jokes where they would choke and howl and snort and cough and gasp, so funny to them and only them. Ronnie isn't going to discuss it.

"Ronnie hates Orlando," Roger says. "He thinks he's some kind of dissident, or like an exile, living in Gainesville. There are plenty of places we could have gone. There's a strip of Vietnamese restaurants here that are awesome, but Ronnie would rather find a place that proves his point."

"Oh, touché," Ronnie says, sneering, booze already kicking in. He grabs a handful of tortilla chips, throws them at Roger's head. Roger laughs, tosses the chips aside, combs out his hair.

"You think you're an exile?" Portland Patty says. "Try living here when you're from Portland."

"People always come to Gainesville from Portland," Roger says. "It's like a whistle stop on the Trustafarian circuit."

"Whatever," Portland Patty says. "Anyway, none of this," and here, she extends her hands out to the décor of Jalapeño Larry's, out to the concrete beyond the restaurant, "is Gainesville. We can agree on that, right?"

"No," Ronnie says. "It isn't."

"I've been everywhere," Portland Patty continues. "Not much out there is better than Gainesville."

"That's fucking depressing," Roger says.

"Maybe it is," Ronnie says. "I mean look at this." Ronnie points at the menu. "Even these menus. This desperate striving idiocy of these United States."

"You shouldn't be so cynical," Portland Patty says.

"Only when I'm here," Ronnie says. He turns to look her in the eyes. "Normally, I'm a lot of fun." And here, ok, there's something in the way Ronnie Altamont says this which makes Portland Patty start thinking that maybe Ronnie is really and truly different, and not the different of all these other guys hanging out and hanging around on the streets and front porches.

"Gainesville's meaner than you think," Roger says. Ronnie laughs. By "mean," Ronnie assumes Roger means all the gossip and inevitable petty horseshit indigenous to every small town.

"I'm serious," Roger says.

"It's not that bad," Portland Patty says. Ronnie notices, really notices, her smile. It's never triggered by anything in particular, but by everything in particular. "People are always talking, but you don't have to listen."

"You'll see," Roger says. Ronnie and Portland Patty look to each other. They both start laughing. It's nervous laughter, seemingly apropos of nothing.

"Excuse me," Portland Patty says, standing up, a little wobbly, as Ronnie notices. "My muy loco drink is making me have to use el baño, comprende?" She giggles. Ronnie giggles. She walks away.

The moment Portland Patty is out of earshot, this is the moment when Roger leans in, whispers, "She's a total acid casualty."

"Really?" Ronnie says. "She seems alright." The food arrives, a tamales dinner for Ronnie, a taco salad for Roger, and guacamole for Portland Patty.

"I heard she's tripped hundreds of times, dude. Thousands." Roger leans back in his chair, speaks louder, "So you don't get any ideas. She's not a, you know, punk rock nnnnugget, and I know what that means to you."

It is too late for Ronnie not to get ideas. Sometimes, the entire state of Florida seemed like one big acid casualty, the way people talked about spending their entire high school and early college years on daily acid trips. If Roger is trying to get Ronnie to think twice, he's failing.

"What about Maux?" Roger adds.

Ronnie shrugs. When Portland Patty returns, it's Ronnie's turn to excuse himself. He can only imagine what Roger is about to say about him. He'll probably bring up Maux. Asshole.

Inside the door marked "CABALLEROS," Ronnie washes his hands, breathes in, breathes out, tries not to look in the mirror, tries not to think about anything. He is in love again, the way he always thinks he's in love again. He thinks he knows what is next. He isn't worried about Roger. All he needs to do is get back to Gainesville, and it will be alright.

"How's the food?" Ronnie asks when he returns.

They both shrug.

"I need another drink," Roger says.

Another round for Roger and Portland Patty. Ronnie switches to water. Rather than trying to get the girl drunk, as so many other dipshits do, Ronnie wants to get his roommate drunk. He'll talk and talk, and get increasingly surly, all of which finally culminates, as Ronnie knew it would, in him standing up and announcing over a quarter-eaten taco salad:

"Let's leave this dump. I need to get back. This place sucks."

"Alright," Ronnie says, smiling. "Let's go." He picks up the bill, glad to, just once, actually take care of a bill.

Through Orlando's inexcusable early rush hour traffic, they eventually make it back into the countryside, in the light of a grape and honey hued sunset. Roger talks, and talks, and talks. Turning back to Portland Patty, he talks of screenplays, of films he's seen, of films he wants to see. He goes on lengthy tangents, following every thread of his thoughts, devoid of filter between brain and mouth. Roger is going for it, using everything he has—his brains, his thoughts, his intellect. Ronnie has tuned him out; Portland Patty throws out the occasional "Really?" or "Oh," and this encourages him. Roger is drunk. He gets drunk easily. Ronnie knows this much about his current roommate. Two cups of Fun y Spontaneity, and he's in blotto speech, telling it like it is about film, about films, about film criticism. He goes on, and on, and on, until the halfway point of the trip—in beautiful Leesburg, Florida, while passing an orange juice processing plant, he turns and immediately falls asleep. When Ronnie sees he's asleep, he looks up in the rearview mirror, to Portland Patty, who smiles at him. Ronnie smiles back, makes the "whew!" gesture of a right hand wiping imaginary sweat off his forehead. Portland Patty

BRIAN COSTELLO

laughs at this gesture. The Meat Puppets get them home, back into the beauty of North-Central Florida.

Ronnie drops off Roger first. He wakes him up. "We're home, buddyboy!" Ronnie says.

Roger opens his eyes, makes that jolt-gasp sound people make when they wake up on travels to find they've arrived at their destination. "Oh! Here!"

"Yup. Home. See you soon." Ronnie says.

Roger looks to the backseat. Portland Patty is still there. "Bye, Roger," she says.

Roger looks to Ronnie. Ronnie gives a barely perceptible nod, as if to say, "Time to go now. Time to go."

Without a word, Roger opens the car door, steps out, slams the door. Ronnie immediately puts the car in reverse, leaves NW 4th Lane for Portland Patty's house, north on NW 13th Street, past the high school, the Wal-Mart. She lives in a brown duplex. Ronnie pulls in the driveway, about to ask her out, when she looks at him, in the rearview mirror and asks, "Do you want to come inside, listen to music?"

Ronnie shuts off the car.

Music is always the catalyst for getting the boys and girls into each other's homes, the ostensible, weighted, lines you read between. The wine helps—in this case, a jug of unlabelled Chablis poured into *Empire Strikes Back* collectors' glasses from Burger King—Ronnie sipping from a Boba Fett glass, Portland Patty from Lando Calrissian.

Music. Drinks. It was the only diplomatic way we knew how to get to sex.

(The blasé coldness, the self-preserving cynicism of the smug mid-20s onward hasn't sunk in yet.)

•

"What's a Volvo-driving pirate's favorite radio station?" Portland Patty asks. She sits across from Ronnie at Long John Silver's, cardboard pirate hat pulled down across her forehead.

"Pirates don't drive Volvos," Ronnie says between bites of hushpuppy.

"Will you just ask 'What?' please, Ronnie?" She looks so perfect in a pirate hat, he thinks, the long blonde-brown hair flowing out and around the brim. (Maux would never go to LJS with him: quote, "That place sucks and it's nasty.")

"Ok, Ok, what?" Ronnie manages between chomps of tartar-drenched fishflanks, flakes and chunks dripping out his mouth. "I mean, I know, but I want to hear you tell me."

"NPArrrrrrrrrrrrrrrr." She laughs and snorts at her own joke, laughter an exhaled melodious tittering hee-hee-hee followed by inhaled free-jazz saxophone goose honks.

Ronnie laughs, more at her reaction than the joke itself. "Jesus, that was awful."

"Aw, c'mon, Ronnie!"

He reaches across the greasy table, swipes the cardboard pirate hat off her head, hair trailing behind the hat and above the table. He puts it on, yarrs out an, "Avast, why aren't ye eating any seabiscuits, ya scallywag?"

"I told you I'm vegan. And you took me here anyway."

"Yawn." Ronnie cannot explain his sudden obsession with Long John Silvers. It occurs to him that it's one of those fast food chains that are everywhere, but it doesn't seem like anyone actually goes there to eat. Even this afternoon, lunchtime on a Saturday, no one's eating here except for this pink-faced flat-topped overalled farm-boy-looking kid, sitting in the front, looking out the nautical windows at 8th Avenue. Thinking this way, Ronnie got it into his head that it would be hilarious to take girls here. On dates. As a litmus test. Because if they couldn't put up with Long John Silvers, they wouldn't be able to put up with much of anything else about Ronnie, and it would save the trouble of attempting a relationship.

"I can't eat anything here."

"Yawn."

"Shut up, Ronnie."

"Yawn." Portland Patty reaches across the table, punches Ronnie in the chest, with a right arm swirling with kaleidoscopic, even hypnotic tattoos from shoulder to wrist, retakes the pirate hat.

Ronnie laughs. "What are you going to eat then, matey?" he asks.

"I'll eat later." She refits the pirate hat on her head. "I had heard you liked this place."

"You heard I think it's funny to go here?"

"Everybody knows about Ronnie Altamont."

Ronnie shrugs, expels a bitter pshaw. He has a first and a last name here now too. He can't escape it. "Everybody hates me here," he says. "I'm not emotive enough. Too weird. Too drunk. Something."

"You seem nice." Portland Patty, she means this, trying to hide her amusement at the way he eats this greasy fried offal. "You're different, I think." She's almost convinced, by virtue of being here at Long John Silver's as opposed to all the more obvious spots they could have gone to eat. But then, maybe they would see Maux, so maybe he isn't that different. Maybe he thought of the one place he knew he would run into no one.

"I'm nice. I'm different," Ronnie repeats, deadpan. He looks at her, bugs out his eyes, stabs one of the tartar and malt vinegar-soaked fish flanks with the plastic spork he holds in his left hand, holds the fish flank aloft and loudly proclaims, "I AM THE AYA-TOULLAH, OF ROCK AND ROLLAH!"

"Put that down," Portland Patty says. "You're ridiculous. I've seen that movie."

"It's who I am, and that's what you haven't heard about me yet," Ronnie says, slowly lowering the fish flank. "That's my rank, baby."

"Whatever."

Ronnie wonders how long until she discovers the truth. How will he blow it this time? With Maux around, and that other girl he spent the night with, he can definitely guess.

Ronnie drives Portland Patty home. They exchange phone numbers. Kisses in the car, as the same Meat Puppets tape from yesterday still plays, Curt Kirkwood moaning, . . . *there's a lot out there but don't be scared / who needs action when you've got words?*

This is too easy. They both think this—Ronnie driving away, Portland Patty standing in the driveway, watching him leave, tattooed right arm upraised in a brief wave, fingers up and down, up and down.

•

Mac Arthur's Park is melting in the dark / all that sweet green icing / flowing dowooooon . . .

It's one of these typical Florida afternoon downpours, where the drops hit like thousands of water balloons. Ronnie is walking home from the used college textbook store gig, belting out the Richard Harris classic "Mac Arthur Park," an attempt to laugh through the rain soaking his clothes and glasses, to laugh at the realization that the job is now, officially and inevitably, finished, and the money would be running out very soon. The students are settled in their classes—books purchased, books returned, books sold. The copypack orders are filled. Ronnie had hoped to stay on permanently—for once, after finally learning, through the magic of asbestos removal, that he was a hard worker, and, also for once, his bosses liked him—but it was seasonal work, and the season was over.

Someone left a cake out in the rain / and I don't think I can take it / because it took so long to bake it / and I'll never have that recipe uh-gayne / oh noooooooo.

Jobs. Oh, the jobs. And the guitar. It hasn't been touched in months. Ronnie thinks he hid it in the closet before a party so it wouldn't get stolen, but he's really not too sure. The writing. Only when thoroughly drunk, home from whatever, he scribbles illegible words in ninety-nine cent notebooks on whatever drunken drama feels so terribly important at that moment.

What now, what now? Ronnie walks down University for home. He passes the feminist bookstore. A familiar voice behind him. "Where are you going jerk? And where have you been? Jerk."

Maux stands in the threshold, cracking the door open and closed enough so the motion detectors continually beep.

"Lost my job today," Ronnie says, standing in the rain, beyond the saturation point, accepting that he is going to be drenched until he finds shelter. He shrugs, holds out his arms, points at the rain. "Stuck out here. What are you doing?"

"Nothing." With a tip of her head to the store behind her,

a wicked smile spreads across her face, and she adds, "I'm just checking out what the dykes are reading these days."

"Wow. That's really classy, Maux." Maux laughs that mean-spirited preteen boy laugh of hers. Ronnie would like to have a meeting between his mind, his heart, and his dick, in which the mind and the heart collectively kick the dick's ass while saying, "Walk away. Turn around and walk away," but the dick still—still!—trumps everything, and says, "Look at her. Look at those long white legs and that short black dress and the tight yellow t-shirt and the pale skin and the indigo hair uh humina humina humina . . . "

Thus conflicted, Ronnie says nothing.

"Aw, I'm kidding, Ron," Maux says. "Get outta the rain, dumbass."

Ronnie is about to step into the shelter of the feminist bookstore, when he hears the Teutonic buzz of a Volvo car horn. He turns. The passenger side window scrolls down.

"Need a ride?" Portland Patty asks, leaned over, peeking through the half-opened window.

Heart, mind, and dick, for a refreshing change, are in unanimous agreement.

"Sure!" Ronnie shouts, runs to the green Volvo station wagon. "See you later," he waves to Maux, opens the door and hops in.

"Who's the hippie, Ron?!" Maux yells behind him. Ronnie doesn't answer. Portland Patty pulls back into University's traffic.

•

In Portland Patty's, her tiny duplex that smells of soy sauce and incense sticks, there are posters and fliers on the wall, of Jawbreaker, Husker Du, Minor Threat, Fugazi, Rites of Spring, dozens upon dozens of local bands. Ronnie, drenched, sits on Portland Patty's couch and studies the names, the images, the Sharpie writing, the fonts, the faces.

She hands Ronnie a Mickey Mouse beach towel. As he dries off, she warms up leftover soup, some vegan concoction Ronnie will find impossibly flavorful.

"Feeling better?" Portland Patty asks, setting the soup bowl on the coffeetable, sitting next to Ronnie on the couch.

"Feeling good!" Ronnie says, leaning forward, towel wrapped around his shoulders, slurping up the soup. On the record player, some overly distorted, overly whiny modern punk song, a lament offered up to the Bitch Goddess responsible for all this unrequited love plaguing our world.

He finishes the soup in no time. Ronnie Altamont turns to Portland Patty, smiles. He places his damp head in her lap, and falls asleep.

For the second time in three days, Portland Patty watches Ronnie sleep. Inhale. Exhale. He's so disheveled. Dirt eating into the hinges of his glasses. Broth crusted along the edge of his mouth. Crumpled, unwashed, undry clothing.

What will she do with a boy like this? There is Maux, and there is Roger telling her he's sleazy. What she knows for sure is, is that he's some kind of goof. Will he leave Maux? Is he worth the trouble? The time?

She removes his glasses, sets them on the coffee table, places her hands on his not-clean hair as he sleeps. "Are you different, Ronnie?" she whispers. "Are you really different?"

MAUX CALLS RONNIE

"Hey! What're ya doin'? Fucker." Maux sounds drunk. Vodka-drunk.

"Sleeping," Ronnie yawns into the blue corded phone plugged in by his mattresses. "It's 4:30."

"So did you call or somethin'?"

"No." Ronnie turns, pulls himself upward, wakes up, realizes why she's calling. Yes, of course. "But come over."

"You're weird." Ronnie yawns a second time, almost hangs up. "I'm just callin' ya back. Fucker."

"I told you I didn't call."

"Oh. Well." Darkness. The every-night looped cassette of Television and Flipper is on the guitar solo to the Television song "Elevation," a fierce electric bounce before the song quietly implodes, puts itself back together. "Why can't we talk? Who's the hippie?"

"The hippie?"

"Yeah, that twat I saw you with who had the long hair and the Volvo. In the rain. Fucker."

Silence.

"Guess what?" Maux says, every word a sloppy slurred groan.

"What?"

"I hate hippies."

"I don't care."

"What?"

"Nothing, man. Are you coming over or what?" Ronnie turns onto his back, phone pressed to his left ear, reaching the pinnacle of his 4:30 a.m. alertness, returning to weaving in and out of sleep.

"No, Ronnie."

"Then what do you want?"

'What about that hippie?"

"Then I'm going over there."

"No, Ronnie, but please tell me about that hippie—"

Ronnie yawns. "She's a friend. You're a friend. We're all friends."

"Friends."

"I don't know. What do you want from me, Maux?"

"I haven't seen you in a while. We're hanging out, right?"

"Hanging out? Sure."

"So what are you doing with that hippie?"

"I'll call later," Ronnie says, hanging up before Maux's drunk ass can respond.

What's funny about it is that even if Ronnie had told her everything, she wouldn't remember what they talked about in the morning. He closes his eyes. Out of the speakers, Tom Verlaine sings, *This case is cloooosed*. Ronnie cannot sleep. What does Maux want? What does Ronnie want? And Portland Patty. He needs to say something, do something. Make a stand. Make a choice. The last definitive choice Ronnie has made was moving to Gainesville. Everything else has been reaction, chance, a passive going with the flow Ronnie is almost foolish enough to believe is "Zen." What is it really? Ronnie is afraid of the answer. It's easier to let it happen. It's easier to spend time with both, to avoid classifications, to not think and to ride it out and let the events take care of themselves. So why worry? Go to sleep.

Marquee Moon ends; the tape deck whizzes through the silence afterwards, flips the tape to the other side. Ronnie cannot go back to sleep. The only way is to roll out of bed, go into the living room, throw on one of Roger's artfilms, some three-hour

Bulgarian epic, stretch out on the living room couch, and not think about any of this. Within five minutes, the film knocks him out.

HIPPIES . . . CHEAP WINE . . . INDECISION

"Look at you, all dressed up," Portland Patty says. "You almost look employable."

"Almost," Ronnie repeats, and then lets loose a "Pffff," exactly like his old roommate Alvin. For once, he has combed his hair, is wearing clean clothes, has removed the gunk eating into his glasses. He's in khaki slacks, a red Oxford shirt, and a green necktie as he trudges up and down University filling out job applications. Only the dirty black low-cut Chucks—and the general air of looking like a temporary department store employee in a department store at Christmas—give him away as someone who might not be just another regular normal collegiate looking to have a regular normal job. Even if he had the money, Ronnie would not think to buy a new pair of dress shoes.

He runs into Portland Patty as he's en route to inquire about a bus boy position. She's standing in the Gatorroni's parking lot, conversing with a group of hippies. Gingham-dressed, tie-dyed, Birckenstocked, dirty-dreaded hippies. Six of them, smiling and laughing, playing with those stupid flippity sticks hippies are always playing with. Some are even barefoot. The air is poisoned with fucking patchouli.

Ronnie is happy to see her, even as she interacts with these disgusting creatures from a rival subculture. She introduces him to them. They smile and wave. Ronnie nods and glares. Ronnie looks around. It's bad enough he's dressed like this, but to be seen consorting with the enemy—well—that would be the end of Ronnie Altamont. There were too many neo-hippies in Gainesville, passing through on their way to commune with the Ocala National Forest. While they weren't as abundant in Gainesville as they were in other college towns, there were too many for Ronnie's liking. He has to leave. He has to leave now.

"Later," Ronnie grunts, walking fast, back to the sidewalk, back to University, anticipating the ugly gossip of fellow travelers in the rock of punk, seeing him in such unsavory company.

"Hey wait!" Portland Patty calls after Ronnie. Ronnie walks, looking straight ahead.

"Friends of yours?" he asks when Portland Patty catches up, past the bookstore where Ronnie used to work, walking past the school newspaper offices. All thoughts of applying for the bus boy gig vanish. He has some money left. The financial situation is not as dire as it could be. This is so much more important. He can't/won't be involved with no hippies.

"Ronnie!" Portland Patty says, laughing. "We went to high school together. They're traveling the country, stopping off for a drum circle somewhere. We met for lunch. Now they're leaving."

"Drum circle?" Ronnie shakes his head from side to side as he walks, brain a bubbling cauldron of 1980s hardcore rage. "What the hell. You're a hippie?"

"A hippie?" Portland Patty stops and faces Ronnie. "You're not actually joking, are you? You're trying to come across like you're joking, but you're not."

"A hippie," Ronnie insists, turns to walk.

Portland Patty grabs him by the arm. "This is stupid," she says. "They're old friends, Ron. Not that this matters, but in middle school? I tried to be a hippie. Then in high school? I tried to be goth. In college? Here? I went to punk shows. Then, I grew up, and now I do whatever the hell I want. That's how it goes. Last June, I graduated. Now, I work at a daycare center." She steps back, begins to pivot to leave. "This is so stupid. But if it makes you happy—fine—I'm punk rock. I've been going to shows at the Nardic Track since I moved here in 1990. You've seen my posters, you've seen my fliers. I'm the biggest goddamn punk rocker you've ever met. I'm sorry I didn't stab my old acquaintances who happened to be passing through right in their stupid hippie faces. Ok? Because punk fucking rock. That's the best, right Ronnie?"

Ronnie looks down, sighs, stammers, "I don't know, man." Hands on hips. Then he gesticulates as he says, "I guess so. But jazz is good too. Some country. Glam. Hard rock, under the right circumstances. I don't even mind psychedelic music, as long as it's got an edge to it . . . "

Portland Patty laughs. "God, you're a dork," she says. Thinking about it later, it was one of those answers that make powerful arguments in either direction re: is Ronnie any different from the rest of these jerks circled around the bands, shaking their heads as they cross their arms and watch.

"Let's go," she says. "Did you drive?"

"Naw," Ronnie says. "I've been walking around trying to get hired. I'd rather spend the money I have left on beer instead of gas."

"I'm parked at Gatorroni's. You can lead the way, since you're so punk, so full of your punk convictions."

"That's right," Ronnie laughs. "I am." Along the sidewalk,

Ronnie smirks with Sid Vicious lips and yells, "I 'ate Thatchuh!" at passersby. She laughs, but she really laughs when he yells this to a group of gutter punks stomping down the street, even flashing the two fingered "Piss off" sign with both hands before one of them answers, "Whatever, yuppie. Give me your money." In his shirt and tie, Ronnie joins in the laughter, throws them his spare change, and Ronnie and Portland Patty walk off arm in arm, singing "Anarchy in the UK," with the Johnny Rotten "Rrrrrright! Now!" rrrrrolls and everything.

·

On the way to her house, they stop at the liquor store. Ronnie buys a bottle of Wild Irish Rose. It's all he can afford; he counts the money in his wallet and the change in his pockets, standing in front of the XYZ Liquor Store counter as Portland Patty waits in the parking lot. The bottom shelf is where the cheap wine is. There's Night Train, Boone's Farm, Mad Dog 20/20, Thunderbird . . .

"What did you get?" she asks when he returns.

"You don't want to know," is all Ronnie says, and off they go.

Indeed, as Ronnie tastes it once again, and Portland Patty is given her first exposure to Wild Irish Rose, the only way they can keep from complaining about it, the only thing keeping Portland Patty from being "flus-trated,"[8] is to joke about the taste, acting like parodies of aficionados in Napa Valley.

"There's a syrupy consistency, conjoined with a high octane fuel bouquet," Portland Patty says, as Ronnie looks through her

[8] When, later, during an argument more about him instead of dirt-cheap wine, she tells him that that means, you guessed it, flustered and frustrated all at once, Ronnie answers, honestly, "Yeah, I've made a lot of people close to me feel that way."

records, finds Galaxie 500s *This Is Our Music*, and throws it on the box, still obsessing over that expression and what it means.

"Yes," Ronnie says, joining her on the couch, sharing and sipping from the same *Empire Strikes Back* collector's glasses—Lando Calrissian and Boba Fett. "There's a bilish finish that leaves a chunky film on the roof of your mouth."

"Ah, yes," Portland Patty says, "with just a hint of river bottom sediment."

Ronnie Altamont laughs, a happy kind of laughter he hasn't had since Maggie left him. From the stereo, Dean Wareham sings of the Fourth of July, and Ronnie and Portland Patty taste the cheap slime of the Wild Irish Rose on each other's tongues, and it isn't so bad, it isn't so bad at all. He kisses her and thinks, yes, I should end it with Maux, whatever it is we're doing, I should end it. This is entirely too perfect. To be here in this house, laughing and drinking wine and kissing, it's better than anything that has happened or could ever happen with Maux. He could start here and leave the past, all of it, behind. With Portland Patty, he could stay here in Gainesville. He could build a new life, forget about Orlando, forget about this directionless living masquerading as what he had called the "sweat jam," and move forward.

Yes. He could. And he would meet with Maux tomorrow and let her know. Ronnie was a punk with conviction, and he would give it to her straight.

MAUX DRAWS RONNIE

At Maux's. All day before this, hiding out in his room from Roger and his films and the outside world's tendencies to simply open the unlocked front door and let itself in, Ronnie planned on not coming in, on standing in the doorway and saying "Let's just be friends . . . it's not you, it's me . . . you deserve someone better . . . I'm not ready . . . it's just not working out . . . ," walking home, then calling Portland Patty to see what she's up to. But then Maux stood there, looking like she did—black t-shirt sorta covering black panties and clearly no bra underneath, and that's it—and he couldn't.

So. Instead, he sits on Maux's ancient sofa, kissing-gropes interspersed with silence, sipping vodka tonics as her muted television plays Fellini's *Amarcord*.

She shows him the only record she owns, a copy of *Thriller*. "I got this for my eighth birthday," she tells Ronnie. "Look at what I drew on it."

Ronnie takes it from her, holds it closer, tilting it to get better light. The word "POOP," drawn as a black-markered thought cloud next to Michael Jackson's Jheri curled brain.

"See! Even then, I had it," Maux says, taking the cover back from Ronnie.

"You sure did," Ronnie says. "You sure did."

"I have something else to show you," she says. She runs into her bedroom. Ronnie thinks, "Ok. This is it." He has to say something. This must end.

Maux returns with a thick scrapbook. She retakes her position on the couch, flips from page to page. It's every cartoon she has ever drawn for the school paper. Dozens, if not hundreds, of drawings. He doesn't focus on any particular piece, but instead soaks in the vast output, the collection itself. For all her faults, Ronnie thinks, Maux is the only person in Gainesville he knows who actually produces something seen by thousands each week. She is always producing. Always drawing. In Gainesville, the bands come and go. Aspiring filmmakers talk more than they film. Poets don't rhyme. Dancers don't dance. And Ronnie, he isn't doing a thing. But Maux is always drawing something.

She flips to the last page. "Look at this one."

A fresh white sheet glue-stuck to the page. It's a sketch of Ronnie, drawn from memory, of a photograph he gave her of him wearing a fake Japanese headband while making the "Hi-yah!" gesture with his hands. For once, the drawing is more realist than caricature. Surrounding the drawing are ten of Maux's favorite haiku taken from the haiku wall in Ronnie's room—haiku about Sanford and Son, Dee Dee Ramone, Emmanuel Lewis, EPCOT Center, and the wonder of large breasts, among others.

"It's going to be in the paper next week," she tells Ronnie. "I wanted to surprise you."

Ronnie smiles. He wants to tell her that this is the nicest thing anyone has done for him in a long time, and while it's true, the words don't formulate. "I'm speechless," is all he can muster.

"You hate it?"

And there's so much Ronnie could say and should say but doesn't say right here, because he broods on the question, on this lowering of that hate-filled wall she's always putting in front of him, and everyone else. Ronnie understands her. He thinks he understands her. She has to defend this gift—this vulnerability, this gift of observation, this something beyond what most people have.

"Naw," Ronnie manages. "It's awesome." (He wishes he can say more, has forgotten why he was going to tell her that it was over.)

Maux leans in, hugs Ronnie, kisses him on the cheek. "I'm

glad you don't hate it. I thought you would. Hate it, I mean. Most boys hate my renderings of them."

Instead of dumping her, he spends the night. Not even Ronnie Altamont is obtuse enough to dump Maux—here, now. The classifications and the labels—as he opens his eyes at sunrise, as she sleeps in gentle breaths to his left—they strike Ronnie as idiotic. Some social construct designed by locust-eating Christians 2000 years ago. Why can't we be polygamists? Who gives a shit, if everyone's happy? Why can't we have harems; why can't we have, as Lou Reed sang in "I Wanna Be Black," a "stable of foxy little whores?" Who made these rules, and why do the people who enforce them look so miserable as they sing their hymns? Why do we have to have these definitions: "friends," "more than friends," "boyfriend/girlfriend?" We know what we want and need, so why all the complications and lovesong hokum?

Oh, Ronnie. Is there anything you won't rationalize away?

SALTY SNACK TELEMARKETING OR PIZZA DELIVERY

You know the job market is bleak when your best options are between telemarketing or pizza delivery. Into the semester, as all the other positions have been filled, there is nothing in the classifieds other than these two. Ronnie thinks, often: Man! Dude! If I could only get a real gig in Gainesville, the place would be as perfect as I could ever hope for. To have a real job, like, some kind of office job with all the usual benefits, would be, with Gainesville's low cost of living, like being a millionaire! True enough. But his choice is down to the only available options: Telemarketing or Pizza Delivery.

Telemarketing. He is hired, quickly trained, given a cubicle in a large windowless room filled with hundreds of other cubicles, where he sits in front of a green computer screen as the phone calls random numbers. Ronnie is hired to survey callers about, you guessed it, salty snacks.

There is a bleak gray Orwellian pallor to the call room. The walls reverberate with the dull chatter of questions like:

"When shopping, how often do you purchase salty snacks?"

"What kinds of salty snacks do you buy?"

"Salty snacks salty snacks salty snacks?"

Ronnie Altamont's entire career in the field of telemarketing lasts seven calls (and seven hang-ups), one hour, three minutes, and forty-two seconds. For the first time, he cannot reconcile that he spent five years to earn a college degree, in part to avoid shit work like this, and here he is in some forlorn callbank center on the outskirts of this town he moved to so he could plug away at his "art" with less hassle, but instead he's asking probing questions to the American public re: their spending and relative infatuation with salty snacks. It's not even that he thinks he's too good for the gig, but he simply can't do it, won't do it, doesn't want to ask anyone about salty snacks. He feels the seconds ticking away in his too-short life.

He walks out of the large dismal room without a word, never more happy to step outside into the parking lot of a rundown shopping center.

This leaves pizza delivery. Ronnie is hired by the General Lee's Pizza Cavalry chain, driving around with a car full of piping hot peetz made in their Newberry Road location. What Robert E. Lee has to do with pizza is anyone's guess, but people generally appreciated the tip of the hat to their southern heritage. Until the late 1980s, there used to be more of a "Dukes of Hazzard" theme to the place, the name as much a nod to the speedy automobile Bo and Luke Duke drove on the TV as it was to the great Civil War General. This was back when General Lee's Pizza Cavalry promised in their commercials, "Hot and Fresh Pizza Delivered to Y'all's Door in Thirty Minutes or Less or It's Free." Before too many drivers, not wanting to cost their employers any business-slash-lose their jobs, wrecked their cars, hit pedestrians, died.

Ronnie spends a dinner shift getting trained, riding shotgun in this black Celica driven by a high school senior named Kenny. Kenny gives the grand tour of Gainesville's gridded streets, and like many involved in the lower echelons of the pizza delivery industry, Kenny smokes dope like a Rastafarian.

He wears a peppermint-striped mushroom cap, black Stone Temple Pilots t-shirt, too-big jeans hung halfway down his ass, exposing red boxers, the chain wallet dangling to his side. Clearly, General Lee's Pizza Cavalry didn't bother with uniforms.

"Don't smoke, huh?" Kenny says, after Ronnie declines the joint Kenny holds out, the joint he damps down with wet thumb and forefinger before opening the door and running the pizza to some parent, some college kid, some party.

"Nah," Ronnie says. "It makes me paranoid, neurotic, and miserable, but, ironically enough, it curbs my appetite. I smoke pot, and I can't eat for days."

"Take it from me, my man," Kenny says as they turn into some neighborhood on the heretofore unexplored west side of town, "it's an indispensable tool in this profession."

"You're an indispensable tool in this profession," Ronnie

wants to say, but keeps quiet, taking in what passed for suburbia in Gainesville. Pot. It is impossible for Ronnie to conceive of doing anything like working while high. Even breathing while high was a neurotic endeavor.

They pull up to some house in some neighborhood far west of anyplace Ronnie would ever want to go in Gainesville. As Kenny goes to the front door, Ronnie stares at the Bob Marley air freshener dangling from the rear view mirror, green black and yellow, Bob Marley exhaling a smokestack of dope smoke. On the radio, alternative rock growls and blares from some lousy station out of Jacksonville. Ronnie kinda hates Kenny the way he kinda hates 98 percent of this immediate world. Like so many Floridians and so many teenagers, so many people, Kenny thinks he's much more clever than he actually is. Ronnie sits in the passenger seat of this Celica, brooding on all the wrong moves he's made in life to end up here. He didn't think that this was how it would turn out, thought the book and the band would wow the world to the point that he could get by, doing what he loved.

Well. It didn't.

Back to delivery. After the training sesh with this high school kid Kenny, Ronnie is ready to deliver the peetz. Ronnie worked in this gig back in Orlando for a summer, delivering for a contemptuously unmentionable corporate chain, before quitting then writing about his boss in his school paper opinion column, calling the man "a lazy lump of shit for brains plopped onto a lazy shit for heart and soul." Delivery was like riding a bike, only now, said bike was a sputtering blandy apple green sedan on its rapid descent into being driven into the ground through a combination of Ronnie's negligence and utter automotive incompetence.

The shift: Saturday, Game Day, 10:30 a.m. to 1:00 a.m.. The customers: collegiates and post-collegiates and families all about the gimme gimme pregame show slices, gimme gimme game day pizza, gimme gimme post-game party food. *Gimme gimme this, gimme gimme that*, as the late great Darby Crash once barked. To the suburban homes, moms with their seven year old sons, moms opening the doors, sons always yelling, "It's the pizza dude!" and the moms smiling in that indulgent way moms smile, saying, "Hey, it is the pizza dude!" and Ronnie tries smiling at this heartwarming tableau as the mom next says, "Give the pizza dude the money, dear!" and the kid gives Ronnie the cash and Ronnie gives the kid the pizza and the mom says "What do you say, dear?" and the kid says, "Thanks pizza dude!" and everyone laughs and the mom gives a "Thanks for tolerating us" kind of nod with her head and Ronnie thinks of a) what he will invest in with his one dollar tip, and b) how they really train them young in Gainesville re: conducting the pizza transaction. There's the suburban homes, and then there are the collegiate apartment complexes up and down Archer Road and Tower Road, nestled far away from the crime and crack and horror of real poverty lurking in the residential neighborhoods on the outskirts of the UF campus. Game day parties where the hosts and partygoers become increasingly generous with their food and beer as the day goes on. They answer their doors, "What's up, pizza's here!" and let Ronnie in, leading him through narrow hallways past fresh new all-off-white living rooms packed with orange and blue adorned football fans yelling at the TV screen or laughing at the commercials on the TV screen and Ronnie leaves the pizzas on the inevitable Kitchen Island as they try and talk to Ronnie about the "big game" and Ronnie tries pretending he isn't too, you know, like, punk rock to give a shit about it, takes the money and hustles out the door, and the tips are usually a little bit better than most places, especially as the day goes on. The tips from upperclassmen parties or recent graduates are always better than the underclassmen, who almost always want exact change. Game day: Some SEC bigdeal the people have been looking forward to all week, and as Ronnie walks through apartment complexes and courtyards, up and down these residential streets, he hears the cheering, the curses, the slow hand-claps for the good plays. Interspersed between the game day, calls not football-related: Pre-med students on study breaks—twenty pound anatomy textbooks, bleary eyes, gifted with an unfathomable (to Ronnie) drive and motivation; metal kids in black Megadeth t-shirts taking the pizza at the door, cumulonimbus marijuana clouds behind them, guitars wrapped around them; weekend mechanics emerging from underneath the hoods of their El Caminos, paying in oil-smudged money; bridal showers where the ladies drunkenly flirt and inform Ronnie that only one of them is getting married; senior citizen book clubs, day care centers full of kids who dash from their Twister and Chutes and Ladders and converge upon Ronnie. They all want pizza. Everybody wants pizza on Game Day Saturday.

The cassette in Ronnie's car: an endless loop of Bad Brains, Flipper, Spoke, Television, Sonic Youth, Thin Lizzy, Crime, Gary Numan, Guv'ner, Superchunk, Crowsdell, Thinking Fellers Union Local 282, Polvo, Urge Overkill, Naiomi's Hair, Melvins, Unrest, Beat Happening, Fudge Tunnel, Tsunami, Bratmobile, The Scissor Girls, Spinout. Fourteen straight hours of nothing but, one side to the next, morning to afternoon to night to late night. Ronnie was on the older end of the spectrum of delivery drivers at General Lee's. He had worked with older drivers. They were generally lost souls, struggling to make ends meet and/or lost in a permanent marijuana cloud that makes everything that's just ok eternally tolerable. Alone with nothing but this mixtape for company, four hours in, Ronnie finds this an alien, alienating gig—he's too old to do it, but too young to be good at anything else. Soon enough he's started taking people up on offered beer.

As the early afternoon progresses to mid-afternoon, it is clear from the general spirit of the parties he is delivering pizza to that the Gators are winning, and winning big. The tips from the apartment parties and backyard or courtyard barbeques are increasing. Everyone wants to be Ronnie's—The Pizza Dude's—buddy.

"Hey man, sucks you gotta work today," says some shirtless guy with short blond surfer hair and aviators, conveying the authority of the host who's having this party outside in the back space between the clusters of apartments.

"What can you do?" Ronnie shrugs, hands the dude the pizzas.

"Well the Gators won. Ya want a beer?"

"Sure." Maybe it will make him feel better.

"Hold on, dude!" the guy says. "Set the pizzas on the picnic table." To his friends, he announces, "I'm gettin' the pizza dude a beer!"

Everyone cheers at this. This is Ronnie's last delivery before going back to the store for the next round. Why not? He sets the pizzas on the picnic table. This beautiful blonde—so so so Floridian with her tan and fluorescent green bikini, not like beautiful in some California centerfold polyethylene kind of way, but in a natural, not even trying, not even caring kind of way—turns to Ronnie, holds out a thermos. "Hey," she slurs. "Pizza dude. You want some FloCo?"

Floridian Comfort. Ronnie takes the thermos, unscrews it, takes a healthy swig.

"Sucks you gotta work," she says.

Ronnie says, "Yeah," and before he can even start to think he has a chance, the host shows up with the inevitable blue Solo cup of foamy beer, hands it to Ronnie, leans in, kisses the blonde. Blond on Blonde. The pinnacle of Floridian beach culture.

"Yeah, I used to deliver at General Lee's," the surfer host tells Ronnie. "The Game Days were the worst. And you don't even make any money."

"What?" Ronnie had already made twenty something deliveries and the day wasn't halfway through. He was eagerly anticipating returning to the Myrrh House with a small fortune.

"No, you get tips, and what, seventy-five cents a run?"

"Right," Ronnie says.

"Yeah. Fuck that. Between what you pay in gas, and the wear and tear on your car, you'll be coming home tonight with less than minimum wage."

Ronnie says nothing.

"Which is fine, if the tips are good, and the deliveries aren't a long way to go, and you got a new car. Then maybe you'll make money. But this is Gainesville."

Ronnie says nothing.

"Looks like you could use more beer," the surfer host says, and his girlfriend laughs, holds out the thermos of FloCo, adds, "This too."

Ronnie takes the thermos, extends his emptied blue Solo cup.

"Yeah man, it's tough to make a living here," the host says, returning with the filled cup.

"No shit," Ronnie says, and he's never meant it more. "What do y'all do?"

"School," the host says, and his girlfriend nods and says, "Yup."

"I'm really a musician," Ronnie says. "And I write. I have parties. We have a big house in the student ghetto. Y'all should come by." He holds out his cup. "And give me one more. For the road."

"You got it," the host says, taking his cup.

The party is clusters of surfer types talking about the usual party topics. Ronnie wishes he could stay. "Give me some more of that," Ronnie says, pointing at the blonde's FloCo thermos.

"You sure you'll be alright to drive?" Her concern breaks his heart.

"Totally," Ronnie says. He smiles. "I'm fine."

"Well. Ok." Ronnie grabs the thermos, sips again, feels that rush. "Whoooo!" he says.

"Here ya go, brah," the host says returning with the newly filled blue Solo cup.

Ronnie takes it. "Yeah, dude, I live in the Myrrh House. It's on NW 4th Lane. Look for fliers, ok?"

"You got it dude," the host says. "Later. Thanks for the pizza. Good luck with it."

Ronnie shrugs, walks back to his car. The sharp-dull numb from the beer and FloCo leaves him in a giddy eternal-now focus. The host gave him a ten dollar tip. Ronnie takes note of that in the car, as the mixtape returns to life. Ronnie honks as he pulls away, one last sight of that blonde, there on the picnic table. The party waves back. As Ronnie leaves, he bites his fist like Squiggy from *Laverne and Shirley*, one last tribute to that girl he knows he'll never see again.

Ronnie drives back to General Lee's to pick up another round of pizzas, muttering about "No money? Fourteen and a half hours for less than minimum wage? Fuuuuuuuck that, man. Fuck that." He sneaks sips of the beer as the car moves, keeps it hidden at stop lights, wedged between his sweaty thighs.

He decides to give it one more round, to see how it goes, and if the tips are bad, if nothing's as good as that party, he will go home. Deep breath, look normal, look sober, now run back into the store.

"Finding your deliveries alright?" the manager asks, some husky nineteen-year-old-looking-guy, standing behind the counter, conveying an authority, but a lax, stoned authority Ronnie doesn't mind and doesn't hate.

"Totally," Ronnie says, collects the stack of six pizzas next in the delivery queue, and hustles back to his car.

The city's grid is easy navigating. Streets run north/south, avenues east/west. And then, between, there are places and courts and terraces and circles, to say nothing of the winding depths of the serpentine apartment complexes. You kids today, with your GPS systems and cell phones. Pizza delivery has benefitted so much from 21st century technology. You would have to really try (or live in Boston) to get turned around and lost delivering pizza these days. But way back in the fall of 1996, the pizza delivery driver settles for maps pinned to the front of the store, with directions shouted by the dispatcher like a quarterback in a touch football game: "Ok, run straight, turn right there, go straight there, then turn left can't miss it." And if you did miss it, there were payphones, if you could find them.

Ronnie figured it out easily enough. But then, he had a few

drinks. He knew enough to not get so drunk, he'd wreck the car, get pulled over, hurt himself or others, but there was enough alcohol to impair his sense of direction. Halfway through the run, he'd confused his trails and lanes and so ends up at a payphone in front of the entrance to the Publix on University and 34th. Usually, what happens is, you calmly explain the situation, and the customer calmly gives you directions and everybody's happy.

"You're where?! Where's my pizza?!"

On the other end of the phone, this young, entitled college male voice. So demanding. So serious with the pizza.

"I'm at the Publix, on 34th Street . . . "

"Wait a minute. You're all the way over there?! I want my pizza! Now!" (In later years, Ronnie will hear a similar tone from one George W. Bush.)

"You'll get it, dude. Give me directions and I'm there."

"I'm not eating cold pizza—duuuude!" George—let's call him George—exaggerates the word "dude." Ronnie has spent a lot of time thinking of the expression "The customer is always right," and after years toiling in customer service, he has learned that the rest of that expression goes, "The customer is always right, but the customer is quite often a fucking asshole, regardless."

"Are you stupid?" George continues. "I want my pizza! Now!"

"Well fuck you then," says Ronnie's mouth, before his buzzed brain puts up any roadblocks.

Silence. Then: "What did you say to me?" A shrillness to match the entitlement. Shock. George wasn't expecting this.

Ronnie follows his instincts, which tell him to press forward and make no apologies. "Look dude: You're a pussy, and your pizza's still warm, so I'm going to eat it. No pizza for you."

Ronnie hangs up, looks around. The salmon and teal-aproned bagboys push shopping carts into the store. Families waddle through the automatic doors. Blasts of air-conditioning. Smells of produce and bleachy mop water. A little girl in a pink dress bounces up and down the scale on the entryway to the store.

Ronnie wants to recall exactly where he is as he does this.

On the drive back to the Myrrh House, Ronnie removes the six pizzas in his car from the two insulators, places them in the front seat, tosses the two stars-and-bars clad red pizza insulators out the window. He has six pizzas, and while he feels sorry for the people on the route after George who wouldn't get their pizzas until they called the store to find out what happened, the anticipated pizza party that will soon happen, when Roger sees what he has, when Ronnie calls almost everyone he knows (except Maux and Portland Patty), trumps everything.

Ronnie is sobering up. He stops at the XYZ Liquor Lounge. Before entering, he takes one slice from George's pizza out of the box in the passenger seat. Not too hot. Not too cold. Delicious. Unconsciously, Ronnie knew that this was the only way to deal with fools. Not just in writing, but in person. It was a turning point, a good turning point, whether Ronnie was aware of it or not, and now he will go home and eat pizza with friends, chased with Old Hamtramck tallboys.

LOST, LOSING

In her kitchen, Portland Patty rolls the dough for the vegan pizza. A glass of red wine—Shiraz—to her left, a mixtape flipping from one side to the next, a mixtape she made then titled *oreGONE, xmas, '95.*[9]

Waiting for Ronnie, the tape reminding her of home: Last Christmas, with the mixtape finished, she'd borrowed Mom's car and drove to Sauvie Island, lost in the once-familiar of the scenery, of summers between high school years with long-gone friends, driving out of the city, through the railyards and industry on one side and the mountains (mountains!), cliffs (cliffs!) and woods (Ok, Florida has that, but c'mon! It's not a foregone conclusion like it is back there . . .) on the other, getting baked at the beach (on real weed, not this North-Florida skunky-dirt oregano), then floating in the Columbia River, the evergreen trees, the blue of the sky a blue you don't see anywhere else but in the Pacific Northwest, floating in the water, spinning in circles, Washington state right there on the other side, the Walton Beach crowds packed in in the mid-afternoon beach, the dune behind them, the Van Gogh farm-land behind all that. Or at Collins Beach, drunk, stoned, horny, seventeen, "clothing optional" with a whole crew of friends, but with Miranda, they hold hands and conveniently drift away far enough from the pack to kiss, and to act on it for the first time, and why was that the only time? With Miranda, with women. She stopped off at both empty beaches last Christmas and wondered about this, among many other things, as people do when they go home for the holidays and get away from family and all the other obligations long enough to take stock of the distance in time between when you lived your life here and when you come back and see how you don't live your life here and the stupid places don't

---

[9] See Appendix F for the track listings

change in the same ways. She knew herself, even then, enough to know that when she wasn't drunk, stoned, and horny at a "clothing optional" gay and lesbian beach, it wasn't an honest feeling. It was kicks, in the moment. And they drifted apart—her and Miranda—her oldest friend, going back to fourth grade—because, as her friends told her in the drama of the days after, Miranda wanted so much more. And over time, through the transition to high school to college (and choosing to go as far away as possible, to start completely fresh, thinking you actually could start completely fresh, as if genetics and memory don't have something to say about your identity) to post-college, everybody goes their own ways, to the point where even at Christmas and New Year's, nobody gets together anymore. So at Christmas, it's too cold and there's been too much time passed to do much of anything but drive around Sauvie Island and listen to this tape and confront the sinking realization that Portland isn't home. Not anymore.

She's waiting for Ronnie to finally show up. Dinner, wine, this Cassavettes movie she rented. It's almost 8:30, and she'd been expecting him at 7:00.

She rolls the dough (the yeast lives, and the wine lives, but she sleeps at night just fine even if she's slaughtered bacteria . . . everyone has their limits, Portland Patty concluded, the first time she was confronted by one of the more fundamentalist members of the vegan sect about her role in the bacteria holocaust), cuts the green, red, and yellow peppers. Soy cheese. Tomato sauce. The important thing is to keep moving. Listen to the tape, think of someplace far away, like Oregon, last Christmas, alone in the car where nobody knows you and nobody sees you and you have no name, no nickname, no one to be and nothing matters and nothing hurts.

He's with Maux. Why? And why does Portland Patty care? What is she doing, anyway? To see the big picture, to think of the endless succession of losers she's dated in this town, who drink and play in bands and say a lot of nice things until she lets them into her bedroom. When it's done, they look like they want to take on the world and win—alone—and she's left in bed wondering why she went on the ride and why she can't just enjoy these fleeting moments for what they are. Older now, she's become how Miranda was, eight years ago, always wanting something more, behind the words, the faces. And just like with Ronnie, she always wants to know if they are different, and so far, they never have been different.

Sip the wine. Preheat the oven. To think about them—that bitch—who everyone in town knows is a total bitch—together—in any capacity—is enough to make her end it. Tonight. No. Not tonight. But the later he is, the more likely it will end tonight.

No calls. Not from Ronnie. Not from anyone. Evenings like these, if you're not careful, it's like vertigo, to be so far from home, and to know that home as you knew it no longer exists. In bed, it overwhelms you, almost asleep. It's a jolt that shakes your chest and legs. You're nowhere, and no one's around to make that go away.

She slides the dough into the oven when the doorbell rings. Finally. She shuts the oven, walks to the front door.

The fucker smiles as she opens the door, and he immediately waddle-bumbles inside. A smile, a squeezeless hug, and it's "Hey lady, can I come in?" even as he's five steps in the door. "Sorry I'm late," he says, "I was at the Drunken Mick getting berated by Neal and Paul. They won't shut up about . . . "

"Who?" Portland Patty interrupts, shuts the door, walks towards him, "oreGONE xmas '95" continuing behind her.

"Nothing." Ronnie stumbles to the couch. "No one. Maux. But . . . "

"What about her, Ronnie?"

Ronnie falls backwards, lands on the couch, leans back, puts his hands behind his head with fingers clasped, smiles the smile of the overserved. "Aw, you know, they think we're dating. But we're not dating. We're friends. That's all. Ffffffffffffriends!" He laughs, he smiles, he unclasps his fingers, extends his arms into an embrace and says, "I like you. They like you. Isn't that nice? Isn't it? Nice? Right?"

Portland Patty has to smile. Beneath the attempts at charm, the rumpled yet almost "punk" clothing, there was a lush—a great big comical lush—like the kind they used to draw in caricature in the 1930s—with red clown noses and floppy holey shoes and a stick with a knotted handkerchief holding his meager possessions. Portland Patty recalls a song from when she was a kid, a song from the kids' show *The Electric Company*—"I'm just a clow-wow-wow-wwwn / who's feeling dow-wow-wowwwwn / since my baby left tow-wowwwwwn." They were teaching kids about the "ow" sound in words, but maybe it was about Ronnie, or Portland Patty, or everyone in Gainesville flopping around doing nothing all the time. Ronnie the Lush. She promises that, no matter how annoyed and angry she gets with Ronnie, to keep that nickname to herself. She doesn't want to saddle him with it, as someone with a faraway, long ago, hardly remembered hometown in front of her name.

"Well. The pizza's almost ready if you want some."

"Hell yeah, brah."

Ronnie picks up the VHS cover of the movie Portland Patty rented. *Opening Night* is the title. He flips to the back, closes one eye so he can focus on the words, laughing in perceived recognition as he reads:

"*. . . The master narrative of all of Cassavetes' films is to force characters to shed their own skins . . . the discovery of who we really are can begin only when our routines are disrupted . . . we must be forced out of our places of comfort . . . not to break down, to maintain your old routines at all costs, to hold onto an established definition of yourself with a death grip . . . is to be truly damned.*"

Portland Patty removes the pizza stone holding the newly formed crust from the oven, sets them on the kitchen counter. She spreads the tomato sauce, sprinkles the soy cheese, plops the peppers, puts it back in, as *oreGONE, xmas '95* plays "24" by Red House Painters and the lyric *and I thought at 15 I'd / have it down by 16 / and 24 keeps breathing in my face / like a manhole / and 24 keeps pounding at my door* . . . And now, she's twenty-five. Years of never having it down, years of fleeting thrills and nothing substantive.

When it's cooked, removed, cooled, she cuts the pizza into slices, divides it between two plates. She carries the plates into the living room. Ronnie's head is tilted back. He smiles as he snores, mouth agape. It is too ridiculous to be angry. She sets the plates down, goes into the kitchen, stops "oreGONE xmas '95," carries the bottle of Shiraz into the living room, turns on the TV, the VCR, starts the movie, cranks the sound to drown out Ronnie's snores, eats, drinks, drinks, drinks, tries to enjoy this fleeting man and this fleeting moment, so far from home, so far from home.

•

Yes, at the bar, Paul and Neal were trying to give Ronnie all kinds of shit about Maux and Portland Patty. It was the primary topic of conversation during the Drunken Mick's all-you-can-drink Happy Hour from 5:00-8:00 p.m.

"Maux's gonna kill you," Paul said, seated to Ronnie's left, facing Ronnie, slapping him in the arm with each gesticulation, black Caesar cut and sideburns, hunched over the bar, head tilting to Ronnie, to the mirror behind the liquor bottles, back and forth in nervous darts. "She knows about this, and she's going to kill you. Then, while your body is still warm, she's going to draw a brutal caricature of you in the paper."

"Haw haw haw," Ronnie said. Both brothers were plying him with whiskey shots, Paul on the left and Neal on the right.

"And Portland Patty's cool," Neal said, less fidgety than his brother, but no less strident, concerned, nagging. Neal's approach is to buy Ronnie beers, shots, to make up for the awkwardness of talking this way, after they showed up at Ronnie's house and flat-out told him, "We're taking you to the Drunken Mick to let you know how fucking stupid you are."

"You can't do this, Ron," Neal added, waving to the bartender for another shot, another beer, fingers pointing in Ronnie's direction.

Ronnie downed the shot. "You don't understand, man. Maux, she doesn't really wanna date. Portland Patty, I just met her. So so what?"

"So you're a dumbass," Paul said, slapping Ronnie in the arm.

"What would Doug Clifford do?" Neal said, then to the heavens, shouted, "Why can't you think of Doug Clifford?" Hairy black arms in the air, hairy black hair, hairy black eyebrows, lamenting upward, "Why doesn't anybody think of Doug Clifford?"

Ronnie laughed, numbed into drunken intuition, but no less resolved. That final shot pushed him over the cliff. The mouth and the brain were in sync, and Ronnie talked and talked and talked, gibberish along the lines of:

"Haw haw haw, naw I can't decide because actually it ain't a bad arrangement you know because Maux she keeps the distinctions blurred like and really at the end of the day I like being in her apartment and I'd do more with Maux if she only gave me the chance but then there's Portland Patty she's great too and yes greater than Maux I think but I don't like to you know unattach myself to girls to like breakup and end things and not only that but having two bodies makes up for having, heh heh heh, nobodies, got me? Haw haw haw?"

Nevertheless Neal and Paul continued to berate him in a steady stream Ronnie only half-listened to, llllllloaded as he was, not feeling all that happy in this alleged Happy Hour. Through the whiskey and beer haze, Ronnie caught phrases like "fucking moron," "juvenile excuses," and "selfish drunkard." The last phrase catches his ear and sends his thoughts spiraling down, down, down. Why did he have to drink like this? Christ, he was lllloaded! Was it mere boredom, Floridian boredom? Was it believing he was a writer, believing that this is what writers did—they drank, almost as much, if not more, than they wrote? Because he was still young—even if 24 was pushing it? Tradition? Genetics? Personal choice? Maybe it was all of that, but really and simply: Ronnie enjoyed it. He laughed a lot, felt relaxed, made connections he believed he could not get any other way. He gained experience. It got him to the state he wanted to reach as a person, someone who could freely talk, who could be fun, someone with the confidence to trust his intuition. It melted frivolous annoyances and stresses. It put life firmly in the present. Righting the balance of the world. Or, as it did in the past year, it numbed pain. It left Ronnie ok with sitting in his room despondent and disconnected, blasting the Germs, the Stooges, Crime, DMZ, Television, Flipper, tuning out bad breakups, finding and losing jobs he hated, awkward transitions into the world of post-college. He hadn't done anything terrible—yet—and the great times far outweighed the surly and alienating times. He didn't physically *need* it. More than anything, it was, you know, just something to do.

Blacked out. Neal and Paul dropped Ronnie off at Portland Patty's. They were still telling him what to do and how to be as he opened the passenger door and lurched down her driveway to the front door, turning, yelling to them, "There's nothing to end! Doug Clifford thinks you guys are fags!" He fell over, onto the grassy-dirt of the front yard, stood, brushed himself off, knowing that inside, there is pizza, and Portland Patty will be ok with this. Why wouldn't she be? Everything was alright.

. . . So when he wakes up on Portland Patty's couch, in total darkness except for a VCR digital clock reading 3:36 a.m., it is still alright, even with the slight headache and the massive dehydration. He feels through the darkness, finds the hallway, finds Portland Patty's bedroom. He climbs into her bed.

"Hhhhhey," Ronnie mumbles, nasty old booze breath, clothes reeking of bar smoke. Portland Patty turns away as he pulls up the covers, tries draping his arm around her shoulders. She stares into the darkness, looking away from Ronnie, as much on the mattresses' edge as she can be without falling out of bed.

•

In the morning—is it morning? afternoon? does it matter?—Ronnie feels a poke and a nudge. He is awoken from dreams of sitting in sunset jungles underneath palm fronds blowing in hurricanes. He opens his eyes. Portland Patty stands over him, saying, "Ronnie? Ronnie? I think you should leave."

Ronnie stretches, yawns. "Leave? Why? I'm still tired. I was kinda drunk last night, huh—heh heh?"

"I just. I don't know. I've been thinking."

"Thinking." Ronnie repeats. He looks at Portland Patty. She looks serious. Grave, even. Sad. "You look serious, Portland Patty. Grave, even. Sad."

"You should stay with Maux. You like her." Portland Patty steps back from the bed. To say those words, her sad mood melts. Confidence takes over as she says, "I can't go along with whatever it is you're doing, here, with me, with yourself."

"What am I doing?" That sinking feeling of knowing he would be leaving a bedroom, a girl, probably forever.

Portland Patty opens the blinds, lets in the ever-present sunshine. "Well, you're not doing anything, Ronnie. That's the problem. I like you. But you're not doing anything." She wants to tell him he's like all the others, which is what's so disappointing, disheartening.

"I do like you, Ronnie Altamont," she continues, "but I think I want to be alone now. Please leave."

Ronnie, half-asleep, fully hungover, rolls out of bed, lands on his feet, pats his body like someone trying to recall in which pocket he kept a pen. He moves like some slapstick goof in a forgotten silent movie. Portland Patty stands by the window, reminded of why she liked him. She wants to laugh, comes close to taking it all back, wants to keep him. But there is Maux, and this slacktastic lifestyle of leisure just like all these boys in Gainesville. She wants to forgive him his youth and inability to think beyond today, as he looks in the mirror and ruffles his hair like he's trying to straighten out bedhead in the clumps of that growing-out brown mess.

He turns from the mirror, looks to Portland Patty. "I'm sorry." he says. "You're right." He extends his arms, makes doe eyes, and in a move Portland Patty suspects is practiced, he asks, "Friends?"

She nods. "Friends." She steps away from the window, around the bed, to Ronnie. This shouldn't hurt.

He steps back. "Well. Goodbye," he says. He smiles, like he doesn't believe her, like this isn't real. "See you at the shows." He turns, walks out of the bedroom. She hears his steps across the carpeting through the living room, to the foyer, the open and shut of the front door. She falls into bed. Tears. It isn't Ronnie—not entirely—it's hope meeting reality, the way it always does with her.

Ronnie begins the long walk through the heat, humidity and sunshine down 13th Street, south towards home. Portland Patty will change her mind. Even if she doesn't, there's always Maux, or that girl on her bike there, or those girls on the sidewalk, or the girl in the Volkswagen next to him at the stoplight. Nothing is serious. Nothing is ever serious. To take anything serious means taking life serious, and why would you do that? There is only fun. Fun is the ideal. Fun is the center. If it isn't fun, there's no need to bother.

It feels like hours, but it's really only 45 minutes until Ronnie makes it to NW 4th Lane, but instead of going into the Myrrh House to brood on Portland Patty in hungover agony, he thinks the better move, the smarter move, is to keep walking, past the Myrrh House and through the parking lot shortcut, two blocks to Maux's. Maux will make this ok. He wants to be with Maux anyway, and who cares what anyone else has to say about it? Her apartment will be nice and dark, vodka will be in the freezer, and she'll show him her latest drawings. Then, they will climb into bed and ignore this stupid, stupid world.

He parks, walks up to the second floor of her dismal apartment building with its motel walkways and motel railing, knocks on her door.

"What do you want, douche?"

"Let me in."

"Why aren't you with the hippie?"

"The hippie? She's just a friend. Let me in."

Maux opens the door. She's wearing this silver-sequined miniskirt, newly-dyed indigo hair. He wants her. So. Bad.

"I'm not letting you in," she says. "I can't do that."

Ronnie smiles, digs deep for the charm. "Aw, c'mahhhhhn. I'm only friends with her. That's nothing. I want to see you, Maux."

"You're like the rest Ronnie." She looks past Ronnie, in the direction of UF it seems, but it could be anywhere behind Ronnie. "I mean, I don't hate you, but what we've been doing? It's a farce. I mean, friends of mine—and I do actually have some friends here, Ron—overheard your drunken bullshit last night at the Mick and told me all about it. They always thought I was too good for you anyway." She looks at her watch. "I need to graduate. I need to get out of here. I can't waste any more time." She looks at him, sneers. "I mean, this is a college town, Ronnie. You graduated college. What are you even doing here?"

Ronnie wants to answer, "To write! To play music!" but he can't say that. He shrugs. "I like it here. I'm going back to school."

"No you're not," Maux says, shuts the door.

Ronnie faces the gray metal door where Maux had just stood. He knocks three times. "Maux? Maux? Hey, I just want you to know? This is fine. I mean, I understand, but I'm wondering. You're not going to draw me, are you? I don't want to be in the paper. I mean, the haiku drawing is fine. I just don't want a caricature of me like, I don't know, a flounder? Floundering around as a medium fish in a small pond? I'd say you could use any of these ideas, but I'd prefer you didn't. All I'm saying is, these things happen, but don't draw me, 'kay? Maux? Maux? Alright. Well. Later."

Maux sits in the dark of her living room, listening to this nonsense on the other side of the door. She wants to laugh at what he's saying, almost wants to let him in, to tell him, "Get in here, jerkoff. You're not even worth drawing, and I wish I hadn't drawn you and all those stupid haiku you write."

Instead, she listens to him walk away, turning her thoughts towards graduation, to escaping Gainesville, to whatever is beyond all this dumb childish futile whatever.

JULIANNA

Julianna reclines on the couch, watching the sunset light filter through the sliding glass back patio doors of the apartment she shares with her boyfriend. She has almost finished the fourth tall glass from a now-emptied box of white wine, holding the glass with both hands on her fatter-than-it-used-to-be midsection.

Some '70s cop show, all sideburns and implausible shootouts, sto-ry-arcs to its predictable outcome on the unwatched muted tele-vision in the corner. New Zealand indie-pop from the early 1980s whispers out the speakers in every corner of the room. After com-ing home from work today, a quick glance in the rear view mirror revealed her first gray hair, a barely perceptible white thread in the blond, but there just the same.

The apartment is on the third floor, in a beige and pastel building surrounded by the twelve identical buildings that make up the apartment complex. Julianna straightens up, finishes the white wine, takes the five steps from the couch to the tiny back patio. The breeze is a warning of the cold to come. This is only the beginning. She has never been outside of Florida for the fall and winter months. How do people stand it? Why do people stand it?

The view from the patio: parking lot, swampy retention pond, and, directly across, an apartment building. It wasn't even a bad day at work. It was a nothing day. Julianna's boyfriend of ten years waits tables at night. Since the summer months, he has been com-ing home from work later and later. New friends from the restau-rant who Julianna has yet to meet. In the morning, as she leaves for work, he's asleep, hungover, guilty of something he's too dumb to hide. Scott reluctantly moved up here when Julianna got the job, but he's hit his stride—friends, a new life, reinvented as someone he wasn't in Gainesville: a dick. At least that's how Julianna sees it. When he comes home, she knows he's been cheating, but doesn't say anything, and she knows that when Scott sees her, he sees a past he'd rather forget. He has carved out a niche here, but for Juli-anna, there is nothing but this too-small apartment, and their bas-set hound, Charlie, who always looks how she feels anymore.

There is nothing to do in Charlotte, North Carolina.

There is nothing but this job for the tiny academic press, translating Russian Criticism into English for advanced Russian Studies students sprinkled across the North American continent. She sent them her resume on a whim, not thinking it would be her ticket out of Gainesville. Finally. It was the change she thought she needed. Seven months later, after doing nothing but translating all this criticism, she's not sure. It isn't simply criticism of literature, existence, the government. It is criticism of everything. Toilet paper. Bank tellers. The tonality of door bells. Nothing escaped the critical eye of these Russian theorists. Every facet of existence, no matter how mundane, should and must be critiqued. Julianna has nightmares of a world like this, filled with people yelping yelping yelping about every interaction in the consumer economy. Wasting their intellectual capacities, their advanced educations, on assessment. To waste your life on knocking down rather than building a better world. What if everyone fancied themselves a Russian critic? Pop culture. Restaurants. Toll booth operators. Cheese graters. Bars. Dandruff shampoo. A world of critics. The job, immersing herself in this level of criticism, is nightmare enough.

It is tedious, lonely work, sitting at a desk in a windowless corner, the only non-native Russian working in the pale dusty windowless office. But it pays better than any job she ever had back home, by far. With benefits and everything. And there was talk—drunk talk, yes—of marrying soon, buying a house, having kids. That thought, now, makes her laugh the laugh of the beyond-bitter.

She starts shivering as the sun fades behind the apartments. 45 degrees is the low tonight. It rarely gets this cold in Florida. She thinks of home. Is this everything? Benefits and security. Plans. A lifetime of translating Russian Criticism.

Across the parking lot, beyond the retention pond, in the third floor apartment in the building across from her back patio, the lights are on and the blinds are open in the living room. College students in backwards ballcaps and oversized sweatshirts—three men, two women—play the drinking game Quarters, howling like morons every time a quarter bounces off the coffeetable, hunching over the action like gamblers at the roulette wheel.

Julianna had never played Quarters, always thinking of it as that stupid game high school slutty girls play with frat boys instead of just getting drunk, but she can't stop watching. As the night goes on, they're louder, more animated, the noise echoing across the spaces between the apartment buildings. It isn't the drinking game, and it isn't even their excitement—their ridiculous excitability with each bounce of the quarter—that has her entranced like a voyeur.

"You're having fun!" she yells, an accusation, although not loud enough to resonate past the parking lot and retention pond.

Charlie gallop-flops to her side, barks, then moans in a way that has always sounded to Julianna like abject resignation to his fate.

Where is the fun here, she thinks? The parties? The shows? The records flipped from one side to the next all night long. The . . . cute boys.

Yeah. The cute boys.

The impulse hits Julianna like an instinct. A conviction. She needs to leave. Now. Otherwise, she'll be like this at 35, 40, until death. That one gray hair is only the beginning. And Scott . . . he's practically done everything but come home with the proverbial lipstick marks on his collar to show that he's cheating, that he's moved on, away, become someone else, somewhere else. She has money saved. Credit cards. That blue Corolla in the parking lot below. If she leaves, she'll make it to Gainesville by morning. She doesn't know if that's where she'll stay, but Gainesville's where you go when you don't know where else to go.

She brews a pot of coffee, drinks glass after glass of water to sober up. She packs her clothes, CDs, plates, glasses, utensils, books, as much as she can cram into the Corolla. Without the least bit of coercion, Charlie walks down the three flights of stairs, climbs into the passenger seat.

On scrap paper, Julianna scribbles a quick note, tapes it to the door:

"I need to leave. I'm not happy. You're not happy. Goodbye."

Interstate 95 South is desolate, black except for the distant red circles of the far-off semis. She drinks coffee after coffee. Each mile closer to home, each passing hour, the decision feels better.

In the dark orange sunrise, she crosses into Florida, sees the longed-for scenery, the lonely pines and live oaks, the Jesus billboards and Zero Tolerance for Drugs signs. She pats Charlie on the head as he sleeps through the trip.

Sunshine glares off the vacant early morning Jacksonville skyline. Gainesville is one backwoods backroad away, and all she knows is that whatever happens next won't be boring.

FOUR: NO SEASONS

"No. Calm down. Learn to enjoy losing."
—Hunter S. Thompson

SUNNY AFTERNOONS

Ronnie approaches the mic, check-one-check-twos it, announces, "Hi, we're The Sunny Afternoons."

·

On Rae's upper left arm, there is a tattoo of the outline of Florida with a hand emerging from the center of the state holding a British flag. The hand and flag are meant to be a replica of the hand and flag on the cover of the 1969 Kinks album *Arthur, or the Decline and Fall of the British Empire.*

·

Crammed into the very corner where they practice, here in the Myrrh House—plugged in, setting the levels. At the peak of the party, as the beer-buzzes reach a fine collective plateau before the inevitable spiral into a mindless lack of self-control.

·

It is October. After the rent is paid, Ronnie is broke. The last of the cash from the temp gig at the bookstore is spent, Ronnie is spent, and his days are spent alone in his room, reading book after book, happy tomes from, say, Louis-Ferdinand Celine, as the Stooges' first album plays over and over again.

•

Outside, they stand in groups of four or five up and down NW 4th Lane, leaning against cars, retelling anecdotes. Young voices bouncing around the Floridian no-season of autumnal summer.

•

Rae lets herself into Ronnie's room, carrying his guitar with her left hand, and a beige Fender Squire in the right. "Look what I just bought," she says.

•

They learn five songs: "Victoria," "'Til the End of the Day," "I Need You," "Dedicated Follower of Fashion," and "Where Have all the Good Times Gone?"

•

Two friends, playing unamplified electric guitars.

•

"I've been practicing," she says. She starts to play that three chord intro to "Where Have All the Good Times Gone?" Strum. Strum. Strum. Two of the strings (B and D) are beyond out of tune, but this only enhances the charm.

•

Of the many many rock and roll lyricists you're supposed to admire in your admiring youth, Ronnie Altamont had always idolized Raymond Douglas Davies over all the others.

Why?

Here's why: Boozy visions of British Walter Mittys struggling and suffering and finding the briefest moments of joy in the most mundane. Less about the in-your-tits sexual innuendo of blues bands, and less about the spiritual yearnings of psychedelia, less about classic rock ego and more about the anti-ego of the reticent trying their best to get through the day-to-day.

And then, the music. It never had to go out-there to tremendous lengths to get the point across—no drum solos, no synthesizer solos, no violin bows to the guitars. Actually, from their earliest to the end, you quite often hear borderline hack attempts at the proverbial "hit song." —But at their best, nobody does the three minute pop masterpiece better. No one has written a better song than "Waterloo Sunset." *No one.*

The demeanor. The idea of the man as an underdog overlooked genius, the Kinks usually rating fourth or fifth behind the Beatles, Stones, Who, and Zeppelin. The Beatles have plenty of champions, and most of them are insufferable bores. The Stones have plenty of champions, and most of them are shit-drunk white males who look and act like Jim Belushi and don't even care about pre-1969 Stones and get sappy at the mere mention of Charlie Watts. Zeppelin. You can't throw a dead dick at a radio without it finding some classic rock station gettin' the goddamn Led out. Seriously. I mean, I like them too, but enough already with the Zeppelin, America. There are other bands. Like The Who, another classic rock staple, and they have plenty of champions, and that's fine, because in Ronnie's mind, The Who and The Kinks are in a constant neck-in-neck for Best Band from Those Days. But Ray, he's the one-true genius of them all, and this genius is compounded in how Ronnie sensed that more than the others from the British Invasion, Ray Davies believed himself to be a vaudevillian . . . and saw the irony in it. The dichotomy of writing a song as beautiful as, say, "This is Where I Belong" (among so many others), then going from town to town and leading

American audiences in the call-and-response of "The Banana Boat Song," or even calling an album *Give the People What they Want*, or *Something Else*. Art. Showbiz. The eternal tug of war.

Anyway. Ronnie could go on and on about The Kinks. But before we move on, it's worth noting: since first hearing them at age ten—the song "Predictable," on an HBO music video program that predated MTV coming to town—Ronnie wished he could croon like Ray Davies . . . and to live someplace where he has the chance to play Kinks songs, with others who like them almost as much as he does . . . wow, man! Just wow! Gainesville!

•

The songs hold together. Somehow. The rhythm section chugs along.

•

He leaves his room each day long enough to walk the one block to the Floridian Harvest minimart and purchase one twenty-five cent Little Lady snack cake for brunch, and a second Little Lady snack cake for dinner.

•

Bradley wears slacks with leather weave belts and French flaggy Tommy Hilfiger shirts. He aspires to one day write a best-selling book on effectively managing your money. He is the drummer for The Sunny Afternoons.

•

"And I know the choruses now, too," she says. With tiny wide fingers, her left hand barres the frets, back and forth between B and A, over and over again. Ronnie cannot help but sing softly, "Won't you tell me / where have all the good times gone? / Where have all the good times gone?"

•

"Right now, the working title is *Effective Money Management*, but that might change," Bradley says to Ronnie shortly after meeting for the first time, at some dreadful party Rae almost literally dragged Ronnie to, some apartment deep in some complex off of Archer Road filled with the noises of bouncing quarters and shots and gratuitous yelling. "You're a writer. You know how it is with works-in-progress."

•

No shit. Where have all the good times gone?

•

They run through the song, from beginning to end. They play it a second time, now with Ronnie singing along, louder now, what he remembers, which is most of it. The third time, Ronnie puts more feeling into the vocal delivery. It has been too long since he has picked up the guitar and played something.

•

On the bass is Mitch, this big lug of an expatriate Midwesterner from Austin, Minnesota, the town where Spam is manufactured. He wears a worn Twins ballcap, white t-shirt, khaki shorts. With a thick red pick he plucks a pink bass guitar he's borrowed from his younger sister, who isn't using it anymore since her ill-fated feminist grunge band Bitch Slap broke up last year.

•

"That's a very functional title," Ronnie says before drunkenly burping. Rae punches him on the arm.

•

Played nonstop, the set is a nice and tidy fifteen minutes. With Rae's incessant worrying factored in, the set pushes the half-hour mark.

•

"Here's your guitar back," Rae says. Her speech is a rapidfire torrent, tinged with the phlegm of the chainsmoker. "At one of your parties you showed me how to play the beginning of 'Lola,' and then you told me I could borrow your guitar and learn the rest because you said you didn't need the guitar anyway and that it meant nothing if you had or didn't have it."

•

Her name isn't even Rae. It's Lauren. She changed it in honor of Ray Davies.

•

Heckles—smart, dumb, funny, and unfunny—were Gainesville's "Bravo! Encore!"

•

Rae's hair is red ringlets looping to her shoulders. Freckles dot her face and arms. Hazel eyes under horn-rimmed cat's eye glasses worn only by elderly diner waitresses and hip girls. Short. Thin. Bouncy. A green t-shirt silkscreened with the minimalist child-scrawl of some Pacific Northwest indie-pop band. Black skirt. Doc Marten boots. And the tattoo.

•

They run through their five songs as they have every evening now for nine days straight, in preparation for playing here at the Myrrh House this upcoming Saturday. Ronnie feels like some kind of grizzled veteran you see in old sports movies, the kind of grizzled veteran who knows he's washed up and turns to boozing, but these ragtag kids with their sugary heads filled with dreams give him a new lease on life, so he puts the bottle down and decides to give the game one more shot.

•

Ronnie downstrokes a first position A chord, then flamencos the strings like Townshend, then stops and says, "The Sunny Afternoons. That's what we're called."

"I thought we could be called Ronnie, or, The Decline and Fall of the Floridian Empire," Rae says.

Ronnie laughs, says, "No."

•

Rae rescues Ronnie from this miserable, uncreative, self-inflicted youthfully naïve funk. Every night for two weeks, Ronnie sits on the patchwork rug in her living room and she sits across from him and they strum their five Kinks songs. Ronnie enjoys her company. She does all the talking. Ronnie is sick of talking, sick of being the one who does the talking. For too long, he hasn't listened, opting instead for the mindless barf of alcoholic chatter leaving his mouth before the brain steps in and says, "Whoa! Easy!" On her walls are Pavement promo posters, pictures of the Kinks gallivanting around London, tiny paintings clipped from the pages of art history books. The TV is always softly playing one of those movies that's always on in these Gainesville houses—your Hartleys, your Jarmusches, your Jadorowskys, your Godards, your Trauffauts. You know. The red curtains are shut and that outside world of Ronnie's mistake-filled life doesn't exist in here. In here, Ronnie feels like a teacher; it's not an unpleasant feeling. He enjoys spending time with Rae and has no interest in anything more than friendship. He has blown it so many times with the people he cares about. He doesn't want to be like that anymore.

•

There will be no scathing music on the stereo, no scathing French literature dog-eared on the floor. Instead, Ronnie stretches out on the mattresses, strumming first position chords on the guitar until he falls asleep, and if this action isn't one of the secret pleasures afforded to guitarists, Ronnie will make a meal of his guitar and use the strings as dental floss.

•

She stands in front of Ronnie. Facial tics contort her mouth. Their guitars hang off their shoulders, clanging into each other.

"Ronnie," Rae says, turning away from the dozens beginning to concave around them as the set is about to begin. "I can't do this. I'm too nervous."

•

On some nights, he stares at the typewriter, but no words come. And that guitar, this same guitar Rae holds in her hands as she steps into his room, well, Ronnie had been wondering whatever happened to that thing in the same way you might try and figure out what happened to that book or record that's missing that you're not terribly concerned about, seeing how you didn't really like the book or record that much to begin with.

•

In the middle, Ronnie stands, running through the songs, singing into a microphone on a stand, cable plugged into a Peavey amplifier as he strums his guitar again, and the simple joy of being here, doing this, is enough.

•

After practices, Ronnie turns up the stereo loud enough to be heard up on the roof, where he climbs up with a four-pack of Old Hamtramck tallboys. Roger works weeknights now—when he's not at the library studying—and the neighbors expect the Student Ghetto to be loud. Mitch sticks around after practice, follows Ronnie up an easily-climbed tree next to the roof, steps across.

·

It holds together. Not tight, not loose. Bradley usually knows his twos from his fours. Mitch's Pete Quaife bass guitar imitations are solid enough. Rae plays better than she thinks. With each practice, they sound closer and closer to being ready to play the Myrrh House.

·

"I'm out of tune," Rae says after every song.

"You're fine," Ronnie insists.

"Yeah. See?" Mitch plucks the E-string of his sister's pink bass. Rae plucks the low E-string on her guitar. "In tune," Mitch concludes.

"Am I playing it right?" Rae moves to the next concern.

"Yes. You are." Ronnie answers. He finds a boundless patience for Rae and her endless worries, for the three in this room making music he loves.

·

"No worries," Ronnie says. He sips from the Old Hamtramck can, the sudsy water fogging his brain into optimism.

"Nahhh, I ain't worried," Mitch says, in the flat Midwestern accent that had never left him. "I'm more worried about Rae."

"I ain't worried about her," Ronnie says, in the early stages of speaking in a very affected Chicacalgo El-a-noy accent, for the move he plans on making sooner rather than later. "Cahmahn! Ya know it won't be a prah-blum."

"People are talking, Ron." (And yeah, Mitch says "Ron" like "Rahhhhn.") "She's notorious for flaking out."

"It's not gonna happen." Ronnie says.

•

"Look at me," Ronnie says. "You're going to do fine. Just play it like you did at practice."

"I think I'm gonna throw up."

"Good!" Ronnie says. This was something she had said during every practice, and the practices always ended up vomit free. "Wait until you're done, then we'll get you to the hospital.

"Oh," Ronnie adds. "And have fun."

•

All these people, so easily filed under "your so-called friends," validate Ronnie and the rest of the Sunny Afternoons with their vacant-drunk smiling faces. Should Ronnie feel too high on himself and his ego, friends in the audience are quite willing to yell stuff like "Hey look! It's Maux!" or "Hey look! It's Portland Patty!" or "Hey look! It's Maux and Portland Patty together, making out in your bedroom, Ronnie!"

•

"What if I forget how to play the songs when we get shows?"

"You won't."

"What if I play a part from one song in a different song?"

"It won't happen."

"What if—"

"It'll be fine!"

•

His favorite heckle is when William yells, "Play that one Stones song again!"

•

In Gainesville they stare at you with their arms crossed, smiling, basking in the magic. To Rae, to do anything more than offer a silent positive support would reduce her to a quivering neurotic twitch of tears. Ronnie gladly receives any and all heckles.

•

Ronnie plays and sings. He never gets nervous. Performing never scared him. Not once. Everything else in the world fills him with anxiety and apprehension, but when the guitar goes on, all that disappears. Their friends, they watch Rae, because they want her there, playing a guitar. They want this to work.

•

The view from Ronnie's roof: The ramshackle student ghetto houses. The unstoppable Florida foliage—the live oaks, pines, palms. NW 13th street—the traffic, the giant green-squared MOTHER EARTH sign above the organic market. The stars and the moon. Ronnie spends more and more time here when the heat dies down and the roof shingles aren't blistering.

•

There will be no stars in Chicago. Ronnie does not know this yet.

•

Tonight's post-practice record is "The Kinks are the Village Green Preservation Society."

•

Ronnie hasn't felt this happy in months, if not years. Smiling. Singing. Strumming. An imitation of the cynical, almost-hack tone of Ray Davies: *I need you / I need you more than birds in the sky / I need you / it's true little girl / you can wipe the tear from my eye.* Pure joy.

AT THE NOISE SHOW

"Shit's gay," Mitch repeats. He stands on the front porch with Ronnie, passing a flask of whiskey back and forth, taking a break from all that Art inside.

"Don't be homophobic now," Ronnie says, taking the flask, sipping, exaggerating the ol' burn (oh! The burn!) of what you could charitably classify as "the cheap stuff" by tilting his head from side to side, twisting and twitching and convulsing.

"I ain't homophobic," Mitch says. "If this was gay—like as in, really actually gay—it would be interesting." He grabs the flask from Ronnie, tips it to his mouth. "But no. Shit's gay."

"G.A.Y." Ronnie says.

"If you talk, they shush you!" Mitch says. "It's a fucking party, and they shush you."

"Shushy shushy shushy," Ronnie says. He sips, twists, twitches, convulses, then laughs.

"Shush, you heathen! Can't you see we're making very important white noise feedback from our amplifiers?"

Ronnie starts hopping around like a monkey caveman. "Me like rock. Me no get noise." This, punctuated with armpit scratches and lots of "ooga booga" onomatopoeia.

Mitch laughs, joins in with the hopping and the monosyllabic grunting. It's too easy, laughing at these homespun avant poseur noiseicians, or, as they insist on being called, "soundscapers."

•

Here in 1996 AD, noise music is a one-way ticket to underground credibility. Make your guitar produce shrill feedback through various effects pedals and your amplifier, and—voila! You now work with noise the way other capital-A Artists work with clay or marble or wood.

One day back at the Myrrh House, after Ronnie cracked one too many jokes about some swooshy ethereal Morse code bleeps coming out of the living room stereo while Roger sat on the couch leaning forward in an "intent listening" posture, Roger turned to him and said, "You're not smart enough to get it."

"Aw, bullshit," Ronnie muttered. "What's to get?"

"It's thought and expression that can't be expressed any other way."

"Sure, dude," Ronnie laughed before going into his room to listen to something slightly less noisy and a lot less pretentious, and a lot more structured.

Yes, it is all quite serious; the dozen-odd geniuses who comprise the Gainesville Noise Community sit around and watch each other make twittering screeches while wearing stern expressions, thinking of highly intellectual comments to make when it is all finished.

This is what is happening inside, as Ronnie and Mitch are on the porch cracking funnies and drinking too much whiskey. It's a cleared-out, average-sized living room in a typical student ghetto house, filled to capacity, most dressed all in black, and/ or wearing masks (papier-mache homemade, or rubber custom shop-bought).

Ronnie and Mitch were standing in the back, trying not to laugh at Roger, "performing" with a strobe light, controlling a theramin with his right hand and a box with knobs he twists and turns with his left hand. All the while, he wears a black robe and nothing else, his face painted all white, looking like some kind of surfer druid, dancing a strange kind of hop-march-jig with his right and left feet kicked up at random intervals.

"It sounds like gerbils mating," Ronnie thought he was whispering to Mitch, before the audience turned and collectively gave a shush noticeably louder than Ronnie's whisper.

It was an unrelenting hour of pompously smug guys (all guys) who had no problem talking about how they had "outgrown punk," and are "far beyond rock and roll," "fully embracing a post-music landscape," before making sounds that, to Ronnie's untrained ears, sounded like highpitched and beepy old telegraphs on sinking oceanliners.

.

"You're not profoundly inspired by this?" Mitch asks.

"Let's go," Ronnie says. "We'll walk to the Drunken Mick." He inhales, exhales, smiles. "It's a nice night."

As they turn to step down from the front porch, the front door opens and a familiar voice yells, "Heyyyyyy Ronnnnayyyyy!!!"

Mouse steps up to Ronnie, hugs him. "I never see you anymore, Ronnnayyyyyy!" Mouse wears an off-white suit, too-tight, covered in a multitude of splotchy stains, a very wrinkled black collared shirt, faded red tie. Behind him is Icy Filet, wearing red panties, red sequined pasties, and giant white-framed glasses. "We were hiding in the back getting ready to perform," she tells Ronnie and Mitch. "But you're here now, Ronald, and Mouse is right. We never see you."

"Aw, you know," Ronnie says, stepping back from the hug, trying to take them in in the numb spin of the whiskey. "I've been busy."

"Heh heh heh, you've been busy," Mouse says. "I can tell."

BRIAN COSTELLO

Ronnie shrugs. "I'm doing a lot of thinking."

"And a lot of drinking," Mitch has to say, since it's out there, free for the taking. Ronnie turns and punches Mitch on the arm. Mitch hasn't taken his eyes off of Icy Filet's breasts.

"That too," Mouse says. "I hear you just sit in your room all night, drinking alone."

"I've been thinking," Ronnie repeats, as if that should settle everything. "And we're just leaving."

"But we're about to play," Icy Filet says.

"Yeah, she's—they're—about to play," Mitch says.

"Heh heh heh," Mouse says. "Ronnie just wants to drink."

Ronnie steps off the front porch. He holds out his arms and spins like he's in a musical, says, "I just wanna dance! And sing. And write."

"And drink," Mouse says.

"That too," Ronnie says.

"You're a mess, Ronnie," Mouse says.

Ronnie is stomping down the street now, turns long enough to yell, "Who isn't?," continues trudging down the street.

Mitch still stands on the front porch steps. The interaction's knocked him out of the male-dumb haze of gawking at the red-se-quined pasties covering Icy Filet's nipples. He looks up at Mouse, at Icy Filet, says, "I'm sorry. I'll look out for him."

"Heh heh heh," Mouse laughs his laugh, as if to say, "No, you won't," and Mitch stumbles off in pursuit of Ronnie, who's half a block away trying to imitate Robert Plant's banshee wail in "Immigrant Song" and concluding each yell by either knocking over a garbage can and/or karate kicking a mailbox. Mitch catches up to him, joins in with the banshee wail, kicking and chopping and laughing before turning left onto University, whiskey-fearless, yelling their conversation:

"What does she see in him?" Mitch says.

"Who?"

"What's her name. Icy Filet?"

"Yeah."

"Yeah. What does she see in that Mouse guy?"

"No man . . . no . . . it's like . . . they're good for each other. Hang on a second." Ronnie turns to the curb, bends over, throws up, keeps walking, continues talking. "No, they're good for each other. Totally."

"How did you do that?" Mitch says.

"What?"

"Umm . . . nothing. Never mind." A moment later: "I just like her tits."

"Icy Filet's?"

"Yeah."

"Cool."

"You see those things, Rahhhhn?"

"Yeah," Ronnie yells. "She has breasts. Women have breasts. And with the pasties? You could almost see them in their . . . fuckin' . . . entirety." They approach the darkened doorway of the Drunken Mick. "And now, to celebrate the only pair of tits I'll almost see tonight, let's drink."

Vomit-breathed and dizzy, Ronnie enters the Drunken Mick, sits at the bar. Mitch follows, sits to his right. A shot and a beer, a shot and a beer.

"To the Midwest," Ronnie proposes, raising his shotglass to toast.

"...Ok," Mitch says, clinks his shotglass to Ronnie's, drinks.

When the shot is choked down and Ronnie shakes it out and around his head, he says, "Can't wait to get outta here ..."

"Why the Midwest?" Mitch has to ask, because now, really. Cahmahn.

"Why not?"

"Why?"

"Better than here ..."

Mitch raises the pint glass to his lips, drinks, sets it back down on the bar. "It doesn't matter where you live."

"Sure it does," Ronnie says, wobbly on the barstool, slurring his speech. "Makes a huge difference."

"Naw, not really, Rahhhhn. It's the same bullshit everywhere." Almost as if on cue, almost as if to bolster his argument, that one Bad Company song about how the vocalist is, well, he's bad company, and he can't deny, starts to play on the jukebox.

"You're saying Chicago is the same as Gainesville?"

"Naw, of course not. You're missing the point. You can be happy anywhere, or unhappy anywhere. That's all I'm sayin'."

Ronnie belches. Laughs. Raises his pint glass. "Ok, yeah: You can make the best of it, like here, for instance. Or Orlando. Or Chicago. Some people need more from the people and places around them. Some don't."

"I guess, Rahhn. I'm also saying that Chicago is exactly the same as this, only there's more of it."

"Look," Ronnie says, "look, *scientifically,*" he burps, continues, "there are big cities, small cities, suburbs, college towns, beach towns, factory towns, and ski towns. Each has their own ratios of boredom to excitement, danger to safety, vibrancy to redundancy, despair to hope. Sure, under the right set of circumstances, you can find your own version of happiness in almost any of these . . . " Ronnie stops, laughs. Turns to Mitch. "Look at us. Trying to solve the problems of the world."

"I'm just tryin' to figure out why you you cheersed the Midwest, Rahhhn. That was your toast, not mine."

"I don't know. I got my reasons." Ronnie laughs. "Let's get another beer, another shot, hmmm?" Ronnie nudges Mitch in the arm, punctuates the gesture with added "Hmmm?! Hmmm?!"

"Naw, I'm drunk. I'm walking home."

"Alright. I'm staying."

"You're staying?" Mitch stands, starts to walk to the door. "Camahhhn. You're drunk already. You don't need to get drunker."

"I'm stayin'," Ronnie says. Mitch shrugs, shakes his head, walks out the door, leaves Ronnie to his drunken drooling brooding. Dumbass. Thinks the Midwest—thinks Chicago—is any different. And now Mitch has gotta get home and sleep this off and make it to class tomorrow for an exam, and what does Ronnie have? Nothing. Not a thing.

TWO ON A FARTY[10]

Naw, dude, he had no idea the age of the nnnugget, Julianna, but she definitely wasn't some puppy-eyed punkette younger than Ronnie, now floundering somewhere in his mid-twenties. There

---

[10] Yes, this is a stylistic/structural parody of the Tennessee Williams short story "Two on a Party."

were some hungover mornings when he could believe his mind's jive turkey talk—that he was you know hanging out with some older Anne-Bancroft-Mrs.-Robinson-scotch-and-Virginia-Slims-panty-hose-and-blouse-type, but there were nights when the malt liquor was really kicking in, and the bands were hitting their strides three to four songs into their sets, her blue eyes were you know Bambified wonder, and she would shake that curvy-enough body up and down round and round, and Ronnie's hormones sang Beefheartian lyrics on the order of "Rather than I wanna hold your hand / I wanna swallow you whole / and lick you everywhere that's pink / and everywhere you think," she looked younger than Ronnie, younger than the clove-smoking dorm girls in their CRASS t-shirts. As he got to know her, Ronnie no longer thought about Julianna's thirtiness (thirtiness!), and he even forgot that on the night he met her, he contemptuously regarded her as "an aging yuppie." Natch, when Ronnie first met Julianna, she was looking notso hotso. It was at The Drunken Mick; she swiveled on the stool next to Ronnie's and she had lost a twenty dollar bill and was accusing the Irish bartender of shortchanging her on her last drink. She kept swiveling in her chair like a drunken manatee bobbing and weaving in a lagoon scanning the dark dirty bar floor for any sign of the bill, mumbling and swaying as the barstool squeaked each time she spun a 360, leaning forward, back of her blouse bunching upward and revealing the promise of two glorious asscheeks. As she spun, Ronnie was getting the feeling he was on the verge of being accused of reaching across the bar and stealing the twenty when she left it there while stumbling off to use the ladies'. Each time she spun his way he felt nausea in his stomach; he totally thought she was a stupid-ass aging yuppie. Actually she didn't think Ronnie Altamont had anything to do with it; her only suspect was the bartender, tallying her drinks with her hands—wwwwwun . . . twoooo . . . thhhhreeee . . . fffffff-four . . . fffffive . . . sssssix . . . ssssssseven . . . —repeatedly, obnoxiously asking why they don't teach subtraction in Irish schools.

Then Ronnie found it as he was about to bail, irritated and depressed with his decision to waste the evening drinking when he could have been trying to write; he spotted the twenty folded in half, pressed against the bar and the floor, far below the range of the swiveling yuppie's double-sight. With the kind of self-righteous elitist snobbery one gets when knowing that the independent rock and roll music you're fond of is billions of times better than the dependent rock and roll music the masses are spoonfed, Ronnie plucked the bill from the floor, made a sarcastic production of showing her the discovered twenty, and slammed it on the bar without saying a word. Two events prevented him from leaving The Drunken Mick right then and there. Three Gainesville scene nnnnuggets entered the bar one . . . two . . . three, and they knew Ronnie from his parties, and he knew them because they were nnnnuggets and anytime he saw them—individually and collectively—he bit his fist like Lenny from "Laverne and Shirley," and as they said their Hahhhhowareyewws in that syrupy southern way of theirs, at the same time, the woman, Julianna, wouldn't stop thanking him for finding the twenty, wanted to repay him in whatever he wanted to drink. Well? Sure. Ok. He returned to his seat, she bought him the drink, the nnnuggets seated to his right bought him drinks, the yuppie bought the nnnuggets drinks, the nnnuggets bought the yuppie drinks, and Ronnie made charming promises to repay them all when he finally found a job, and in no time it was like the beautiful bright celebration Ronnie wanted to throw when the lead singer of U2 finally up and died.

Within minutes, she was no longer an aging yuppie but someone decently attractive, who spoke knowledgeably of Belgian indie-pop and Nova Scotian hardcore, who actually knew the older members and the older bands of the scene inside and out, who had moved to Charlotte, North Carolina on a whim, and moved back to Gainesville, Florida on a whim, someone even more to Ronnie's taste than the nnnnuggets with their fake IDs could ever be. Seeing them, Ronnie and Julianna, in the long bar mirror behind all those multi-colored liquor bottles, he saw all the makings of a fellow flounderer, the perfect companion to kill these empty Gainesville afternoons, evenings and late nights. She could pass for an almost-haggard Swedish stewardess, short blonde hair, pale skin, almost statuesque save for the slight arm flab, a barely perceptible unfirm around the middle, tiny purple veins beginning to emerge in the thighs. Have you ever heard the song "Lady Midnight" by Leonard Cohen? Well, if you have, she—and it—were a lot like that. Ronnie had uneven short black hair from one-too-many friends who were amateurs with hair clippers. He had a darker inevitable Floridian tan—even though he rarely ventured outside. He wore black-rimmed glasses—handles covered in grime eating into the hinges. He kept his stained baby blue Oxford shirts untucked to camouflage the emerging beer belly. Unfortunately for Ronnie, the belly would kind of, you know, hang over the shorts he was forced to wear nine months out of the year, and by the month, it was getting harder and harder to hide, no matter how much he sucked it in. Of course, behind the bar, the nnnuggets didn't notice it, but when he stood . . . I mean, did The Ramones have beer bellies? That's how he explained it to Julianna. She said, Dude, find something else to drink besides all that stupid beer, get some exercise! Why do you care so much about it? I'm older than you; I should be the one complaining! Beyond the floundering and the drunken belligerence, Julianna was usually well-intentioned in her honesty, even if Ronnie would never argue with someone as much as he did with her. She would argue over anything—literally anything—especially when drunk—and she lived in France for two years and knew everything about pre-fusion jazz—knew more about music than even Ronnie's extensive knowledge, spoke fluent Russian, graduated Magna Cum Laude at the University of Florida. Easily, she was the smartest woman Ronnie had ever met, but there was nowhere for that energy to go, so she drank, and that would have been depressing to be around, if Ronnie hadn't matched her drink for drink, time and time again. Totally, when he stopped thinking of her as some yuppie, he thought of her as a serious drinker—not a drunk or a lush or an alcoholic—not yet, and maybe not ever—but as someone equally as bored as Ronnie by what his surroundings had to offer anymore. Her intelligence simply didn't exist with the women in the Gainesville punk scene. Some came close—Maux, for instance—but they were too young, masking their inexperience with a self-invented world-weariness.

Fortunately for Ronnie, he had broad shoulders. If he could hold his shoulders back and try not to slouch, the beer belly practically disappeared, but unfortunately, years of playing and seeing loud music had dulled his hearing. To listen to what the nnnuggets were saying, he needed to slouch inward, towards them. He had no money—living a hand-to-mouth existence from plasma donations—so joining a gym or even buying running shoes was completely out of the question. To be in shape meant not playing music, not writing, not going out each night, because it meant finding a full-time job, and Ronnie Altamont, in case you didn't know it, was destined to be a great writer and all that shit. Yes, all that shit!

Being a little fat and a little deaf, and more so by the month, it seemed, Ronnie would lean into conversations, shoulders slouched, belly poked out, if he wanted to hear what the nnnuggets were yapping about. It isn't nice and it isn't cool to not listen to the nnnuggets, because the way they talk and what they talk about is almost as important as how they look in determining whether or not they're really and truly a nnnugget, or some run-of-the-mill cute girl with the grave misfortune of being a fan of Alice in Chains, and Ronnie hated making that mistake. So he leaned inward a little bit, and the gut popped out enough to make Ronnie inwardly cringe, ashamed at what the floundering was doing to his body, making him age ungracefully, someone who could no longer hang with nnnuggets, with anyone younger than he. But, as he often said to Julianna, it's important to know if they're, you know, punk, or not.

Julianna disagreed, and they had many arguments about it. But Ronnie was obsessed with this, and would go on and on about it, like some Maximumrockandroll columnist delineating what is and isn't punk and why and why not and Julianna would surrender the argument out of outright boredom, simply not caring one way or the other, as Julianna had slowly moved away from younger punk rock obsessions in ways Ronnie had not.

About her own looks, Julianna was equally depressed.

You know, Julianna would say, I used to be a nnnugget myself. Before I thought I had grown up. I can hide years, and sometimes, when they're drunk enough, I think the boys actually think I'll be off to take my core classes the next morning. Assuming they even care about it, and many of them don't. How can they not see this fatty ass and this fatty face and this sagging everything else, Ronnie?

Bull. Shit. Ronnie would counter. You're beautiful and I know it, and they know it, and if you don't know it, I'm gonna keep telling you! Kee-rist, lady! Get over here!

And Ronnie would stand, extend his arms into a hug the way he would when he thought he was being charming, and he'd put his arms around her and embrace, hands touching her back where the Carolina pale was darkening into Floridian permatan, and it was always around closing time, when the bars or shows or parties were ending and this youthful life they had lived for far too long felt exhausted and they didn't know where to go or what to do next, that tasty guitar lead to the Dan's "Reelin' in the Years" came on like it always does, somewhere, on a jukebox. Another night where you go out with so much hope and come back feeling older than you actually are. The world is against you, and so are the nnnuggets, who are as coy as you are drunk and the teasing is the worst, the unconscious coy teasing that inspired so many of those emo songs from the emo bands of that emo town. These temporary early twentied sorceresses of the nanosecond, the boys and girls at the height of their beauty, and after this, it would be over for them the way it would be over for Ronnie and Julianna, and only Ronnie and Julianna knew this secret, and it killed their hurt along with the booze—the bottle and the wisdom a futile solace wherever they ended up. This brought out the "Reelin' in the Years" talk, the regrets of wasted lives with wasted lovers, forgetting they were still young and not unattractive.

Really, they batted about .300. Usually once a week one of them succeeded in what Ronnie called "prospecting for nnnuggets." On the awesome nights, they were both successful. The awesome nights weren't as rare as snow, but they weren't as frequent as frat boys, but it was obvious they were a good pair, setting off the latent charms inside each other that nnnuggets picked up on immediately and responded accordingly. The nights were bright brilliant parties of bands and booze and pizza and singing and the ol' awoooooga! Julianna's arrival into Gainesville led Ronnie to reserves of vast energy, to places Ronnie never knew existed. It was the best of times, papa papa papa ooo mow mow papa ooo mow m-mow, even when it was notso hotso. Even if the worst happened, if there were no nnnnuggets around and it was only Ronnie and Julianna sitting on Ronnie's roof—bored, drunk, and arguing—hey, it beat sitting at home watching television, waiting for work the next day. Good or bad, it was living.

That first week, they were inseparable, seven days and nights of binge-drunk self-destructive hilarity! Kicks! Ronnie thought, in the Kerouac-mindheart of these moments. The break-ups and the frustrations of not fitting in in this alien land melted and out of all that Ronnie reemerged as a goof with a fellow goof, a goofette, and her arrival in town brought all the dudes around and all the nnnnuggets appeared around Ronnie, because it seemed they were together but they weren't together, it was like that first dusty grizzled prospector sticking his tray into the crick, sifting out the dirt and the water and he sees it and screams "GOLD! IT'S GOLD IN THEM THURR

HILLS! HOORAY FOR 1849!" and you and her are the only ones in the crick and it's simply a matter of how many nnnuggets you can carry off because they're there ready for you to take them home.

What a great week that was, when they were first inseparable. Starting at The Drunken Mick, when Julianna had lost her twenty dollar bill that Ronnie found. Clinton was reelected. The Gators were bound to win the National Championship in football. There was a safety to the mid-90s, between decades full of apocalyptic gloom and doom, and there was relatively less to worry about. With few responsibilities and a time to get out there and enjoy life, why the fuck not? Everyone was apathetically blissful, ripe for adventure. Yes, ripe!

By the end of the week, when the 70 percent unsuccessful rate would happen, Julianna was crashing on Ronnie's couch rather than staying in her depressing studio apartment in some "high-rise" (six stories, a veritable skyscraper for Gainesville) close to campus. The second week was nowhere near as good as the first week. Julianna was beyond drinking for fun and relaxation. In the morning, she shook. She would vomit. She wasn't eating. Her face puffed and sagged, and bags the size of tumors hung below her eyes. She was, as she said, the living embodiment of the Iggy and the Stooges song "Your Pretty Face is Going to Hell," and Ronnie had to agree. She never looked older, and she lived in a constant cycle of pass out, vomit, pass out, vomit, and somehow nevertheless back to the studio to feed and walk her poor dog.

Then on Friday night, Ronnie's roommate Roger had had enough. Ronnie figured it would only be a matter of time, but Julianna was oblivious, moving from one drink to the next. Eventually,

Ronnie knew, that stressed-out aspiring film critic roomie of his was going to flip out over Ronnie and all these new weirdass older and younger friends coming and going at all hours, on morning drunks, afternoon drunks, night drunks. And Ronnie couldn't afford to pay the bills, the rent. When he'd enter the Myrrh House with Julianna and whoever tagged along behind her who wanted more of whatever "their thing" was—whatever it was these new friends Julianna introduced to Ronnie were doing, Roger would turn away from his precious artfilms and send a deathglare that grew more severe with each passing day. Then one night, they brought back to the Myrrh House some nnnugget who wanted Ronnie to teach her guitar, and some ponytailed freshman who caught Julianna's eye, some collegiate claiming he would be the next Scorsese, Roger snapped, raving like a Führer in a traffic jam.

What the fucking fuck fuck! he screamed. I live here! I work and go to school and when I get home I need to study and watch films! This isn't The Drunken Mick! You're the most selfish, thoughtless people, and you, Ronnie, are the worst roommate—

A nasty scene. Roger wanted everyone out, immediately. Julianna yelled, Sorry about your luck, fag! Ronnie lives here too! Roger swung a right hook, connecting with Ronnie's jaw. Ronnie fell backwards, Julianna stuck her right index finger in Roger's face, screaming, Why are you such an asshole, asshole?! and her new friend—the Next Scorsese, stepped in and started swinging.

Oh my God oh my God! screamed the nnnugget, standing over Ronnie, who bled and stared blankly at the ceiling. Scorsese stood over Roger, who had also fallen backwards to the floor.

As drunk and everything else as she was, Julianna always had a deep reservoir of composure when it was absolutely necessary.

She could control her thoughts, her brain, into passable, rational sobriety.

You two should probably leave now, Julianna said to the nnnugget and Scorsese.

All the nnnugget needed was an I'll be ok from Ronnie for her to step out the door, but Scorsese wanted more punches, even if Roger was already prostrate on the ground, holding back tears. Just leave, Julianna insisted, whispering, I'll call you later. (The only time they ever saw those two again was at some party by the train depot two to three weeks later, where the nnnugget and Scorsese touched and groped and kissed like boyfriend and girlfriend while Ronnie and Julianna rolled their eyes. Kissing in public. How disgusting.) She gave Ronnie a dishtowel of ice for his jaw, and wiped away the blood and the tears from Roger's face, making harmless jokes the entire time, so incredibly charming in that way only southerners have, when their voices are smooth soft and sugary and total and complete bullshit. You silly boys, she kept saying. All heart, no brains, no muscle. As a peace offering, Julianna offered Roger her collection of Jodorowsky videos. He agreed, but only if Ronnie agreed to stop having strangers over well into the early morning hours on weeknights. Fine, Ronnie sighed, through the drunkenness and the swelling jaw, as he was starting to believe that, more and more, he could actually date Julianna, if she would have him. That night, after they left Ronnie's and actually spent the night in Julianna's studio, she did.

The next morning, they talked about it in terms of its inevitability. Bound to happen, Julianna said. Wanted it to happen, Ronnie insisted. Now they could move on to other thoughts, other people.

Dating was out of the question. She refused to be with anyone, after leaving Charlotte, and Ronnie refused to take anything—especially this—seriously. But they would talk about it, indirectly, with a giggly reticence proving neither had grown up completely.

Fantastic, Julianna would later say, as they drank malt liquor on Ronnie's roof, as the sun set over the student ghetto.

I always wanted it to happen, Ronnie said. From when I first met you and everything. It was better than I expected.

Aw, c'mon, Julianna said, punching Ronnie in the arm. It was awful. I was awful. Dranking (She called it "dranking." She liked how it sounded more, you know, winoish?) too much made it awful, but it wouldn't have happened any other way.

No, I was awful, Ronnie said, leaning in to kiss her on the cheek as she pulled away. We'll never try it again. I was so bad.

You were great. The best. Julianna said. But we're friends. Friends can't do this.

It gets dramatic, Ronnie agreed. There's too much of that here already.

I can't be monogamous now, Julianna sighed. It's too much trouble.

I don't care that much, Ronnie said, finishing his quart of Brain Mangler malt liquor then watching the bottle roll off the roof and shatter.

They never officially got together again, but unofficially? Ok, sure. In those weeks they were the closest and most unorthodox of friends, there were some blacked out moments, when waking up was a jigsaw puzzle missing most of its pieces, one or the other waking up to the other's snoring, an arm trapped under or draped over the other's semi-nude body.

We didn't, she'd say, waking up in her new place, some prefab house she rented on a month-to-month basis in the Duckpond, realizing she had more money saved from her Russian translation job in Charlotte than she realized. Money went further in Gainesville than in most places. God bless towns with cheap costs-of-living. (The month-to-month at the studio was far too depressing, surrounded by all those dumbass college kids yelling. Simply deplorable, ugh, she said. And besides, there was so much more room and a backyard for Charlie, her dog.) (She paid for everything. Food. Drinks. Once she happened to drive past as Ronnie was walking along. Where are you going? she asked. To donate plasma for money, he answered. What? What?! No, you're not doing that. Get in here! Ronnie climbed into her car. If you need money, she says, I have money. You shouldn't do that. It's not good for you. And Ronnie never donated plasma again.)

Oh we did, baby! Ronnie would laugh. And you were, like . . . rrrrroar! Animal! Sex kitten! All that shit! Meow!

As much as she drank? Really? I must have been like a corpse!

Well, Ronnie said. What are you? Thirty-one? Thirty-two? You're not far off, har har har . . .

Shut up, kid. Get your clothes on. I wanna bloody mary.

Oh, a bloody mary! My gout! My hernia! Ronnie laughed and laughed until Julianna yelled STEAMROLLER!!! and tried rolling over Ronnie, Bob and Doug McKenzie style.

Sometimes, they would break out what Dylan called "your useless and pointless knowledge," but typically, neither wanted to talk of anything much deeper than where they would go to drink, where were the parties, and bands, bands, bands. Ronnie didn't want familiarity. Familiarity hurt. For the first two weeks, Ronnie didn't even know Julianna's last name. Wasn't interested. And for that first month, neither realized the other had a brain, you know, for thinking? Then, they would start talking of their recent pasts, their almost-glory days (if they were dumb enough to believe life peaked before you were twenty-two), when she was straight As and living in France, when he was editing the school newspaper and writing highly-regarded yet notorious humor columns. Over time, they learned they had more in common than the floundering, that they were older than the college crowd, smarter, yet dumber, and stuck in this town and they had no idea where they were going next.

It was a partnership of necessity, because nobody else around them was going through what they were going through, and they were connected in part because they shared a weariness with everything and everyone around them—for Ronnie, the culture of the South, and for Julianna, youth culture. They did not dislike anyone; they simply found it all too funny—punks, vegans, rednecks, indie-rockers, emo kids, co-workers, roommates, students. They would sit on Ronnie's roof and they would laugh at all of them, and for all the right reasons. These kids were all so serious, thought everything mattered, thought life and living was all so very important. Ronnie and Julianna were the only ones in Gainesville who saw through all the pretentiousness of everyone. Ronnie and Julianna were real. They had lived. They weren't in college anymore. Ronnie, for his part, had taken to speaking in an exaggerated Chicago accent, throwing out words like "yer basic," and "jagoff" whenever the opportunity was there. On the roof, they were like Statler and Waldorf on The Muppet Show, heckling from their balcony. On the ground, at parties and shows, it was a mutual bitterness and frustration with where their lives were going . . . Excuse me, scenester jerks! Ronnie would yell as he moved through parties. Why do you whine so much? Why do you feel the need to whine your songs? Julianna would ask of bands during and after their sets. They hated these uniforms these Gainesville punks all wore—their stupid short hair and their beards and their tattoo sleeves and their black band t-shirts and their cutoff army fatigues and their wallet chains. They lived to be as obnoxious as possible around these people. And on the classic rock radio stations of the world, Steve Miller sang "Time keeps on slippin, slippin, slippin, into the future. Tick tock tick. Doo doo doo doo . . . "

Yes, with each passing night, the awareness that this really could not last. They would have to grow up already. Knowing this lessened all inhibitions. Because these opportunities would not happen again. Ronnie wasn't going to act this way when/if he made it to Julianna's age, and beyond. And there was only so much money Julianna had saved, only so much she could use to buy Ronnie food and drink. She would need to find a real job eventually.

And Ronnie still considered himself and still wanted to be a writer. He thought of people he would never see again, of an Orlando that no longer existed.

This can't last, Julianna said. Someday soon, we're going to move on. We need to.

Why? This is fun.

You write. Your bedroom is full of scribbled journals and stacked pages. When I'm around you all the time, you do nothing but sit on this roof and drink and talk shit. It's not healthy or right for you not to be writing. I've read what you've written.

No you haven't.

One afternoon, while you slept off a late night, I grabbed the manuscript off your desk and read the first fifty pages while drinking coffee with Roger. I told him you were actually a pretty good writer. He agreed, didn't understand why you weren't trying anymore.

Cah-mahhhhhhn, Ronnie said in his best grew-up-in-Bridge-port-next-to-the-Daleys-accent.

I see you, observing all of this. You think it's all one big Bu-kowski scene, and you're Chinaski himself, but you ain't that. No way. You've had it too good, overall. But you're shifty-eyed, Ron-nie Altamont, and I see you observing these places, this town, and I know you're writing a book in your mind. And someday soon, you're going to give up this farty-fart fartaround and get serious with it.

And if I do, Ronnie said, you're getting serious with me. Move to Chicago.

What am I going to do in Chicago? Seriously.

No idea. Because they knew, when this floundering exis-tence ran its course, when one or the other or both said Enough! they would drift apart. Ronnie even knew it would go down the way Julianna predicted. In upcoming weeks, months. He would move on, and Julianna would either stay on the binge and find another partner in the floundering fartaround, or she would move to a real city and get a real job. The only conceivable way Julianna could get serious with life right now was if she fell off the roof, or crashed her car, or when the proverbial sauce and the proverbial dressing did to her outsides what it was doing to her insides. The Floridian climate makes the easy, unchallenging life very comfortable, seductive, and it isn't something you can simply change overnight, wake up and say Ok world, let's get to work. Only when you run out of money does that happen, and Julianna had no shortage of money.

Let's tour Florida! she said one fine hungover afternoon on Ronnie's roof. I'll drive. I'll pay for everything!

The motherland? You wanna explore the motherland?

We're taking a Gainesville timeout. Let's dress like tourists and see what happens. We'll go through the panhandle, both coasts, the Keys. Everywhere!

At the thrift store, they found a nice pair of sandals to go with Ronnie's black socks. Swim trunks at the mall that looked like Bermuda shorts. A tan-gray short sleeved collared shirt with a penguin embroidered on the right breast. A light blue fishing hat with a navy blue brim. Flip shades for his glasses. An old camera necklaced over the front. *Sticky Fingers* by The Stones on cassette on a perpetual loop. (I'm sick of all this played out punk rock garbage, Julianna said. Me too! Ronnie hollered.) Singing "It's just that demon life / gotchoo in its sway." Maybe Julianna went overboard with it, too undeniably a native Floridian to really look like a tourist, so when she dressed in a pink Minnie Mouse long-sleeved t-shirt, tucked into tight khaki shorts, she looked like an alien from the planet Camel Toe. The purple cruiseship visor and the sunglasses permanently wedged behind into the bleach blonde hair was a nice touch. Perfectly new white Keds tennis shoes. It didn't even occur to them to bring a change of clothes. Initially, Julianna drove her blue Honda coupe like a tourist, or like a retiree, sputtering down the Interstate at five to ten mph below the speed limit in the left lane, cutting across two-to-three lanes of traffic to hit an exit at the last second. But they grew bored with this, and it was too much work. Florida! Up and down the Atlantic coastline, where the past of seafood shacks, boiled peanuts, and neon motels gave more and more ground to the hot pink hotel skyscrapers. The old fort at St. Augustine, and the winding little walkways where the bars were filled with Conch Republicans listening to beach bums strum "Margaritaville" on nylon strings on beat-up acoustic guitars on tiny wooden stages. Across and down the peninsula, south of Orlando, driving through all the theme parks. A replica of the Bates Motel seen from the highway, on top of a hill, in front of a setting sun. Highway signs reading "HOLY LAND WET AND WILD/ NEXT EXIT 2 MILES." Everyplace, every sign, reading, in essence: WELCOME TO FLORIDA. GIVE US YOUR MONEY! Decorative palm trees, Seussian in their postures and presentations. Ferneries and grapefruit groves. And it's the no-season of 70 degrees. The absolute miracle of the nature when it isn't ruined by overdevelopment. The dreadful towns. The backwoods. The Born Agains. The pick-up trucks with "NEVER APOLOGIZE FOR BEING WHITE" bumper stickers. The feeling of being on what amounts to a narrow stretch of land, memories of Bugs Bunny taking a chainsaw to the Panhandle, pushing Florida away and proclaiming, "Take 'er away, South America!" Through Tampa, the glows of televisions visible in all the tiny shacks along the highway, no promises of anything worthwhile for a couple of pretend tourists like Ronnie and Julianna, no disappointments nor regret for driving straight through.

Stopping in St. Petersburg to check out the Dali Museum. Watching *Un Chien Andalou* several times, fascinated by how people get up and leave when the music has its triumphant finish though the film does not. Humbled and inspired to continue living, and that's how it went with them when they found the few artistic statements humbling and inspiring in their semi-affected jadedness. Seafood and wine by the water as piped in Caribbean music steeldrummed all over the place. Yah mon, Gulf Coast irie, Ronnie said, and Julianna laughed. They checked into a hotel for the night, planning to drive farther down the Gulf Coast before cutting across Alligator Alley, check out Miami then drive all the way down to the Keys before the long return trip to Gainesville. It's a search for what Florida's all about, Julianna said. The Floridian Dream! Whatever, Ronnie said. They reclined in separate beds, drinking wine, watching late-night television, Ronnie flipping through the hip alternative weekly paper. Says here there's gonna be something called The St. Petersburg Margarita and Ribs Blues Fest tomorrow afternoon. Oh really? Julianna said. I could do this, Ronnie said. We'll check out of the hotel, go see what this is all about. I do love all three of these, but together? That's madness. Yes, it is crazy, Julianna said. Maybe we'll learn something of our Floridian motherland.

And—hoo boy!—here comes the gremlin, the weasel, the Joe Lieberman of destiny to mess up all their plans, even though they really honestly had no one to blame but themselves!

Downtown St. Petersburg, among the strange mix of the bank buildings and old man bars. The streets are closed off. The margaritas are cheap, too cheap, and the ribs don't cut into the tequila enough. At first, this is enjoyable. Fat Floridian Rush Limbaugh-type guys looking like they just stepped off their yachts, faces smeared with barbeque sauce, spilling their 'ritas with every sway to the white man bluesbands singing "I went down to the crossroads" and so on and so forth on the stage draped in corporate sponsorship banners. Wristbands and handstamps. Clowns making animal balloons. Police. Ronnie and Julianna dancing like crazy, front and center, alone like Druncles at weddings, on their fourth, fifth, and sixth 'ritas, not as watered down as they should be.

Wheeeeeeeeeeeeeeeeeeeeeeeeeeeeeeeeeeeeeeeeeeeeeeeeeeee
eeeeeeeeeeeeee!

Was it the ribs or the 'ritas or the bummer jams the white-
man blues bands were laying on their ears? It could be any or all
of the above, as everything turned a little, then a lot, disorienting,
sloppy, gross. How they didn't wind up in jail is anyone's guess.
There were all these kiosks selling things like pirate hats and plastic swords and rainbow-lensed John Lennon sunglasses. Ronnie,
bored and drunk, thought it was funny to shoplift everything that
wasn't nailed down, and through the audacity and total belief that
nothing bad could ever happen to him on that day, he continued
getting away with it, to the point where he was walking down the
street trying to speak in a Liverpudlian pirate accent. Oh, and then
there were blackouts:

(Julianna making out with one of these Rush Limbaugh guys, one
fattyass hand on her ass, the other fattyass hand holding a cigar.)

(Ronnie on the curb, singing a cappella Steely Dan songs like Michael McDonald for spare change that was not forthcoming.)

(Ronnie wearing dozens of colorful beaded necklaces, exchanging
these for views of tits of varying size and quality.)

(. . . . .)

. . . And then they're in the car, on some back road between St. Petersburg and Gainesville, Julianna driving, screaming (screaming!) You're a shitless piece of worth, Ronnie! You're the worst! I'm pulling over at the next town, and you can get the fuck out!

What did I do?

What did you do? What did you do?! I don't know what you did! You were running around screaming "Tits!" at the top of your lungs, and "Blues!" and "Tits Blues!" and it was all I could do to drag you out of there to break up the fight that was about to happen, the arrest that was about to happen.

He needed to remember to thank her for tapping into her sobriety reservoir when the going turned ugly. He could remember very little of this. You're drunk too, he said.

Yeah, but we're leaving. You're getting out at the next town. I hate you Ronnie Altamont! Then, a ten minute tirade: You are a terrible writer, Ronnie, an awful musician, a lazy ass, no friends, no girlfriends. You destroy everything and everyone around you. You ruin people. You fuck up everything you touch, Ronnie. Everyone you touch. Jerk. Dick. Cock. Pussy. And on, and on, and on, Julianna broke out the big guns, so much so, Ronnie couldn't accept it as anything more than Julianna too far gone on the 'ritas to be rational. Ronnie took out his wallet, tossed bills on the dash. Here's gas money. Please drive me back to Gainesville, and that's it. We don't have to ever talk again. No! I'm pulling over now! She pulled over in the middle of Florida cracker ranchland—flat green earth and cattle only broken up by clusters of jungle. Aw, dude, Ronnie said. Please. Get out! No, I won't! There's my money. Take it. Just give me a ride home. And then, as the standoff in the heat and humidity was really about to start, Julianna calmly rolled down her window and barfed. Ronnie looked away, staring at the ranchland. Violent retchings. Splatter onto the dirt shoulder of the road. That smell. What does this all mean? What were they doing here? In the backseat, a gallon jug of water. Ronnie reached back, grabbed it. Here. Drink this, he said. She turned around, wiped the puke off with her ironical Minnie Mouse t-shirt. Ok. Three large gulps. The fourth a swish around the mouth and a spit out the window. I'm drunk, she said. I shouldn't be driving. We'll go to the next town. Get a room. Ok.

After twenty minutes of nervous silence, they find a motel, and of course, like most east coast motels of this type, it's called The Sunrise Motel. It's evening when they check in. One bed apiece. Squiggly color TV. Wood-paneled walls. Julianna orders a pizza before passing out. Ronnie eats a slice before passing out. Hours later, he wakes up. Julianna spooned in next to him. He pulled her closer. On the floor, their now-wrinkled, stained, and stinky thrift-tourist clothing. None of this makes any sense to him. It isn't supposed to. It's the end, isn't it? he thinks. The end of the fartaround. Ronnie was wide awake when the heralded sunrise attacked the motel room window, as the A/C unit wheezed like an asthmatic. He kissed Julianna on the back of her blonde head before falling asleep again. They would wake up and leave minutes before checkout time.

Hungover.

The day of the week did not matter, but from the serious driving of the mail trucks and delivery vans, it was a weekday late morning. A little remorse, but no regret, and a lot of recovery in Julianna's car. These low-energy post-mortems always put Jimi Hendrix in Ronnie's mind, singing "I don't live today." How did we get to that hotel, exactly? Julianna asked. Ronnie shrugged. You drove. I did something to piss you off. You wanted to leave me on a ranch. What?! Yeah, you were screaming. Said I was awful. Really mean. Oh. Ronnie. I'm so sorry. I didn't mean anything. I don't remember much. Yeah. Sigh. We should go back to Gainesville. Yeah. You're right.

Two hours later, they were back up the peninsula entering Gainesville's city limits. Ronnie marveled as he always did about how innocuous the place looked when you pulled off the highway. The world Ronnie lived in was hidden when you came into town like this. It was hidden. It always looked sad to Ronnie. Transient. Magical, but fleeting. Like Julianna, who would leave very soon. He would never forget the look when she dropped him off at his house, the unwashed touristy clothes and unwashed hair. But the eyes. So bittersweet. At the time, Ronnie would be too hungover, too exhausted, to give it too much thought, and he figured they would be on the roof this time tomorrow, laughing about their arguments, piecing together what they would recall of the Ritas and Ribs fest, and everything after. Wow. What happened? That was crazy! Yeah. I'm sorry, Ron. I already accepted your apology. We were drunk. Ridiculously drunk. It went too far. But I've never met anyone like you ever. I . . . no, I'm not going to say love, but couldn't we try? Who else is there around here? Kids. And you know I'm not like them. I hope. We could try, right?

She would call Ronnie, on the fourth day upon returning from the ersatz search for the Floridian dream. I'm leaving for Tallahassee, she said. I'm going to take the GRE and get into grad school there, and, clearly, I can't be here anymore. There's no reason for me to stay here. What little I have is packed. I'm gone. Ronnie, flabbergasted, blubbering like the Big Bopper, uh

whuh . . . whuh . . . will I whuh? He would think of all the right
things to say in the upcoming weeks and days, but she left town
more abruptly than she arrived, Lady Midnight, and Ronnie sat
in his room, listening to the song "Days" by The Kinks, over and
over again . . . "Thank you for the days, endless days, sacred days,
you gave me . . . you're with me every single day, believe me,
although you're gone, you're with me every single day, believe
me. " Someone once described "Days" as the only heartbreaking
song in which the person had no bitterness towards the person
who split. "Days you can't see wrong from right. It's alright. I'm
not frightened of this world. Believe me."

And so alone, in his room listening to The Kinks, on the
streets, at the parties, riding around the great space coaster aptly
named The USS Great Lost Dickaround, Ronnie would think of Julianna, and half expect her to tumble into some dumb scenester
party with a six-pack yelling WHAT'S UP NOW, SELLOUTS? WHO
WANTS A WINE COOLER? But that Julianna wasn't coming back,
and Ronnie knew, somewhere in his head, that their connection
was a brief bright moment, a mutual respite from the uncertainty
of impending adulthood. But alone on the roof, looking northwest
to Tallahassee, across the miles of Florida, he forgave and he loved
and he thought of old Julianna, he thought of old Julianna.

FROM THE MYRRH HOUSE ANSWERING MACHINE

Looking south out to the ocean, Sally-Anne Altamont watches the
blue-gray waves roll in and debates whether or not to call her son,
once again, and leave an answering machine message, once again.

It has been two and a half weeks since they've talked, and even then he sounded distracted, depressed, short in responses, annoyed with the most basic questions of conversation. Answers almost grunted. Like the teenager he no longer was.

Speed dial. Three and a half rings. And there it is again, ten seconds of the intro to "Eighteen." The worst thing about this is that she can't even hear his voice, even speaking something as simple and generic as a "We can't come to the phone right now, please leave a message."

BEEEEEP.

Sigh.

"Ronnie. Call us please. This is the third message we've left with you. And do you think anyone will want to hire you with that Alice Cooper song on your answering machine? Yes, your mom knows who Alice Cooper is. Call us. We're getting worried."

Push the off button. Sigh. With no job, what could he possibly be doing?

It's too cold to swim—in the pool, in the ocean. Charley is at the driving range. Too early in the day for a drink. Maybe she should buy him a plane ticket for Thanksgiving. Get him out of there. Maybe let him stay here until he's back on his feet. Maybe. Maybe? Maybe.

It's a lot to consider. The ocean is God. The ocean is the Buddha. Ronnie is in the wilderness, and he must make his own mistakes, and learn from them, and Sally Anne, she stares at the waves rolling, listens to the surf, stares out to the horizon line and the gray-blue sky and the gray-blue waves and none of the world's insights trump how much, on a pure emotional level, she misses her son, her son of today, and the son she used to have.

THE WHITE ROACH

The roach is cradling a crease in the white painter's tarp spread across the living room carpet in the room Andy—no longer Professor Andy—has just finished. It is impossible to miss. Brown with black wings, concave, antennae pulsing in sick throbs. Andy was moving his equipment—paint cans, brushes, rollers, trays, ladder, and, finally, the tarp—into the master bedroom, when he spotted it there.

Andy approaches it, towers over it, shrieks like a little girl in a dodge ball game after he taps the nasty thing with the edge of his boot, and its wings sputter towards him in an ominous droning buzz.

The roach jumps two feet backwards, lands on a different bump in the tarp. Its body expands and retracts like it has giant lungs under its shell. Andy shrieks again, runs into the master bedroom, slams the door.

Andy waits for his pulse to return to normal. If he can find a can of roach spray, there's a slight chance the thing will die. The property managers have their offices at the entrance to the apartment complex, in that trailer where all the red white and blue "WELCOME" flags wave around at the top of poles stuck in the dirt-grass every five feet. But he would prefer not dealing with them if he can avoid it. They are in late middle-age. Husband and wife. Overweight. Andy suspects they are swingers. Unattractive swingers. There's nothing overt about their behavior when Andy interacts with them, and he knows he's being a shallow and judgmental bastard when he's forced to consider them, but it's like they're the kinds of people you'd expect to go off and meet similar-bodied enthusiasts in some exurbian hotel located next to a business/industrial park near the airport. The kinds of people you don't want to see but are inevitably the only ones frolicking at the nude beach.

It is there, in the creepy emptiness of the vacated apartment building's master bedroom, when Andy sees the tray covered in hardening white paint with the brush dipped inside, he hatches a plan so completely idiotic, it just might work.

(But first, a brief, vaguely Melvillian discussion about the Floridian cockroach.

The Floridian cockroaches are nothing like those tiny German cockroaches you see on the walls of large northern city kitchens in the summertime. Floridian cockroaches are FUCKING MONSTERS! They are as large as a toddler's shoe. Larger. Fucking Gregor-Samsa sized. Stomp on them. They live! What is crushed of them gets on your shoes, or, worse, in the case of Andy, the roach guts stain the off-white carpeting of the apartment that needs to be completely finished before the end of the work day so the property managers can show the place to prospective renters tomorrow morning. This is why Andy does not and cannot simply squash the roach with his painter workboots and get on with his day.

They've even been known to fly, and when they do fly, they fly straight for your face.

The Floridian cockroaches are one of many ungentle reminders of the jungle lurking beyond the civilizing effects of air conditioning. Developer's delusions to the contrary, it is the Floridian cockroach who rules Florida. It was here before people moved in, and it will remain when we are gone.)

Andy scrapes the Wite-Out-consistency paint with the brush

off the tray, holds the brush in his upraised right arm like an Olympic torch. In the living room, the roach has not moved from the tarp. If he picks up the tarp and shakes it, maybe the roach will leave, but it is just as likely to fly towards him and attack. Floridian cockroaches know no fear. They don't scurry when the lights are turned on. They don't run when they hear footsteps. They possess Viet Cong patience.

Andy stands over the vile bug, nausea typhooning his chest when his eyes meet the thing. It twitches. Andy steps backwards, flings the paint on the brush at the roach, white blobs landing on it with papery thuds. Another paint fling. Another. Five, ten seconds. The thing's still breathing. It is now a white roach. It still breathes. It flaps its horrific wings, tries to fly, but can't, weighed down by the gloopy paint.

"Oh God oh God oh God!" Andy says, stepping backwards. The white roach crawls two inches forward, deeper into a fold in the tarp, then stops. It inhales and exhales, antennae swaying to and fro.

"They're swingers, but they must have roach spray," Andy says aloud. Out of the living room window, the unused swimming pool, walls covered in paintings of upright alligators in orange and blue helmets encircled by a happily cursive "GO GATORS!" Through open windows, that carsick feeling of stuffy heat. These roaches. Academia. Painting. Life. Life in Gainesville. Andy wants five o'clock, home, the desk, the writing. The writing trumps all of this. All of this.

•

These days are rooms and rooms, walls and walls. Each workaday, Andy tapes off the trim, throws tarp over the greasy white carpeting, rolls white paint over stained, chipped, and tack-holed apartment walls. Fresh coats, for fresh faces. These days are the wet gloopy sounds of the rollers, the chemical pungence of the paint, the classic rock from the kitchen counter—fuzztoned guitar riffs from an old gray boombox covered in splotchy white blobs like a seagull-turded pier—existing in purgatorial fifteen song rotations that have sucked away whatever grandeur these songs once possessed, Aerosmith banished to hell and forced to sing "Sweeeeeeeeeeeeeeeeeeeeeeeeeeeet Emowwwwwwwwwwww-shuuuuuuuun" for all eternity.

Most days, Andy actually loves the work—perhaps more than he should—pleased with the undeniable evidence that something—no matter how minor—has been achieved each and every working day. Left alone to do a job. To paint, to simply work and look forward to what he has to work on when he gets back home.

An old friend who runs a successful house and apartment painting business gave him the job the summer before last, while Andy was deep in the dire poverty all adjuncts go through between semesters. Everyone else, out painting interiors and exteriors, are college kids. The potential indignity of being, by far, the oldest man on the job, was offset by the pleasant solitude.

So far, this life outside of academia has proven to be the change Andy so desperately needs. There are no shortages of houses and apartments that need repainting. The summer is always the busiest—everyone moving out at the end of May and moving back in in August, but the work never stops. Kids flunk out, screw up, get evicted. Gainesville is not a rich town, and it is transient. It is always hot, always sweaty in these empty apartments, but Andy does not mind. With teaching you are never fully off the clock, but with housepainting, going home for the day means leaving work at work, where it belongs.

•

In the property manager's office, the woman sits her fat ass at a desk, punching buttons on a calculator with fat fingers, excessive purple eye shadow sweating in the humidity. Her husband is plopped on one of the two folding chairs in front of the desk, gray-black armpit hair bushy out of a lumpy purple tank top, gray Michael McDonald hair and beard, flipping through a magazine. Was he reading something like *Southeastern Swingers Quarterly*? Probably.

"Roach spray? We just sent in the exterminators!" the man drawls, standing up, tossing the magazine on the desk. Andy sees that the magazine is actually called *Modern Property Manager*. But that doesn't mean they're not swingers, doesn't mean they're not going to ask Andy to join them in some sick shit. Andy's 37 after all, not much younger than they. It's not that they're swingers. It's a free country, etcetera. But the way the woman always looks at him, giving him something like what the English call "the come-hither look," as in, "Andy, come-hither! Me and my husband want you to join us in the heart-shaped bed!"

"Let me get you some spray," the man says. He steps into the storage closet. Andy avoids the woman's gaze the way he tried to avoid looking at that goddamn roach.

"How's the painting coming along?" the woman asks. She peeks up from the calculator through perm-curly gray hair.

"Fine," Andy says, eyes cast downward as if he's studying the fascinating patterns from the off-white paint splotched on his workboots.

"Do you need anything?" She leans backwards in the office chair, chubby hands folded behind her fat head.

"Need?" (Need?) "No, I'm fine. Thanks."

"You sure? It must get hot up there. You by yourself today?" That come-hither look.

"I'm fine," Andy says, looking to the storage closet.

She swivels to Andy, exposing curdish white cellulitic thighs. "Guess you can't escape the bugs down here, hmmmm?"

"Guess not," Andy says.

"Happy hunting." The man reemerges, tosses Andy the giant cylindrical roach spray can.

Andy nods, leaves immediately.

•

The roach has not moved from its spot on the tarp—still inhaling and exhaling, antennae quivering, alert. Andy shakes the full can of roach spray. "Kills Bugs Dead" is what the can promises. Andy has little faith in the can's self-assurance. This is a Floridian cockroach, after all.

Andy pops the top of the can, stands above the roach, extends his right arm, aims the nozzle, sprays with a right index finger. A chemical mist envelops the white roach. It starts twitching. Five seconds of spray. Andy stops. The white roach curls, flips on its back, legs twitching in every direction, antennae in forward lunges like swimmer's arms. Andy waits another fifteen seconds. He is fascinated by the white roach's struggles, its ceaseless movement. The white roach has not died yet. Andy sprays again, for ten seconds. Steps back. Observes. Fewer legs twitch, the antennae hang limp. But the legs keep moving. The hiss of the can, hollowed as the spray empties. Andy shakes the can. It won't die. He sprays for ten more seconds, soaking the spray up and down what passes for its face, this row of legs, that row of legs.

Andy stands over the roach between his workboots, pleads, "Why won't you die?"

It is down to one leg moving in a slow counterclockwise motion. This goes on for five minutes. Ten minutes. The antennae hang limp; the other legs do not move. That one leg, refusing to drop.

Andy is fascinated with the roach, how it finds this roach life so much more preferable to the unknown, even painted white, with a nervous system choked with pesticide. If I was covered in white paint and paralyzing poison, I would offer no struggle. I would surrender. Die quickly. But the white roach, it wants to live. What do I care if it's in here? I don't live here. It wasn't bothering me until I panicked.

Maybe I could save it. Give it some kind of hospice comfort before he passes on. Andy's mind searches for symbolism, for the metaphor of the great white roach, forgetting how much he hates symbolism for the jive speculation of halfwit high school English teachers that it is. He could unroll what remains of the toilet paper in the bathroom, gently pick it up, take it outside, leave it in the shade of a bush.

The white roach's last twitching leg drops. With the toilet paper, Andy picks it up, flushes the white roach down the toilet, watches it circle and circle, bobbing defiantly from the hole before it's swept away.

From the kitchen, the 7/8 shuffle of Pink Floyd's "Money" plays for the sixth time that day. The master bedroom needs a fresh coat of paint. And I've wasted too much time. I need to leave.

Andy stands there thinking about what he has and has not done so far. When the anxiety subsides, he opens another gallon of paint and pours it into the tray.

•

"Damn, son," says the Michael McDonald property manager/ swinger when Andy tosses him the can. "Musta put a hurtin' on that thing!"

"It wouldn't die," Andy says.

"Don't gotta tell us," the woman says, still tapping buttons on the calculator, scribbling numbers in a ledger sheet.

It's nearly five when Andy finishes painting the apartment. He returns the ladder, leans it against an open wall in the office. "Alright, well, see you tomorrow. I'll start on the next building then."

"Wait a minute," the woman says, punching a final sequence of buttons on the calculator. She looks up at Andy. Smiles. "Any plans tonight?"

"I have plans!" Andy blurts out, stammers. "Big plans. Tonight."

"Oh, well, that's too bad. We wanted to invite you somewhere."

"Can't!" Andy blurts out again. He wants to vomit.

"On Wednesday nights," the woman says, that come-hither look in full effect, "we have our weekly prayer meeting, at our house."

"Bible study," Michael McDonald adds.

"Yeah. Busy," Andy says, smiling, almost laughing that this is all they want from him.

"Hand him them little books we got," the woman says. Michael McDonald opens the file cabinet, sticks a hand inside. He walks up to Ronnie, hands him six of those Chick Tracts, insanely Christian comics that equate everything on God's green earth with Satanism—rock and roll, homosexuality, Jews, Islam, Catholicism, consumerism, Marxism, mainstream Protestantism, etc, etc.

"Oh, so you're . . . " and Andy really wants to say "not swingers after all, but run-of-the-mill Florida religious nuts?! Whew! What a relief!"

"That's right," Michael McDonald says. "We're evangelicals. Pardon us, but we thought it seemed like maybe you need some spiritual guidance, the way all of us do."

"You're so quiet!" the woman says. "We thought this would help you in your times of trouble. Have you been saved?"

"Oh. No thanks," Ronnie says.

"Well, when you change your mind, when you're ready to let the Lord into your heart, we're just a phone call away," McDonald says.

Andy nods. "Yup."

"Go forth in the Lord and Savior Jesus Christ, and stay blessed, Andy!" she says as Andy leaves.

·

A glass of red wine—Malbec—the bottle within arm's reach. John Coltrane's *Impressions* on the box. A typewriter in front of him, the page left off at that point he couldn't wait to return to all day, as he painted and killed the white roach and brooded on life, death, and whatever spiritual guidance meant and how it applied to him, exactly.

Andy raises the glass. "To the white roach," he says. He sips the wine, the sleepiness, the annoyances of work disappearing. He sets the glass down, leans into the typewriter, fingers on the home row, thumbs on the space bar, dives in. He's going to leave town. Soon. He needs to save money, needs to write and have some stories to show for all the wasted years, all the time and energy dissipated and squandered when he should have been here, doing what he's doing now.

GATORRONI'S IN SOHO

Once the six-week whirlwind with Julianna has ended, Ronnie wakes up one warm mid-November weekmorning alone, emotionally drained, and as financially wiped out as he has ever been in this past lost year.

Ronnie could almost believe she never happened. He spends two days and two nights in his room, drinking cheap wine with scrounged change she'd left behind, laying on his back, staring at the ceiling. Shortly after the sunset of the second night, Mitch comes by with a twelve-pack.

"I heard what happened," he says. "Put some music on and we'll go up on the roof."

Ronnie shrugs.

Before climbing the tree up to the roof, Ronnie turns on and turns up the stereo, throws on *Destiny Street* by Richard Hell and the Voidoids. On the roof, they split the twelve-pack.

"So. Gone like that, huh?" Mitch works up the courage to finally ask, around beer three.

"Yeah," Ronnie chugs a deep guzzle, tries formulating what he wants to say, but the words leave his mouth before he can check himself. "That was real, right? I mean, I have no proof, except a memory constantly assaulted by this stuff," he says, pointing to the beer can in his hand. Julianna's friends who used to come around are gone. Neither of them took any pictures of their travels; they didn't take any pictures at all.

"Yeah, Rahhhn. What the hell happened to you?"

"Don't know," Ronnie says. He stands, and for two seconds—one, two—he considers jumping off the roof. Or, better yet, rolling off and seeing what happens. But it isn't high enough. He wouldn't die. He'd only get hurt. And he has no health insurance. It would only make everything worse. He drains the can of Old Hamtramck, steadies himself, rolls it down the roof in the exaggerated manner of a professional bowler, burps.

"I gotta get some sleep," Ronnie says to Mitch. "You can stay up here if you want."

"Cool," Mitch says. He watches Ronnie edge downward on the roof to the edge, step across to the tree, climb down. "Jesus," he mutters, then repeats, "What the hell happened to you?" Ronnie. Mitch is nineteen, Ronnie is 24, and anymore, Ronnie is becoming everything Mitch doesn't want to be, with living, with women, with working . . . shit, with everything. Actually, everyone around him is everything Mitch doesn't want to be. The students. The co-workers at the restaurant where he busses tables. The customers. His friends. It's like nobody knows what the hell they're doing. No mentors. No paths to follow. He finishes his beer, tosses it over his head, listens to it roll down the roof's opposite slope. This could be him in five years, and the very thought of it sends him clattering down off of the Myrrh House roof and straight home.

•

Late morning, Ronnie wakes up. As the coffee brews, he stands in the living room, noodling around the fretboard of his guitar in Black Flag-style solos. Thinking.

Rent. Bills. In the middle of this binge, Ronnie Altamont had managed to find the time to apply to every restaurant, retail store, and bar he could find. Eviction looms, as usual. He wouldn't put it past Roger to pile up his belongings on the curb on December 1st. Maybe it's all over here. Leave a goodbye note and flee like you did from Chris Embowelment back in Orlando.

Why not? There are no jobs here. The music scene isn't what it was, and is transitioning into something he isn't interested in. He isn't writing. The reasons he moved here don't exist anymore. So leave then. Go back to Orlando and follow Kelly's advice from way back at the beginning of this futile endeavor: Save money. Move to Chicago already. Why the hell not? After eight months of under-, un-, and temporary employment, survival here ain't in the cards.

One Greg Ginn style chromatic solo later, Ronnie unplugs the guitar, turns off the amp. The coffee is ready, and as the pop and hiss fades from his amplifier, he hears the voice of rescue on the answering machine, ". . . from Gatorroni's in SoHo. You turned in an application to us earlier in the month, and we were wondering . . . "

"Hello?"

Early morning prep cook. 20-30 hours per week, depending on the season and upcoming reservations. Starts at 7:00 a.m. Sharp. You want it?

All plans to leave, poof, like that, gone. What is this, his eighth job in as many months? Who's keeping score?

•

For what little it was worth, this would be the best job Ronnie would work in Gainesville.

Gatorroni's in SoHo is not in the art district of Manhattan. It's on University Avenue, in a small shopping center by the railroad tracks, between a sporting goods store and a shop with the unusual name of "Stoney O'Bongwater's: Purveyors of the Wackiest of Tobaccos."

Ronnie has to admit: It feels pretty good to be a productive member of humanity again, to wake up at 6:30 in the morning and have someplace to be. From his house, it is a fifteen minute walk to the restaurant, past dew-drenched windows in the pale early morning sunrise. (Ronnie cannot recall the last time he had seen a sunrise and wasn't too blind drunk to appreciate it.) The smells of food prep fill the air: Zesty Glaze Donuts, Viva Taco, Sesame Happiness Chinese, Szechwan Gator, Party Burgerz, This Can't Be Hummus. The lingering tinge of the recently ended late night—stale beer and garbage. Nobody else on the street but construction workers and bums. The no-season Florida mornings are perfect, especially in Gainesville, the precious daylight hour before most people are out of bed.

His co-workers—among them, "Sweet" Billy DuPree, former late-night DJ for 1970s FM classic rock station BJ 103 "The Tongue," and current disc jockey for "Rock and Bowl" nights at Gainesville Lanes—are perpetually stoned. Before work, break time, before clocking out, they pass around an endless supply of joints, sneaking off into the dining room in a quiet corner booth while Ronnie follows the caffeine rush and keeps working. Ronnie cannot partake. His boss—Jack, Jack the Fencer, a former world champion fencer for UF before faulty protective gear let through an unfortunate thrust to his right shoulder, robbing him permanently of the speed and accuracy he needed—always asks Ronnie if he wants to get high with him. He never comes right out and says, "Hey, wanna get high?" but couches it in the most ridiculous of insinuations:

"Hey Ronnie, we're about to, uh . . . hop on the Mary Jane Train to Green Town, you in?"

or

"Hey Ronnie—we're fixin' to, uh . . . blaze a nature trail straight into the rec room of our minds. What do you say?"

or

"Hey Ron. We're gonna take a little break so we can, uh, remove the dandruff from our psychic shoulders and face the stresses of the day with a clean scalp. Wanna join us?"

. . . To which Ronnie naturally replies, to any and all of these questions:

"What do you mean?"

At which point Jack the Fencer would lean in and whisper, "We're going to smoke some marijuana. Would you like to join us?"

"I can't, man," Ronnie always says. "I can't function stoned."

Here Jack the Fencer would always chuckle, like he was privy to some top-secret information, then repeat the word "Function . . . "

While his co-workers get high, Ronnie drinks cup after cup of coffee, often exhausted from the previous night's fun—wired enough to fill buckets with marinara sauce, plastic bins with white bean salad, tubs of white rice (eating bowls of it on breaks with co-workers, drenching the rice in spicy Sriracha sauce). It feels good to be locked into the ethic he was learning while removing asbestos from schools in the Crescent City heat. His co-workers are two-to-twenty years past college age, and for that, Ronnie is grateful. They are interested in DJing or fencing, in fishing or bondage, in biking or boating—their only goals in life being comfort and the flexibility to devote time to what they love. The job is a laid-back trap, deep in the heart of the laid-back trap that is Gainesville.

But it is quiet, steady work, thankfully lacking the unpredictable annoyances of customers. It is enough to keep Ronnie busy, to forget Julianna, Portland Patty, and Maux, to try and move on with life, to pull out of the depression, to pay Ronnie enough money each week to keep him living in the Myrrh House, to keep him living in Gainesville.

THE LIGHT IN THE DORM ROOM

It's one of those days at the record store when you're reminded of that line from Monty Python's *Flying Circus*: "Never kill a customer."

Who are these people who walk through our door on Sundays? What planet are they from? Why don't they bathe on that planet? Why do they have such shitty taste in music on that planet? You would think the customers at a record store would be cool, you know, rock and roll? Not here man, and not on Sundays. *On the Corner* by Miles Davis gets me through the tedium, the mindlessness, the assholes and jerkoffs and douchebags who come in here and stink up the place and don't buy anything.

"Sounds like pimp music," some teenager in all black looking up to my perch behind the counter says, and it's all I can do to not hit him on his zitty head with a hammer until his cretin brain squishes all over the grimy floor. Instead, I glare. "Never kill a customer," the

Pythons warn, and they're right. Just sit here and lock into these fantastic beats. Tune out everything else unless these jerks actually need to ring up something they're actually going to buy (on Sundays, it's always something cheap . . . a two dollar used VHS tape, a one dollar punk rock button, a one dollar alternative rock patch to sew on their bookbag), and look forward to the evening.

"Ya wanna beah?" Boston Mike asks, the wet six-pack of Old Ham-Towns soaking through the brown paper bag.

"Y'know . . . I shouldn't," I say. I'm really trying to cut back. Yeah, ok, it's about the girl. I don't wanna be "Drunk John" anymore. I've been good. Better. No, really: I've been good! But this day man, these fucking . . . fuck it. "But perhaps maybe I should," I say, reaching into the wet bag and pulling out a can. Boston Mike laughs as I pour it into my usual black mug used more for these beers than for coffee.

Two hours left before closing. I will drink two beers, be sober by the time we clockout. Until then, I'm going to pray for minor time travel. To be locking up the front doors, saying "Later" to Boston Mike, and walking out of this plaza, crossing the street, stepping onto campus as the sun sets behind the football stadium and those brick buildings housing all those academic departments. In twilight, past dutiful students marching to the library, past groups of students talking of their usual big-deal collegiate concerns.

I'll round a corner and see her dorm building. It's getting dark now; the streetlights are turning on. Second light from the right. Third floor. I'll be up there very soon. Her dorm room, where she has spent the day studying, and (I hope) waiting for me. Up the stairs, past barefoot students lugging laundry. Down the third floor hallway. Knock on her door. I'll hear her footsteps, running. Locks unlock. The door opens. She will hug me. She will look tired and I will look tired, but it'll be alright. All the irritations will fade away. We'll order pizza, play a boardgame, watch movies. The beer stores and bars and even Boston Mike will have to get by without me. I'm sure they will.

The nursed beers help the time pass as fewer and fewer jerks come in to bother me. All I really see is that dorm room, her dorm room. That light. These aren't the things I'd like to talk about with Boston Mike, or the jokers over at Gatorroni's by the Slice, but I don't have to. For the first time in a long time, something good has happened, and we've only been together for three months, so I don't wanna put too much into it, but I can't help thinking this is the beginning of something better. Finally.

DEEP INTO THE WHAT-NOW

"Yeah." Sigh. "I don't think I can see you anymore," your latest girlfriend tells you, over Sunday brunch at Gatorroni's in SoHo, seated at a table plopped at the edge of the curb and the parking lot of what they call the front patio on an otherwise perfect late November afternoon. You're on your second bloody mary, third cup of coffee, second carafe of water, and the tiniest of scrambled eggs and toast from the buffet—all of it free of charge, a fringe benefit from working at the other Gatorroni's. Your friends serve all of this on this fine, fine day.

"Ok," you say, somehow expecting it, not asking "why," because you have a feeling you know why.

"It's like, you haven't been sober since before Halloween. Now it's almost Thanksgiving." She leans in, speaks in a near-whisper. "I wanted to take you home to meet my parents." She scoffs. Leans back. "That's not going to happen. I can't even imagine it."

"Ok," you repeat, staring at the glasses and liquids that are supposed to get you back to functioning like a productive member of the human race. You're scheduled to work tonight. You'll probably phone it in. No, you will phone it in. Sundays are dead anyway at Gatorroni's by the Slice.

This brunch isn't agreeing with you, or, more to the point, it isn't agreeing with the beer, the whiskey, the wine, and the vodka you guzzled last night over six nonstop hours.

"Wait," you say, leaping from the chair and rushing to the men's room.

When you're done, your insides are a dizzy dry delirium. Now, this is the part where you're supposed to leave the stall, wash your face and hands in the mirror, wipe the puke off your chin and your shirt, stare at your proverbial bloodshot eyes and five o'clock shadow, the greasy hair, the dirty clothes, and whimper, "What am I doing? What am I doing with my life? I need help!" With the notable exception of wiping the puke off your chin and shirt, you do none of these things. You shrug, you laugh a desperate "Hee hee hee" about the way it's going, and think about that Bloody Mary on the table.

No, it's no surprise that she's gone when you return. You can't blame her, can't explain what's been going on in your mind. As a boy, going with your father on weekends to the bar, drinking Coke after Coke after Coke while Dad talked to the bartender, surrounded by all those other old guys at the bar who kept yellowed newspaper clippings in their wallets of this play or that play they made in some high school game from their high school years so long ago. Telling their varsity stories. And when they'd start to get really drunk, they'd remember a few years beyond high school—what happened with girls at college or what happened in the service fighting wherever whichever president saw fit to send them. This tacit, unspoken agreement between all of them that the best years in life were over, and it was enough to sit here and make the best of it beneath the ESPN's 1 through 4 broadcasting the eternal strivings of Youth on the bar televisions. Make the best of it, and wait to die. Over the years, as your dad got drunker, and the men got older, and you grew up so slow, too slow, always that silent envy of the old men, who always referred to you in third person, "How old's Will getting to be now, Tom?" "Pretty soon, Will's gonna be chasin' girls, eh Tom?" Their lives were over, aside from these vicarious twinges from the next generation, and that bar was a pleasant-enough waiting room before death. You saw this, weekend after weekend, until you were old enough to have the option of saying no, you're gonna go skate, and by that point, your Youth had a caustic air of insolent truth that no one in the old man bars wanted to face or confront. You vowed never to be like that, to think like them. It sounds so corny now, but when you wrote those three Xs on your hand with the black marker, it was your line in the sand, that you would always be young, no matter what, Straight Edge for Life, and time as portrayed by society with its Hallmark-greeting card parameters of "old" and "young," was meaningless. Even after giving up on being straight edge around the time you realized the beer made it much easier to talk to girls, you always kept that belief that NOW was the best, and to look back was death.

Lately, since returning from the tour, you think you understand those old guys your dad drank with every non-working/sleeping hour. You see nothing—absolutely nothing—to look forward to. These hours are empty, directionless. Those guys delayed it by having children. You don't want children. So what now? You drink your bloody mary, drink her bloody mary, stare at the remnants of a post-breakup Sunday brunch, all you want—all you really want—is what you had on Halloween.

You were dressed as that stand-up comedian from the 1980s whose shtick was to smash fruits and vegetables with a comically large mallet. Vodka drunk and dressed in black beret, black mustache, black curly-haired wig glued to the beret, black and white striped shirt, black pants, black shoes, and a garbage bag filled with produce, in the front yard of the Righteous Freedom House, you smash tomatoes, grapefruit, cantaloupe, watermelons, and the unveiling of each new piece of produce brings louder applause and laughter to everyone circled around you. With vodka, the body is light—indestructible—and it is nothing to swing the mallet as the rinds and pulp and juice spray all over the front yard, and it's fun slipping in the mess. Inevitably, the front yard becomes a massive food fight, with produce remnants hurled into anyone who dares get involved, until the produce is too pulpy, too disintegrated, to pick up. Fun. Laughter. In the immortal words of Mick Shrimpton: "Have a good time, all the time."

There isn't much that is more ridiculous than the walk of shame on the morning after Halloween. Walking back to your house—dizzy and nauseous, heavy and destructible—you keep all of your costume on, the clothing stained, the mallet broken. On the couch, back at the party, some girl dressed like a Plus-

Sized Wonder Woman, not your girlfriend, laying on top of you. Walking past Gatorroni's, friends wave pitchers of beer to you. Of course you take it. You're tired and you're shaking and your body wants more, more, more. Kill the night. What else is there? The band is finished. Just this job in this kitchen . . . water bottles filled with vodka. What do you want? What do you need? What's missing here? Nothing's missing! Everything's alright! It's there, and I will drink it. To drink like this always leaves the element of surprise, the possibility that life will be less boring. Maybe those old guys remembered the time a beautiful woman once set foot in that bar—years ago—and hoped that such a momentous occasion would happen again, or perhaps they wanted to hear a new joke, a new twist on the sports on TV, something spontaneous, anything but the routine of responsibility. Yes, you understand. You never know how it will turn out when you drink. What impulses you will act upon, for good or ill. Too old to sing in bands anymore, like those guys are too old to play varsity football.

You feel that brainrush of the booze coming on once again, here at the brunch table on this otherwise perfectly warm late November afternoon, you're reminded of that song you heard in a movie somewhere, that 1920s song where the characters happily drone *What's the use of gettin' sober / if you're only gonna get drunk again?* You belch. Ha. Ha. Harrrrrrrr.

The server, whatshername, in the fancy white shirt and black tie and black apron, that reddish brown hair long, curled, ponytailed. Nnnnnnugget! She fills your pint glass with the bloody mary mix she carries in a pitcher.

"You're the best," you say, smiling your smile. She will do. Yes, she will do.

"Rough night last night?" she asks. You know what you smell like, what you look like right about now.

"Well, you know, ha ha, you weren't there, so yeah, it was rough, you know." You almost visibly cringe at this corny dumb line, but you're charming—you still have your charm—and you can make this work.

"Ha," she says, an emotionless laugh. "I can't go out, then work here the next morning. I stayed in and watched movies."

"Sounds like you need a rough night then. When are you done?"

"A couple hours," she says. She gets more and more beautiful, with each sip of the bloody.

"Meet me at Gatorroni's later," you say, still smiling that smile. "I'm working tonight. I'll hook you up. Pizza. Drinks. Whatever. It'll be nice to talk."

"What about . . . ?" she says, pointing at the empty chair across from you.

"Her?" Scoff. Pshaw, pshaw! "Just a friend. Seriously though, meet me after work."

"Ok definitely," she says, and you know that's Gainesvillese for "I'm probably going to flake out on you."

You laugh. "See you then."

She leaves you to your hangover cures and your thoughts. The future. It'll be like this, only it will get worse, until you become what you always hated. You may as well embrace it. It is, after all, your birthright.

INCREDIBLE MARINARA, AND WHY
"SWEET" BILLY DUPREE LEFT RADIO

"Ladies and gentlemen, may I have your attention please," Jack the Fencer announces, right hand on Ronnie's shoulder, tongs in left hand upheld like an Olympic torch.

The morning crew gathers around Ronnie's section of the kitchen, between the cooktops with bubbling pots and the cutting boards lined in front of industrial-sized containers of herbs and spices.

"I beseech each and every one of you to feast, first, your eyes, and second, your palette, on this incredible marinara sauce contained inside this rather ordinary looking clear plastic bucket," Jack the Fencer announces, with a little too much Shakespearean flourish for 7:30 in the morning, heightened by the fencing stabs he applies with the tongs.

Everyone in the kitchen gawks, Ronnie standing to the right of Jack the Fencer, waiting for the other shoe to drop, wondering if it already has.

"Note the bold red, contrasted with the perfect arrangements of whites and yellows from the onions and garlic. The interplay between the smooth and rough between the sauces, juices, and the chunks of diced tomato. A hint, a tantalizing tease, if you will, of the green flakes of herb sprinkled delicately, sublimely, across the top."

"That's great, Jack," the dominatrix of the crew said, a towering Scandinavian beast of a woman covered in tattoos.

"Hold on, hold on, my alpha female mistress of the dark," Jack continues, still swinging the tongs in his hands, like he was in the UF gymnasium and these were the Southeastern Conference Fencing Championships, and not an ordinary Tuesday at Gatorroni's in

SoHo. "Note the confident swirls of the sauce, the inevitable intangible results of assertive stirring and accurate measurement.

"This bucket of marinara sauce, my friends and colleagues in the culinary arts, is the desperate, hard-earned expression of an artist at the peak of his powers. But let us sample and confirm with our mouths what our eyes have already told us." The crew grabs spoons, scoop samples, tastes.

"Please," Jack announces. "One spoonful and one spoonful only. This must be shared with our patrons, who probably don't deserve and will most certainly not appreciate the glory, the enchanting wonder that is this marinara sauce."

Ronnie watches as the rest of the kitchen crew sample the sauce, each silently nodding in agreement with Jack's eloquent, bombastic words as they let the sauce cover their eager taste buds.

"It's really good, Jack. You're right," the dominatrix says. "Nice work, Ronnie. Now can we go get high?"

"Yes, we can go get high now. Ronnie: Well done," Jack adds, one last pat on the back before everyone leaves him in the kitchen to continue tending to the rice, the sauce, cutting the artichokes, the tomatoes, the cherry tomatoes, and so on.

Only "Sweet" Billy DuPree remains, chopping parsley in the next station over.

"That sauce rocked," DuPree says, in the low, gravelly, grave yet celebratory voice innate to all classic rock DJ's, especially those who work for the more serious "rock is art" stations. "It was delicate yet dangerous, like David Gilmour's guitar work." DuPree looks up from his stack of half-cut parsley. "You like Floyd, right?" DuPree looks away, coughs out a laugh. "Shit, what am I talking about, you probably haven't even heard Pink Floyd."

"I like some of it," Ronnie says. "The Syd Barrett stuff, mainly. I like *Meddle* and *Soundtrack from the Film More.*"

"*Meddle*?" DuPree laughs, wheezes, laughs, coughs. "Wow man, haven't even heard that since they first did *Meddle*." DuPree laughs again. "I almost can't remember, man. Know what I mean?"

Ronnie had no idea, but ventures a guess. "You mean, it came out so long ago, you don't remember it that well, and besides, you were high on drugs at the time?"

"Right," DuPree says. Ronnie is fascinated by DuPree's classic rock radio timbre—that voice you never hear or see, in the flesh. "Still man, if I had a dollar for every time we played 'More Than a Feeling' when they still had BJ 103: The Tongue here, I wouldn't be cutting parsley right now, that's for damn sure, brother."

"I always wondered that," Ronnie said. "Like, do classic rock DJs ever get sick of playing the same old songs, over and over again? I mean, I went through a Zeppelin phase, and a Pink Floyd phase, but I could easily go the rest of my life without ever having to hear 'Black Dog' or 'Time' ever again."

"Sweet" Billy DuPree stopped everything he was doing to stare at Ronnie. For a moment, Ronnie thinks DuPree is going to fling his knife at Ronnie's forehead for such blasphemy, but instead, DuPree coughs out a laugh and says, "That's why I left, man. I mean, the station was going under anyway, but the DJs had less and less power every time somebody new took over the station.

"After a while, I had the feeling all they wanted me to play was Pink Floyd and Led Zeppelin, with a bit of Skynyrd thrown in here and there, over and over again. Like a whole generation that prided itself on having an open mind and an embracing spirit decided they'd had enough change. Not that anybody wanted to hear that DEVO crap . . . "

(And here, Ronnie wants to laugh, because he loves DEVO.)

". . . But still, there were plenty of new bands out there worth playing, but management, and even listeners, didn't want to know. I mean, radio gave the world 'Surfin' Bird' and 'Louie Louie!' Do you think something like that could happen today? Hell no!

"And it's not because the '60s were so much better than today. They weren't. Maybe even worse in a lot of ways. It's because accountants, instead of DJs like me, run the show now.

"So fuck 'em," DuPree says, returning to the parsley chopping with a couple crunchy thwacks with his knife. "I'd rather work here, pick up money on the side at the bowling alley for anybody who remembers me, instead of all that FM jive."

Throughout DuPree's spiel, Ronnie tosses in words like "Right" and "Right on" and "Yeah" and "Totally" and "Uh-huh" and "Oh for sure" and "Yeah man." The rest of the crew returns to their stations, as high as they were before. There is so much more Ronnie wants to say to "Sweet" Billy DuPree, but he doesn't know where to begin, and besides, there are white bean salads to make.

Rock and roll. If it doesn't kill you, it tosses you out of the tour bus at top speed and leaves you on the side of a desolate Death Valley highway to rot. Or, to spend your late middle-age years chopping parsley at sunrise.

Same diff.

HOW NOT TO ACE THE GRE'S

First, don't prepare. In bookstores, you've probably seen those Vollman-sized test prep books filled with practice questions. Don't buy them. Don't even look at them. They will only help you succeed. Same with tutors, computer programs, CD-Roms, and DVDs.

Now to the night before. You haven't been prepping up to this point, and there's no reason to start now. In fact, why not throw a huge party? Ask one of your friends' bands to play, the friend who recently quit being straight-edge, because you know he'll have enough beer and liquor to knock out 10,000 Marines (or Keith Richards). His band will stink—coming up from Orlando and all—but no matter. Drink what he offers you, and try not to laugh at the other band—vegan jokers from Pensacola some scenester woman in town asked you to help out, soy ham and soy egger happy hippy punks who used your kitchen before the party to make sauceless pasta then sat in your bedroom staring at your haiku wall covered in haiku about Boom Boom Washington and Bam Bam Bigelow and asked, "This is cool, but have you ever heard of Charles Bukowski?"

Continue drinking. You don't want to be alert and refreshed for the GRE, do you? If there are other drugs on hand, take those too, but nothing that requires serious time commitment. Showing up to take the GRE on, say, LSD, doesn't sound particularly pleasant. But, as they say, whatever Christmas-trees your Scantron is fine.

Watch the bands. One of them should be at least decent. It is your house, after all, and this is a Gainesville houseparty. Tell everyone how you're taking the GRE the next morning. Look how respectfully everyone looks at you. So punk! Way to go, Sheena!

Feel that beer, dulling your brain. No matter. It's important to have total and complete faith in your unshakable intelligence, the kind of brains that slept through high school and still made it into a Florida state university. Don't worry about it! You're gonna ace this thing!

Now is the time to use this looming standardized test to your advantage. Since it is a party—your party—there should be girls there. There's that girl you've had the hot-tot-tot-tots for a couple months now.

With the GRE, you have a readymade excuse to leave your party (but not too early—like 2:00 or 3:00, instead of 4:00 or 5:00). Ask that girl if you can stay with her tonight—you know, just so you can get a good night's sleep before this very-important-my-whole-life-hangs-in-the-balance examination. She'll naturally take pity and say yeah, and you know she has no couches in her house, only that magical miracle of a bed, and soon enough, you have to (awwww . . .) leave your own party to the care of your roommate, and walk to her place, using what remains of your brain on this fine fine early early morning not towards any final prep for this test, but for thinking of how you will get her out of that black miniskirt.

Don't sleep now. Whatever you do, don't sleep. Stay up all night and put the moves on the girl you like so damn much. Maybe you'll be luckier than Ronnie Altamont in this situation and not be with a girl coming out of a four year relationship and not ready for any kind of rebound sex just yet. No, not just yet, and not with you. But that's ok, because it's all in fun. Fun fun fun fun fun fun fun fun fun.

Now get up early and don't eat breakfast. Why start trying to do well on the GRE now? Don't bathe. Walk to the nearby campus and line-up for your seat. You won't be hungry. You'll be too tired, too hungover, for breakfast.

Only half-listen to the test proctor, who looks like a smarmy prick anyways with his clean clothes, combed hair, and glasses.

Now you have the GRE in front of you. Do your best, but by this point, your best couldn't get you through the arithmetic quiz Walmart lays on its job applicants, so, you know what? Hurry it along. It's multiple choice, and the odds of getting each question right aren't the worst. You have better odds guessing these questions correctly than you did hooking up with that Gainesville scene nymphette earlier this morning.

Your goal is to be the first one done. It makes those around you, those driven fools determined to live out their dreams of facing thesis committees of tenured assholes, quite uncomfortable.

Now you're finished and now you're free. Enjoy the rest of the day, and don't be surprised when, a few weeks later, you get your GRE test scores in the mail and you're in the bottom third of almost everything. Hey, at least you tried, right? No. No you didn't. But it's fine, because you didn't really want to stay in Gainesville, did you? And this stupid test, while lining the pockets of the college standardized test industry, failed, like school has always failed, to adequately assess your intelligence. On the other hand, it clearly showed your total inability to handle the demands of graduate school, then and there, a nonstudent in the student ghetto of Gainesville.

THANKSGIVING

At dusk, Ronnie walks around the Student Ghetto, thoroughly enjoying the desolation of cleared-out Gainesville on Thanksgiving. Ronnie turned down a flight to Hilton Head to stay with his parents because he is scheduled to work early Friday morning, but really, he turned it down for the same reason he turned down various invites to attend "orphan" Thanksgiving dinners—he would rather be alone.

Not since summer has he really felt that Gainesville was his. The stillness of the streets makes him smile. He passes Maux's hideous giant cinderblock of an apartment building, wonders how she's doing. This leads to thoughts of Julianna, Portland Patty, Maggie. There's no emotion guiding the thoughts, as he walks through the silence, the darkened little houses with the bombed-out dirt yards littered with lawn furniture, the chipped-paint porches, the tree-canopied strange streets he never bothers exploring. He hopes they're well, wherever they've gone.

At University and 13th, the streetlights are almost pointless. Ronnie jaywalks east across 13th, passes the gas station, Gatorroni's by the Slice. The bookstore. A different General Lee's Pizza place. What's Ronnie thankful for?

Of course, his mother asked him that when she called earlier. He couldn't say at the time, grunted an "I don't know. Nothing?" but then said he was thankful to have a job again, but it wasn't a definitive answer, and Ronnie, now, really wants to know.

He turns right where the Boca Raton Subs store is empty, dark, and closed. Back onto an empty residential street, he's thankful for all of this. For everything. For being alive. He's thankful for heartbreak and failure and for getting the chance to learn from them. He's thankful for getting the opportunity to teeter on the edge of bankruptcy. To teetering on the edge of sanity, sobriety, stability. For the adventure possible in each waking moment. If he could ever get things right again, he would be more appreciative, now that he's seen the opposite of success, wealth, long-term love. He would appreciate those who smiled, no matter how much they suffered from within and without. He would be a better person than that snarky prick who acted like he was some kind of hot shit on-campus genius big shot destined for great things.

These aren't the kinds of words Ronnie's parents—or anybody's parents—really want to hear on Thanksgiving. But Ronnie is thankful for all of these things, and thankful for everything Gainesville has shown him, and now that he has learned what he needed to learn here, Ronnie walks back to the Myrrh House, and begins to plot his escape from this life.

MAUX, ONCE MORE

"Where have you been, asshole?"

Good ol' Maux. Indigo hair. Indigo clothing. Swigging vodka. She follows Ronnie into the kitchen as he stands at Mitch's counter, pouring more nog—thick, off-white, boozy, and potent—from a clear green glass pitcher.

"Nice to see you too, Maux," Ronnie says. She is within striking distance. Or kissing distance. From the living room, the party chatter of the Yankee gift exchange. In Mitch's kitchen, a wiped down orderly arrangement of someone who actually uses their kitchen to cook, as opposed to Ronnie's kitchen, which was more of a place to store beer, brew coffee, and throw away fast food wrappers.

"Aw, you know I'm kiddin'." She taps him on the right bicep with her right fist.

"Wocka wocka," Ronnie says.

Maux steps back. "Seriously though. Where have you been?"

"Around." He sips from the nog. "Out. About. Here. There. Thinking about moving. The girls here are bonkers." Ronnie smiles at Maux, punctuates his remark with a loud and lengthy belch.

Maux smiles at this. "Hey man, you were the one who went off with that Portland Patty fee-male." The way she says "fee-male" makes him laugh. He can't help it.

"Yeah, well . . . you know."

She punches him on the arm again. "You disappeared, Ron."

Mitch invited him three days ago, as they sat on the roof before another Sunny Afternoons practice, telling Ronnie to "Bring a shitty gift because it's a Yankee gift swap." Fair enough. Ronnie brings a round fake porcelain goose that doubles as an egg holder, ends up with a VHS compilation of videos from the glamorous metal band Trixter. He breaks about even.

Throughout the party he avoids Maux, avoids looking at her as the guests sit in a circle in Mitch's cramped living room. Paul, Neal, William, Siouxsanna Siouxsanne, Mouse, Icy Filet, Rae, and a dozen-odd others Ronnie doesn't really know that well talking and laughing in the sluggish bright hazy throb of a nog-buzz. Ronnie doesn't want to try and iron out whatever happened between him and Maux. He knows he's partially at fault, but only partially. If that.

But the funny thing is that, of course, as the hours whiz along and the party evolves into rolling laughter and loud talk, the bad ideas start to turn into totally awesome ideas. So the next time they happen to be in the kitchen alone, as she opens the freezer to take out more ice for the nog, he stands next to her, leans in, whispers, "Sorry I disappeared, Maux. Let's get caught up. Let's get outta here. Let's listen to mus—"

"Listen to music?" Maux scoffs. "That line is as phony as your Chicago accent." She turns away from the freezer to face him, smirks, scowls. "But let's get out of here. Drinks at Drunken Mick. My treat. Since I'm assuming your writing career is still nonexistent?"

"Hey, you're hurting my feelings." They walk out of the kitchen and pass through the living room without anyone realizing they had left until whoever is stuck with the fake-porcelain-egg-holding goose will pick it up to take it home, and someone will ask "Where's Ronnie?", and no one will know and it will suddenly occur to them that he hasn't been seen for a while now, and Maux isn't around either, and then Mitch will say, "Oh no. Them two, again?" and someone else will see the Trixter VHS on the coffee table and point out that he left it there, and by the time they put it all together, Ronnie will be at a stool at the Drunken Mick next to Maux, both slurping from pint glasses filled with more vodka than tonic.

The bar isn't terribly crowded. It is December and finals and the final end-of-semester celebrations aren't in effect yet. Groups are scattered around the tables spread throughout the room, plus a couple old drunks near the front door.

"So," Ronnie says.

"So," Maux says.

"Let's talk," Ronnie says, leaning in, placing his hand on her thigh right above the knee, moving up . . . up . . . up.

"Yeah, talk," Maux says, grabbing Ronnie by the wrist and pulling away the horny hand. "I just want to talk to you, Ron. I don't really have any friends around here anymore."

Ronnie laughs, leans in, tries repeating the move with the hand, and as Maux blocks the thigh-grab with her hands, he says, "You know . . . that's not my problem."

"Not your problem?!" Maux swivels away from Ronnie, stands off the barstool.

"Goodbye, Ron." She starts to walk past Ronnie to the exit.

"Aw, c'mon! Why do you gotta be so bitter all the time?" Ronnie asks.

She turns to Ronnie, each word out of her mouth slow-slurred and carefully annunciated: "Don't be one of them. I thought you were better than that."

Ronnie chugs what remains of the vodka tonic Maux bought him, steps off the stool, stands up, faces her. "I don't understand you."

"I understand you," she says. "You're a loser. Goodbye."

Ronnie raises his right arm, waves his right hand like he's bon voyaging on a cruise ship, hopes she doesn't turn around, even goes so far as to think, "Don't look back." And when he thinks "Don't look back," it makes Ronnie think of Bob Dylan playing an electric guitar for folkies, and he's drunk enough to yell to her back, in his best/worst/most parodic Dylanese: "I don't belieeeeve yew. You're a LIAR!"

At the exit, she turns, one last time. All that indigo. Nnnnnnugget. Ronnie smiles at her. Maux smirks at him. Stupid Ronnie. Of course this is how it would play out. When she sobers up, she'll blame the drinking, holiday loneliness, how they can't give what the other one wants, her inability to hate Ronnie as much as she should. But now, she knows and he knows it can go one of two ways as they look at each other in these challenging smiles and smirks. She walks out the front door.

Ronnie will never see Maux again. In two months, she will move to Atlanta. Around that time, Rae will inform him that Maux scribbled a list in one of the ladies' room stalls of The Puzzled Pirate Saloon of "People I Will Miss in This Shit-Shitty Town," with Ronnie's name in the top two.

There will only be two names, but hey.

FIVE: NICE WINTERS

"You are a lost generation."
—Deputy Dawg, to Patti Smith

NEW YEAR'S EVE

If you've ever dropped acid at a party where most people are sticking to beer as their drug of choice, you know there is a point when
you branch off and eventually move away from the 'faced behaviors and sloshed actions of those around you. Ronnie recognizes
this fork in the road early in the last hour of 1996, as he sits on the
upraised platform of the abandoned train depot where this New
Year's Eve so-called "sex party" was supposed to be happening behind him, inside. "Sex acts" would be filmed. So the rumors went.
It sounded incredibly stupid to Ronnie, as Mitch told him about it
earlier in the day at a barbeque, but the early afternoon beer buzz
convinced him enough to shrug and say "Why not?" and the added beers and the flasks passed around at this so-called "sex party"
from strangers and near strangers, to say nothing of what Ronnie
thought was a bit of a dogshit year, convinced him that the best
way of putting this year to bed and starting 1997 with a squeaky
clean slate was to, as Bill Hicks put it, "squeegee his third eye" and
accept the tab of acid given to him, gratis, from some Orlando girl

he used to like way back in high school before she dreadlocked her hair and took to wearing giant candy-striped Cat in the Hat hats and shooting black tar heroin.

But as the Fork in the Road begins, Ronnie regrets this spontaneous act. Oh, Christ. This is going to be a long commitment, and it won't be pretty and it won't be fun. But the drinking lessens the fear inherent in seeing the lines in the denim of his jeans expand and contract, to say nothing of the splintered wood of the platform he sits upon. What are we doing here? The five foot drop from the platform to the rocky dirt darkness below is beginning to look like a perilous fall. He can't look down anymore, so he opts instead to try and observe the crowds—dozens of stumbling young sloppy-loud revelers spending their last moments of 1996 milling about and trying to pack into the long-abandoned depot to see . . . what? A boob or two? Intercourse through strobe lights?

Over the oontz—oontz—oontz of the techno behind him, Ronnie hears Mitch's "HAW HAW HAW" as he approaches Ronnie, leans in close to Ronnie's face, makes sci-fi theremin laser noises, wiggles his fingers, and yells, "YA TRIPPIN' BUDDY?! YA FREAKIN' OUT YET?!"

Ronnie smells the booze sweat, the cheap beer breath, calmly turns to Mitch, looks up at him and smiles. Mitch sees Ronnie's half-dollar pupils, the paranoid vacancy on his face, and steps back when he speaks in an unRonnie soft-spoken eerie drone, "That's not what's freaking me out here, Mitch. It's everything else you're doing but that."

Mitch bursts out into another round of "HAW HAW HAW." He puts his tallboy of Old Hamtramck to his lips, chugs . . . chugs . . . c hugs . . . and when it's drained he throws it as hard as he can into the black of the ground below, the street beyond it, and as Ronnie follows the end over end trail (*dude . . .*) of the can, Mitch burps long and loud, then says, "Looks like these weirdos are about to go do it. Ya wanna check it out, Rahn?"

If he can stick close to Mitch, everything will be fine. Because: Mitch will remind him that everyone around him is drunk, and therefore, everything is ridiculous and absurd and therefore ok.

"Sure," Ronnie says, feeling the perfect kind of distance from everything and everyone, in spite of the sheer aggressiveness of the hallucinations. "This will be hilarious."

Ronnie follows the path cleared by Mitch through the crowd and into the depot. Through Promethean will and focus, Ronnie ignores the grotesque visuals of the white stabbing strobe lights and the horrifying patterns in the shadows on the ceiling, the demonic voices shrieking.

They stand as close as they can before the audience is too thick. Ronnie stands on tippy-toes. What is, in actuality, two women in Bettie Page wigs, matching black pasties with red tassels on their breasts, matching black lace panties covering their hindquarters, and fishnets, looks to Ronnie like a flabby-cellulitic overly tattooed multi-limbed monster twitching on an old stained mattress as giant insects stand on their back legs, hold cameras, and circle the beast.

"Kill it!" Ronnie screams over the techno. Mitch laughs, and before Ronnie has time to register the amused/bemused expressions of the drunks around him, he turns around, tries to figure out how he can get back to where was sitting before, outside, on the depot platform. Home, The Myrrh House, trying to get back there, that would be impossible.

"This party is a batch of bullshit," Mitch yells in Ronnie's ear. "Ya wanna get . . . "

"Yes!" Ronnie yells. "Let's go!" As he starts to step away though the crowd gathered around watching this, Ronnie screams, once more, "Kill it!", in case those around him were unsure of what to do with that . . . thing they were watching.

As Mitch stomps off past him, drunk and surly, and Ronnie knows it's because he was hoping to you know find some girl to . . . fuckin', take home or whatever, Ronnie formulates a "To Do" list in his head:

- get out of here (somehow)
- get home (somehow, and hopefully not run into anyone)
- do some serious thinking
- listen to Side 2 of High Time by MC5
- do some more serious thinking. About everything.
- wait it out/make it to the morning

"Camahn, Rahn!" Mitch yells from somewhere out there away from the depot, in the dark. To get to him requires getting off of this platform somehow. For who-knows how long, Ronnie stands there, dreading the free fall, dreading the hard landing, doubting he can even land on both feet.

"Jump, Rahn!" Mitch yells. "Look, I know you're on acid , but quit acting like a pussy!"

Others behind him chant, "Jump! Jump! Jump!"

It takes the countdown, the "5 . . . 4 . . . 3 . . . 2 . . . 1 . . . HAPPY NEW YEAR!" for Ronnie to close his eyes and leap off the platform, the freefall of it, even in those nanoseconds, like the time he sky-dove while on assignment for the school paper, the vast stretches of green squares bisected by Interstate 4 as the wind blew through his face and the hard Wile E. Coyote death of the land between Lakeland and Orlando awaited him if this parachute didn't work—or like the plunges off high dives as a child, trying not to belly-flop, trying to cannonball all the adults past the yellow line on the concrete that kept the kids out of the pool during adult swims, or like stage diving in those flashes when you worry whether your friends will actually catch you this time.

But unlike those other flirtations with vertigo, this time Ronnie is actually stunned to land, stunned to make contact with the grassy gravelly dirt so much sooner than he anticipated, and on both his feet, without injury.

Adrenaline cuts in through everything else currently circulating his bloodstream. He feels a tremendous sense of accomplishment, getting off that horrible abandoned train depot where mutants made love for the entertainment of cretins—but before he can get too far, Mitch yells, "Alright champ. You landed. Let's bail already."

SATURN'S RINGS

"Ya wanna stop in here, Altamont?" Mitch asks as they pass Tweakies, the rave club, as excessively sweaty large-pupiled jaw-grinding adults with pacifiers and baby tees run in and out. "Grind on some nnnnuggets lllloaded on ecstasy? Start the year off right?"

Ronnie forces out a laugh, smiles a smile borne out of paranoia and sensory overload as the inescapable oontz-oontz-oontz-oontz fascist lockstep jackboot beat marches ever onward, spilling out Tweakies' front doors. Don't look at anybody as you pass. Stay focused on Mitch—drunk Mitch—who's drunken belligerence reminds you—hey, it's going to be fine because everybody out on the streets right now is as far gone as you are, dude.

Yes: Follow Mitch. He led you away from the depot and its scenes of cheesy quasi-debauchery. Follow the breathing street lights and noise along Main Street—the loud bars and restaurants screaming tepid alternative rock.

"Alright, Wavy Gravy," Mitch yells over the din. "Where we headed?"

"Um . . . " Ronnie, trying to choose his words, because every spoken word has ramifications.

"I'm not gonna lie," Mitch says. "I wanna go kick some ass."

"What?" The very thought of fighting sends bolts of fear flashing from his brain and heart and out to his extremities.

"I wanna have some fun tonight. Find a party. Drink some beers. You know: Kick some ass."

Kick some ass. At the intersection of University and Main, the demon dogs in the sirens of the roadblocks. Amber death heads peeking out of the streetlights. The frenzied amorous ravers, the howling agitated rednecks, the shrieking dramatic college students. "I'M SOOOOOOOOOOO FUCKING DRUNK!!!!" Every college girl within a ten mile radius seems to be yelling. Ronnie wants to tell Mitch how close to insanity he feels right now, but if he can make it to his room and get the MC5 on the stereo, and if he can keep his eyes straight ahead, manage the slightest of nods when people shriek HAPPY NEW YEAR DUDE! at him, Ronnie might survive.

"I got beer at my house," Ronnie manages to squeak out. "Help me get home, dude, and you can have it. It's all really . . . um . . . crazy, right now."

"Yeah, these people are idiots," Mitch says, forcing his big lug body through the crowds. Ronnie follows in his wake. "Amateurs. We gotta find our friends. The professionals."

Ronnie, relieved that Mitch doesn't realize he's freaking the fuck out, but maybe he should tell him, because he has to explain what's going on:

Saturn's Rings. That was the name of the acid the Orlando junkie gave him two hours ago. And sure enough, the tab had a circle with a ring around the tab. Ronnie finds a comfortable headspace where he can watch the visuals from the streetlights, focus enough on Mitch so he knows it's all one big joke of and on the desperately festive, and turn inward and recall the beach at Christmas. As his parents jogged or swam or meditated, Ronnie walked the beach, trying to think of ways to apologize to his parents. For everything. For everything that went wrong this year. For following vague and under-defined ambitions. For fleeing Orlando like some immature, irresponsible coward. For really having no reason to be in Gainesville. Low tide, high tide.

The crowds have picked up again; the waves of yelling, honking cars, fireworks, sloppy stumbling. Younger, more monolithic packs of dorm kids with fake IDs, drunk on Jell-O shots and their own youth. Some combination of Mitch's yelling and the intense trails from the street lights rattles Ronnie's equilibrium. He doesn't/can't answer Mitch, he reaches out, grabs the nearest solid object he can lean against—a streetlight post—feels himself wrapped up in the coolness of the concrete, his eyes move over the textures of the chipped marks and the black splotches, stickers of bands, show fliers taped at eye level, and Ronnie laughs, because everyone around him right now, and all the time, they take their roles so seriously, as if they're unaware of the futility of existence, and who knows, maybe they are unaware of this—Mitch has never tripped so what does he know about it?—and they never-ever ask "Can you see the real me?" because they're not above hiding it and faking it and being inauthentic to get by. They're fellow Americans and they only care about being number one.

"Rahnnie? Rahnnie?!" Mitch leans in. "You alright, buddy?"

Ronnie doesn't/can't turn away from the lightpost, nods, slowly, nods again.

Mitch takes him by the arm, says, "Good. We gotta keep going. C'mon, we're almost there . . . "

Angry loner dudes stomp home drunkenly swearing at the world because they didn't pick up any women, lonely women sloppy in heels, the usual catalog-clothed, ballcapped collegiate packs you see in any college town from Cambridge, Mass to Eugene, Oregon. It's not just that they're drunk, Ronnie thinks. It's their futures. They know they have futures. They are here to get degrees, passports to good jobs and the bounteous Floridian future of palm trees in the yards, tanned children, Baptist church on Sundays, trips to the beach. What would 1997, 1998, and on and on, hold? Nothing will change. He can't conceive of a way to leave Gainesville.

Maybe this is the best I can hope for, Ronnie thinks, walking while staring up into the dark, into the least visual, least textured scenery he can find, the patch of black sky overhead. It is an exciting-enough trap, surrounded by people who know you and will always know you. Gainesville is the kind of place where, when you return, you feel the painful pull of the routine, the comfort, the security. If he did manage to leave, it would take every fiber of his being to keep driving when he got on the exit ramp, to not turn around and stay. He could imagine returning, many years later, looking down any of these empty streets on Sunday afternoons, there, see the nineteen year old lesbian on her bike—DYKE POWER in big black letters on the book bag strapped across her back, peddling in an unrushed zig-zag below the canopy of trees, and he will know how much the passage of time hurts, because Gainesville has moved on to the next batch of eager Florida kids trying to figure themselves and their world out. What was once the only world Ronnie knows will be no longer that world, and the 1996 into 1997 nice winter will no longer exist. The blizzards and hurricanes and the spinning planet in spinning galaxies have their own way of making you realize how insignificant you are. Here and now, Ronnie can't fathom this being any different, except for the very real possibility that this acid will leave him insane, and he will be like any other casualty you see on weekday afternoons sitting on bus benches, muttering and laughing about some gibberish concerning Saturn's Rings.

PEAKING, BRAH

"The fuck you doin', dude?"

Normally, this is an easy enough question to answer—for Ronnie, or anyone else. But as the acid peaks, the question fills with peril, with nuance. What does he mean, and what do I say?

Roger kicks open the cracked door to Ronnie's bedroom, starts laughing; there's Ronnie, sprawled, studying the fractals in the purple and pink floor and how the purple and pink crests decorating the floor expand and contract and break apart from each other—how the floor wobbles like the ocean—then suddenly, terrifyingly interrupted.

"Uhhh . . . uh . . . tripping?" Ronnie manages to say, sits up. "Where's Mitch?"

"Tripping?" Roger yells, in a tone filled with mockery, anger, belligerence. Roger's hair moves in blond Medusa hisses, the frays at the ends of his jeans writhing like white worms, and everything in between is too horrible to comprehend. "Not here, but the front door was wide open when I got here, so thanks for locking up, guys." Roger steps closer, leans in and over Ronnie, asks, "Have any extra for your roomie?" Roger turns down Ronnie's stereo, snickers at the drawn lines and circles on the ripped pages scattered around Ronnie.

"No!" Ronnie gasps, like someone accused of a crime, because that's what questions—any questions—sound like to Ronnie right now. "I got it from some girl, at some party."

"That stupid sex party?" Roger yells, standing in the middle of the room below the ceiling fan and the light, fan fluttering like dreadful insect wings, the light heightening the opening and closing pores on Roger's face. "I was there, didn't see you." Unnecessarily, he adds, "I'm drunk."

Ronnie cowers against the couch, knees pulled up to his chin, hugging the legs of his jeans, tries not to look at the throbbing cracks in the walls, the spider webs on the ceiling, the wavy flowers on the floor tiles.

"Well," Roger says. "You're obviously no fun right now. Good night, Ronnie. Happy new year." He steps out of the room, Medusa hair and wavy frayed jeans trailing behind him.

Ronnie leans against the cowboy couch, moans "Oh God oh God," while suffering through throbbing undulating hallucinations at every turn. At his side is his journal, where he's tried to write what he had been thinking on the walk home, how he has to leave Gainesville before the law of diminishing returns exacts its ugly costs, but it was more entertaining to draw curvy lines in the journal's pages, to follow their shapes as the patterns emerged. He forgot to put on Side 2 of the MC5's *High Time* and instead plays the Flipper song "Life" on repeat—over and over, finding a surprising tranquility in the music's plodding cacophony as Will Shatter yell-pleads "LIFE! LIFE! LIFE IS THE ONLY THING WORTH LIVING FOR!" over the glorious din. It is almost cold in the Myrrh House. Ronnie could wear a long-sleeved shirt and not sweat. Ronnie tries imagining Chicago cold, a January in Chicago cold, a frozen gray lake facing thousands of buildings gushing smoke. He does this in spite of where the acid wants to take him—bleak eyelid visions of melty-faced Julianas and Mauxs and Portland Pattys and Maggies. The cracked case of the MC5 CD, opened, and the back cover, yellow with red lettering, the song title "Future/Now" hovers over the rest of the text. Two words, separated with a slash, and the meaning is obvious and requires no thought, no brooding, no reflecting. No more of that. He has to go. Just go. Leave. Where? Anywhere. Future/Now. Future/Now. Future/Now. Future/Now. It is time to make this potential energy kinetic.

If only Saturn's Rings would leave. As the hours pass, Ronnie finds fewer and fewer vantage points in which to view his room, fewer objects he can look at without feeling profoundly disturbed by what he's seeing. The lamp on the desk. The Lara Flynn Boyle poster on the wall. The cracked plaster. The guitar. The typewriter.

All the little pieces of paper taped to the Haiku Wall. He crawls to his mattresses, falls back, eyes looking upward at the tiny square of window above the horrifyingly jade green curtains; as the sky changes from black to purple to blue, Ronnie can finally close his eyes without seeing ex-girlfriends and all the corny trails and throbs that go with your standard trip, can go back to imagining the beach at Christmas, walking along the shore, feeling quadrophenic, always and forever.[11]

•

"Steal the cue / achieve succeed / place in line / position it in time / make the effort / hey it's worth the effort / sure it's worth the effort / A conversation / a contradiction / you make no sense / you got no position / what you need is a validation / go ahead you got my permission"
—Minutemen, *"Validation"*

"No no no, look: It's like, because of last night, I figured it out. What I need to be doing," Ronnie says, as Ronnie plus you, Neal, and Paul plow through your fifth pitcher of Old Hamtramck, in the middle of a twelve-hour all-you-can-drink Happy Hour at Unknown Pleasurez, a New Wave-themed danceclub on University east of Main that has, for today, transformed into a sports bar, because the Florida Gators football team are winning . . . something? The SEC? The National Championship? You don't know nor care, and of your friends, only Mitch is interested. And he's

---

[11] Over the course of six and one-half hours, Ronnie Altamont listened to the Flipper song "Life" eighty-one and a half times. Not sure if that's a world record. Of the song, the *Trouser Press* has this to say: ". . . Flipper can be uplifting. Underneath the tumult you'll find compassion, idealism and hope, best represented by "Life" ("the only thing worth living for"). That kind of moral statement takes courage."

off watching it at a real sports bar with his jock-tendencied Tommy Hilfiger-shirted friends from back home. But for today, because business is business and so on and so forth, the TVs here at Unknown Pleasurez that are normally tuned to static—because that's, as any UCF fraternity lad in the early 1990s would tell you, alternative and like . . . post-modern?—are tuned to the channel broadcasting The Big Game.

"Ok. What?" you moan, sigh, can barely hide your annoyance with Ronnie. Not so much with Ronnie, but with so much talking-talking-talking right now. After all, it has been a twenty-four hour binge of—what?—beer, whiskey, Jaeger, pot, coke, hash, Xanax, Vicodin, with maybe a quick nap on a couch along the way—to Happy New Year Dude, to more of this, to bloody marys, to here, the twentieth bar or party you've been to since getting off work at 4:00 p.m. yesterday.

"What what?" Ronnie says.

Sigh. "What do you need to be doing?"

"William's a little bit tired," Paul says. "In case you haven't noticed."

"I think we're all pretty spent here, Ron," Neal says. "So tell us why today is different from any other day in your life . . . "

Ronnie, in the shaky gray twitch of an acid hangover, isn't any less exhausted than the rest of you, but in the mania of no-sleep, coupled with the recent addition of Old Hamtramck on draft, he begins talking and talking and talking, as the dozens at the bar and the surrounding tables cheer and slow handclap the touchdown on the screens.

Like so many, Ronnie exaggerates and romanticizes the insights and epiphanies he claims to have had while on acid, either forgetting or refusing to discuss the nightmarish aspects to it—the dark thoughts, the insufferable paranoia, the joyless hallucinations. You've heard variations of this story for so long now. Some drug "cleaned the slate"—and Ronnie will use that expression no less than five times in this spiel. From what you can gather, last night Ronnie figured out that he really-really wants to be a writer, that, once again, he feels the possibilities of life, of what can still be accomplished as they face down baby New Year 1997. He woke up his roommate Roger to tell him this very important news, but Roger (sensibly) moaned and went back to sleep.

Even if it's a cloudy pale gray day, all the colors in the spectrum are so much brighter in Gainesville today, because Ronnie has finally figured out to move on from his past in Gainesville, and his past in Orlando, and it's a new day, and it's time to do it, time to go for it, this is it, it's time to be a writer, blah blah blah blah blah, because that's why he's on this earth—to write—he needs to write and write and . . .

"Well go then!" you say.

"Go where, William?" Ronnie says.

"Go write," William says. "I like you, but all you're doing is talking right now. You're not writing. You're wasting time. With us. You're wasting time. Here." And as you extend your hands, gesturing, Ronnie gives a confused look around, like he doesn't know if you mean Unknown Pleasurez, or Gainesville. "You don't even have a pen with you, do you?"

Ronnie doesn't even bother with putting his hands to his pockets. Shakes his head.

"Ronnie. Go. Go write."

•

Ronnie walks down University, crazy University where, like all over Gainesville, cheers are erupting. Cars line up and down the street, honking their horns, drunks hanging out of windows screaming "WE'RE NUMBER ONE!" as the cars swerve close enough for the passengers to high-five each other. Seems like the only ones who don't care about this game are the crusties outside Gatorroni's by the Slice, who seig-heil the honking cheering cars or give them the finger, one with the words GAY GOATERS written on his ass cheeks in black Sharpie large enough to be viewed across the street, which gets even funnier when the police grab him and hustle him off, presumably to jail. Ronnie turns right down 13th towards the Myrrh House, doubting he explained himself very well as he starts muttering to himself, lost in thought, lost in validation—William told him to go but Ronnie would have should have left anyway.

Back in his room, on the floor, journal in his lap, he stares at the minutes ticking away on the digital alarm clock. Will it always be like this? What is he doing here? He stretches, thinks WHAT DOES THIS MEAN? To live this way, to talk to people about your dreams of being a writer or a musician or whatever it is Ronnie wants to do with his life—and the world keeps spinning and it is 1997 and pretty soon the decade will be done and Ronnie if you're going to give up, give up, but if you're going to live, you better live and live right. You better start scribbling something, anything.

On that unhinged January 1st evening, Ronnie takes a deep breath. He laughs, he smiles, and then, Ronnie writes everything that enters his mind, no longer caring if it is good or bad, publishable or un-.

Maybe you expect the climax of this big mother of a book

to be something like Ronnie puking all over a girl, or deciding to stay or leave Gainesville, or getting published, or getting a band to some level of success, but really, here's your climax, folks, completely lacking in titties or whatever else you might prefer. It's Ronnie scribbling words into a $1.99 composition pad.

It's Ronnie in his room every morning and most evenings for the remainder of the so-called winter, and onward into the spring and the beginnings of that long Floridian summer, writing whatever comes into his head, not caring that it's awful, filled with missteps and failed experiments and worth nothing but the inevitable rejection slips, year after year. But it doesn't matter. Forgetting everything else and sitting down to write, that is the important thing. To have the joy of that voice in his head, of these characters, of thinking of what needs to happen in the worlds he creates. To jettison ambition in favor of workman effort.

The pages and the journals stack, some better than others. The ratio will improve over the years. Ronnie thought he was a writer before this winter, but really, "aspiring" hung over him like the specters of favorite writers he wanted to emulate so badly—in lifestyle as well as prose talent. As he really writes for the first time, Ronnie thinks of how ass-backwards he had had it before, thinking he was going to be successful the way he was in college, effortlessly barfing out caustic opinion columns as too many gave him more credit than he deserved. The real world— Thank God—didn't work out that way. It would be a slog through February Chicago blizzards rather than the can of corn that was the Floridian winter.

But for now, in his room with the stacked mattresses and the cowboy couch and the desk with the typewriter and the haiku wall and Lara Flynn Boyle poster, all he needed to do was laugh and write, laugh and write, and try and enjoy the process as much as possible.

SIX: HEY! IT'S SPRING AGAIN

"Whenever spring comes to New York I can't stand the
suggestions of the land that come blowing over the river
from New Jersey and I've got to go. So I went."
—Jack Kerouac

AT THE PAWN SHOP

"Ronnie? That you?" the Gainesville scenester-looking dude standing to Ronnie's left asks as he's checking out the electric guitars hanging from the greasy walls of the pawn shop.

Ronnie turns away from a black Les Paul worth much more than what he has made in the eleven months he has lived in Gainesville. Each guitar has its own story—old, new, expensive, cheap, dinged, shredded, unplayed, missed, unmissed, covered in stickers, covered in Sharpie-scrawls, hollow-bodied, f-holed, whammy barred—these six-strings, hanging by their necks, unloved and quivering in the air-conditioning.

On the floor of the small and inevitably dingy pawn shop, black bulky amplifiers stacked everywhere you turned—faded knobs, knobless, some speakers look razored, some speakers unused. Ronnie is transfixed, making up the stories behind each instrument, the people who pawned their gear and what they bought with the money. Like Frank here, who pawned this electric blue BC Rich when his band, Hollywood Trix, broke up, and used the money to buy a suit for a job interview with the Barnett Bank on University, where they were hiring bank tellers, and he's trying to figure out if the THC has left his system (it has been six months, maybe? Since he last got high? He thinks?). Or Karl, who pawned the red Hagstrom next to the BC Rich after his wife left him for his best friend and he took the money to buy a shotgun because he never played the guitar anyway and besides—what did he have to live for anymore? Somehow, these bleak imaginary tales made the story of Ronnie, who pawned his black and white Squire Fender, his Crate amp, and his gray Smith-Corona fifteen minutes ago, easier to stomach.

"It's amazing what you find here sometimes," the scenester-looking dude says to Ronnie, not taking his eyes off the guitars. What was his name again? He wears the old black denim cut-off below the knee that everyone wears here—soiled blue-black Chucks that get that beat-to-hell look only from miles on skateboards, the wallet chain looped from the side of the cut-offs, the lanky-black-haired pale skinned kid you see in the far corner of every suburban parking lot, sitting on his board, sipping from a Big Gulp cup filled with the contents of a Brain Mangler malt liquor quart.

"Yup," Ronnie says, running his right index and middle fingers across the open strings of the off-white Ibanez Flying-V to the left of the Les Paul. On the opposite side of the room, the pawnbrokers, inevitably orange-skinned, paunchy, and loud, discussing the fish they've caught in their lifetimes, as Rush sings of flying by night away from here on the classic rock radio station playing through the boombox next to the cash register.

It is the afternoon of March 1st.

Ronnie decides to tell him. Out of the three, Ronnie hates mentioning the typewriter most of all, as it was a gift from Kelly before Ronnie left for Crescent City.

The scenester turns away from the guitars, looks at Ronnie. "Damn. Really?" Then, an expression of fearful condescension, of concern mixed with guardedness, his look essentially screaming, Is this guy a junkie?

"Had to make rent, ya know?" Ronnie shrugs, looks down, feeling the hatred and frustration of being here to his bones, the bulge of bills in his wallet going straight to Roger, folded cash for the moment pressing against the left ass cheek of his dirty denim.

"Oh," the scenester says, looking almost relieved, shifting his slouch from the right foot to the left. "Aw dude, you can always get another amp and guitar if you want, and what was it, your typewriter?"

"I feel like I just sold off my limbs," Ronnie oh-so-dramatically puts it.

"Limbs?" The scenester pshaws. "People do this all the time. Our friends do this all the time." He points to the guitars. "Look around. You're not the first."

This is something Ronnie loves about Gainesville. Poverty here is temporary, a condition everyone goes through from time to time, rather than a horrible affliction worthy of scorn.

"It's rent. You gotta pay it," the scenester continues. "It's better than . . . I mean, think of all the guitars here pawned for heroin . . . "

Ronnie nods, knows this guy is right, but not over the hurt of having to pawn off his most-valued possessions. He thinks of that old chestnut on TV shows, those trips to the pawn shop, when the hardluck protagonist pawns some treasured object—his watch, saxophone, diamond ring—and gets a pittance from the conniving pawn broker, who will not negotiate any better deals, the poor guy having no choice but to take the spare change he's offered, and as he leaves the pawn shop, putting the coins in his pockets, the pawn broker immediately sets the prized possession in the display window with a price tag twenty times the amount he paid the poor bastard for it.

The thing about it was that he used the typewriter only to write haiku. Since receiving it from Kelly, he was more inspired to sit and write haiku than to write short stories or anything else publishable. Instead of that proverbial Great American Novel people were always making jokes about when Ronnie told them what he did ("So, ya writin' that Great American Novel, heh heh heh?"), Ronnie wrote haiku about the cast of *What's Happening!!* A disgrace, in light of all the things he imagined he would write when he first lugged the machine to the car. Ronnie brooded, often, on what kind of muse he was stuck with that was never around when he had something he was aching to say, but was always there to come up with silly, unpublishable horseshit.

And the amp, well, maybe the scenester was right about that one. After all, The Sunny Afternoons had broken up the day after playing another party where they were well-received, but not as well-received as they had been earlier. (There is a law of diminishing returns at work with cover bands.) Besides, Bradley the drummer needs to graduate, wants to spend more time on his finance book. Rae has found a boyfriend, prefers getting high and watching movies with him in her living room over learning new Kinks songs. Ronnie can't blame her. She has done enough for Ronnie, and he is grateful. This leaves Ronnie and Mitch free to sit on Ronnie's roof to drink beers, but even that is infrequent these days as Ronnie opts, more and more, to scribble whatever thoughts are in his head.

The amp was taking up space in the corner of the living room by the front door. It was good to have around when the mood struck him, as was the guitar, but eviction looms, once again. The part-time gig at the restaurant is conducive to a hand-to-mouth existence, but it didn't make rent this time—Gatorroini's in SoHo has been in a down time between major sports seasons, the cold, and the students hunkering down to study.

"Well, I'm gonna go pay the rent now," Ronnie says to the scenester, extends his hand. They clasp at the fingers, pull away, snap. "Take it easy."

"Hang in there, alright?" the scenester says. "Hey wait," he adds. "If you're around this weekend, my band Marcus Aurelius is playing at the Righteous Freedom House." He pulls out a small flyer from his pocket, hands it to Ronnie. The flyer artwork is all Mondrian lines and lower-case Helvetica fonts.

"Sure, dude," Ronnie says, knowing he isn't going.

Walking to the front door, Ronnie takes a passing glance at that gray typewriter on the glass counter between the two pawn-brokers who still talk of fish in this lake versus fish in that lake. It's what he already misses the most.

Out the front door, Ronnie feels the warmth of the spring sun, the breeze. The depression lifts. Ronnie has a notebook and a pen. He wants to go home and work. He will drive his dying car through this perfect weather, leave his share of the rent money on the kitchen table for Roger, then retreat to his bedroom, open the windows, listen to Chuck Berry, and write.

RONNIE FINDS A SECOND JOB IN THE ELECTRONICS
DEPARTMENT OF THAT ONE DEPARTMENT STORE THAT IS
QUITE OFTEN THE SOURCE OF CRUEL JOKES AMONGST
THE PRE-TEEN SET AT THE EXPENSE OF THOSE BELIEVED
TO BE OF A LOWER SOCIOECONOMIC STRATA

Into the whoosh of the automatic front doors, that first kiss of
stale A/C air, past the wet-moussed cashiers, through the racks of
prismatic t-shirts, shorts, blouses, pants, slacks, dresses, and Florida Gator leisure wear, past the cologne and perfume cases, mixing with the lotions to add that chemically floral tinge to the air,
and contrast that smell with the automotive aisle (keep walking,
keep walking) with its stench of the various automotive lubricants
stocked in rows six feet high, and head straight to the cacophony
of sixty televisions—five down, twelve across—showing, on an endless loop, the films *Space Jam* and *Independence Day* over and over
as the CD sampler machine plays ten-second snippets of the same
ten songs—Young Country numbers about girls with hearts as big
as Texas and drinking establishments where the domestic beer is
served cold mixed with alternative rock and roll songs about relationship troubles and stuff. In the middle of this squared-off section of this department store—part of this nationally-known chain
notorious for being the butt of so many jokes among kids, the very
idea of kids' parents shopping there the epitome of cheap poverty—rows of compact discs, cassingles, VHS tapes, even movies in
the exciting new DVD format arranged alphabetically, more or less,
and shrinkwrapped. At the entrance to the territory marked off as
the Electronics Department, two employees in matching red vests,
black slacks, white Oxford shirts, and black ties stand behind the

BRIAN COSTELLO

glass display cases containing wristwatches and beepers stand and pretend to look busy amidst this cacophony—the one on the right seemingly studying the pages of a clipboard, and the one on the left standing behind the register while holding a broom.

The employee on the left has clipper-shaved stubbly black hair, patchy in some parts and overgrown in others because the person working the clippers was on her seventh glass of boxed wine. His glasses take up a large amount of facial territory—two squared circles above the eyebrows rounding downward to above the cheeks. When he scowls, he looks like he could be insane, definitely weird, as he says to his co-worker, "I can't believe you've never seen the punk rock episode of *CHIPS*.[12] Pain is one of my all-time favorite fictional bands. No, they are my favorite. Let me sing it for you again: "I dig pain . . . the feelin's in my brain . . . " and here, the employee sounds more aggressive and, well, barky, with each new lyric. "the scratching, the bashing, the clawin', the thrashin', the givin', the gettin', the total blood lettin' drive me insane . . . " and here, the employee bellows out, "I DIG PAIN!"

"Shut up, dude!" the other employee whisper-yells, nudging the bespectacled creep employee in the arm. "I know you like that song. You've only told me about it for three months now." This employee has blond, surfer-style hair with plenty of West Coast rock and roll shag. In spite of the laidback hair and the tan that looks imported from the nearest beach, his general demeanor here at the department store is one of harried annoyance with everything and everyone around him, especially his co-worker here, who happens to also be his roommate.

[12] "Battle of the Bands," first broadcast on NBC, January 31, 1982

"Well I have the whole episode recorded," Ronnie says to Roger. "You need to watch it, and get hip to the music of Pain."

"You've turned down every invitation I've ever extended to watch films with me, but you want me to watch a *CHIPS* rerun."

"Yeah, but this is different."

"Gotta study," Roger says, pointing to the clipboard, which contains thirty-four pages of the screenplay he's working on for class—scenes from a project about, in Roger's words, "the one and only man living in the United States who is 100 percent happy with the spectacles and entertainment and choices presented that are filed under 'lowest common denominator.' For instance, this Phil Collins song we're hearing right now over the loudspeakers—nobody really likes it, but this guy, he really likes it, and he likes anything and everything about our culture that is intended to make as many people as possible at least somewhat happy . . . so in this mass-produced post-industrial capitalist society that's just ok, if not worse than ok for most people, this man is in paradise."

"I can relate," Ronnie says, trying to understand.

Roger laughs. "You don't relate, but you understand, right?"

"I think so," Ronnie says. "Dude's happy with . . . " and Ronnie extends his hands outward to the department store, "this crap?"

"Yes," Roger says. "That's right."

•

Ten minutes down 13th Street, in the car he will sell soon, southbound through the too-quiet weeknight, softly singing T. Rex's "Life's a Gas." Past the deserted parking lots of the plazas, the lugubrious high school, the old houses where lawyers and accountants and music schools have set up shop. The scuba store. The trophy makers. In the cold of January, the palm tree fronds turn a pale green. There is the slightest tinge of what many places would call "Autumn." Ronnie wonders if he really wants to leave, for all his talk about it. There are times when Gainesville feels like home, someplace he could settle down and live.

Closer to the Myrrh House, he stops off at the Floridian Harvest, buys the usual two dollar four-pack of Old Hamtramck tall-boys. He exchanges pleasantries with the clerk. They know him here. On nights he turns to home, up and down NW 4th Lane, neighbors wave from windows. It could never be like this in the north, in January. Maybe he should stay. He will mull this over while pretending to watch the movie.

ON THE PHONE WITH MRS. ALTAMONT

"Yeah, I guess it's all right," Ronnie says. Before dinner (cooked tonight by Charley: steamed kale on hummus-covered bruschetta, with sliced grape tomatoes over that, drizzled with balsamic vinegar) before meditation, Sally-Anne talks to her son on the phone. "I'm left alone at both jobs. So that's nice. Not so much at the department store. You should see these people who come in. Stupid. Fat. Annoying."

"Ronnie," Sally-Anne takes on a scolding voice she hasn't used since Ronnie was a smart-aleck tween. "Right speech, right thought . . ."

"Not even Buddha can help me there," Ronnie says. "But hey: it's a job, and it's money to get me out of Gainesville."

"To where, Ronnie?" Sally-Anne asks, stress, the fight-or-flight tension in the nervous system building with each passing second.

"Chicago," Ronnie says, as if he's simply running an errand and will be back within the hour. "I thought I told you that."

"No. You didn't."

"Sure I did. At Christmas."

"I would have remembered that, Ronnie."

"Well, that's what I'm doing."

"To do what?"

"To do what?"

"Yes, Ron. To do what."

"I don't know."

"You don't know?"

"Write. Play music."

"That's what you said about moving to Gainesville."

"I'm saving up money."

"You haven't been able to afford Gainesville. How are you going to afford Chicago?"

"I'm on the right track," Ronnie says, and for once, Sally-Anne not only wants to believe him, but there's something in his certitude this time.

"Ok, Ronnie," Sally-Anne says, after a pause long enough to take in this news.

"Ok?"

"Yes, Ronnie. Ok."

"Supper!" Charley bellows, comedically, in the tone of a grub-cook in a trite Western. He adds, "Hey, Ronnie."

"Hey, Dad."

"Well talk soon, Ronnie. This is a lot to take in."

"Ok."

"Soon."

BRIAN COSTELLO

"Yes, soon."

Sally-Anne turns off the phone, walks to the dining room, where the bruschetta is plated, and she softly mutters the word "Chicago . . . " every ten to fifteen seconds. She stares out to the ocean and repeats it. "Chicago . . . . . . Chicago . . . . . . Chicago."

"What?" Charley says when he emerges from the kitchen. "Chicago?"

"Pour me some wine," Sally-Anne says.

THE FUTURE

In faded black t-shirts advertising bands with names like Defiled Ballsac and Infested Turdgobbler, the Gatorroni Losers spend their days and nights seated at the front patio of Gatorroni's by the Slice, emaciated ghost-like half-human half-junkie apparitions. Living on Xanax, Vicodin, Rohypnol, and free refills of iced-tea, the Gatorroni's Losers sit like lonely impoverished old men in late-morning fast food restaurants as they stare at what passes for the action of University Avenue—the bleary-eyed students pulling all-nighters for upcoming finals, the crackheads and winos panhandling change with cardboard signs reading "WHY LIE? I JUST WANT A DRINK," the busses and bikes and cops and hicks, the rich and poor, young and old, southern and northern—in a hazy unfocused state of near-bliss.

At the shows and the parties, the over-25 crowd linger on the edges in an undefined bitterness—in their words, their observations. Increasingly paunchy, thinning hair, clinging to another time, older and wiser in spite of all best efforts to always remain between 18-24, frustrated that the real 18-24 year olds can't be anything more or better than 18-24 year olds. Long out of college, but still in the college town. More jaded than anyone between 25-40 had a right to be. Acting like the music scene existed solely for their own scorn and ridicule. In a town were Youth rules, Not-Youth clings to what they had when they were in charge, compares it to today, finds it lacking.

CHICAGO. CHICAGO? CHICAGO.

"Why would you leave?" Mitch wants to know. He's up on the roof with Ronnie, the usual routine of two-dollar four-packs of Old Hamtramcks, as the Kinks play from the speakers below. "It's easy here. Girls everywhere, bands, parties." He smacks Ronnie's side with the back of his hand. "What more do you want?"

"I gotta leave now before I hate it," Ronnie says, stretching out across the tiles, breathing in this clean air he finds so invigorating. "And I will hate it if I stay."

"Cah-mahhn, Rahn! You can write anywhere! It gets cold in Chicago!"

Ah, yes. The eternal Floridian belief that snowfall and sub-freezing temperatures are far, far worse than plagues, pestilence, genocide. The mere thought of cold weather sends the average Floridian reaching for their smelling salts.

Winter and spring are rapidly passing into summer. Jeans and long-sleeved shirts are put away until next December. Ronnie drains the second tallboy, revels in the cheap beer bliss, the warmth of the evening sun, regrets that The Sunny Afternoons never covered "This Time Tomorrow." Ronnie reclines, head on the tiles, croons along, "This tiiiime tomorrrowwww / where will we go / on a spaceship somewhere / watching an in-flight movie show . . . "

"It's not gonna be as much fun when you leave," Mitch says, looking out to the sun setting, yet again, over the student ghetto. Only now, these days, over the trees are the construction cranes, there to help construct sore-thumb apartment buildings. One by one, the old houses are razed, replaced by high-density several storied buildings designed in the ugly tasteless pastel architecture aesthetic Ronnie thought he had left behind in Orlando and points south. For two years, Mitch has watched friends arrive and leave, and he never understands—can't fathom—why anyone would want to get out of here. Gainesville has everything you could want in a town. And even if Rahnnie—way too often—gets hung up on some crazy broad, or disappears into himself to write in his room for hours and days on end; even if the dude is weird, off-centered, a thoughtless floundering goof-off, the times here are good.

"I need something new," Ronnie says. If he thinks of Chicago in any kind of tangible way besides Not Gainesville and Not Florida, he imagines it as he is here-now on the Myrrh House roof: A dark rock and roll bar, playing guitar on an acoustically perfect stage at some lucrative gig that will pay at least one bill, if not all bills, and as he plays, instead of these invigorating breezes, cold bracing wind blasts through the opened front doors as more and more people pack in to listen, to really listen, because, finally, Ronnie will be around hundreds (rather than handfuls) who share his frame of reference, the same cultural heroes, the same underground language. With that kind of perfect fit, why would Ronnie stay in the Great State of Florida?

"You can always come back," Mitch says, bummedoutedness increasing in a direct relation to his drunkenness.

"Nah," Ronnie says. "But, you know, I'm hoping people will visit."

"Oh, we'll visit," Mitch says. "We'll go see the Cubs lose, then console some baseball sluts in their Ryne Sandberg jerseys when the game ends in typical heartbreaking fashion."

Ronnie laughs. "Yeah, that sounds about right."

RONNIE AND WILLIAM

Rolling off this greasy urine-stenched couch, finding your wallet and your keys in a puddle of bongwater on the coffeetable, opening the front door to meet the painful Florida glare, stepping onto the mulchy mucky front yard for home. It's early—too early (with only a sunrise peeking over the trees, to give you any kind of guess at what time it is), but you don't want to know what happened the night before, don't want to piece it together via the predictable post-mortems with friends. The booze hangovers, those are bad enough, but the cocaine hangover on top of it is suicide-inducing. You can almost remember when this kind of thing was fresh and exciting, as everything promised in the 1980s party college movies HBO played incessantly came to life, and it was like those hilarious bits where the characters would wake up with panties wrapped on their heads, naked blondes passed out on either side, limp pizzas spinning on turntables. Now, it's waking up to snoring tattooed gutter girls you've known for way too long, muggy sweat on your aching forehead, and the fourth of five CDs in the CD changer, some factory-grade heavy metal pummeling, the double bass like pistons pounding your weary skull.

Uhhhhhhhhhhh ... shield your eyes, gain whatever bearings you can. Across the street is a field, the parking lot of a crumbling white wooden church. Stand on the empty street, listen for traffic. Nothing happening in either direction. Another tree-canopied sidestreet with houses like this one, full of people you know are always throwing parties. If you squint through the glare and the humid haze, if you listen past the birds and insects, there are cars, whizzing back and forth. It must be University Avenue. University will take you home.

The soft air blowing through the trees is some help, some protection from the sun's already-nasty blaze, as you hobble along like a bum (a bum!), a dizzy sweaty creep squinting one eye like a hungover Popeye on shore leave. These mornings are piling up. Here's where you should believe that you are tired of always picking up the pieces, of always trying to recall what happened the night before, trying to recollect how you ended up where you woke up in the morning and why you feel the need to leave so quickly, but instead, it's all part of this ha-ha-ha-larious routine.

Down this random street, you sing a Replacements song— "bring your own lampshade / somewhere there's a party / here it's neverendin' can't remember when it started / pass around the lampshade / there'll be plenty enough room in jail." You sing it with atonal gusto, with volume and heartiness, and no one's around to appreciate it. Your best performance yet!

On University Avenue, you mock yourself and the situation, all like, "Oh! Sure! That's right! *Now* I know where I am!" to no one, because no one's on the sidewalks this early. You read the street sign, in your best parodic North-Central Floridian drawl, you say, "Les' see, 'cordin' mah calcuhlashuns, Ah'm fahve blocks uh-way." You sound less like a native of the region and more like Mick Jagger when he "goes country" on the occasional Stones song. That's funny to you, so you decide, fuck it, to belt out a few lines from "Faraway Eyes"—"cuz if yer down on your luck / and life ain't worth a damn / find a girl / with faraway eyes . . . and if yer downright disgusted / uh yeah yeah yeah / y-yeah, girl, faraway . . . fuck it." Christ, you smell. What is that? Stale whiskey/coke sweat, cigarette smoke, old-ass couch musk? Yes. Yes it is. You want to puke, but instead, you continue singing.

"Ah wuz drivin' home early Sunday morning through Bakersfield listenin' to gospel music on the colored radio station . . . "

You look up from your hungover daydream. It's Ronnie Altamont, singing along with "Faraway Eyes," laughing at you, at something, at nothing. He's gotta be as hungover as you. You really don't want to see anyone right now, but at least you can bond about the night before.

You duet a few lines of the chorus, burst into laughter by the time you sing, "So if yer downright disgusted," and you drop it long enough to say, "What are you doing awake?" (No one should be awake right now. No one.)

"Going to work," he says, and now that you actually pay attention, he looks too . . . awake, to be hungover. "Preppin' the food," he says. "You?"

You manage a burnout "heh heh" laugh that transcends your usual ironical imitations of burnouts. "Leaving a party," you shrug.

Ronnie laughs a sympathetic laugh. "Fun?" he asks. Fun.

Another "heh heh." You find that laugh disconcerting. You try shifting gears. "You know," you say, a bit sharper. "Where've you been lately, Ron?"

Ronnie tells you. Working. Writing. Planning a move to Chicago. And the way he says it, it sounds so casual, like he's planning a weekend camping trip or something. Like he has no idea what he's in for. That much you can sense from the way he talks. You give Ronnie three months, tops, before the crime, the weather, and his friends beckon him homeward. You don't say this. Instead, you say, "Well, I have some friends up there. If you want, I could see if you could stay with them until you find a place."

The look on Ronnie's face? Too bright, brighter than this goddamn day, as he speaks all goshwow and oh really and wowthatwouldbeawesomes.

"I'll call them later," you say. "I'm sure they'll find something." Sharp pains stab all the major organs. "But I gotta go. I had a—heh heh—late night."

"Thanks, dude," Ronnie says, walking to work with an even brisker stride, and you almost hate him for it.

ANDY'S ESCAPE

The completed manuscript is the last thing Andy carries out of the now—officially—vacated house. The query letters and novel samples mailed away to agents yesterday, are somewhere between here and New York, and so are the movers, and so is Andy.

He shuts the front door, locks it, the sound of that final dry slide and click sends his thoughts reflecting on how when you move, it's the sounds, and, by extension, the sights, smells, tastes, and touch of all that you take for granted that make you realize that everything you had written off as wornout, tedious, and commonplace, was actually unique, special, a miracle of math, dimensions, resources, humanity, evolution, entropy. Which, almost reluctantly (nineteen years in the same town and it's over, just like that) he removes the keys from his key chain and hides them, of course, under the soiled welcome mat. He has been planning this move since the faculty meeting meltdown, looking forward to this day when he could leave, all the time spent in between saving money, writing, dreaming, planning, and now that it's here, even the twist of the deadbolt is cause for sentimentality. Because, in spite of the self-pity, self-destruction, anger, and bitterness, he knows something bright emerged out of this house, and the years living here were not in vain.

Andy walks to his packed-up, packed-full Volkswagen. To his right, past the small strip of dead grass between their homes, Andy's neighbor, this overtanned brown-mopped ACR[13] landscaper named Rick, sits in a teal tanktop and cutoff shorts, under his front door awning, watching the sprinklers jettison water across the lawn. Between burnt red thigh-skin, he wedges a silver beer can stuffed into a blue koozie.

"Moving?" Rick bellows across the twenty feet of humid air between them.

"Yup," Andy says.

"Stayin' in town?"

"No. Off to New York. Brooklyn." Since New Year's, he had made

---

[13] "Alachua County Resident"

three trips, falling in love with the pace, the places, the possibilities, hours upon hours of walking around, taking in each new block.

"City?"

"Yup."

"What's up there?"

"Got a new teaching job." (Indeed, Andy has enough money saved for the summer, before starting the new teaching gig in the fall. If he can resist the temptation, the ease, of spending money every single time he sets foot outside of his studio apartment (literally one-fifth the size of where he has lived here in Gainesville, for, literally, twice the price), he can make this work. Difficult, but not impossible.

"They got key lime pie up there?" Rick asks.

Andy smiles, turns to face Rick after plopping the manuscript in the passenger seat. "I'm pretty sure they do."

"Is it good?"

Andy laughs. And to the mix of sensory details unique to here, Andy adds sweet tea, seafood, and, why not, key lime pie to the ever-growing list of what he will miss. He steps into his Volkswagen, turns the ignition. "Good luck."

"Wanna smoke out before you go?"

"No. Thanks." Andy gives a final wave before shifting into reverse, hearing that final dirt crunch of the driveway.

On the drive out of town, Andy takes in University Avenue's little stores and restaurants, the bustle of the collegiates, the unknown familiar faces of the smalltown streets. He stops at the Chevron for gas. From the sidewalk, two students—a purple-haired punk rock boy and a pink-haired punk rock girl, shout his name, smile, wave, approach.

"Remember me? Doug? I wrote the story about the chess-master with, um, chronic flatulence?"

"I do," Andy says. In a class filled with stuffy English majors, Doug was a welcome bit of comic relief, a bouncing gawky goofball.

"And I'm Lisa," she says. "I wrote that story about that guy who's addicted to betting on jai-alai and loses all his possessions?"

"Ah yes," Andy says. Andy recalls how—this was the fall semester before last—they sat closer and closer to each other with each new class—purple hair on the left, pink hair on the right, slowly moving until they were next to each other, hand in hand in the center of the auditorium by the final class. They were serious without being serious, productive but not pretentious . . . Andy's favorite kinds of students. "Still together, I see?" Andy asks, and he hates how, well, professorial he sounds here. But, at the same time—dammit—he loves it.

"We started dating in your class," Doug says.

"Where are you going?" Lisa asks.

Andy tells them. They are impressed. "You belong there," Lisa says. "You were the best teacher we ever had."

"What?!" Andy laughs.

"No, really," Doug says. "You were different. You cared. You acted like you didn't care, but you cared."

Andy doesn't know what to say. "Thanks," he manages to mumble.

"Well good luck!" Lisa says.

Gas tank filled, nozzle replaced, Andy steps inside the Volkswagen, starts the car, drives off. In the rearview, Doug and Lisa wave. It's almost enough to make him want to stay, but instead, he takes in University Avenue one last time—the buildings, the people, the flora and fauna, the sun, the light, the breeze—before the turn onto Waldo Road, and the start of the thousand-mile drive to the north.

WHERE DO YOU GO?

Each passing year, the bands and the fliers and the seven inches look more and more quaint, not as timeless as we believed them to be—but what is timeless is what it is between our ears. What it did to us, for us, when we needed it most. (As d. boon once howled: "mr. narrator? (this is bob dylan to me).") This final house show Ronnie attends as an actual Gainesville resident is less an A-to-B movement and more a blurry blurred transcendent glimpse into better worlds. It doesn't move in a real-time so much as that time and how it exists today beyond mere nostalgia, beyond the so-called "classic rock" of misbegotten youth that "Sweet" Billy DuPree spins at the bowling alley.

Because, you see, Ronnie and me, we miss those days, we miss cramming into muggy living rooms watching our friends transcend genetics, background, conditioning, socialization, for those precious moments before we grow up for good, and we will grow up, no matter how we fight it into our 20s, and even our 30s.

There would be so many parties after these, in so many different places, and they were never that much different from town to town, and after a while, it is easy to grow jaded as we get older, but in the precious fantastic moments of youth, these house shows border on sacrosanct, tempered from piousness thanks to the accompanying wanton hedonism. When it's really right—when I'm playing or Ronnie's playing or you're playing—don't you wish you could hold those moments a bit longer? When people like you and me forget the mundane daily existence and become something else? An honest expression, even when it's ironic.

Music was the center of our lives.

Ronnie won't remember the bands who play tonight at Righteous Freedom House, he won't remember the so many acquaintances he will never see again, the sort-of friends with whom he hardly exchanges words, but they share what we share no matter what becomes of us later. Some died way too young, some become too boring for words. But in the forever-now of the 1997 Gainesville house party, we're still there, downing beers and cheersing friends and sweating in our own juices as the bands put it all out there.

Yes, the bands in Chicago and elsewhere are much better, but the house parties were never as glorious, because these were the first. It was the miracle—the goddamn miracle—of your friends expressing themselves.

It's as real as this February Chicago morning—me, looking out the front windows of the rehabbed two-flat, the dirty snow on the ground, the leafless trees, the cadaver sky, as King Uszniewicz and His Uszniewicztones counter it with their cover of "Land of 10,000 Dances" honking out the stereo. It is the shortest of body highs, but a lifetime of mental shifts forming you into what you thought you could be.

In our own small ways, we reached our American dream for a nanosecond or two, and it had nothing to do with money or property or sports or cars, and everything to do with simply getting ourselves right in our place in the world, expressing the heretofore inexpressible through music, and when you do get that right, it's hard to go down from that, back to the world of dishwashing, of the cubicle, of balancing the books.

Maybe there is more to life than starting bands, seeing bands, listening to music, but we didn't think so at the time. What the hell did we know then, besides living for these frozen moments, these chances that the band plugging into the sockets of these old houses, trying to tune while their friends stand there heckling and laughing, would be the greatest thing we would ever see? You never know, right?

And to come down from that . . . Where do you go . . . where do you go?

IN THE PARKING LOT, LISTENING TO "HOOTENANNY"

You're sitting in your car in the afternoon sun crying while listening to, for the fifth time today, the Replacements' album *Hootenanny*. The engine is still running, max A/C blows against your not-cool tears. "Treatment Bound." The last song on the album. Yeah. No shit. Your organs throb in pain and you feel sick and sweaty and shaky. Parked in the far corner of the hospital parking lot, drunk and high and cored out.

What will they say when you walk in? On the passenger seat floor, an Evian bottle filled with vodka. You reach across and down, unscrew it, put it to your lips. There. Better/Not Better. *We're gettin no place . . . as quick as we know how*, Westerberg sings. *We're getting' nowhere . . . what will we do now?* It almost makes you laugh. Yeah. No shit.

What would be easy to do—the easiest thing—would be to go home and sleep it off. You'll be fine. You're too young to be anything but fine, even as your old friends are starting to look away when you enter the room. Night after night after night of hazy—if outright nonexistent—recollections. You need all of this simply to maintain. You finish the vodka, toss the Evian bottle out the window (it's fun throwing bottles when you're vodkafucked) and the eighteen-year-old self, the one who rejected all of this to create something on his own, that kid—that kid you've been doing your absolute best to ignore since returning from the tour—shouts in your head that no, this is not alright, and no, you will not be fine, so instead, you shut off the car, and *Hootenanny* is silent. Don't look in the mirror. Don't look in the reflections. Move. Out of the car. Stumble across the lot to the hospital's front doors and try to come up with the words to say it.

DRUNK JOHN AND SICILY

That's right, shitdicks, we're leaving town—me and Sicily. We're moving to New Orleans. She's transferring to Tulane, and I got nothing keeping me here. Sooo . . . as we say here in Gainesville: "Screw it."

I'm removing the second of the two speakers from the front windows of the apartment, and it's a little sad, to think of all the incredible times I've had when all I did was sit on the front patio of this house, going inside only to flip records and grab more beers. But it can't last and I can't stay. I can't.

"Looks like the last of it," my girlfriend says from the middle of the front room, holding a broom, sweeping away the years of accumulation under now-removed couches into one scoopable pile.

I smile, cradling the giant speaker. To leave Gainesville, it's like launched rockets requiring so much force to overcome the gravitational pull. Into the unknown. Because New Orleans, to me, might as well be one of those planets Roger Dean was always painting on Yes album covers (yeah, I worked at a record store!) for all I know about it.

We talked about it and talked about it when Sicily got accepted. Aside from me, Gainesville wasn't working out. I'm applying to grad school. I'd like to teach college. I could see myself doing that. Easily. Anyway, it's way more appealing than ringing up compact discs purchased by morons as I'm perched behind the counter of that fucking record store, muttering under my breath to avoid completely losing it.

The bedroom, my old bedroom, is empty now. Even the fliers have been taken down, most thrown away. The records are boxed up and packed. With the last speaker pushed inside, the U-Haul is filled.

I take one last walk through the house, trying not to dwell on the memories in each room (even the bathroom), the ghosts of old friends I may never see again. It's that time of year when everyone leaves for summer, some never to return. I always kept track of who came and went, who had moved on, and who, like me, never left. Until now. This girl. She saved me. I could have been Drunk John forever. At 30, 35, 40, and on and on. She saved me from my own stupidity. From a comfortable life filled with regret and past-tense talk.

I don't mean to sound too dramatic here, you know, I mean, I may end up back here within three months. Maybe I'll miss it, and maybe I'll hate New Orleans, and I'll find I actually belong here. Nothing wrong with that, right? Happens all the time.

"It's getting late," Sicily says, standing on the patio as I lock the front door for the last time. "We have a long drive ahead."

I pull her in for a long hug, a long kiss. It's a late morning, and I've spent it noticing everything I may miss, and I try not to think about it. This quiet familiar little student ghetto street where every fourth or fifth passerby is an old friend. I gotta remember that my future isn't here. It isn't sitting at Gatorroni's after a shift at the record store, scoring pitcher after pitcher until I'm standing up on the table karaokeeing Angry Samoans songs. I mean, I'm sure I could do that in New Orleans anyway. Easily—ha!

Most moments, you want to forget as quickly as possible, and you try and beer it away and hope the beer replaces it with some better time. Not this moment. I want to hold onto it like I hold onto Sicily. Hold this moment close, a last toehold on the familiar, the feeling of being saved and set free all at once. I love her.

And she is right. It is a long drive ahead. We let go. The future is one step off a rickety wooden front porch away. She holds my hand and I don't look back.

SUMMER OF WORK

Bobby stacks the moving boxes by the front door of the common room of what the University charitably classifies a "dorm suite" as *Youth of America* by the Wipers blasts out the speakers of his boombox, when his dad—the very picture of suntanned venerable grayhaired pink-Oxford-shirted Floridian success, steps into the doorway and says, "What the hell's this you're listening to?"

Bobby shrugs, nearly expels a long, dramatic, "Fuuuuuuuck," but checks himself.

"The guy ain't even singin'," Dad says, and now Bobby holds back a few other choice phrases.

It's going to be a long summer.

"Let's hurry it up," Dad says, picking up two of the lighter boxes, walking out of the common room, towards the minivan.

There isn't much left to pack. Throw the remaining clothes into a garbage bag, and that's it. His dorm room is back to how he found it back in August. Thin-mattresssed bed frames. Two desks facing each other, a kind of barrier between Bobby and his now-former roommate. On his roommate's side, gone are his cheesy posters of Lamborghini Countaches and Pamela Anderson. On Bobby's side of the room, gone are the flyers of the local shows he attended. In the common room, gone is the ironical beer can wall.

Bobby remembers when summers were fun. When he was really young, when you could get out of school around Memorial Day, and the idea of ever going back to school seemed unfathomable. Summers when going inside for anything was the worst kind of punishment. Now, the summers are working and saving money, living at home, stuck in a boring town with no more friends.

He walks down the sidewalk between his dorm building and the girls' dorms. Girls lugging laundry baskets downstairs to their own summer fates of hometowns, jobs, the drearily familiar. Everyone takes one final glance at the new and the youthful. Bobby crosses the sticky blaze of the parking lot, tosses his things into the back of the minivan. His dad waits, impatiently.

Back to the sidewalk, he hears the last thing he needs to snag—the boombox. Bobby indulges one last glance at where he spent this past year, shuts the door, jogs out.

The long lithe sinewy women lounge around in the university's grass in cut-off shorts, absorbing the summer sun. It's so easy, really. College. Even when it's difficult, it's learning new things around somewhat intelligent people. It isn't the front counter of Eckerd's Drugs, ringing up purchases from the pissed-off elderly, the depressing break room with its desperate no-talk to fill the tedious hours. Summer is now a waiting game of earning money, saving money, going back to his bedroom at home and listening to The Wipers, counting down the days to go back, X-ing the calendar's passing days.

Bobby climbs into the minivan's passenger seat and Dad pulls away before the door's completely shut. "Have a good semester?" he asks.

"It was fine," and Bobby could talk about, say, losing his virginity in that room, the girl he met who started talking to him at that party in the student ghetto, where the bands played, where the partygoers shouted along to every word. He could talk about discovering punk rock in Gainesville, of all the people he met from it, but none of that will be discussed.

"I hope your grades are good," Dad says as they pull out of the campus, south onto NW 13th Street. Bobby turns, looks. Out the minivan's dirty back window, the campus—with its girls, youth, energy, epiphanies, discoveries—fades away. Summers suck now. Summers are working, sleeping, sweating, looking and finding nothing to do. Already, Bobby is planning ways to get through it. Maybe I'll learn guitar while back home. Write some songs. Start a band. Why not?

Until then, Bobby turns back around, away from the campus, through the love-bug smeared minivan windshield as Dad steps on the accelerator, into the Floridian countryside. Bobby's heart sinks.

RONNIE AND CHARLEY

"Now, Ronnie: Are you sure you want to do this?"

His dad (oh, good ol' Charley) waits until it is way past too late to ask this question. Because it is, after all, way past too late.

Ronnie has sold his blandy-apple green sedan for the equivalent of two month's rent in the Chicago apartment. He has made all necessary arrangements with his roommates-to-be, has let them know he will be in Chicago this time next week. He has begun packing his books and records into boxes collected from the XYZ Liquor Store.[14] He has reserved a U-Haul. Put in his two-week's notice at both jobs. Has spread the word about the Going-Away Party. Compared to the move to Gainesville, the move out of town is a calm and deliberative process. And yet, somebody still has to ask, "Are you sure?" Arriving, it was Kelly, and leaving, it is good ol' Charley Altamont, retired teacher, born-again Buddhist and practicing vegan, and Ronnie's father.

---

[14] Will future generations know the joys and sorrows of packing and unpacking hundreds—if not thousands—of LPs and books? Of knowing that the place you live isn't really your "home" until you've unpacked the LPs and books? This was one of the reasons why the double-wide trailer was never quite a home for Ronnie, but the Myrrh House was . . .

Before Ronnie can answer, Charley laughs his little southern-style chuckle-while-talking "I know . . . I know! All I'm saying, son, is that if you're not sure, and if it doesn't work out—because it might not, and that's ok—you can come back."

"Ok, Dad," Ronnie says, but inside, Ronnie thinks of how there have been so many times he felt bad about what he did. How he left Orlando. How he lived in Gainesville. But what if Ronnie hadn't moved into that trailer and followed Kelly's advice? What if he broke down and admitted to his father, "No, I'm not sure I want to do this." After all, in a few short months, Ronnie could be lonely and miserable. And very, very cold.

There is safety and warmth in the womb, security in what you know and who you've known. But then they want to tell you who you are and what you can and cannot do, and how you'll always be, and when Ronnie senses that happening in his environment, his first reaction—from his skin, to his bones, to way down deep in the coiled double-helixes of his DNA, is to get the hell out.

He isn't sure he wants to do this, but he isn't sure he has a choice, and not only because the process is already underway. He isn't coming back. Not for a long long long long time. Maybe never . . . but . . . he has always imagined he would end up in the same retirement home with his friends . . . somewhere in what's left of Florida after the glaciers melt. Shuffleboard with Neil and Paul, followed by late-night panty and/or girdle raids. Arthritic hands strumming a guitar, teaching Rae side two of *Kinda Kinks*. Ronnie and Mitch will find a way up onto the roof, with a six-pack of Futro-Hamtramcks (or whatever they'll be called in the 2050s) and a Boombox 2000 playing all the 20th century rock and roll of yestercentury. Movie night, curated by Roger, who will hate the snoring. Mouse and Icy Filet, recording in the Rec Room, drafting the other residents, the nurses, the doctors, to play kazoos, recorders, and detuned electric ukuleles. Kelly . . . Magic Jensen . . . Willie Joe Scotchgard . . . Chuck Taylor . . . Macho Man Randy . . . everyone will be there.

Bingo with William, and as they half-pay attention to the caller's announcements of letters and numbers, they will think back on it all, all those frivolous times in Gainesville, 50 years ago, in those last years when you still had the time space and distance to fuck up and fuck up royally without a Mr. Google to hold your hand and tell you no, Internet Buddy, you're not as alone and confused as you think.

Ronnie, in the retirement hot tub, watching the elderly nnnnuggets practice their water calisthenics. Maggie will be there, and so will Maux, and Siouxsanna Siouxsanne, and Portland Patty and Julianna, and the distant past will be funny to everyone, almost forgotten, and with the warm jets on his achy old limbs, Ronnie will fall asleep, and then he will die in the hot tub, smiling, with no one noticing for a good half hour, at least.

THE GOING AWAY PARTY

Earlier that week, Roger had gotten word that the owners of the Myrrh House—a glass company the next street over—were going to tear it down for a parking lot once their lease expired—or Roger left, whichever came first. Bulldozers will crash and topple these flimsy walls, the neighborhood itself will become another high-density, high-profit bland-ass nothing. You can

vandalize, you can set the buildings on fire, you can scream your angry songs, but the Floridian developers march on, and on, and on, and on, and all you can do is dance this one night away before leaving the state of Florida behind.

On NW 4th Lane, bottle rockets whiz and explode everywhere. On opposite ends of the street, Neil and Paul hide behind cars, taking careful aim at each other, shooting, firing, missing. Laughter.

A dizzying array of near friends gather to say goodbye. Ronnie is in constant motion, trying to talk to everyone but too drunk, too overwhelmed, to express how grateful he is.

"You know you're fucked, right?" Kelly says to Ronnie during a short break between Ronnie giving his goodbye "Gonna miss you guys . . . c'mere, gimme a hug" spiels to anyone and everyone who stopped by to see him off. Kelly, who spent the entire day debating whether to show up—because, after all, Ronnie will be back here by Thanksgiving. Even if he somehow stuck it out in Gainesville, Chicago is something else entirely. Kelly had work, but after some internal debate, he called in sick, jumped into his car, and made it to the Myrrh House.

"Yeah, I know," Ronnie says.

"Good," Kelly answers. "As long as we're clear on this . . . "

Ronnie runs off, returns to the keg, cup after cup after cup, emerges from his bedroom with an acoustic guitar, ends up somehow on the roof screaming and strumming "Real Cool Time" by The Stooges, yelling the words at the groups of people clustered up and down NW 4th Lane, and the jungle trees towering over the streetlights will soon be no more, and neither will the street, these friends and near-friends, and Ronnie Altamont could end it—right now—he really could—he could run off this roof and dive headfirst and save the trouble, but so much remains unanswered, and all of this is simply a beginning (when he thought the whole time that this was the end) for better things to come.

Mitch joins him on the roof, followed by Rae, followed by Paul, by Neil, by Mouse, by Icy Filet, by Kelly, by Roger, by Siouxsanna Siouxsanne . . .

"Hey Rahhn," Mitch says. "Play 'Lola.'"

And so Ronnie plays "Lola" on the acoustic guitar, and in the sea-shanty chorus, he and Mitch and Rae and Paul and Neil and Mouse and Icy Filet and Kelly and Siouxsanna Siouxsanne, along with the dozens spilling out of the Myrrh House, sing along—"Lola / Luh-Luh-Luh-L-Lola / Luh-Luh-Luh-Luh-Low-Luhhhhh" on repeat, and that's the way that Ronnie wants to stay and always wants it to be that way. He will remember this, and over time its meaning will grow, playing music on the roof with friends, this, what it meant to live in Gainesville for thirteen months in the mid-to-late 90s . . . Later, he will go skinny dipping in some apartment complex pool with 30-plus equally intoxicated revelers, but the apartment pool skinny dip is nothing, and the abundant late-night and early morning antics are nothing, and the going home with the blue-haired tat-sleeved nameless one-night stand, while definitely not-bad, that too will be nothing . . . compared to that roof, that street, that town . . . Compared to youth.

Singing with friends, Ronnie basks in the treacherous ecstasy of transition.

12/26/2005—9/3/2013
Longwood, FL—Chicago, IL

APPENDIXES

APPENDIX A:

Ronnie Altamont's April 23, 1995 column in the UCF *Unicorn:*
"Fired again..Another Lazy Boss, This One with Obvious Apartheid Sym-
pathies . . . The Differences Between Being a Cocksucker Who Does't Suck
Cock and a Motherfucker Who Doesn't Fuck His Mother . . . Nasty Winds
Blowing in From Alafaya and Lake Underhill . . . "

So I got fired from my job. I don't know if you, gentle reader, have
ever been fired by a racist South African cocksucker (not that he
literally sucked cock, and even if he did that's not what made him
a cocksucker and if he was a bona fide real-deal cocksucker that
wouldn't matter to me because hey: to each his own, right?), but
lemme tell ya, bro: NO FUN.

I'm not really sure why I lost this particular job. I know he
wasn't exactly a fan of all the stuff I was writing about for your
delight and edification here in el column for el papero.

"Your language is disgusting," he informed me at the start
of one shift, shortly after the staff got wind of what I was doing
(writing about my nights behind the front desk, the drunks, the
quickie sex of our customers, the sleaze, the found porno mags,
the junkies, the flunkies, all of it . . . c'mon, you remember, right?),
because Geoff (his name was Geoff, if that's any 'ndication) (and
sorry if your name is Geoff) (not apologizin', just sayin' sorry your
name is Jeff with a "Geo") is obviously, from his lofty vocation as
live-in manager of that fleabag hotel, a man of Belles Lettres, gettin' down to your Dostoevskis and Camuseses and the like.

Geoff did this high-larious imitation of the Latino workers
he had back when he was working some other blow-tel down in

Miami, where he would talk about it by saying stuff like "You tell them to get to work and they say, 'Iss not my yob, mang.'"

Hey-ohhhh!

What. A. Fucking. Asshole.

And, in hindsight, I should apologize for showing up drunk from parties for my 11:00 p.m. - 7:00 a.m. shift. But I had my trusty compadre Kelly to co-work with through the night, and he could cover for me while I slept it off in a vacant room. And sure, there were plenty of times when Kelly wasn't around and I didn't know what I was doing, didn't know how to fix the printer when it jammed, would forget to enter in all the information into the ol' computadora, but seeing how he's the Live-In Manager, you'd think he'd come down to help out when his assistance was required. But no. Didn't want to be disturbed. Can you believe it: Men and Wimmin? To get the motherfucker (because that's what he was, I mean not literally, but unlike if he was a literal cocksucker, if Geoff had sexual relations with his mother (and who knows, when you get right down to it . . .) I would hold that against him) out of bed to do his job was such an or-fucking-deal. Oh, Geoff. The buck never does stop with you does it? You are the "Slack Motherfucker" Superchunk warned me about.

My former boss is a very sweaty man. This Central Florida climate does not suit him. He smells like rancid eggs. Sweat stains crescentmoondampturd across his shirts. Our guests hated the very sight of him. And I hated the very sight of all of them. I just wanted to go home . . . at the end of the shift, I would look out the front windows and there (there!) would be Maggie's car, waiting to take me home. Through the dew drenched windows as the sun rose over the good ol' smothered and covered Waffle House we shared the parking lot with. And speaking of Camus . . . I'm glad this sysiphusian nightmare is finished, once and for all, and I can go back to doing what I want to . . . which hey, by the way, my band—The Laraflynboyles—have ourselves a sweet li'l ol' (as they say in the music biz) "gig" at Coffee Creamerz, which is in the Alomarod Plaza next to Palm Frond Steve's Oyster Emporium, so you know it's gonna get p-u-n-k so rock on, homie!

. . . OK, I know there was more I wanted to say about my former boss before calling this a column and going off to drink a couple quarts of Brain Mangler malt liquor . . . but really, all you need to know is that he's just your run of the mill cheating lying lazy ass scumbag, as good a representative of "the dark shattered underbelly of the American dream" that good ol' HST warned us about as anyone.

So (Maggie don't read this) if the wind blows from the vicinity of Alafaya and Lake Underhill, and should you detect a smell redolent of a retarded abortion, with hints of diarrhea from a llama's leaky asshole, know that that smell you smell comes from my former boss, who should do the world the humble favor of putting a gun to his mouth and pulling the trigger, eliminating his horrid presence on this horrid planet once and for all.

OK. Sorry! I'll try and write something funnier and nicer next time. Until then . . .

This column is finished.

APPENDIX B: KELLY'S RESIGNATION LETTER

MARCH 30, 1996

GEOFF:

I am writing this letter to inform you that, effective immediately, I am terminating my employment as Night Auditor and Front Desk Clerk of this hotel you allegedly operate.

In the two years I have been employed here, I have known you to be nothing but a thoroughly reprehensible and incompetent boss. Your verbal abuse of the cleaning staff leads me to believe that you have Nazi sympathies, and if the opportunity had presented itself to you, you would be leading any number of oppressed minorities to their gruesome deaths in concentration camps, willingly, gladly, and unreservedly. Your demeanor around the women who work at the Front Desk and in the office is just this side of prosecutable sexual harassment, and while you no doubt fancy yourself to be a suave and debonair member of male humanity, I can assure you that no one else—women, in particular—sees you this way. You are vile and corpulent, a malodorous pervert, a cheap hustler all-too-typical here in The Sunshine State.

Had you any shred of human decency, any sense of compassion or empathy or sympathy for anyone or anything, your first response to finding me pistolwhipped and bleeding would not be, "How much did they take?" but, rather, oh, I don't know, "Are you ok," perhaps? Did that thought ever cross your mind? No. You know and I know that I am expendable here in this service economy state in this service job, so why even make the attempt to trouble your nonexistent conscience? I cannot and will not work for someone of your ilk. You embody everything wrong with capitalism, with America, with the world. The feces you void each morning, the waste of your Big Gulps, your KFC, your nonstop diet of fried everything for breakfast, late breakfast, lunch, late lunch, dinner, dessert, and late night snack, has better qualities than you will ever have.

You think you are charming. You think when you crack your corny and hateful jokes with your ripped-off customers, with your overworked and underappreciated staff, that you are amusing. You think you are enjoyable to be around. You are not. No one likes you, Geoff. No one working for you, no one paying to lodge in that filthy squalored vermin infested pit you call a hotel, no one you meet here, there, and everywhere, from Florida to South Africa and back again, thinks you are anything more than an arrogant fool, the kind people instinctively know to tolerate to the best of their abilities. This is why you live alone in a hotel halfway around the world. No one likes you.

Go ahead and rationalize these words, but know that when you look in the mirror, my words are the truest words you will ever read. Scoff, huff, and ignore it. But I can assure you that Ronnie Altamont was right about you, and as inarticulate and as self-absorbed as he was and is, he got you right to the best of his limited abilities. Your delusions are pathetic and sad, and you will die lonelier than any man who has walked this earth.

Have a nice day,
Kelly
Cc: Ronnie Altamont

APPENDIX C: NICHOLAS J. CANBERRY'S SHORT STORY
'ZOMBIE NARC' (WHAT HE HAS TURNED IN "SO FAR")

When anybody asked him, Smokey most defiantly would proclaim that he and Stoney had become the best of friends. At their houses they would get each other high and hang out and tell jokes. Smokey grew hydroponic bud in his closet. One day, after they got high together, Smokey showed Stoney the amazing surprise he had stashed away in his closet.

"I got a surprise for you," Smokey said.

"Yeah?" Stoney asked. "What is it?"

"You'll see," Smokey said, smiling like he was high. Smokey was high. So was Stoney. "It's over their, man," he said, pointing to his closet.

Smokey lead Stoney to his walk-in closet. Inside, Stoney couldn't believe his eyes. That is, if he even has eyes. Because, Stoney had a secret or two of his own.

"Check it out!" Smokey said.

"Wow! Is that what I think it is?" Stoney curiously asked.

"Yup, it defiantley is" Smokey triumphantly exclaimed. "It's a closet filled with hydroponic bud!"

"Oh, man," Stoney rubbed his eyes. His eyes were bloodshot because they were so high. "What if we smoked all of that at once? We'd get so high and shit."

Smokey laughed. "Most defiantly, bro. I'm gonna keep enough for me to get high, but I'm gonna sell the rest in the park to all the little kids playing in the playground. I always taught that was a good idea, right bro?"

Stoney laughed. "Yeah. Except there's just one problem."

"Problem?" Smokey asked questioningly. "What are you talking about."

"Oh nothing," Stoney said but the way he said it sounded different like he was lying or had something more. "I need to go to the front door real quick. Then, let's smoke out some more from this mary jane in the membrane."

"Cool," Smokey said as Stoney made his way out of the walk in closet and moved his way to the front door.

Suddenly, there were lots of footsteps that Smokey could here in his apartment. He seemed to be hearing sirens and walky talkys. The next thing Smokey new, the police were in his walk-in closet. They told him to freeze and that he was under arrest.

"Oh no." Smokey said.

"Oh yeah." Stoney said.

"I taught you were our friend, man!" Smokey cried sadly as the cops put the cuffs on him and took him away. "We did . . . drugs together. Remember?"

"I am your friend, man!" Stoney pleaded insistently. "But there's one thing, you don't know."

Smokey spat at the ground as the cops led him away. "I know everything I need to know, man. You're nuthin' but a narc! You're just a narc!"

"Not so fast, Smokey!" Stoney announced menacingly. "Watch this!" The skin of Stoney's flesh was ripped by Stoney's hands. His hands tugged at his face, revealing . . . A ROTTING SKULL UNDERNEATH!!!

"I'm a ZOMBIE NARC!!!" Stoney yelled loudly. "And I'm hungry. FOR BRAINS!"

"What the? No! No!!! Please!" Smokey begged as the top of

his skull was being chewed by Stoney's mouth. Blood shot everywhere, and the cops shot their guns. They had no affect on Stoney. He grabbed the cops and ate them up too.

"Stoney's brain tastes like chicken!" Stoney reflected calmly to himself. "But these cops' brains taste like pigs!" Stoney proceeded to eat his way through all their brains, ralishing each volumtous bite. The fact is, Stoney was hungry, hungry for brains.

[I didn't finish this because I had other work I needed to get done and when I tried to get back to it I lost the flow and my mind wasn't in the right place any more. But I want to finish it soon. I have some ideas about how I want it to end, but I can't decide if I want Stoney to stay a zombie or not. I also can't decide if I want him to stay a narc or not. I think that maybe Stoney will feel guilty for killing his best friend and try to give up drugs. Except pot. That can't. What do u think I should do? Your the teacher. Can somebody not be a zombie if they don't want to be. Any way I no this is passed when it's do but if you can give me an extra days Ill promise to get this to you and it will be somethig Id want too publish. Later, NJC]

BRIAN COSTELLO

APPENDIX D:

"THE OCEAN AND THE SEA"

A POEM BY

NICHOLAS J. CANBERRY

Green waves

Green mind

Bud kind

Life unwinds

The ocean and the sea

It means so much to me

The salt tastes sweet

Feel the sand on my feet

Something 'bout the ocean air

Makes me forget all about my cares

Waking dreams

Are what they seem

The jettys have

The bettys

But the waters kissing the shore

Have my soul forever more

All you hear is radio gaga

All I hear is the seagull's caw-caw!

The fish and the sharks

Swim in the deep, in the dark

If I only had a boat

To leave the shore and all her sea oats

And leave the land for the worker bees

For the ocean and the sea

LOSING IN GAINESVILLE

Is the life for me
For the ocean and the sea
Is the life for me
Peace.

BRIAN COSTELLO

APPENDIX E:

A REPRESENTATIVE SAMPLE OF THE HAIKU WALL

Hmmm: Triumph, or Rush?
Canadian Power Threes
Both? Neither? Neither.

Bar-Bar-Bar-Bar-Bar
Ba-rino. Bar-Bar-Bar-Bar
Bar-Ba-Rino. Jeece!

Welcome Back, Kotter
Arnold Horshack, Juan Epstein
Boom Boom Washington

At Gatorroni's
I saw this nugget today
With tits out to here:

Bam Bam Bigelow
Babyface, or Heel?
Wrestlemania!

Jake and the Fatman
One guy's Jake, the other's fat
Jack and the Fatman

LOSING IN GAINESVILLE

When Darby Crash said
"someone get me a beeyah"
He would then drink it

Maux's drunk on vodka
William's swiped Metrognome
Roger eats tofu

Devo: Mark, Bob One
Bob Two, Gerald V., Alan
Not much is better

The Really Rottens
The Laff-a-lympics Bad Buys
Heavens to Murgatroid!

Mushmouth says to me
"Beeba deeba seeba see,
Soba doba boo."

OJ, OJ, O
J, OJ, OJ, OJ
Jeez, who gives a shit?!

Dee Dee Ramone on
The bass guitar wrote many
Of their greatest songs

BRIAN COSTELLO

I like it when the
Grungy guy in the grunge band
Is all like: "eeeeeeeeeeeyeah!"

It's Sanford and Son
Oh! Elizabeth!
This is the big one!

The Robert Plant bum
Been a long time since he had
A home. Ramble on.

Oh, Beetle Bailey
You are so slow and clumsy
Careful, Sarge is mad.

At EPCOT Center
I got lost at Morocco
Land but bought a fez.

Webster has a dad
It's George Papadapolis
Alex Karras, dude

Curtains and the drapes
Do they match? Well then? Do they?
Folks should just say it

LOSING IN GAINESVILLE

In the tacklebox
There are lures, bait, worms, hooks
At least I think so

Simon and Garfunk
Loggins and Messina, Hall
And Oates. Pro boners.

Steely Dan records
I like em all except the
First and "Gaucho"

Was watching jai-alai
The betters scream at players
Rip tickets, go home

The Jenny Jones Show
Moms and Daughters Who Party
Together, Bad News

We're talkin' big breasts
Here, the bounce em squeeze em kind.
Boobs. Tits. Juggs. Knockers.

My socks are itchy
Will you please scratch them for me
My feet, not my socks

BRIAN COSTELLO

Portobello slice
That's what I want, what I get
I think Neal farted

APPENDIX F: *oreGONE, XMAS '95*

SIDE A

"Isabel"—Unrest

"Driveway to Driveway"—Superchunk

"Baby's Way Cruel"—Guv'ner

"Zurich is Stained"—Pavement

"You're a Million"—The Raincoats

"Window Shop for Love"—The Wipers

"24"—Red House Painters

"Our Secret"—Beat Happening

"Mothra"—Spoke

"37 Pushups"—Smog

"Slugger"—Tsunami

"Parasol"—Sea and Cake

SIDE B

"Facial Disobedience"—Radon

"Image of Me"—Flying Burrito Brothers

"Questioningly"—Ramones

"Game of Pricks"—Guided by Voices

"Twin Falls"—Built to Spill

"Seven"—Team Dresch

"Supreme Nothing"—Tiger Trap

"Insomnia"—Versus

"Port of Charleston"—Seam

"Tragic Carpet Ride"—Polvo

"Sorry"—Galaxie 500

"Realize"—Codeine

ACKNOWLEDGMENTS

Special thanks to Jacob Knabb, Victor Giron, James Tadd Adcox, Leonard Vance, Naomi Huffman, and everyone at Curbside Splendor.

Also, thanks to Ryan Duggan for his work on the cover, and Luke Chappelle, Tim Lampinen, Ben Lyon, and Marieke McClendon for their illustrations.

Thank you to the following for their friendship, support, and inspiration during the years this novel was written: Scott Adams, Randy Albers, Dustin Atwater, Sean Atwater, Shawn Bailey (RIP), Sara Bassick, Seth Bohn, Julia Borcherts, Chris Campisi, Todd Campisi, Pete Capponi, Russ Calderwood, Justin Champlain, *Chicago Reader*—especially Tony Adler, Jerome Ludwig, Philip Montoro, and Miles Raymer, Chris Costello, Deborah Costello, Peter Costello, Brett Cross, everyone at Empty Bottle, Zach Dodson, Chris Erickson, Rich Evans, Matt Flaiz, David Gregorski, Jered Gummere, Brian Hieggelke from *New City*, everyone at The Hideout—especially Seth Dodson, Michael Slobach, and Katie and Tim Tuten, Bryan Hoben, Chuck Horne, Nathan Johnson, Spencer Johnson, Rob Karlic, Ryan King, Rick Kogan, Dan Lang, Mark MacKenzie, Jim McCann, Jonathan Messinger, Kevin Meyer, Kristy Moss, Carin Mrotz, Mike Mrotz, Nick Myers, Wendy Norton, Todd Novak, Outer Minds (Gigi Lira, Mary McKane, Zach Medearis, A-Ron Orlwoski), Brian Pineyro, Trent Purdy, Chris Rice, the Class of 1986 from St. Vincent de Paul Catholic School in Peoria, Illinois, Shame That Tune (Abraham Levitan, Jeanine

O'Toole, Nick Rouley), Tony Sagger, Justin Santorsola, Marin Santorsola, Joel Shaugnessy, Ginna Springer, Matt Springer, John Sturdy, Nicole Torres, Wesley Torres, and Dan "The Fan" Urban.

Boogie Dave was not modeled after any independent record store owner in Gainesville. —BC

(Write your own book. Start your own band. Paint your own picture. Do it.)

BRIAN COSTELLO

is a writer, musician, and comedic performer living in Chicago, Illinois. He plays drums in the band Outer Minds, and co-hosts Shame That Tune, a monthly live game show. *Losing in Gainesville* is his second novel.

THE GAME WE PLAY
Stories by Susan Hope Lanier

"The Game We Play *is a triumph. An outstanding debut that should reaffirm our shared belief in the absolute necessity and imaginative possibility of the short story.*"

—**Joe Meno,** author of *The Great Perhaps* and *Hairstyles of the Damned*

The ten riveting, emotionally complex stories in *The Game We Play* examine the decisions we make when our chocies are few and courage is costly. Topics include a young couple facing disease and commitment with the same sharp fear, a teenager stealing from his girlfriend's mother's purse to help pay for her abortion, and a father making a split-second decision that puts his child's life at risk.

THE OLD NEIGHBORHOOD
A novel by Bill Hillmann

"A raucous but soulful account of growing up on the mean streets of Chicago, and the choices kids are forced to make on a daily basis. This cool, incendiary rites of passage novel is the real deal."

—**Irvine Welsh,** author of *Trainspotting*

The Old Neighborhood is the story of teenager Joe Walsh, the youngest in a large, mixed-race family living in Chicago. After Joe witnesses his older brother commit a gangland murder, his friends and family drag him down into a pit of violence that reaches a bloody impasse when his elder sister begins dating a rival gang member. *The Old Neighborhood* is both a brutal tale of growing up tough in a mean city, and a beautiful harkening to the heartbreak of youth.

DOES NOT LOVE
A novel by James Tadd Adcox

"...Adcox is a writer who knows how to make the reader believe the impossible, in his capable hands, is always possible, and the ordinary, in his elegant words, is truly extraordinary."
—Roxane Gay, author of *Bad Feminist* and *An Untamed State*

Set in an archly comedic alternate reality version of Indianapolis that is completely overrun by Big Pharma, James Tadd Adcox's debut novel chronicles Robert and Viola's attempts to overcome loss through the miracles of modern pharmaceuticals. Viola falls out of love following her body's third "spontaneous abortion," while her husband Robert becomes enmeshed in an elaborate conspiracy designed to look like a drug study.

LET GO AND GO ON AND ON
A novel by Tim Kinsella

"I give Kinsella a five thousand star review for launching me deep into an alternate universe somewhere between fiction of the most intimate and biography of the most compelling. It's like...a pitch-perfect fine flowing bellow, the sound of celestial molasses." **—Devendra Banhart**

Let Go and Go On and On is the story of obscure actress Laurie Bird. Told in a second-person narrative, blurring what little is known of her actual biography with her roles as a drifter in *Two Lane Blacktop*, a champion's wife in *Cockfighter*, and an aging rock star's Hollywood girlfriend in *Annie Hall*, the story unravels in Bird's suicide at the age of 26. *Let Go and Go On and On* explores our endless fascination with the Hollywood machine and the weirdness that is celebrity culture.

WWW.CURBSIDESPLENDOR.COM